GAMES UNTOLD

LOVE IS POWER.

ALSO BY JENNIFER LYNN BARNES

THE INHERITANCE GAMES SAGA
The Inheritance Games
The Inheritance Games
The Hawthorne Legacy
The Final Gambit
The Brothers Hawthorne

The Grandest Game
The Grandest Game
Coming next: *Glorious Rivals*

Games Untold

THE NATURALS
The Naturals
Killer Instinct
All In
Bad Blood
Twelve: A Novella

THE DEBUTANTES
Little White Lies
Deadly Little Scandals

The Lovely and the Lost

GAMES UNTOLD

#1 *NEW YORK TIMES* BESTSELLING AUTHOR

JENNIFER LYNN BARNES

LITTLE, BROWN AND COMPANY

New York Boston

Little, Brown and Company
Hachette Book Group
1290 Avenue of the Americas, New York, NY 10104
Visit us at LBYR.com

Simultaneously published in 2024 by Penguin Random House UK
in the United Kingdom
First Edition: November 2024

Little, Brown and Company is a division of Hachette Book Group, Inc.
The Little, Brown name and logo are registered trademarks of
Hachette Book Group, Inc.

Library of Congress Cataloging-in-Publication Data
Names: Barnes, Jennifer Lynn, author.
Title: Games untold / Jennifer Lynn Barnes.
Description: New York : Little, Brown and Company, 2024. | Series:
The Inheritance games | Audience: Ages 12 and up. | Summary: "Novellas
and short stories set before, during, and after the Inheritance Games series."
—Provided by publisher
Identifiers: LCCN 2024019753 | ISBN 9780316573719 (hardcover) |
ISBN 9780316573726 (ebook)
Subjects: CYAC: Inheritance and succession—Fiction. | Wealth—Fiction. |
Family life—Fiction. | Short stories. | LCGFT: Short stories. | Novella.
Classification: LCC PZ7.B26225 Gam 2024 | DDC [Fic]—dc23
LC record available at https://lccn.loc.gov/2024019753

ISBNs: 978-0-316-57371-9 (hardcover), 978-0-316-57372-6 (ebook),
978-0-316-58278-0 (int'l), 978-0-316-58103-5 (B&N special edition),
978-0-316-58179-0 (Target special edition), 978-0-316-58180-6
(Indigo special edition)

Printed in Indiana, USA

LSC-H

Printing 1, 2024

For Rachel

CONTENTS

TIMELINE

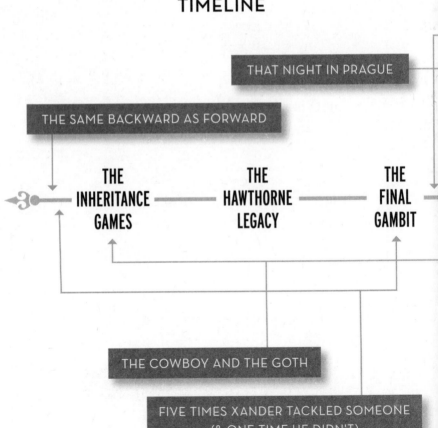

ONE HAWTHORNE NIGHT

$3CR3T $@NT@

THE
BROTHERS
HAWTHORNE

THE
GRANDEST
GAME

WHAT HAPPENS IN THE TREE HOUSE

PAIN AT THE RIGHT GUN

THAT
NIGHT
IN
PRAGUE

*Nothing in this place
was infinite except for
Jameson and me.*

The Morning After

I wasn't worried about him. Worrying about Jameson Winchester Hawthorne was about as useful as trying to argue with the wind. I was smart enough to know that there was no sense in shouting at hurricanes or worrying about a Hawthorne with a love of Hail Mary passes, semi-calculated risks, and walking right up to the edge of incredible drops.

Jameson had a habit of landing on his feet.

"Avery?" Oren announced his presence, a mere courtesy considering my head of security was never far away. "It's almost dawn. I can have my team take another sweep and—"

"No," I said quietly. I couldn't shake the feeling that Jameson wouldn't want me looking for him. This wasn't Hide and Seek. It wasn't Catch Me If You Can.

Every single one of my instincts said that this was . . . *something*.

"It's been fourteen hours." Oren's voice was a military kind of calm: brisk, matter-of-fact, always prepared for the worst. "He disappeared with no warning. He left no trace behind. It happened in an *instant*. We have to consider the possibility of foul play."

Considering nefarious possibilities was Oren's job. I was the Hawthorne heiress. Jameson was a Hawthorne. We attracted attention—and sometimes threats. But deep down, my gut was saying the same thing it had been saying from the moment Jameson had disappeared: *I should have seen this coming.*

Something electric had been building in Jameson for days—an unholy energy, a powerful drive. *A secret.* Memories flashed rapid-fire through my head, moment after moment after moment from the day I'd stepped foot in Prague.

The spire.

The knife.

The clock.

The key.

What are you up to, Hawthorne? You have a secret. What is it?

"Give it an hour," I told Oren. "If Jameson's not back, then you can send out a team."

When it was clear that my bodyguard—and sometimes father figure—wasn't going to argue with me, I made my way to the foyer of our luxury hotel suite. *The Royal Suite.* I took a seat in a chair made of crushed red-and-black velvet and stared at a wall that wasn't just a wall, my mind working its way through this puzzle for the hundredth time.

A decadent gold mural stared back at me.

Where are you, Jameson? What am I missing?

My eyes found the well-masked seams in the wall. *A hidden door.* Its existence was a reminder to me that Jameson's deceased grandfather, Tobias Hawthorne, had once owned this hotel, that the Royal Suite had been built to the exacting, puzzle-obsessed billionaire's specifications.

Traps upon traps, I thought. *And riddles upon riddles.* That phrase had been among the first words Jameson had ever spoken to me, back when he'd been fighting grief and chasing the next puzzle, the next high, determined not to care about anyone or anything.

Back when he'd taken risks in part because he *wanted* to hurt.

As I stared at the wall and the hidden door, I told myself that the Jameson of those early days wasn't the same Jameson Hawthorne who'd pushed my hair back from my face the day before, spreading it out like a halo on the mattress.

My Jameson still took risks—but he always came back.

I know better than to worry about Jameson Hawthorne. And yet...

I willed the hidden door to open. I willed Jameson to be standing on the other side of it.

And finally—*finally*—just before my hour was up, it did, and he was. *Jameson Winchester Hawthorne.*

The first thing I saw, as he crossed into the light, was the blood.

Chapter 1

Three Days Earlier...

The postcard in my hand matched the view out the jet's window. *Prague at dawn.* Centuries of history was silhouetted against a hazy-gold sky, the dark, swirling clouds above the city a deep purple gray.

Jameson had sent me the postcard, a callback to the way his uncle had once sent postcards to my mother. The parallel made me think about what my mom would say if she could see me now: the private plane, the inches-thick stack of documents I'd gone through on the flight, the way I still caught myself holding my breath when the reality of moments like this once hit me with the force of a tidal wave.

Prague at dawn. My mom and I had always talked about traveling the world. It was the one dream I'd allowed myself to hold on to after she'd died, but at fifteen and sixteen and seventeen, I had never let myself daydream for more than a few minutes at a time. I had never let myself want this—or anything—too much.

But now? I ran my thumb over the edge of the postcard. Now I wanted the world. I wanted *everything.* And there was nothing standing in my way.

"One of these days, you'll get used to it," the person sitting across from me on *my* private jet said, then she laid three magazines down on the table between us. My face was on the cover of every single one.

"No," I told Alisa simply. "I won't." I couldn't read any of the words on the covers. I wasn't even sure what language two of the three were in.

"They're calling you *Saint Avery*." Alisa arched a brow at me. "Care to guess what they're calling Jameson?"

Alisa Ortega was my lawyer—and the foundation's—but her expertise went well beyond legal advice. If something needed fixing, she fixed it. At this point, our roles were clearly defined. I was the teenage billionaire heiress philanthropist. She put out the fires.

And Jameson Hawthorne *blazed*.

"Guess," Alisa reiterated, as the jet touched down, "what they're calling him."

I knew exactly where this was going, but I wasn't a saint, and Jameson wasn't a liability. We were two sides of the same coin.

"Are they calling him *Don't Stop*?" I asked Alisa seriously.

Her perfectly sculpted brows pulled together.

"Sorry," I said in a completely deadpan. "I forgot. That's what *I* call him."

Alisa snorted. "It is not."

A borderline Hawthorne grin pulled at the edges of my lips, and I looked out the window again. In the distance, I could still see the spires disappearing into the gold-purple-gray sky.

Alisa was wrong. I would *never* get used to this. This was *everything*—and so was Jameson Hawthorne.

"I'm not Saint Avery," I told Alisa. "You know that."

I'd kept enough of my inheritance that I would literally *never* be able to spend even a noticeable fraction of it, but all most people saw was the amount I'd given away. By popular opinion, I was either a paragon of virtue or about as intelligent as a sack of rocks.

"You may not be a saint," Alisa told me. "But you *are* discreet."

"And Jameson is...not," I said. If Alisa noticed the way my lips ticked upward just saying his name, she chose to ignore it.

"He's a Hawthorne. *Discreet* is not in their vocabulary." Alisa had her own history with the Hawthorne family. "The foundation's work is gaining steam. We don't need a scandal right now. When you see Jameson, you tell him: No puppies this time. No breaking and entering. No rooftops. No dares. Don't let him drink anything that glows. Call me if he so much as *mentions* leather pants. And remember—"

"I'm not Cinderella anymore," I finished. "I'm writing my own story now."

At seventeen, when my life had changed forever, I'd been the lucky girl from the wrong side of the tracks, plucked from obscurity and given the world at the whim of an eccentric billionaire. But now? I *was* the eccentric billionaire.

I'd come into my own. And the world was watching.

Saint Avery. I shook my head at the thought. Whoever had come up with that moniker clearly didn't realize that the biggest difference between Jameson and me, when it came to dares and games and the thrill of the moment, was that I was better at not getting caught.

Within minutes, the plane was ready for us to deboard— security first, then Alisa, then me. The instant I had both feet on the ground, I got a text from Jameson. I doubted the timing was a coincidence.

Very few things with Jameson were.

I read his text, and a surge of energy and awe, reminiscent of what I'd felt when I'd looked out the window at the ancient city below, came rushing back. A slow smile spread over my face.

Two sentences. That was all it took for Jameson Hawthorne to make my heart start beating a little harder, a little faster.

Welcome to the City of a Hundred Spires, Heiress. Feel like a game of Hide and Seek?

Chapter 2

Our version of Hide and Seek had three rules:

The person hiding couldn't ditch their phone.

GPS tracking had to be enabled.

The person seeking had an hour.

In the past six months, Jameson and I had played in Bali, Kyoto, and Marseille; on the Almafi Coast; and in the labyrinthine markets of Morocco. Following the GPS coordinates was never the hard part, and that held true today. No matter how many times I checked Jameson's location, the pulsing blue marker stayed in the same half-block radius, just outside of Prague Castle.

And *that* was the challenge.

My Achilles' heel in Hide and Seek was always how hard it was for me not to lose myself in my surroundings, in the moment—or in this case, in the view. *The castle.* I'd known before coming to Prague that it was among the largest castles in the world, but knowing was different from seeing was different from *feeling.*

There was a certain magic in standing in the shadows of an ancient, massive structure that made you feel small, something that made the earth and its possibilities feel enormous. I gave myself a full minute to take it all in—not just the sights but the feel of the morning air on my skin, the people already on the streets all around me.

And then I got to work.

Per the GPS, Jameson's location had varied between several points, all of which seemed to be located in the palace gardens—or sometimes, just outside the garden's walls. I walked those walls, looking for the entry. It didn't take me long to realize that the garden in question was actually multiple gardens, interconnected, all of which were *closed*—or at least, they were closed to the public.

When I approached the entry, the iron gate swung inward for me.

Like magic. I'd meant what I'd said to Alisa on the plane. I would *never* get used to this. I stepped through the gate. Oren followed at a reasonable distance. Once we were both inside, the iron gate swung closed behind us.

I made eye contact with the docent who'd closed it. He smiled.

I had no idea how Jameson had managed this. I wasn't sure that I wanted to know. My body buzzing with the thrill of the game, I made my way inward until I reached a set of stairs, narrow and steep—the kind of stairs that made you feel as if climbing them might take you back in time.

I made it to the top, looked down at my phone, and then looked back up at the surrounding terrace gardens—and up and up and up. My brain automatically started trying to calculate the number of stairs, the number of terraces.

I looked down at my phone again and took a turn off the beaten path, jogging forward, then turning again. The instant my GPS location brushed up against Jameson's, his blinking blue cursor disappeared from the map.

Technically, that made *four* rules for our version of Hide and Seek.

The hunt was on.

"Found you," I said. Once upon a time, I'd been a more gracious winner, but now I relished my victories like a Hawthorne.

"Cutting it close this time, Heiress?" Jameson spoke from behind the tree that stood between us. No part of his body was visible to me, but I could *feel* his presence, the outline of his long, lean form. "Fifty-eight minutes, nineteen seconds," Jameson reported.

"One minute and forty-one seconds to spare," I countered, circling the tree and stopping when my body was directly in front of his. "How did you get them to open this place early?"

Jameson's lips curved. He turned ninety degrees and took three slow steps back toward the garden path. "How *didn't* I get them to open early?"

Three more steps, and he was on the path. He knelt, picking something up off the stone. I knew before he stood back up and brandished his bounty that it was a coin.

Jameson twirled the coin from one finger to the next. "Heads or tails, Heiress?"

My eyes narrowed slightly, but I deeply suspected my pupils were dilating, drinking it all in. This was *us*. Jameson. Me. Our language. Our game.

Head or tails?

"You planted that." I nodded toward the coin. I had a collection of them, at least one from every place we'd visited. And every single one of those coins had a memory attached.

"Now why," Jameson murmured, "would I ever do a thing like that?"

Heads I kiss you, he'd told me once, *tails you kiss me, and either way, it means something.*

I reached out to pluck the coin from his hand, and he let me—not that I wouldn't have prevailed either way. I looked down at the coin: The outer ring was bronze, the inner circle gold, bearing the image of a castle. On the reverse side, there was a golden creature that looked like a lion.

I twirled the coin through my fingers the way Jameson had through his—one by one by one. I caught it between my thumb and the side of my index finger, and then I flipped it into the air.

I caught it in my palm. I spread my fingers and looked from the coin to him. "Heads."

Chapter 3

Forty minutes later, we were on a rooftop. *Sorry, Alisa.* I still had the coin.

"You could make a wish," I told Jameson, twirling the coin between my fingers again, my lips swollen and aching in all the right ways. I cast a glance back over our shoulders at the gardens below. "There's no shortage of fountains down there."

Jameson did not turn to look at the fountains. He leaned into me, the two of us perfectly balanced—on the roof and with each other. "What fun is wishing?" Jameson countered. "No game to play, no challenge to best, just...*poof,* here's your heart's desire."

That was a very Hawthorne perspective on wishes, on *life.* Jameson had grown up in a glittering, elite world where nothing was out of reach. He hadn't spent his childhood birthdays blowing out candles. Every year, he'd been given ten thousand dollars to invest, a challenge to fulfill, and the opportunity to pick any talent or skill in the world to cultivate, no expenses spared—and no excuses accepted.

I considered leaving the topic alone, but ultimately decided to push back a bit. In my experience, Jameson Hawthorne liked being pushed.

"You don't know what you would wish for," I said, my tone making it clear that the words were a challenge, not a question.

"Maybe not." Jameson shot me a look that was nothing but trouble. "But I can certainly think of some *fascinating* games I'd like to win."

That statement was every bit as much of an invitation as *heads or tails*. Holding back—*just a bit, just for a moment longer*—I pulled the postcard Jameson had sent me out of my back pocket. It was starting to look a little wrinkled, a little worn.

Real, the way most people's dreams never were.

"I got your postcard," I said. "No message on the back."

"How long did you spend trying to determine if I'd written something in invisible ink?" Jameson asked. *Nothing but trouble.*

I countered his question with my own: "What kind of invisible ink did you use?"

Just because I hadn't been able to reveal it didn't mean it wasn't there.

Beside me, Jameson leaned back on his elbows and looked up at Prague Castle again. "Maybe I just considered writing something, then decided not to." He gave a careless little shrug, a very *Jameson Hawthorne* shrug. "After all, it's been done."

For decades, another Hawthorne had sent postcards just like this one to my mother. Theirs had been a star-crossed kind of love—but *real*.

Like the creases in my postcard.

Like Jameson and me.

"Everything's been done by someone," I pointed out quietly.

Jameson's gap year was three-quarters done. Day by day, I could feel him growing more restless in his own skin. I'd been Hawthorne-adjacent long enough to know that billionaire Tobias Hawthorne's real legacy hadn't been the fortune he'd left me.

It was the marks he'd left on each of his grandsons. Invisible. Enduring.

This was Jameson's: Jameson Winchester Hawthorne was *hungry*. He wanted everything and needed *something*, and because he was a Hawthorne, that elusive something could never be ordinary.

He couldn't be ordinary.

"You should know by now, Heiress, that the words *everything's been done by someone* sound a lot like a challenge to me." Jameson smiled, one of those uneven, edged, wicked Jameson smiles. "Or a dare."

"No dares," I told Jameson, grinning right back.

"You've been talking to Alisa," he said, then he cocked an eyebrow. "Saint Avery."

Jameson could read at least nine languages that I was aware of. He almost certainly knew *exactly* what the world was saying about him.

"Don't call me that," I ordered. "I'm no saint."

Jameson straightened and pushed my hair back from my face, the tips of his fingers banishing tension in every muscle they crossed. My temple. My scalp.

"You act like what you did with your inheritance is nothing," he said. "Like anyone would have done it. But I wouldn't have. Grayson wouldn't have. None of us would. You act like what you're doing with your foundation isn't extraordinary—or like, if it is, it's because the work is so much bigger than you. But, Avery? What you're doing . . . it's *something*."

A Hawthorne kind of something. *Everything*.

"It's not just me," I told Jameson fiercely. "It's all of us." He and his brothers were working with me on the foundation. There were causes Jameson had been championing, people he'd brought in to sit on the board.

"And yet..." Jameson dragged the words out. "You're the one with meetings today."

Giving away billions—strategically, equitably, and with an eye to outcomes—was a lot of work. I wasn't naive enough to try to do it all myself, but I also wasn't about to coast on the blood, sweat, and tears of others.

This was my story. I was writing it. This was my chance to change the world.

But for another few minutes... I brought my hand to Jameson's jaw. *It's just you and me.* On this rooftop, at the top of the world and the base of a castle, it felt like the two of us were the only people in the universe.

Like Oren wasn't standing guard down below. Like Alisa wasn't waiting outside the gates. Like I was just Avery, and he was just Jameson, and that was enough.

"I don't have meetings for another hour," I pointed out.

Jameson's adrenaline-kissed smile was, in a word, *dangerous.* "In that case," he murmured, "could I interest you in some shapely hedges, a statue of Hercules, and a white peacock?"

I didn't have to look back at the palace gardens below to know that they were still closed. Jameson and I still had this magical, lifted-from-time place to ourselves.

I smiled an adrenaline-kissed smile of my own. "Alisa said to tell you no puppies."

"A peacock is not a puppy," Jameson said innocently, and then he brought his lips to just almost graze mine—an invitation, a gauntlet thrown, an ask.

Yes. With Jameson, my answer was almost always *yes.*

Kissing him set my entire body on fire. Losing myself to it, to *him*, I felt like standing at the base of something much more monumental than a castle.

The world was big, and we were small, and this was *everything*.

"And, Heiress?" Jameson's lips moved down to my jaw, then my neck. "For the record..."

I felt him everywhere. My fingernails dug lightly into the skin of *his* neck.

"I would never," he whispered roughly, "confuse you for a saint."

The Morning After

There was blood on Jameson's neck, on his chest. It took me a moment to realize that most of it was dry and another small eternity, during which time seemed to stand still, to see the source: a deep cut at the point where his collarbone dipped in the front, right at the base of his neck.

I surged forward, and as my hands went to the sides of Jameson's neck, I realized that although the deepest part of the cut was small, longer red lines traced his collarbone on either side, shallow cuts that gave his wound an almost triangular shape.

Someone did this to you. I couldn't speak. The only thing that could make a cut like that was a blade wielded by someone who knew exactly what they were doing.

A knife? The thought of someone holding a *knife* to Jameson's neck—that close to his carotid arteries—sent a chill down my spine. My voice still trapped in my throat, I skimmed my hands gingerly down his neck to just above the cut. I stared at the delicate rivulets of dried blood on his chest, and then I noticed his shirt.

When Jameson had disappeared, he'd been wearing a button-up shirt, but now, the top four buttons were gone—*cut off?*—exposing the skin underneath.

"*Jameson.*" I'd never in my life said a word that urgently.

"I know, Heiress." His voice was low and hoarse, but he managed a rakish smile. "Bleeding is a good look for me."

Jameson was Jameson, always.

The pace of my heartbeat evened out. I opened my mouth to ask Jameson where the hell he had been and what the hell had happened to him, but before I could get a single word out, I realized...

He smelled like smoke. *Like fire.* And his shirt was smudged with ash.

Chapter 4

Three Days Earlier...

After working nonstop all day, I had only one thing on my mind. One person. From the moment I saw our hotel, surrounded by centuries-old buildings on all sides, anticipation began to build inside me with every step.

Into the lobby.

Into the elevator.

Out of it.

The Royal Suite was on its own floor. I noted two of Oren's men stationed in the hall. There had been a third in the lobby. As far as I knew, that was the entire team he'd brought to Prague.

Threats against me were at an all-time low.

That didn't stop Oren from putting his body squarely in front of mine as we walked down the hall. He opened the door to the suite and cleared the foyer and adjacent rooms before I was allowed to enter. The moment I did, I realized something: From the hallway, the door I'd just walked through had appeared as just a door, but on this side, as it closed behind us, it disappeared into an ornate, golden mural on the wall, creating the impression that the foyer had no entry and no exit—that the Royal Suite was a world unto itself.

The floor was made of white marble, but just ahead, there was a deep red carpet that looked so soft and lush that I gave in to the urge to kick my shoes off and step on it with bare feet. Nearby, two chairs sat facing the mural. The marble table between them was a work of art—literally. The front of the marble had been chiseled into a sculpture. It took me a moment to recognize its shape from the coin. *The lion. A coat of arms.*

"We're clear," Oren told me—in other words, he'd checked the rest of the suite, which raised a question...

"Where's Jameson?" I asked.

"I could answer that question," Oren replied. "But something tells me you would prefer if I did not." He raised a hand to his ear, a signal that someone was talking on his earpiece. "Alisa is on her way up," he reported.

Alisa would want to debrief about my last meeting of the day, which she had been unable to attend. For that matter, Jameson's brother Grayson would want a report on *all* of my meetings—but I suppressed the urge to take out my phone.

I could answer that question, Oren had said. *But something tells me you would prefer that I did not.* Interpreted one way, that sounded ominous. But I knew what it looked like when Oren was coming close to thinking about possibly *almost* smiling.

I walked from the foyer into a dining room complete with crystal chandelier overhead and gold-rimmed china on the table. At each of the twelve place settings, there was a champagne flute. Inside the champagne flutes, there were crystals.

Thousands of them, diamond-like and small. I made my way around the table and stopped when I saw a flash of color inside one of the flutes—green, like Jameson's eyes.

Moving carefully but swiftly, I dumped out the crystals. Among them, I found a larger gem. *An emerald?* It was the width of my thumbnail, and as I picked it up and turned it back and forth in the light, I realized there was something on its surface.

An arrow.

I turned the gem in my hand, and the arrow moved. *Not a gem*, I realized. I was holding a very small, very delicate compass.

It took me less than three seconds to realize that the "compass" wasn't pointing north.

Jameson. I felt my lips curve. I'd never smiled like this before I'd met him—the kind of smile that tore across my face and sent a ripple of energy surging through my body.

I followed the arrow.

Coming into a living room—complete with *another* crystal chandelier, *another* lush red carpet, and windows that offered a breathtaking view of the river—I scanned my surroundings and saw another work-of-art-level marble coffee table.

On that table, there was a vase.

I let my gaze linger on the flowers. *Roses. Five black. Seven red.* I turned back toward the room, looking for that combination of colors, for something to count, and then I realized that I was falling into a Hawthorne trap.

I was complicating things.

Bending down, I reached into the bouquet. *Victory.* My fingers latched around something cylindrical and metal.

"Do I want to know?" I heard Alisa ask Oren in the room behind me.

"Do you really have to ask?" he replied.

Flashlight. I registered what I held in my hand, gave it a twist, and then corrected myself out loud. "Black light."

Jameson wasn't making this particularly hard, which made me think that the challenge wasn't the point. The anticipation was.

"Can one of you turn off the lights?" I called back to Oren

and Alisa. I didn't look back to see which one of them fulfilled that request.

I was too busy having my way with the black light.

Arrows appeared on the floor. It was just like Jameson to not even bat an eye at the idea of invisibly defacing the single nicest hotel suite I'd ever seen.

"Key word *invisibly*," I murmured under my breath, as I followed the arrows out of the room and into another and another and out onto a balcony. The arrows took me to the edge of the balcony—and *that view* of the river—and then they turned back toward the building... and up the closest wall.

The exterior of the hotel was made of stone, not brick—and that meant there were handholds. Footholds. *Possibilities.*

Still barefoot, I began to climb.

"I distinctly remember saying no roofs!" Alisa called after me.

I was too busy climbing to respond, but Oren offered a response of his own: "Threat assessment, low." I stifled a grin, which proved to be a losing endeavor when my head of security continued, "I believe I saw a champagne bottle in the kitchen with your name on it, Alisa. Literally."

Jameson's handiwork, I thought. He had distracting Alisa down to an art form. The last thing I heard as I latched my hand over the edge of the roof was Alisa's response to Oren's thinly veiled amusement.

"Judas."

I might have laughed, if that hadn't been the exact moment that I finished my climb and the rooftop came into view. The tiles were a red-orange color the exact shade of the setting sun. On top of the roof, there was a metal dome that gave way to a spire.

On top of the dome, one hand on the spire, was Jameson Winchester Hawthorne.

Only the gentle angles of the roof and the fact that there was a small stone terrace below the dome could even remotely justify Oren's assessment that there was no danger here. Or maybe he just knew that Jameson and I had a habit of landing on our feet.

Carefully making my way across the rooftop, I arrived at the stone terrace. The railing looked like something an archer might have shot an arrow through, once upon a time. Stepping up onto the terrace, I did a three-hundred-and-sixty-degree turn, taking it all in.

Jameson stayed up on the dome a moment longer, then swung himself down to join me.

"Found you," I murmured. "Twice in one day."

There was something a little lazy and entirely devilish about the way Jameson's lips curled slowly upward. "I have to admit," he told me, "I am becoming very fond of Prague."

Taking in every single detail about the way he was standing there, I noticed a tension to his muscles, like he was primed and ready. Like he was still standing up on the dome.

"Do I want to know how you spent your day?" I asked.

I was sure of one thing: Jameson hadn't spent it here. I doubted it had taken more than half an hour for him to set all of this up. My gut said that something had driven him to do that. Something had put him in the mood to *play*.

I could feel an energy buzzing, just beneath his skin.

"You most *definitely* do." Jameson smirked. I heard what he was really saying: I definitely *wanted* to know how he'd spent his day, and just as definitely . . .

"You're not going to tell me."

Jameson looked out at the Vltava River, then turned in a circle, the way I had earlier, taking in the rest of the view. *The city.* "I Have A Secret, Heiress."

I Have A Secret had been one of my mom's favorite games, one of the longest-lasting games that we'd played together. One person announced that they had a secret. The other person made their guesses. I'd never guessed my mom's biggest secrets, had only discovered them after she was long gone and I'd been pulled into the world of the Hawthornes, but she'd always had a knack for guessing mine.

I let the full force of my gaze settle on Jameson's vivid green eyes. "You found something," I guessed. "You did something you weren't supposed to. You met someone."

Jameson flashed his teeth in a there-and-gone smile. "Yes."

"To which guess?" I said.

Jameson adopted an innocent expression—far *too* innocent. "How were your meetings?"

I could practically feel the rush of adrenaline through his veins. He was so alive—up here, in this moment, right now—that a low, humming intensity rolled off him in waves.

Jameson definitely had a secret.

"Productive." I answered his question and then took a single step toward him. "I don't have any meetings tomorrow."

"Or the next day. Or the next." Jameson's voice went a little low, a little husky. "Feel like a game?"

I grinned, but I was smart enough—and had enough experience with Hawthornes—to approach that proposition with a certain amount of caution. "What kind of game?"

"Our kind," Jameson told me. "A Hawthorne game. Saturday mornings—clue to clue to clue."

Jameson angled his gaze toward the stone railing behind me. I turned, and sitting on top of it, I saw two objects—one I recognized immediately and one I'd never seen before.

A knife. A key.

The knife was Jameson's, obtained during one of those long-ago Saturday morning games with his billionaire grandfather. The key was old, made of wrought iron.

"Just two objects?" I raised a brow. Usually, in games of this type, there were more. *A fishing hook. A price tag. A glass ballerina.*

"I never said that." Jameson mirrored my expression, raising a brow right back at me.

Once upon a time, he had considered me nothing more than a part of one of his grandfather's games. Now, he'd never dream of treating me as anything other than a player.

"A game," I said, eyeing the knife and the key.

"Technically, I was thinking we'd play *two*: one of my design and one of yours."

Two games. Our kind of games.

"We've got three more days in Prague," I noted.

"Indeed we do, Heiress." He had a good poker face, but not nearly good enough.

"You've already made your game, haven't you?" I demanded.

"This place—this city—practically did it for me." There it was again, the hum of energy in Jameson's voice that told me that he wasn't just *playing*. That something had happened.

I Have A Secret...

"One day for my game," the magnetic, adrenaline-drunk, beautiful, *buzzing* boy across from me proposed. "One day for yours. Each game can have no more than five steps. Player with the fastest time sets the itinerary for our final day in Prague."

Jameson's tone made it *very* clear what his itinerary would involve. I had no idea what had come over him in the past few hours, but whatever it was, I could taste an echo of it on the tip of my own tongue, a light and tantalizing thrill. I could feel Jameson's energy pumping through my veins.

You have a secret, I thought. "All right, Hawthorne," I told him. "Game on."

The Morning After

M y fingers stopped just short of touching the ash on Jameson's white shirt. "You smell like smoke," I told him.

"I don't smoke, Heiress."

Jameson Hawthorne, master of deflection. "That's not the kind of smoke I'm talking about," I said, but Jameson knew that, just like I knew from the expression on his face alone that he wasn't going to say a single word about fire or flames or how close he'd come to getting burned.

What happened? I searched his eyes, and then my gaze went back to the cut at the base of his neck—deep at its lowest point, shallower as it went up. *Who did this to you?*

Instead of asking anything out loud, I ran my fingers over the lines of dried blood on his chest—streaks of it, like heavy drops of blood had run down his chest like tears. I could see sweat beaded on his skin even now, and when I brought my gaze back up to his face, there was something guarded about the set of his features.

Jameson was still smiling, but everything in me said that smile was a lie. *Bleeding is a good look for me,* he'd quipped.

"I'm not done asking questions," I warned him.

Jameson reached out and touched me, a light brush against

my cheek, like *I* was the fragile one here. "Never thought that you were, Heiress."

The sound of footsteps alerted me to Oren's approach. My head of security rounded the corner and took in the scene in front of him in a heartbeat: Jameson, me, the blood.

Oren folded his arms over his chest. "I also have questions."

Chapter 5

Two Days Earlier...

On my second day in Prague, I woke with the dawn, Jameson still asleep beside me. *One day for my game,* he'd stipulated the night before. *One day for yours.*

Per the rules we'd agreed to—after a lengthy and not quite G-rated *negotiation* the night before—I had until midnight to make it to the end of his game. As tempting as lingering in bed was, I knew better than to think Jameson might have gone easy on me.

His game was going to be a challenge. I was going to need every minute I had.

Rolling over in bed, I propped myself up and reached across Jameson to the nightstand—and the objects. *The knife. The key.* As I pulled the latter toward the former and closed my fingers around both, Jameson stirred beneath me. For a moment, my gaze was drawn to his bare chest and the jagged scar that ran the length of his torso. I knew every inch of that scar.

Just like I knew that Jameson Winchester Hawthorne played to win.

"Good morning, Heiress." Jameson's eyes were still closed, but a smile pulled at his lips.

I had a split second to make my choice: Did I stay propped up in bed beside him or go for a position that would give me a bit more leverage?

I went for the latter. By the time Jameson's eyes opened, I was straddling him, one hand on his chest, the other firmly holding the objects meant to start off his game.

There were advantages to keeping your opponent pinned down.

Jameson didn't so much as try to prop himself up on his elbows. He just looked up at me with a very particular curve to his lips.

"You are not going to distract me, Hawthorne."

"Wouldn't dream of it." Jameson smirked. "I have scruples, you know."

"*I* know that," I said. "You don't." Jameson had a bone-deep belief that he wasn't the good guy, the one who made the right choices, the hero. On his worst days, he looked at me and thought that I deserved better than him.

This wasn't going to be one of those days.

On top of him, I shifted my weight. Setting the key on his rock-hard abdomen, I turned my attention to the knife. This wasn't my first time seeing the blade—or holding it. I knew for a fact that there was a hidden compartment in the handle.

It didn't take me long to find the trigger.

The moment the compartment opened, I turned the knife over in my hand. A small piece of paper fell out, like a fortune from inside a fortune cookie. I almost rolled off Jameson to read it but decided not to. Keeping his lower body pinned beneath mine, I leaned forward and unrolled the thin strip of paper on his stomach, next to the key.

Jameson's haphazard scrawl stared back at me from the paper. A poem. A *clue*.

"Does finding this count as step one?" I asked Jameson. The night before, he'd said we would each be limited to five steps in our puzzles.

Jameson put his hands behind his head and smiled, like he didn't have a care in the world. Like his body wasn't tense in all the right ways beneath me. "What do you think?" he shot back.

I think that if I don't get off you, I'm never going to make it out of this room.

I rolled off him, off the bed, and to my feet on yet another plush red carpet. "I think," I told Jameson, "that *this* is step one."

I skimmed the words of my first clue—a poem. Once I'd made it to the end, I reread the words slowly, line by line.

Borrow or rob?

Don't nod.

Now, sir, a war is won.

Nine minutes 'til seven

On the second of January, 1561.

I walked over to the window and pulled the massive curtains, staring out at the Vltava River and the city beyond it.

I heard Jameson get out of bed, heard him padding toward me. "What are you searching for?" That wasn't Jameson asking what I was looking at. He was asking what I made of this clue— *his* clue. He was testing me.

I looked back down at the words.

Borrow or rob?

Don't nod.

Now, sir, a war is won.

Nine minutes 'til seven

On the second of January, 1561.

One word jumped off the page, and the gears in my mind began to turn. Maybe I was getting ready to run headfirst down the wrong path, but in a Hawthorne game, sometimes you had to go with your gut.

I stared out at the Vltava for a moment longer, my resolve crystalizing, and then I turned back to Jameson and his question: What was I searching for? What part of this clue did I intend to focus on first?

I met his gaze and threw down the gauntlet. "War."

Chapter 6

An internet search using the terms *Prague* and *war* quickly revealed that most of the search results focused on the same war—World War II. *The Prague uprising. The liberation of Prague.*

Different versions of the same historical account came up over and over again. The dates didn't match the one given in my clue—not the month, not the day, not the year. But I'd played enough Hawthorne games to know that the "date" in my riddle might not be a date. It could very well be a numerical code. And while the Prague uprising hadn't happened in 1561, it *had* coincided with the end of a war.

Now, sir, a war is won.

I looked back down at the clue. If my initial instincts were correct, if I'd zeroed in on the part of the clue meant to start me off, then the meaning of the other lines of the poem might only become clear later, once I was close to the answer.

Physically close.

Jameson had said the city had practically laid out his game for him. I wasn't meant to spend the day in this hotel room. What I was looking for was out there.

The City of a Hundred Spires. The Golden City. Prague. My mind whirring, I refined the search terms on my phone to be specific to World War II, then added two more words: *monument* and *memorial*.

It didn't take me long to find exactly what I was looking for: Six locations marked on a map.

"And now," Jameson murmured, satisfaction clear in his voice, "she's off and running."

I found nothing at the first three locations, but at the fourth, an elderly woman wearing a burnt-red scarf over her hair struck up a conversation with me. I told her that I was exploring World War II monuments in the city, looking for one in particular—I just wasn't sure which one.

The old woman assessed me, not even bothering to hide the fact that she was doing so. After a long moment, she almost smiled, then parted with a single piece of information. "You might be looking for one of the plaques."

"The plaques?" I queried.

"To mark the fallen heroes." The woman fixed her gaze on the horizon. "Some known. Some unknown. They're everywhere in this city, if only you know to look."

Everywhere? I was already two hours into my search, and though I was falling in love with Prague, block by block and mile by mile, I'd gotten nowhere.

"How many plaques are there?" I asked.

The old woman swiveled her gaze back toward me. "A thousand," she told me. "Or more."

The old woman had been right: Once I knew to look for the plaques, they really were everywhere. Most were small and made of bronze or stone. Some bore specific names. Some were dedicated to unknown fighters. One thing was crystal clear: I was going to get exactly nowhere unless I could narrow it down.

I turned my attention back to the exact wording of the clue:

Borrow or rob?

Don't nod.

Now, sir, a war is won.

Nine minutes 'til seven

On the second of January, 1561.

This time, I zeroed in on the number, the only one in the clue written as a numeral. If *1561* wasn't a year, it could be an address. But was that too obvious?

I went back to the beginning of the clue again.

Borrow or rob?

I looked up from the page. The streets were crowded now, bustling. I made my way to a street vendor selling pastries, bought one, then tried my luck at asking a local for information once more.

"Is there, by any chance, a street around here whose name in Czech has something to do with robbers?" I asked. "I'm trying to solve a puzzle."

Borrow or rob . . . It was worth a shot.

"Robbers?" Luckily for me, the vendor spoke English. "As in thieves?" The man handed me my pastry.

"Yes," I told him. "Exactly."

He didn't ask what kind of puzzle I was trying to solve. Instead, he turned to the next customer.

Just when I was on the verge of giving up, the vendor turned back to me.

"If this puzzle of yours involves thieves, you are not looking for a street," he said brusquely, then he nodded toward a spire in the distance. "You are looking for the arm."

Chapter 7

The Basilica of St. James was beautiful, a massive, breath-taking Baroque marvel. The moment I stepped across the threshold of the entry, I felt like I'd stepped into another world. And then I looked up—at the arm.

The thief's arm. I stared at it way longer than I wanted to—an actual, mummified *arm*, hanging from a pole near the ceiling. Ripping my gaze away from it, I pushed down the urge to shiver and shifted my attention to the church around me.

Borrow or rob?

Don't nod.

Did that mean I was supposed to keep my chin up? And look for some marker of the war?

"I thought you might end up here."

Jameson. I turned to face him. His green eyes found mine like a homing beacon, like they'd been made for looking at me. "Guess again, Heiress."

That was as close to a hint as I was going to get: At some point, I'd misstepped. I was barking up the wrong tree. And *he* was smirking.

"You're going down, Hawthorne," I told him.

Jameson took a single step back. "Catch me if you can,

Heiress." He took off, slipping out of the church before I could even blink.

I followed him—out of the building, down, weaving through a crowded street, around the corner, to—

Nothing.

There was nothing there. No plaques. No addresses involving the number 1561. And no Jameson.

It was like he'd disappeared.

I came to a standstill. *Where did you go, Hawthorne?* I whirled, but Jameson was gone. I looked up, expecting to see him scaling the side of one of the buildings lining the alleyway, but he wasn't.

There was nothing for him to have grabbed on to. I looked down the alley. There was nowhere for him to hide.

Where are you? I backtracked around the corner, wondering if my mind was playing tricks on me, if I'd only thought that he'd come this way.

Still nothing. Jameson was nowhere to be seen.

Catch me if you can, he'd said. I was willing to bet he'd known that I wouldn't be able to. He'd had a plan—but I didn't have time to go down the rabbit hole of thinking about it.

That mystery could wait.

I refocused on the task at hand and what Jameson had said when he'd found me in the Basilica. *Guess again.*

That was his way of telling me I was on the wrong track. *With the plaques, the thief's arm, World War II, all of it?* I wondered. *Or just part?*

I stood there, thinking, lost in my own world, for almost a minute. From his position at the entry to the alley, Oren didn't say a word. My head of security knew better than to interrupt my concentration.

Based on experience, I knew that in a puzzle like this one,

when you hit a wall—figuratively or literally—the best thing to do was go back to the beginning and question every assumption and choice you'd made.

I retraced my steps back to the church, but didn't go in. Closing my eyes, I thought back to that first internet search I'd done in my hotel room, for Prague and war.

Most of the results had been focused on World War II. *Most*—but not all.

There were at least two different battles referred to as the Battle of Prague—one that had occurred in 1648 and another in 1747. When I searched for monuments related to those battles, I found three.

I hit the third around noon. *Charles Bridge.* It was one of the most recognizable and iconic locations in Prague. It was also crowded with tourists. At the ends of the ancient stone bridge, there were towers. Carved into one of the towers there was a memorial to the Battle of Prague. An inscription.

I found it just as Jameson found me.

I wondered how long he'd been watching—and then I wondered how he'd managed to lose me before.

Catch me if you can, Heiress. I emphatically shut the door on my memory of that moment and braced myself for his next distraction.

Jameson stepped beside me, his body brushing mine, then nodded toward the words inscribed on the tower. He translated them out loud: *"Rest here, walker, and be happy: You can stop here willing, but..."*

With a smirk, Jameson trailed off and turned his gaze from the inscription to me.

"You can guess the rest," he said, far too satisfied with

himself—and with his game. "The basic gist is that bad guys were stopped here against their will. Victory! Huzzah!"

I narrowed my eyes. "Huzzah?"

Jameson leaned against the stone wall. "For the record, Heiress, you're getting warmer."

I didn't trust the way he said those words. "For the record," I told him, "I know that look."

It was a look that said *I'm going to win*. It said *You don't see what's right before your eyes*. It said *Aren't I clever?*

And yes, he was.

But so was I. "The mention of war," I said, searching his face, reading him the way that only I could, "is a distraction."

A very Hawthorne kind of distraction in a city with a thousand plaques. This time, when I pulled out my phone, I tried different search terms—nothing but the date.

January 2, 1561.

One result came up over and over again—one name: *Francis Bacon*. Apparently, the so-called father of empiricism had been born on January 2, 1561, at least according to some sources.

I glanced up at Jameson, who was watching me with something like anticipation in his eyes.

Narrowing mine at him, I turned back to my phone and did a search for *Francis Bacon* and *Prague*. In less than a minute, I'd discovered that there was an Irish artist who shared the name.

There was also a gallery in Prague that had auctioned off a significant collection of that Francis Bacon's art.

Hitting the gallery took me back through the Old Town Square. Navigating my way down side streets, I managed to find the gallery without too many wrong turns.

Within seconds of my stepping inside, a gallery employee in a very expensive suit fixed me with a piercing look. It was the kind of look that clearly said a teenager in jeans and a worn T-shirt had no place browsing in an establishment like this one—the kind of look that disappeared the moment Oren stepped into the building after me.

There was nothing like a military-trained bodyguard to make people second-guess their first impressions.

As I made my way through the gallery, looking for *something*, the haughty man in the suit tried to mask the way that he was looking at me, but eventually, his eyes widened. I knew that stare. I'd been recognized—and as far as I could tell, there was nothing here.

Another wrong turn. Before the gallery employee could begin rolling out the red carpet for the Hawthorne heiress, I ducked out of the store. I thought I saw Jameson again—through the crowd, on the move. I followed him, picking up my pace, dodging through groups of people. But the second I hit the Old Town Square, I lost him.

As I scanned the crowd, I noticed that all around me, people's bodies were orienting in one direction.

Toward the clock. It was massive, old, a work of art—disk layered over disk, turquoise and orange and gold.

"Here in just a moment," a tour guide said from somewhere behind me, "at the top of the hour, you'll see a rotating procession of apostles. And there, to the right—that skeleton is Death. The other figures you see around the clock are Catholic saints. In addition to keeping time, the astronomical clock lives up to its name. The smaller ring depicts astronomical charts that allow the clock to display the positions of the sun and the moon, while the—"

The clock struck one.

Like the rest of the crowd, I looked up as the "procession" began. Statues emerged from behind a window in the clock. All around me, phone cameras were raised, trying to capture the moment.

And all I could think—suddenly—was *nine minutes 'til seven.* I'd been given a time, and here was a clock—a very famous clock, obviously.

I stopped myself there. I couldn't afford to go down the wrong path again. I'd burned enough time already. I only had eleven hours left, and I was still on the first clue. I needed to focus. I needed to *see*.

I was missing something.

Tobias Hawthorne's games had always had a clear answer. Jameson's would, too. I knew that. I knew it, but I'd been grasping at wisps all morning.

As the procession of apostles continued above, I focused on breathing and clearing my mind. I could do this.

Nine minutes 'til seven. That was *6:51.* Something about that number stuck with me. Unsure why, I took out the clue again and read:

> *Borrow or rob?*
> *Don't nod.*
> *Now, sir, a war is won.*
> *Nine minutes 'til seven*
> *On the second of January, 1561.*

I stared at the last line of the poem. *1561.* My heart skipped a beat. *1561* and *6:51* contained three of the same numbers.

I turned to Oren. "Do you have a pen?"

He didn't—but someone near us did. The only paper I had was the clue itself, so I turned it over and scribbled down the year and the time, and then added two more numbers: The second of January—2 for day, 1 for month.

I stared at my list of numbers: 1651, 6:51, 2, and 1.

And just like that, I saw it. I rearranged the numbers and wrote them out—year first, then day, then month, then time.

156121651.

It was a palindrome. My gaze darted up to the first line of the poem. *Borrow or rob?* I cursed under my breath, half in frustration with myself for not seeing it until now, half in awe at the extent to which Jameson Hawthorne was a tricky, tricky mastermind of a man.

Borrow or rob?

Don't nod.

Now, sir, a war is won.

Those sentence were *all* palindromes—the same backward as forward. *Jameson. Freaking. Hawthorne.* I of all people should have seen it.

I looked up, certain that somewhere in the crowd, Jameson Winchester Hawthorne was watching. And there he was, lifting some kind of cylindrical pastry to his mouth, a very self-satisfied grin on his face.

The moment Jameson's eyes met mine across the crowd, he knew. Just from looking at me, he *knew* that I'd cracked it.

Jameson raised his pastry in salute.

Snorting, I turned to find the tour guide I'd heard speaking earlier. "If I said the words *Prague* and *palindrome* to you, would that mean anything?"

The tour guide puffed up a bit, like after lo the many years, his time had finally come. "Of course it would."

Chapter 8

Back at the Charles Bridge, on the tower on the east side, I found what I was looking for—a number.

135797531.

The palindrome was a date, like the one in my clue. In 1357, on the ninth of July at 5:31 AM, the first stone for this bridge had been laid. *A superstitious king. A mathematical advisor. A palindromic date.*

It was quite a story. Jameson hadn't been kidding when he'd said that this city had practically made his game for him.

"On a scale of one to ten, do you hate me or hate me very much right now?" Jameson said, coming to stand next to me.

That cat-eating-a-canary smile of his made me want to *do things.*

"Very, very much," I told him, but I stayed on task. I was in the right place, but I still needed to find the next clue.

It took me another ten minutes of running my hands over the bridge before I hit paydirt—something caught between two stones. A very small, very delicate, metal *something.*

I lifted it level with my gaze to examine it further. *A silver charm.* The shape was unmistakable.

I flicked my gaze to Jameson. "The Eiffel Tower?"

The Morning After

'm going to need a location," Oren told Jameson. "Specifics. Names, if you have them."

Jameson offered my head of security his most rakish, ne'er-do-well smile. "And *I* am going to need a shower."

This was the Jameson who liked living on the edge, the one who didn't bat an eye at going too fast or too far, the one capable of wielding every little smirk like a shield.

Oren might have bought the act, but I didn't. I could practically feel Jameson's heart pounding from where I stood. He had very few tells—none that I could pinpoint in words—but I knew him.

I *knew* him.

He went to brush past me, and I stopped him with a single word. "Jameson."

He turned his head toward me, like he couldn't help it, like I was his north.

"Avery." Something about the sound of my given name on Jameson's lips, combined with everything else, almost undid me. He said *Avery* like a plea and a curse and prayer.

He said it like he'd said it to himself while blood streamed down his chest.

I saw the rise and fall of his chest as Jameson considered his next words. "You could make me tell you," he said quietly.

No smirks, no smiles, just truth. I knew exactly what Jameson was saying. One little word—*Tahiti*—and I could make him tell me anything. *But...*

"But I am asking you," Jameson continued in that same low tone, "not to."

I could make him tell me everything. That was the rule between us. It was too easy for him to don masks, too easy for me to lie to myself—but *Tahiti* meant no protection, no dancing around the truth, no hiding.

Tahiti meant baring it all.

You could make me tell you. But I am asking you not to.

Jameson Hawthorne didn't ask for much. He tempted. He invited. He created. He *gave.* But he was asking me for this.

I swallowed. "You go shower," I told him, my voice coming out hoarse. "I'll get a bandage."

On my way to find the first aid kit, I shot Oren a look. *We aren't going to push this*, I telegraphed silently. *Not yet.*

Chapter 9

Two Days Earlier...

The Petřín Lookout Tower was a one-fifth-scale, not-quite replica of the Eiffel Tower located on the tallest hill in Prague, overlooking the castle. Decoding the meaning of Jameson's second clue wasn't the hard part.

The hard part was figuring out what to do once I got to the top of Petřín Hill.

Coming to a stop at the tower's base, I looked from the silver charm in my hand up to the real thing in front of me. There were differences, but the resemblance was unmistakable. I was in the right place. Now I just had to figure out what I was looking for—and where exactly to look for it.

Inside the tower? Outside the tower? The surrounding hill?

I summoned an image of Jameson in my mind—a little wind-blown, a little wild. He would have climbed Petřín Hill himself instead of hitching a ride on the funicular, the way I had. And once he'd made it up here, with the city of Prague spread out below, I had no doubt that he would have climbed the tower to the top.

Jameson was fond of heights.

I paid the modest entry fee and made my way inside the tower—and up. Two hundred and ninety-nine stairs spiraled their way around the inside of the tower. *Up and up and up.* When I hit an observation deck, I went into full-on observation mode.

What Would Jameson Do?

I ran my hands over the wood paneling on the walls, examined the framed drawings that hung on those walls, scanned every inch of the floor.

And then I went outside.

Wind whipped at my hair as I walked to the iron railing. A breath caught in my throat. For as gray as the sky had been the morning before, it was crystalline now. The whole of Prague stretched out in the distance, the combined height of the hill and the tower allowing me to see for miles.

"Quite a view." Jameson stepped into my peripheral vision and leaned against the railing.

I turned my head toward him. "Yes. It is." I gave myself a few precious seconds to take in a different kind of view: the tilt of his lips, the dangerous spark in his eyes. Then I turned back and looked up at the peak of the tower.

Steel lattice would be easy enough to climb. "Hypothetically speaking, how many laws am I going to have to break to find my next clue?" I asked.

Jameson flashed me a glittering smile, then produced an apple seemingly out of nowhere. "None." He took a bite out of the apple, then held it out to me. "Hungry?"

My eyes narrowing, I took the apple. Making a study of Jameson and determining that he wasn't lying, I bit into the apple he'd given me. *Crunchy, crispy, sweet.* If there was a law-abiding way of finding my clue, that meant scaling the outside of the tower was out.

Jameson walked to a nearby telescope, mounted on the railing. He bent down to look through it, then adjusted the view.

I knew an invitation when I saw one.

Crossing to stand behind him, I bent to look. Jameson leaned in behind me, nudging the end of the telescope down farther and farther. I felt the heat of his body—and ignored it.

Mostly.

The telescope was pointed at the hillside now, not the view beyond it.

"I prepared a picnic," Jameson told me, and then he turned to whisper directly in my ear. "Come find me once you find the box."

The box. My heart jumped as Jameson took his leave.

A woman on a mission, I searched the observation deck again, then took the remaining stairs all the way up and did the same. *Nothing.* No loose panels in the wall, no loose boards in the floors, nothing wedged in the lattice of the railing.

No box.

A separate spiraling staircase took me down to the base of the tower, and I searched that, too. *Nothing.* The staircase let out into a gift shop. I paused. I could just see Jameson hiding something here, among all the trinkets the shop had for sale.

An electric feeling rising inside me, I perused shelf after shelf, scanning the contents of each one, picking up speed as I went. Jameson had told me what I was looking for, but a *box* could be any number of things.

I stopped in front of one of the largest glass cases, drawn to what I saw inside: A porcelain model of an elaborate labyrinth, filled with arching doors. It wasn't a box. There was no reason for me to linger on it.

But I did.

After a minute—maybe more—I felt someone approach, in part because of the way Oren shifted as they did.

"You like it?" A gift shop employee nodded toward the piece that had captured my attention.

"What is it?" I asked.

"The mirror maze."

My expression must have made it clear that I wasn't following, because the employee elaborated.

"In the chateau next door," she told me.

A mirror maze. I couldn't think of anything more Hawthorne than that, but I pushed back the urge to leap before I looked. I'd already lost hours to impulsivity on this game. Jameson's prior clue—number two in this five-step game—had led me *here*, to the tower.

I wasn't leaving until I'd made damn sure there was nothing here for me to find.

The mirror maze would have to wait.

I paced the rest of the gift shop, continuing my search. Inside the last glass case I examined, there were three items. Two were blown-glass Christmas ornaments.

The third was a wrought-iron box, six inches wide and six deep. The box's design was intricate, but the part that captured my attention was the wrought-iron lock.

At the start of this game, I'd been given two objects: a knife and a *key.*

Chapter 10

I found Jameson on a blanket that matched his eyes—a deep, emerald green. Spread out around him was what could, by some definitions, be considered a picnic, though by most, it would probably have been described as a feast. I counted six kinds of cheese, nine kinds of fruit, five spreads, eight dips, a half-dozen meats, a seemingly unlimited variety of bread and crackers, and what appeared to be the vast majority of the contents of a mid-size gourmet chocolate shop.

I plopped down beside Jameson on the blanket, crossed my legs, and placed the wrought-iron box in my lap. A moment later, I held the key in my hand.

Beside me, Jameson held out an open pomegranate, brimming with jewellike seeds.

"Playing Hades?" I asked him wryly.

Jameson leaned back on his elbows, the sun turning his brown hair almost gold. "Come on, Persephone. What harm could a few bites do?"

Despite myself, I smiled. Jameson Hawthorne was temptation personified—but right now, I was more tempted by the puzzle.

The game.

Our kind of game.

I inserted the key in the wrought-iron lock and turned it. Almost immediately, the box began to unfold, a mechanical marvel of cause and effect that didn't stop until the box had transformed into a flat black square.

Carved into the metal on what had once been the bottom of the box there was a name: *JOEL*.

My gaze went to the two items that sat on top of the square, just under the name. The first object was a glass vial. I picked it up, examining the cloudy white liquid inside. There was a label on the vial: HN_4O.

I glanced up at Jameson, then back down at the second item. Setting the vial aside, I reached for it. The object was a small cardboard cube with a tiny metal crank attached to the side. I took the crank between my middle finger and my thumb and turned it.

Notes played, one after another, for a total of four. *Four notes.* I stopped, then started turning the delicate crank again, and the same combination of notes repeated itself. I didn't recognize the song.

Four music notes. A vial of some kind of chemical solution. And a name.

"Sure you're not hungry, Heiress?" Jameson asked.

Without a word to him, I grabbed some cheese. And some chocolate. And the pomegranate. The last clue had been easy enough to solve, but this one felt more like the first, and I only had eight hours until midnight. I needed fuel.

I also needed to look at the big picture.

Within minutes, I had a working space set up on the blanket. Beside the items from the box, I laid out the ones I'd been given at the beginning of the game. The knife, I had used. The key, I had used.

I thought back to Jameson's response, when I'd questioned the fact that there were only two objects. *I never said that.* It took me a moment to see the catch there—the trick.

I'd been given more than just the knife and the key.

The postcard. If there was any chance that Jameson had been planning this game for more than a day, it had to be included on the list of pre-game items. I pulled it out of my back pocket and put it on the blanket beside the other objects.

A key. A knife. A postcard. And... I wracked my mind and then cursed. "The black light." I hadn't brought it with me.

"I'm a generous man, Heiress." The next thing I knew, Jameson was twirling the black light between his fingers, one by one.

I reached out and nabbed it. "Four objects," I said out loud. "A knife. A key. A postcard. A black light. I've already used the knife and the key."

I turned on the black light, shining it on the liquid in the vial, raking the beam over every inch of the no-longer-a-box. When that yielded nothing, I tried it on the postcard. *Still nothing.* I paused.

Thinking back to our conversation on the palace rooftop above the gardens...Jameson hadn't actually denied that there was invisible writing on the postcard. He'd used the word *maybe.*

Maybe he'd decided against using invisible ink because it had been done before.

And maybe not, I thought. Setting the black light aside temporarily, I uncorked the vial, then dipped the end of my T-shirt into the liquid inside. I went to brush the liquid onto the postcard, but Jameson stopped me.

"Not yet, Heiress."

Not yet? Like the moment when he'd told me I was looking for a box, that hint felt both deliberate and insufficient to give me any insight into what I *was* supposed to do next.

It was a very Jameson Hawthorne kind of hint.

Still lounging on the blanket, he looked up at me, a deceptively angelic expression on his face. "I could probably be seduced into saying more," he told me.

My lips curved, but that didn't stop me from turning his own words back at him. *"Not yet."*

Later, I would kiss that smug expression off his face.

Later, I would let him demonstrate all the many, many reasons he had to be that smug in the first place.

But for now...

"I know a distraction when I see one." I wasn't just talking about *him*. I was talking about the liquid in the vial, about Jameson's *not yet*. If it wasn't time to use the liquid or the postcard—yet—what did that leave?

The music box. The name *JOEL*. And the label on the vial. HN_4O.

I thought through it all—once, twice, three times. I brought my gaze to rest on the label.

"They're letters," I said.

I looked back to Jameson's face and saw the tiniest of shifts, the barest hint of his smile deepening.

I was on the right track.

Using the back of the black light, I drew a series of letters in the dirt beside me. *"Joel,"* I murmured. *"HN_4O."* My eyes cheated up to Jameson's. "Four N's, instead of N_4."

This time, his Hawthorne poker face was impeccable, but it was too late. I knew when I was onto something.

J O E L H N N N N O

I moved, swift and sure, reordering the letters, unscrambling them and writing them anew in the dirt below the original.

J O H N... I paused, then saw the rest of it. *L E N N O N*.

"John Lennon," I said out loud.

Across from me, Jameson sat up and reached for the pomegranate, claiming it back, the expression on his face telling me that he knew exactly what I felt like in that moment.

He knew exactly how good it felt to win.

I did a search on my phone for *John Lennon* and *Prague*. "Bingo."

"Saying *bingo* is a very good look for you, Heiress."

That was yet another invitation—yet more temptation—but I didn't take him up on it. Instead, I collected my objects. *The knife. The key. The postcard. The black light.* I grabbed the vial, too, just in case Jameson's *not yet* meant the contents would come in handy later, even though I'd already used the label.

I picked up the music box last. "One question." I stood, looking down at Jameson, part of me wishing that I was just a little less competitive and little bit more easily distracted. "What's the song?"

I turned the crank—slowly, gingerly—to those same four notes.

"Excellent question, Persephone." Jameson popped an entire handful of pomegranate seeds into his mouth. "As it happens, that particular John Lennon song is called 'Do You Want to Know a Secret?'"

The Morning After

The sound of the shower couldn't drown out the low roar in my ears—or the thoughts swirling in my brain. Something had happened to Jameson, and he was asking me to drop it.

I didn't want to.

Tahiti. I could feel our code word on the tip of my tongue as I entered the bathroom. All I had to do was say it, and he would strip away every layer, every mask, *everything*, leaving only the raw truth behind.

Leaving nothing between us.

Tahiti. I didn't say it. I just stood on one side of the fogged-up glass while Jameson stood under the spray on the other. I could see the outline of his body. Something in me ached to join him, but I didn't.

I let him wash off the blood alone.

He's fine. I knew better than to worry about Jameson Hawthorne. No matter what had happened, he was and would remain fine. But still, I wanted to know.

I *needed* to, the way I needed him.

On the other side of the glass, Jameson turned off the spray. The towel disappeared from the top of the shower door, and I wondered if he was using it to wipe away the last smears of blood on his chest.

I counted my breaths in the time it took him to open the door. *Four. Five.* The glass door opened, and Jameson stepped out, the towel wrapped around his waist.

My gaze trailed up from the towel, along the jagged scar on his torso, to the new cuts at the base of his neck.

"All clean," Jameson told me.

I brought my hand to his chest.

"It's not even going to scar," he told me, like that somehow made the fact that someone had cut him less concerning.

Giving him a look that clearly communicated exactly what I thought about that, I let my fingers lightly trace the lines where the blood had once been. His body was hot to the touch—and wet from the shower.

"All clean," I repeated.

I turned to the counter where I'd laid out the medical supplies and reached for the antibacterial gel first. I smeared some over my finger and then turned back to Jameson. With a feather-light touch, I spread it over his cuts. There were three of them total—the small but deep one at the base of his collarbone, no wider than the width of my smallest nail, and the lighter ones— *no more than scratches now*—that gave the wound its pseudo-triangular shape.

No, I thought, as I pulled my hand back. *Not a triangle. An arrow.*

Chapter 11

The John Lennon Wall was full of bright colors. Spray paint was clearly the medium of choice—and just as clearly, the visuals looked to have been the work of more than one artist. Taking in the colors and angles and images, I wondered how many times this wall had been painted.

"Once upon a time, anyone could add their own paint to the wall." Jameson walked up to lay one hand flat on the mural beside a vivid, neon depiction of Lennon's face. "Now, visitors are limited to markers and specific regions of the wall. Only invited artists are allowed to pick up a can. Anyone else who tries to do so... well, they might find themselves on the wrong side of the law."

If I knew one thing for certain it was this: Jameson was not a particularly law-abiding person. I scanned our surroundings. There was no shortage of cameras.

I could feel a dare coming on. I waited for Jameson to issue it, but he said nothing, and I read into that the obvious: Somewhere on this wall, there was clue.

Given the size of this larger-than-life canvas, finding it was going to be like looking for a needle in a haystack.

I spent a full minute sorting out my strategy, then started at the bottom of the wall, in one of the sections where writing was allowed. I read message after message, in language after language, looking for something that appeared to be Jameson's handiwork, and I found nothing.

Same in the next section.

Same in the next.

Eventually, I stopped focusing on the parts of the wall that people were allowed to write on and started looking at the parts where unauthorized graffiti was no longer allowed.

"I hope you weren't caught on camera," I told him. Alisa was not going to be happy if he had been.

Jameson smiled. "Perish the thought."

Shaking my head, I got back to work. An hour ticked away, then two, as I lost myself in colors and symbols, writing, *art*. And then I heard the music—a busker.

She was playing "Do You Want to Know a Secret?"

I made my way to her. She smiled at me, a nearly Hawthorne kind of smile that had me following her gaze to the top of the wall.

Balanced on the very edge, there was a can of spray paint.

Chapter 12

Scaling that wall was impossible. It was at least twenty feet tall, with no hand- or footholds and cameras everywhere.

But I knew better than most: Some people lived for impossible. *Jameson. Me.*

If I ended up on the news for this, Alisa was going to kill me. And Jameson. Probably Oren, too, for standing by and letting it happen. But what was life without a little risk?

I waited until dark. I made a plan. I executed it.

And in the end, I ended up with the spray paint. I had the distinct sense that even holding the can near the wall might get me arrested, but I didn't have the luxury of hesitating if I wanted to make it through two more clues by midnight.

For what felt like the hundredth time, I scanned the wall. Now that I had the paint, what was I supposed to do with it? A possibility wormed its way into my mind.

I turned my left hand over and used my right to spray my own palm. *Possibility confirmed.* Whatever was in the canister, it wasn't paint. My money was on it being a chemical trigger for invisible ink. That made the next question: What part of the wall did I need to spray?

In between one heartbeat and the next, I suddenly realized that the answer was *none of it.*

When I'd gone to use the liquid in the glass vial on the back of my postcard, Jameson's response had been *not yet.* As in, the postcard hadn't come into play...yet.

Going on instinct, I put ten feet of space between me and the wall, and then I removed the postcard from my back pocket. It was more worn now than it had been before. With a grin, I flipped it over. I shook the canister in my right hand, then sprayed the back of the postcard.

Letters appeared almost immediately—three of them, a single word. *ICE.*

I figured out quickly enough that Prague had a well-known bar where the gimmick was that everything was made of ice.

At the door, a bouncer handed me a full-length parka and a pair of white leather gloves. "Yours to keep," the bouncer told me in a tone that made me think this was very much *not* the normal order of things.

I slipped on the parka. It was snow white and went all the way to my ankles, with a hood lined with faux fur that was mind-blowingly soft to the touch. I slipped on the gloves next—a perfect fit. Clad for deepest winter, I entered the bar.

Small. Sparkling. Freezing.

I pulled up the hood and took a moment to breathe it all in. Everything around me was made of ice—the bar, the lone table positioned in the middle of the room, the walls, the ice sculptures staring at me from all sides.

Jameson was standing behind the bar. He placed a glass on

its icy top, and it took me a moment to realize that the glass was made of ice, too.

Without warning, the lights in the room changed color, casting the ice in a deep purple-blue glow. As small as this space was, I felt like I'd stepped into the arctic.

Like it was just Jameson and me at the ends of the earth.

"What can I get you?" He placed his elbows on the bar and leaned forward, fully committed to playing the bartender. He wasn't wearing a parka, but if he felt the cold—at all—he didn't show it.

I leaned forward and pushed the hood back from my face. "How about my fifth and final clue?" I proposed.

"That you'll have to work for." Jameson smiled. It was cold enough that I could see his breath—and my own—in the air. Separated only by the solid-ice bar, the two of us were close enough that my breath caressed his, the briefest, lightest touch.

"What can I get you," Jameson repeated, "to *drink?*"

"Surprise me."

Jameson turned and reached for a glass bottle on an ice shelf, and my gaze lit on the back of his pants—more specifically, to the chisel tucked into his waistband.

Ice plus chisel plus having to work for my next clue . . . The math there wasn't hard—but getting the chisel away from him might be.

By the time Jameson was pouring a mystery drink into my carved-from-ice glass, I'd formulated a plan.

I took off one of my gloves and ran my finger around the edge of my glass. Slowly. Deliberately. Jameson's gaze lingered on my finger. I picked up the glass and took a drink. As cold as the liquid was, it burned all the way down.

Across from me, Jameson poured himself a drink. I needed to get him to this side of the bar.

Setting my ice glass down, I pulled my glove back on. Slowly. Deliberately. His gaze tracking my movements.

"Feel like a dance?" I asked. There was no music—just the two of us, but that was enough.

Jameson slid over the top of the bar.

I held out my gloved hand. He took it, then pulled me in. Even through my parka, I could feel the hard lines of his body. That was the thing about knowing someone the way that I had come to know Jameson Hawthorne: Every touch triggered the memory of a thousand others.

My body anticipated every move of his. Our breaths met in the air between us like smoke. I could almost hear music starting to play as the two of us began to slow dance. I felt it—the music that wasn't playing *and* the thing rising between us like a living, breathing force.

I, too, was becoming very fond of Prague.

"Feel like playing I Have A Secret?" Jameson asked as we danced. "You still haven't guessed mine."

I recognized the distraction for what it was but didn't shut it down. I knew as well as Jameson did that the two of us were playing more than one game right now.

Earlier, I'd identified three possibilities for his secret: that he'd found something, that he'd done something, that he'd met someone.

"You found something." I made my guess, committing to one possibility of the three.

"Multiple somethings, actually." Jameson dipped me backward. The air in the room was so cold, but I barely felt the chill against my face as he brought me back up, as he pulled my body and my lips so close to his that I felt his next words as much as heard them. "But I think you can do better than that, Heiress."

I knew a challenge when I heard one.

"How long have you been in Prague?" I threw out a question, my tone daring him to answer it.

Jameson Hawthorne was very susceptible to dares. "Not long." He spun me out and back in. "In the grand scheme of things."

In other words, on a scale of months and years and centuries, he hadn't been here long at all. Not exactly illuminating. But given that it had been three days since I'd seen him last, I had to assume he'd spent most of that time here.

"You didn't set this game up in a day," I argued.

"I never said that I did." Jameson smiled. There was absolutely nothing to trust in that smile. It was an *I got you*, clear as a bell.

Something occurred to me—something that *should* have occurred to me much earlier. "And when exactly am I supposed to set up mine?"

Today we played his game. Tomorrow, Jameson was supposed to play mine. It was possible I'd overlooked a key detail in the middle of our *negotiating* the night before.

In my defense, he was a very good negotiator. "Always read the small print, Heiress."

Always look for the catch, I thought. Jameson had been raised doing that every single day under his grandfather's tutelage. Billionaire Tobias Hawthorne had always had an eye for loopholes.

"You stacked the odds in your favor," I accused.

"Of course I did, Heiress, but don't tell me your mind isn't already working at warp speed, plotting out the details of your game while playing mine."

He wasn't wrong, but I didn't have to tell him that. I had his attention—and that had been step one of my plan. All I had to do was keep him distracted just a little bit longer.

"You've been watching me all day. Anything I do, you see." I allowed my arm to wrap just a bit farther around Jameson's back. Next I would slide it down—inch by inch—toward that chisel. "Maybe I can think about my game, but I can't *do* anything."

"That's not why I've been following you," Jameson murmured. "I've been watching you play this game because I want to see it through your eyes."

Neither of us stopped dancing. My head was cradled against his chest, tucked just below his chin, my gaze aimed upward and his down.

"I've seen the world, Heiress. Been there, done that. I'm jaded. But there's nothing the least bit jaded about you. If you could see the way you look when you step into a new place for the first time..."

There was a timbre to his voice that made me ache to listen to it more, but I stayed on task, sliding my hand down his back and closing my fingers around the chisel.

Success! I didn't want to stop dancing, I didn't want to pull away, but I wasn't about to give my opponent a chance to take the chisel back. Over my body's strenuous objection, I put space between us.

Jameson eyed the way I was holding the chisel. "Plotting a murder? *The heiress in the ice bar with the chisel.*"

"Trust me, Hawthorne, if murder is ever on my mind, you'll know." With a smile, I turned my attention back to my surroundings. The bar and shelves were clearly permanent fixtures, as were the walls, which made my best bet for *using* this chisel the ice sculptures.

A castle. A dragon. A swan. A woman. I stopped when I reached the fifth and final sculpture, the one closest to the door through which I'd entered. It was simpler than the others, with less detail, a simple symbol.

"Eight." I ran a gloved finger over the icy outline of the shape, then turned my head sideways. "Or infinity." I looked back at Jameson, memory crashing into me. "The bridge over West Brook."

Jameson and I had found a clue that looked like this once before.

"I guessed that it was infinity," Jameson murmured. "You said it was an eight."

"I was right."

"You usually are, Heiress."

I turned back to the sculpture. "I'm guessing *infinity* this time." Near the top of the ice sculpture, buried deep in the ice, I saw something. *A glint of gold.*

The chisel and I got to work. Five minutes later, I held a ring in the palm of my hand. Rather than a jewel or knot on top, the gold ring bore the infinity symbol.

Jameson took it from me, then turned my right hand over, slipping the ring onto my right ring finger.

A breath caught in my throat. Maybe it was the way his skin had brushed across mine with the motion. Maybe it was the fact that Jameson Hawthorne had just slipped a ring onto one of my fingers. Or maybe it was the knowledge, heavy in the air between us, that in our lifetimes, this probably wouldn't be the only ring that Jameson gave me.

"   e it?"

"You know I do." I met his eyes, and then I narrowed my own. *I see you, Jameson Hawthorne. Multiple birds, one stone.*

I slipped the ring off my finger and turned my attention to the inside of the band.

Four words had been engraved across the gold: *LOOK IN YOUR POCKET.*

I slipped the infinity ring back onto my right ring finger and then did exactly as the note had instructed.

In the pocket of the parka, I found a note, written on spiral notebook paper and folded in half four times, reminding me of the kind of note one middle schooler might slip to another.

I opened it, and the words Jameson had written there took my breath away.

Like the sun and the moon
I loved her.
Saint Avery.
Until death and beyond.

The Morning After

I reached for the bandages on the counter at the exact same moment that Jameson reached for me.

Chapter 13

*L*ike the sun and the moon
    I loved her.

Saint Avery.

Until death and beyond.

I stared at Jameson, keenly aware of the ring on my right hand. *Infinity. Until death and beyond.*

"This is not a proposal," Jameson said quietly. "But it is a promise."

"I'm eighteen," I told him. "You're nineteen."

"You're practical," Jameson replied. "I'm not."

Infinity. Until death and beyond. This is not a proposal.

"The old man liked to say that I was a work in progress," Jameson told me. "That we all were. He acted like someday, Nash, Grayson, Xander, and I would be *done*. That, in his eyes, we would finally be enough. But we never were."

"You are more than—" I started to say, but Jameson pressed two fingers lightly to my lips, and I felt that brush of contact in every inch of my body.

"I'm not done, Heiress," Jameson said intently. "I'm not the person I'm going to be. I know that. But someday, I will be." He took my hand in his. "I'll be that person, and you'll be you, and *this* is what we're going to have."

He looked down at the ring on my right ring finger.

"Infinity," I said. *Until death and beyond. Someday.*

"Now you have a secret, too." Jameson pushed a strand of hair away from my face, then pressed me gently back until I hit a wall of ice. "And incidentally, you also don't have very long until midnight."

"Traps upon traps," I murmured. "And riddles upon riddles."

Jameson meant everything he'd just said. The ring wasn't *just* a distraction. The promise he'd just made me was real. But this—the note, the ring, all of it—was also a part of the game he'd laid out for me.

Our kind of game.

I looked down at the ring. "This isn't your I Have A Secret secret," I said. Earlier, I'd guessed that he'd found something, and he'd responded that he'd found *multiple* somethings. I doubted he'd "found" the ring. He definitely hadn't found the note.

But together, those two items *were* clue number five.

I unzipped my parka and let it drop to the floor, heedless of the cold. An instant later, I'd fished out the black light. It was the only object I hadn't yet used in today's game. I turned the light on, then I aimed it at Jameson's note—his *love* note.

In the purple-blue light of the ice chamber, four words lit up.

*Like the **sun** and the **moon***
I loved her.
***Saint** Avery.*
*Until **death** and beyond.*

"True words," I said, acknowledging that between us. "But they have a second, hidden meaning."

"Very good, Heiress."

I stared at the words. *Sun. Moon. Saint. Death.* And just like that, I knew.

The Morning After

Jameson's hand cupped my shoulder. My fingers hovered over the box of bandages until his wrapped back around to my shoulder blade. Jameson didn't turn me to face him, but *I* turned, unable to do anything else, my shoulders squared to his, the bandages on the counter forgotten.

My arm fell to my side, and he brought his other hand up to my other shoulder. Under Jameson's touch, my shirt felt paper-thin, like the fabric was as insubstantial as smoke.

Like there was nothing separating my skin from his touch at all.

I *felt* Jameson's hands make their way beneath my hair, which was hanging loose down my back. Those hands pushed up to my neck. My breath hitched as Jameson's fingers went up farther—past my hairline, into my hair.

Jameson's fingers curled, grasping my hair, tilting my chin up. I met his eyes, and what I saw there made it that much harder to breathe.

Need. Jameson didn't need me to worry about him. He needed *this*. Brutally. Desperately.

His thumbs worked their way forward to trace the lines of my jaw. And then, suddenly, his hands were tracing their way down my front, past my collarbone.

A promise. A hint. A beckoning.

"No." I found my voice. It came out strong, low, rough.

Jameson stopped the instant I said the word *no*. Before he could even think about stepping back, I brought *my* hands to *his* neck, pulling his body even closer to mine. *I* traced *his* jaw. There was rough stubble along his jawline, and the feel of it under my touch was *almost* enough to make me forget that Jameson had a secret.

"Yes." Jameson gave me *his* consent, his voice lower even than mine, hoarser.

I rose on my toes, and Jameson leaned forward until our foreheads touched. My back arched, and so did his, putting just enough space between our torsos for my hands to continue to work the way down the front of his body.

"Your hair still smells like smoke," I murmured. But he was here. He was fine. He didn't want me to ask him anything.

He didn't want me to call *Tahiti*.

I let my mind linger on the word I wasn't saying as I felt his pulse jump beneath my touch. I searched his eyes. *What happened to you?*

Jameson said nothing, and I reached for the bandages once more.

Chapter 14

Late at night, the Old Town Square was empty. I stood at the base of the astronomical clock, Jameson beside me, Oren a shadow somewhere in the dark. Sculptures of *Death* and Catholic *saints* adorned the clock. The astronomical portion of the clock was designed to show the positions of the *sun* and the *moon*.

Sun, moon, saint, death.

"And so the game ends." There was a richness to Jameson's tone, a depth, an unspeakable *something* that I felt all the way to my bones.

I'd beaten Jameson's game, but there were still more games to play. With the two of us, there always would be.

"Shall we wait for the clock to strike midnight?" I asked.

"As it happens," Jameson told me, "the clock doesn't go off at midnight. Last official procession of the day is at eleven, and right now, it is eleven forty-four." He gave me a loaded look.

In other words, yes, I'd beaten his game—but only just.

"I'm liking my chances tomorrow," he told me.

I took that as an invitation to open negotiations. "Give me until noon." I said, and then I sweetened the deal. "In exchange, I will agree to having three steps in my game instead of five. You'll still have until midnight to solve it."

Jameson looked down at me in the dark. I could barely make out the outline of his face, but my mind filled in everything my eyes couldn't see.

"It's possible that I could be talked into those terms," Jameson told me. "Do go on."

"Well..." I latched my hand on to the front of his shirt and pulled him toward me. "If you don't agree to give me until noon, I'll have to work all night to get my game ready. I won't be going back to the hotel with you."

"Straight for the jugular," Jameson said. "I approve."

I arched a brow. "You'll give me until noon?"

Jameson smiled. "I can live with those terms."

Without a single word of warning, I pushed him back and took off running into the night. "Catch me if you can, Hawthorne."

The Morning After

Bandaging the wound just above Jameson's collarbone, I felt my pulse jump in my own neck—an unrelenting, uncompromising ticking up of my heart rate. Once I was done, I put my palms flat against Jameson's bare chest once more.

"Heiress." This was Jameson asking me to keep going, Jameson asking me for *everything*.

He might as well have asked the sun to burn. No matter the secrets he was keeping, no matter what had happened to him in the past twelve hours, there was an inevitability to him and me.

My hip bones brushed against his body, as I pushed him slowly back against the bathroom wall.

"Tell me you're okay," I ordered.

"I am," Jameson said with unmatched intensity, *"better* than okay."

I brought my lips to his. *Tahiti. Tahiti. Tahiti.* It took everything in me not to say it. Instead, I dragged my hands down his chest. *Down. Down. Down.* My heart sped up. Time slowed down.

Jameson pushed off the wall. The next thing I knew, his lips were devouring mine.

"If you're going to say it . . ." Jameson pulled roughly back, and I could feel the intensity with which he *didn't* want me to call *Tahiti.* "Say it now, Heiress."

He didn't want me to—but I could.

Chapter 15

One Day Earlier...

Laying out my own Hawthorne-style puzzle sequence confirmed what Jameson had said about Prague. There was just something about this city. It was made for our kind of game.

On the roof of the hotel, on top of the dome at the base of the spire, I gave Jameson four objects—the knife and the black light, recycled from his game, and two others: a steamer and a marker. With just hours to plot things out, I hadn't been able to get *that* creative.

I had, however, managed to be sufficiently devious.

Beside me, Jameson gave each object its due. He started with the pen, examining the words embossed on its side in raised lettering. A VERY RISKY GAMBLE. Alisa hadn't even asked me why when I'd requested she procure it.

Jameson uncapped the pen and lifted his eyes to mine. "A pen with your name on it?" *A Very Risky Gamble*, rearranged, was *Avery Kylie Grambs*. "Give me your hand, Heiress."

I schooled my face not to show the stab of victory I felt when he interpreted those words the way I'd meant for him to.

"Which hand?" I asked innocently.

An hour and a half later, Jameson had ascertained that the pen wrote in invisible ink that was revealed by the black light. He had also ascertained that there were no clues inked onto my skin— anywhere—invisible or otherwise.

His search had been... thorough.

"You are *fiendish*, Avery Kylie Grambs. As far as distractions go, that one wasn't even fair."

I shrugged. "I play dirty."

"You know what Nash says," Jameson told me. "*There's no such thing as fightin' dirty if you win.*" Even just mentioning one of his brothers seemed to bring out Jameson's competitive streak. He shifted his attention back to the pen. "Hypothetically speaking, what would happen if I asked you to write something with this pen?"

"Hypothetically speaking," I told him, "that would depend on when you asked me to do it and how much time had passed since the start of the game."

Jameson studied me and didn't bother to hide the fact that he was doing so. He relished taking in the lines of my face, the tilt of my lips. "In other words: The pen doesn't come into play yet," he concluded.

With a twisted little grin, he set it to the side, then did the same for the black light. He spent five minutes on the steamer, then turned his attention to the knife. Inside the hidden compartment, he found a bronze chain. On that chain there dangled eleven small charms, each one a bronze letter.

Alisa also hadn't asked *why* when I'd requested she help me find the right artisan to get them done in time.

As I watched, Jameson unhooked the chain, then held it up, allowing the letters to slide off, one by one, into the palm of his hand.

A

O

U

I

Y

X

W

V

T

M

H

The instant the last letter fell off, Jameson closed his fingers around the entire collection. And just like that, he had a plan.

Chapter 16

A, O, U, I, Y, X, W, V, T, M, H.

Watching Jameson try to work his magic on the letters was better than being a spectator at almost any professional sport. He wasn't a person made for stillness, especially when he was thinking.

And thinking.

And thinking.

WITH MAY VOX U.

MOUTH IVY WAX.

MOUTH WAY XIV.

"Xiv?" I said, drawing his eyes to me.

"Roman numeral fourteen." Jameson lifted his eyes to mine. "Though based on your expression and the fact that you just asked that question, Heiress, apparently not."

Eventually, Jameson followed the maxim he'd once taught me: *Whenever you get stuck on a game, return to the beginning.* In this case, he picked up the marker. "Hypothetically speaking, what would you do if I asked you to write something with this pen now?"

I checked the time. He'd been working long enough. I

wanted to get out of this hotel room and into the city as much as he did.

I shrugged. "I would say take off your shirt."

A few minutes later, the same collection of letters from the charms was written on Jameson's chest.

A, O, U, I, Y, X, W, V, T, M, H.

I checked my work with the black light, then capped the pen.

"Seriously?" Jameson asked me. "*That's* my hint?"

"That's your hint."

Jameson threw back his head and laughed. He laughed the way he ran or drove or flew—with abandon, holding nothing back. "Remind me not to get on your bad side, Heiress."

"Tell me something about your secret and maybe I'll be a little more generous."

Jameson's eyes sparkled. "Now where would the fun be in that?" He paced the room, circling it with an almost feline grace, and then, suddenly, he went still. He looked to me, then took the black light from me. He aimed it down at his chest. *Eleven letters, all capitalized, all written in a plain hand with not a single flourish, all very difficult for him to see from his current angle.*

"I cannot help but notice," Jameson said, an undertone of energy building in his voice, "that you didn't exactly make these easy for me to read." He paused, and something about that momentary silence felt filled to the brim with an unspoken *something.* "Clever, Heiress."

An instant later, he was scaling down the rooftop and swinging himself back down onto the balcony. I followed suit.

Inside our hotel room, Jameson stopped in front of an ornate gold mirror. Brandishing the black light, he flashed it on his own chest. The letters I'd written on his chest were reflected back—*exactly*.

"Even with the help of the black light, I couldn't fully read what you'd written on my chest, due to the angle, but given that you burned two of your remaining three objects to write it there, it was obvious there had to be some significance to it, beyond what you wrote." Jameson paused. "It occurred to me that the significance might *be* the angle. Perhaps I was not meant to read them by looking down. Perhaps I was meant to read them in a mirror."

Yes. I didn't say that out loud, just let him continue on.

"There are only eleven letters in the English alphabet that have perfect vertical symmetry." Jameson arched a brow at me. "Just eleven letters that look exactly the same when reflected in a mirror."

A, O, U, I, Y, X, W, V, T, M, and H.

I waited for Jameson to make the next leap.

"A *mirror*," he murmured. I saw the exact instant that he realized where he was supposed to go next.

"Don't forget your last object," I told him. "You left the steamer up on the roof."

Chapter 17

Seemingly countless columns and arches stretched out in every direction. I felt like I'd been transported into a fairy tale or a myth where magic was real and labyrinths were infinite and alive. Logically, I knew that it was an illusion, that nothing in this place was infinite except for Jameson and me.

But the mirrors were very convincing.

Beside me, Jameson turned three hundred and sixty degrees, and all around us, his reflection did the same.

"A mirror maze," he said. "Very us."

I smirked. "I thought so." There was a distinct chance that I got more pleasure than I should have out of turning the tables on him. "I ordered a picnic, if you get hungry," I told him.

And then I left him to navigate his way through the maze, to find the clue I'd left for him among the mirrors.

I was really starting to understand why billionaire Tobias Hawthorne had loved his traditional Saturday morning games so much.

It took Jameson three hours to find what he was looking for and meet me on the picnic blanket I'd set up at a point overlooking the castle. He sat down next to me, then flashed the black light at his arm, where he'd written the clue that he'd found:

NOT OUT

←————————

I looked from Jameson's arm to his eyes. "How long did it take you to realize you needed the steamer?"

He snagged a chocolate-covered strawberry off a tray in front of me and brandished it in my direction. "Longer than it should have, not as long as it could have. It also took me some time to find the right mirror. And then I spent far longer than I would like to admit trying to treat your clue as a map."

I snagged the black light from him and aimed it at his arm again:

NOT OUT

←————————

I repressed a smile.

"The arrow is pointing due west on a compass," Jameson said. "But inside the maze, it was pointing north-north-east. And incidentally, it was pointing directly at another mirror, not an exit."

"So you're saying it wasn't pointing out?" I knew he'd hear the challenge in my voice, plain as day.

He answered it by rising to his knees, closing the space between us, and bringing his lips very close to mine. "*Not out,*" he said, his voice low and smooth. He studied my face. I stared right back at him.

"Has anyone ever told you that you have an excellent poker face, Heiress?"

I knew better than to take that to mean that my poker face was working. "What do you see?" I asked, another challenge.

"You're happy." Jameson sat back on the picnic blanket and stretched his long legs out. "A little smug." He let his gaze travel over my poker face once more. "A lot smug."

I shrugged. "I'm smug," I told him, "and *you're* on the clock."

We ate. He worked. I watched him.

"Not out." Jameson returned the favor and watched my reaction to his words. "Also known as *in*."

My face gave away nothing, even to him. I was sure of it.

"*In*," Jameson repeated. "Say it out loud, and you might as well be saying the letter. *N*."

He was almost there—so close he could taste it. I could, too.

"*N*," Jameson reiterated. "And an arrow."

N plus arrow equals... It took everything in me not to give him the prompt, but I managed to do nothing but lean back on my elbows on the picnic blanket, the way he had the day before.

"*N. Arrow*." Jameson smiled. "Put them together..." He snagged one last strawberry. "And you get *narrow*."

He wasn't wrong. The question was, having decoded the clue, did he know where in the City of Spires he was headed next?

With liquid grace, Jameson rolled to his feet. "Race you there."

The Morning After

I didn't call *Tahiti* as I pushed Jameson backward into the bed-room. I didn't say that magic word as I pushed him down onto the bed. I didn't say it as I straddled him.

I didn't say it as he turned the tables and flipped me over onto the bed.

The blood. The smell of smoke in his hair. I have a secret.

I could have forced the issue, but I didn't. I wasn't going to—not now, not ever. Because sometimes loving a person meant trusting them. Sometimes it meant taking a *no* even when you knew there was a way to get a *yes*. Sometimes it meant knowing that what he needed mattered more than what you wanted.

I *wanted* answers. He needed me not to ask.

"If you're going to say it," Jameson repeated hoarsely, "say it."

I surged upward. Kissing him was like unleashing a tidal wave, a hurricane, a wall of fire—power and heat and *more*.

"Like the sun and the moon," I said, my lips on his, his every breath ripping through me, the touch of our skin electric. "I loved him."

Jameson looked at me like *I* was the force of nature. Like *I* was the mystery for the ages. Like he could spend a lifetime solving *me*.

"Avery." My name escaped his lips. *"Heiress."*

For better or worse, this was us.

Us.

Us.

Us.

Chapter 18

There was a famous street in Prague, less than twenty inches wide. Vinárna Čertovka. It was more like a staircase, really, barely wide enough for one person to walk down, so *narrow* that it had its own traffic light to ensure that two pedestrians, headed in opposite directions, would not get stuck in the middle.

Jameson got there first. He waited for me by the traffic light, in the midst of the oldest neighborhood in Prague. The moment I arrived, he pushed the button to indicate to pedestrians on the other side that he was getting ready to walk through.

I doubted he'd find my next—and final—clue on his first pass. I followed behind him, and even though I was well-accustomed to secret passages and hidden rooms, this lone staircase passageway felt too narrow even for my liking.

The moment Jameson approached the far side of the passage-way, he stopped—not just stopped but jerked to a halt, like his entire body had just been turned to stone.

"Jameso—" I didn't even get his full name out before he threw himself forward. *Running.*

I jogged through what was left of Vinárna Čertovka. But when I came out the other side—not more than two seconds after he did—Jameson was nowhere to be seen.

He was gone.

I waited for him to reappear.

I waited.

I waited.

But he never came back.

The Morning After

Y ou never finished my game." My head was on Jameson's chest. I listened to his heartbeat as I waited for his reply. "I waited, but you never came back, never found the final clue."

"Do you still have it?" Jameson asked, and I felt the quiet rumble in his voice.

I'd left it there in the narrow staircase passageway from whence he'd disappeared. "Can you at least tell me how you did it?" I asked Jameson.

He was silent for so long, I didn't think he was going to reply— but then he did. "How else?" I could hear an echo of a crooked little smile in his voice, layered over something else, something he was trying to hide from me. "A secret passageway."

I thought back to the guesses I'd made about his secret—the secret that had filled him with an indescribable energy, that had put him in the mood to play. "You found something." I repeated my earlier guess, then his correction. "Multiple somethings."

Multiple passageways.

"They're everywhere in this city," Jameson murmured. "If only you know to look."

The hairs on the back of my neck rose then, only I wasn't sure at first why. Then I remembered—the woman in the burnt-red scarf, the one who'd told me about the plaques scattered throughout the city.

She'd used the *exact same* words.

"You won our wager," Jameson said, and I craned my neck to look at his face without sitting up. "You solved my game before midnight. I never finished yours."

What did you see at the end of the narrow passage? Why did you take off? What happened once you did? What the hell did you stumble into, Jameson?

"By the terms of our wager, that means I get to decide what we do our last day in Prague," I said. I pushed myself up off his chest, crossed my legs, and sat there in bed for a moment, just looking at him. "Do you *want* there to be a last day in Prague?" I asked.

Do we need to get out of here?

Jameson responded like someone who hadn't a care in the entire world. He stayed exactly where he was in bed, looking at me with a smile I knew all too well. "I hear Belize is nice this time of year," he said.

That was Jameson, pretending that this didn't matter. Pretending that he didn't *need* to leave.

I got out of bed and sent a brief text to Alisa, then turned back to the boy on the bed. The boy with the bandages at the base of his neck.

Jameson Winchester Hawthorne. "Belize it is," I said.

THE SAME BACKWARD AS FORWARD

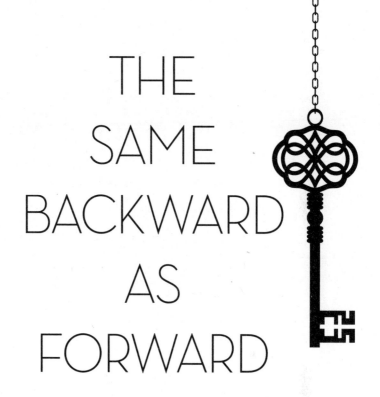

"Sometimes, when I look at you,
I feel you, like a hum
in my bones, whispering
that we are the same."

Chapter 1

There was an art to being invisible. In this town, with my last name, it took effort to be nobody, to make people look right through me. I was quiet. I never wore makeup. I kept my hair just long enough to pull back into a nondescript ponytail. When I wore it down, its sole purpose was falling into my face. But the real key to being the right kind of invisible, the thing that mattered far more than making myself quiet and nondescript, was keeping the world at arm's length.

I was a master at being alone—but not lonely. Loneliness would have been a vulnerability, and I was Rooney enough to know how that would end. Weakness of any kind was nothing but blood for the sharks. At twenty, I'd survived by keeping my head down and my eyes open. I'd made it out of the house—and out of the family in every way that mattered.

Except for one.

"Kaylie." I didn't raise my voice as I called out to my sister, who was currently dancing rather enthusiastically on top of a pool table. She shouldn't have even been able to hear me over the dull roar of small-town drunks on a mission to get drunker, but Kaylie and I had always had a sixth sense for each other.

"Hannah!" My sister kept right on dancing, as delighted to

see me as she'd been when she was three and I was six and I'd been her favorite person in the world. "Dance with me, you beautiful bitch."

Kaylie was an optimist. For example, she thought there was a chance in hell that I was joining her on top of that pool table. My sister's knack for misplaced optimism was half the reason she had a rap sheet. The other half was that, no matter how good I was at fading into the background, I'd never been able to shield her, too. Kaylie had been born dancing on tables and shouting her joy to the moon—and sometimes her fury, too. Her fearlessness suited our mother.

Some of the time.

"I'll have to take a rain check," I told my still-dancing sister.

"Your loss, you glorious thing, you." Kaylie twirled in a circle, adeptly avoiding the half-dozen balls scattered over the table's surface. The trio of guys holding pool cues, whose game she had presumably interrupted, didn't seem to mind.

Collared shirts. Expensive shoes. Prep-school looks. Those three weren't locals. In this bar, that spelled trouble.

"I'll race you home." I tried to tempt Kaylie off the table. She had a competitive streak.

"Last I checked, it's not your home anymore, O Serious One." Kaylie walked along the edge of the pool table, her arms held to the sides, her long hair streaming down her back. When she reached the end, she bent at the waist to place a hand on the shoulder of one of the pool-cue-holding boys.

"My sister," Kaylie confided in him in a stage whisper, "is faster than she looks."

Faster. Stronger. Smarter. I was a lot of things that Kaylie didn't need to be advertising. Luckily, the guy on the receiving end of her attention, who didn't look older than eighteen or nineteen himself, couldn't have glanced away from her leather-clad torso if he'd tried. As for his friends, one of them was relishing the view of Kaylie from behind, and the other one...

The other one shifted his gaze languidly toward me.

His hair was a dark, almost reddish brown and long enough to hang over his eyes, which did absolutely nothing to mask the way they roved over my body. I could feel him taking in my faded blue scrubs, my dishwater blonde hair, the exact set of my mouth.

"I have to ask," he said with the air of a person to whom everything was a very dark joke, "exactly how fast are you, Hannah?"

My instincts, honed from years of watching and trying not to be seen, told me two things: first, that he was drunk or high or both, and second, that, even inebriated, he missed nothing.

I gave him no visible response. My quiet was the kind of quiet that didn't blink. Didn't flinch.

Dark green eyes, shining with the light of bad ideas and worse ones, locked on to mine. "It's nice to meet you, too," he said dryly.

We hadn't *met*, and we weren't going to. "You're not from around here," I commented. That was a warning. He didn't heed it.

Instead, he picked up a piece of pool chalk and spun it through his fingers, one after another. "What gave me away?" he asked mockingly.

That was a rhetorical question, but my brain generated an automatic response. *Your tan is too even. Your hands aren't calloused. You're wearing a button-up shirt.* The top three buttons were undone, his collar more rumpled than popped. Smirking, he leaned against the pool table, as casual as a demigod who found some amusement in sizing up little mortals. There was a canny looseness to the way he moved, not even a hint of tension visible anywhere in his body. It was all too easy for me to imagine him as an ancient royal sprawled across a litter, being carried around by servants.

Or soldiers, I thought. Something in me whispered that he was spoiling for a fight. And in this bar, as an outsider, he was likely enough to find one.

Not my problem.

"Kaylie," I called. To everyone else in the bar, my voice probably sounded exactly the same as it had before, but my sister heard the difference. The two of us had been forged in a different kind of heat. She hopped off the pool table and sauntered around to my side, slowing as she passed the guy who'd zeroed in on me.

"Maybe I'll see you around." Kaylie's smile was trouble.

"You won't." I directed those words at the outsider.

"Will I not?" Eyes on me, he set his whiskey glass on the edge of the pool table, partially overhanging the edge, just daring gravity to make itself known.

The glass stayed exactly where he'd placed it.

"And what about you, palindrome girl?" The stranger's hair still hung in his face, casting his razor-sharp cheekbones in shadow. "*H-A-N-N-A-H*. Will I see *you* around? We could have a little fun, set the world on fire." He held a hand to his heart and lowered his voice. "If you're a *Hanna* without the *h* on the end, I don't want to know."

I was a Hannah with two *H*'s, and I was supposed to be invisible. The two of us definitely wouldn't be seeing each other again. We wouldn't be setting the world on fire.

He never should have *seen* me at all.

Fifteen minutes later, Kaylie was walking along the rocky shore the same way she'd glided over the edge of the pool table, like she lived life on the high wire. As I walked behind her, she looked up at the night sky, not even bothering to watch where she was stepping. There was an energy to my sister, an unspoken *something* that was a little frenetic and utterly full of life.

"You took their wallets, didn't you?" I said, resigned to the answer before she even gave it.

Kaylie glanced back and smiled. "Only one."

I didn't have to ask *which* one. She'd slowed as she'd passed him on the way out, the two of them a study in contrasts—his darkness, her light; razor-sharp angles versus full, teasing lips.

"Do you want to know his name?" Kaylie's grin deepened, bringing out twin dimples as she brandished the stolen wallet between two fingers.

"No," I said immediately.

"Liar." She smiled again, wickedly this time. Based on past experience, I had about a hundred reasons not to trust that smile.

"You need to be careful," I told her quietly. "You have a record now."

I needed her to keep her hands clean for another year. That was all. By the time I finished nursing school, Kaylie would be eighteen, and I was going to get her out. We'd move far, far away, to a place where no one had ever heard of Rockaway Watch or the Rooney family.

She just needed to keep her head down until then.

"Honestly, Hannah? I'm not the one who needs to be careful. You *don't* have a record." Kaylie did a little one-footed spin to face me. In the moonlight, I could see the thick kohl rimming her cornflower-blue eyes, the dark lipstick she'd somehow managed not to smear. "You should go before we get much closer to the house," she said. "You don't want anyone to see you. Out of sight, out of mind."

Kaylie was the one chink in my armor. She always had been. I'd given in to the impulse to check up on her tonight, but we both knew that I was never more visible than when I stood in range of her glow.

"Be careful, Kaylie," I repeated, and this time, I wasn't just talking about stealing wallets or dancing on top of tables. I was talking about the rest of it. The family business.

With a roll of her eyes, my optimistic little sister tilted her face skyward once more, brave and brash and invincible, always, until she wasn't. I couldn't help thinking that maybe I should have left her at the bar, dancing and free and beckoning trouble toward her for the hell of it. But even if Kaylie had made it through the night without incident, even if she'd walked away soaked in adrenaline and unscathed, word of her night out would have gotten back. It always did.

And Kaylie being wild and free only served my mother's interests—the Rooney family's interests—to a point.

Chapter 2

My apartment honestly wasn't much of one. I could reach the kitchen counter from the bed. My three measly kitchen cabinets held more books than pans. On good nights, I read until I fell asleep, wrapping myself in fantasy worlds like they were blankets. Tonight, I fell back on an older habit instead. Ripping a blank page out of one of my clinicals notebooks, I folded the top right corner of the paper down—and then I just kept folding.

Growing up, there had been times when having my nose in a book would have made me a target. I'd had to find other ways of being *elsewhere*, tricks for daydreaming without ever losing track of the here and now. I'd taken to carrying scraps of paper in my pockets—a focus, something to occupy my hands.

Even now, alone in the apartment where I'd lived for the last two and a half years, there was something steadying to me about the familiar motion of folding a piece of paper in on itself again and again and again in different ways. The end result this time was an odd, jagged little shape.

I threw it away when I was done—and went to sleep.

In the dead of night, a voice jerked me back to consciousness like ice-cold water tossed over my prone form. "Get up."

The voice was gravelly. *This is not a dream.* I had no recollection whatsoever of opening my eyes, but suddenly, they were open. My kitchen lights had been turned on. My mother was standing over me, and she wasn't alone.

"You." Her voice hardened. "Get up." Eden Rooney wasn't in the habit of asking anyone to do anything twice, so I took that as the warning it was and slipped out of bed, putting space between us and taking in the person standing in my mother's shadow.

My cousin Rory was scowling—and bleeding.

"Fix him." My mother didn't make *requests.*

I eyed Rory's injuries, but all I could think was that it had been two and a half years since I'd moved out. I hadn't asked for my mother's permission to leave. She hadn't come after me. She'd *let* me get comfortable, and now...

Fix him. I kept my heart rate even and my face carefully blank. The worst of Rory's injuries—that I could see—was a deep cut on his cheekbone, maybe two inches long. It wasn't the type of injury that people in my mother's line of work typically concerned themselves with. I'd seen one of my uncles dig a bullet out of a guy's shoulder with a *spoon.*

This was clearly a test.

I was a nursing *student,* but I was deep into my clinical hours, and I'd buried myself in internships almost from the moment I'd started. What my mother wanted was within my capabilities, but the test wasn't what I *could* do. The test was whether I would push back, and the one thing I knew for certain was that if I did, I'd never be invisible to Eden Rooney—or the Rooney family—again.

"Supplies?" My voice was muted, unemotional. I knew how to

make myself disappear even when she was staring right at me. *No weakness. No rebellion. No emotion at all.*

Wordlessly, my mother dropped a black pouch on my bed. I unrolled it. Inside, there was a rudimentary surgery kit—scissors, scalpel, forceps, needle, suture thread.

"I suggest you make yourself useful, Hannah."

I heard what my mother didn't say: *I let you go because it suited my purposes to do so, but you're still mine, body and soul. You always were.*

All I said out loud was: "There's no anesthetic."

"He doesn't need it." My mother's diamond-hard gaze traveled from me to Rory. "Just like I didn't need this little asshole getting himself injured in a bar fight tonight of all nights."

Bar fight. My mind went immediately to a preppy boy with a dark aura, to green eyes and sharp cheekbones cast in shadow, to a glass placed precariously on a pool table's edge.

"I need to wash my hands." I bought myself some time going to the kitchen sink—but not much, just enough to focus on the fact that my mother apparently wasn't doing this just to teach *me* a lesson. She was using me to teach Rory one.

He had five years and at least a hundred pounds on me, but he would sit there while I dug a needle into his face over and over again without anesthetic, because the alternative was doubtlessly worse.

I turned off the faucet and made my way back. I didn't want to do this. If anyone found out, I'd get kicked out of my program. And, possibly worse, I would be complicit in whatever the family had going on right now that made Rory's choice to get into a fight *tonight* of all nights that much more objectionable to my mother.

But if I didn't do this, she might, and that would be so much worse for Rory. My cousin looked like he wanted to spit on me and vomit, in that order.

"Sit," I told him. I had to hope that if I could do this without faltering, without showing a hint of weakness or rebellion, that might pacify her into forgetting me again—or, if not *forgetting* precisely, at least putting me on the back burner for a while.

Long enough for me to finish school. Long enough for me to find a way to get Kaylie out.

Rory sat. I tilted his chin back. Buying myself one last reprieve, I went into the bathroom and grabbed some antiseptic. I applied it, then opened the needle and the thread. At least they were pre-sterilized.

"Get on with it." My mother took a single step toward me.

Do it, I told myself, but getting started was made harder by the lengths Rory was going to *not* to flinch. Lifting the needle, I didn't bother telling him to relax and opted for distraction instead.

"Which one?" I said.

"Huh?" Rory was not, by any measure, the smartest of my cousins.

"The rich boys slumming it at the bar tonight," I clarified. "Which of the three of them did this?" The question commandeered enough of his attention that I was able to start.

The needle was just a needle. Skin was just skin. My hands were steady.

"Doesn't matter." Rory spoke in a low voice, his face barely moving. "I'm gonna kill all three of the little bastards."

In my family, statements like that weren't always just for show.

"Hannah? Stop." My mother's voice ricocheted through the

room like a bullet. But all I could think was: *Do no harm.* I finished the stitch, and *then* I stopped.

My mother bent until her eyes were even with Rory's. She pressed her thumb into the flesh of his cheek, right below the partial line of stitches. "Do you have any idea who those boys are?" When Rory didn't answer, my mother snorted. "Didn't think so."

She pressed her thumb into his face a little harder, then slid her gaze to mine.

"Let's see if Hannah here can work it out. Rich boys in Rockaway Watch. Heads up their asses and looking to commission a boat in the morning. Who are they?" The last stitch I'd done popped, tearing through Rory's skin.

I forced myself to focus. *A boat.* There was only one place close enough to serve as a destination from Rockaway Watch, a private island owned by a billionaire. *Hawthorne Island.*

Who are they? I answered my mother's question. "Hawthornes."

"At least *she* has a brain." My mother swiveled her gaze back to Rory. "One Hawthorne, two friends, and the Hawthorne in question would be Tobias Hawthorne the Second. Toby. The only son of one of the country's richest men. Little bastard might have a death wish, but we won't be the ones granting it. *Will we, Rory?*"

"No," Rory gritted out.

My mother dropped her hand from his face. "You'll want to fix that last stitch," she told me, her voice utterly devoid of feeling.

I swallowed back bile as I finished the job. To keep myself steady, I retreated elsewhere in my mind. *Tobias Hawthorne the Second. Toby.* I thought about the boy with the reddish-brown hair and his emperor-lounging-on-a-litter looseness. He was the

Hawthorne of the group, I was sure of it, and apparently, I had his overprivileged, trouble-starting ass to thank for tonight, too.

I finished the last stitch. My mother didn't linger. On her way out, Rory following like a dog on her heels, she paused in the doorway and looked back at me. "You have a steady hand," she said.

That didn't sound like a compliment. It sounded like a promise. She would be back.

Chapter 3

I didn't sleep the rest of the night and left my apartment at sunrise. It was my day off, but I had to do *something*. I needed to clear my head, so I went to the grocery store and then headed to the outskirts of town—farther, even, than my own apartment. I couldn't afford rent in any of the towns closer to the community college or hospital than Rockaway Watch, but I'd chosen to stick to the very edges. The only thing farther out was an abandoned lighthouse and terrain so inhospitable that no person in their right mind would have tried to live there.

Which is not to say that no one did.

I knew better than to approach Jackson's shack, so I left the groceries I'd bought on the steps of the lighthouse, which had been built sometime in the eighteen hundreds and looked like it had been battered by saltwater and storm-force gales every day since. The roof had, at one point, been blue, the tower some shade of white, but the whole thing was faded and overgrown now. The beacon hadn't worked for decades. The stone walls were literally crumbling.

It was my favorite place in Rockaway Watch.

Lighthouses had always felt like something out of a fairy tale to me—a warning not to come closer, a liminal space between here and there. This one wasn't easy to get to, but I made the climb every two weeks, groceries in hand.

"I oughtta shoot you."

I turned to face the gruff, copiously bearded fisherman who'd just spoken those words. "Please don't," I said calmly.

Jackson Currie wasn't technically a shut-in. He left his house to go out on his boat and interacted with others when necessary to dispatch his fishing haul, but he loathed people—all people, myself included.

He scowled at the bag I'd left on the lighthouse steps. "I told you to stop doing that."

"How's your arthritis?" I asked. He couldn't have been older than forty or forty-five, but a lifetime of fishing had wreaked havoc on his hands and wrists.

"None of your damn business."

"About the same, then," I said as I reached out and took his right hand in mine, gently prodding the joints at the base of his fingers, lightly flexing his wrist, rubbing my thumb over it, then up the adjacent bone. "Do you need any more cream?" I read his answer to that question in his expression: *None of my damn business.*

I checked his other hand. When I finished, I expected him to storm off—*with* the groceries—but he didn't. He didn't curse at me or threaten to shoot me again, either.

"Storm's coming." Jackson turned toward the ocean. The sky was clear, stretching down to meet the gently rolling blue-green waters of the Pacific. "Gonna be a big one."

Something in his tone made it hard for me to doubt him, no matter how blue the sky was. "If there's a storm coming, I'm assuming you're in for the day?" I said. "Or that you'll be going out and coming back in before it hits?"

Jackson snorted. He was the type of person who would have arm-wrestled a lightning bolt if he could have. He turned his head to look at me, his brown eyes executing a grid search of my features. "What's wrong with you today?" he demanded.

Bringing Jackson Currie groceries had never felt like letting the world in, specifically *because* he hated people, myself included, so much. His question was gruff, but the fact that he'd asked it at all hit me hard.

"Nothing," I said. If I didn't think about what had happened the night before, maybe I could pretend it away—for a few hours, at least.

Jackson gave a little nod. "None of my damn business," he concluded.

Hours later, I drove two towns over to the hospital, even though it was my day off, and even though I'd told myself I wasn't going to. If I'd been certified, I might have been able to pick up a shift, but instead, I headed to the cafeteria.

Hospitals were an easy place to disappear. Everyone had something else to worry about.

By late afternoon, the sky outside had turned—not just purple but black. It hadn't started raining yet, but the wind was a feral creature. The hospital was far enough into the mainland that I couldn't see the ocean, but in my mind's eyes, I conjured an image of dark waters. Lightning tore across the sky.

Surely Jackson wasn't out in this. *Surely.*

I stood and grabbed my tray, and it was only by chance that I was still looking out the window when lightning struck again in the distance and what looked like a massive fireball shot up into the sky.

An explosion? It had come from the direction of Rockaway Watch. I broke into a run, my heart pounding in my throat with every step. I made it to my beat-up old car in record time and drove until I made it back to town, then kept driving until I could see ocean. A fire raged in the distance, out on the water, like a mansion-sized torch in the dark.

Hawthorne Island.

Chapter 4

J ackson showed up on my doorstep eighty minutes later, soaked to the bone. The second I opened the door, he spoke. *"Hannah."*

He'd never said my name before, had never sought me out—never sought *anyone* out, as far as I knew.

"You need to come with me." The recluse's voice was raspier than normal. He didn't appear inclined to explain his demand.

I didn't ask.

It wasn't until we were halfway to the lighthouse that Jackson spoke again. "I should have most of what you need," he gritted out.

I had to push myself to keep up with him. "Most of what I need for what?"

"Boy's half-dead." Jackson picked up speed, his stride and his words both erratically paced. "Head injury. Burned. Nearly drowned."

Burned. Drowned. Boy. My mouth got there before my brain did: "Hawthorne Island?"

"Explosion threw him from the cliff," Jackson practically growled. "I fished him out of the water."

One of the outsiders. In my mind, I could see a boy whose dark green eyes shined with bad ideas and worse ones. I could hear a dry voice inviting me to have a little fun—to *set the world on fire.*

"It's a damn miracle the kid survived." Jackson's voice grew hoarse. "Fishing's good on that side of the island, especially during a storm, so I was close. The way that the mansion blew when the lightning struck—there was nothing natural about it."

"What are you saying?" I came to a halt. "Jackson, when you find someone half-dead, you take them to a hospital!" Why hadn't I ever bought a cell phone? The money hadn't seemed worth it, but... "We need to turn back and call nine-one-one."

"Can't." That one word was as harsh as a blow.

"Why the hell not?" I demanded, and for once, there was nothing quiet about my voice, nothing soft or understated.

Jackson grabbed my arm, pulling me onward. "Only word he's said—screamed—since I pulled him out is *kerosene.*"

Kerosene. Set the world on fire. Nothing natural about it. My brain churned like stormy waters. "There were three boys," I said. "Three outsiders. The others—"

"There are no others anymore." Jackson's voice broke the way the surface of an icy pond breaks if you hit it with a hammer, cracking in unexpected places. "They're all dead, except him."

Which him? I didn't ask the question. What did it matter? "We have to go back to town," I said. "We have to call—"

"Four." Jackson came to a standstill. I stared at him, not understanding what he was saying. "I saw the boat that took their group over to the island this morning." The fisherman's words came out stilted. "There weren't three passengers on that boat, Hannah. There were four."

Suddenly, I *knew*. I knew why Jackson's voice was cracking. I knew why he kept saying my name. I knew who the fourth person on Hawthorne Island was.

Maybe I'll see you around, my sister had told the outsider boy.

"Kaylie," I whispered.

Jackson Currie might have been a recluse, but he still knew the people in this town, and everyone knew the Rooneys.

And Kaylie—she *glowed*.

"*No*," I said. Jackson was acting like there weren't any other survivors, like there couldn't have been, but there was more to Hawthorne Island than the mansion. If she'd been far enough away when the house blew—

I wrenched my arm from the fisherman's hand. I had to find a boat. I had to get to my sister.

"Coast Guard's out there, fighting the fire," Jackson told me. "Cops'll be there soon—if they aren't already. And I'm telling you, Hannah...there's no way." He closed his eyes. "Four kids went into the mansion. Only one came out, right before it blew."

Only one—and not her. Air felt like shards in my lungs. The world threatened to spin.

Jackson caught me by both arms this time, forcing me to look at him. "He's in agony, Hannah. He's dying. And if he and his friends cost a member of the Rooney family her life..."

My ears rung. Who the hell did Jackson Currie think he was to talk about my sister being *dead*?

Not Kaylie.

Not my Kaylie.

"What do you think happens if I take him to the hospital?" Jackson pressed. "If we so much as call an ambulance or the cops, what do you think happens next?"

I didn't want to hear that question. I didn't want to give it purchase in my mind. All I wanted to do was prove to myself that Jackson was wrong. Kaylie hadn't gone out to Hawthorne Island with those boys. And if she had, she'd survived. She was dancing—*somewhere*—with wild abandon. Or she was at home, sleeping curled in a little ball beneath the covers, the way she had since she was a little girl. She was laughing or hungover or both.

She was *fine.*

But my brain answered Jackson's question, all of its own accord, like she wasn't. *What do you think happens next?*

My family had a saying: *blood for blood.* My mother had ordered Rory to keep his hands off the outsiders. She hadn't been interested in the trouble that the wrath of a billionaire could bring to a town like this and an operation like hers. But if Jackson was right, if a Rooney was dead—if Kaylie wasn't dancing, wasn't sleeping, wasn't laughing; if my sister wasn't *anything* anymore; if Kaylie was dead—all bets were off. The person responsible wouldn't be safe in a local hospital. He wouldn't be safe with local cops. My family ran the drug trade and the weapons trade, all up and down this stretch of coast. They *owned* the cops.

Blood for blood.

If my sister was dead, and one of the people responsible was alive, he wouldn't be for long.

Chapter 5

I went with Jackson. No part of me wanted to, and a big part of me said to let whoever he'd fished out of the water die—alone, in agony, it wasn't my concern. But I kept thinking about what I'd been forced to do for my mother the night before. I kept thinking, *Do no harm.*

I kept thinking about Kaylie—and trying not to.

So I went with Jackson. I didn't ask or even wonder which of the three outsiders had survived, but when I stepped through the metal door of Jackson's shack onto a knotty wood floor, when I saw the unconscious body on a pile of blankets on that floor, the first thing I noticed was his hair.

Reddish brown.

It no longer hung in his face. It was matted to skin so pale I thought he might already be dead. Instinct took over, and I knelt beside him. I was in no way qualified to do this. I wasn't a doctor. I'd never worked in a burn unit or emergency room. I didn't even have my nursing degree yet.

But I was here, and he was on the floor.

I pressed my index and middle finger to his carotid artery. His pulse was racing. A jolt cut through my body with every beat. I held a hand over his mouth. He was breathing. I lowered my head and turned it sideways, listening to those breaths with my face close to his.

His breathing was labored—but clear.

I pulled back enough for my hand to snake in and put pressure on his chin, opening his mouth. The next thing I knew, a flashlight had been placed in my free hand.

Jackson. "Tell me what else you need," the fisherman grunted.

I needed a doctor, an actual nurse, anyone with the experience to do this, but barring that, I needed to finish checking my patient's airways—*clear.*

What now? I looked for the head wound, pushing my fingers back into a thick and tangled mess of damp hair, prodding gently until I found it. *Back of his head.* If there was any internal bleeding, we were screwed, but I tried not to dwell on that as I used my fingers to spread his hair, taking measure of the wound.

"I need to clean this," I told Jackson. "I'll need something to cut his hair with, a clean washcloth, antiseptic, butterfly bandages if you have them." I withdrew my hands from the boy's hair and turned my attention from the head wound to the rest of his body. "Second-degree burns on his arms and over his collarbone," I noted.

Very little remained of his shirt, but what there was, I tore off, except where it stuck to burns.

"I'm going to have to clean this and dress his wounds. Chest and torso, *here...*" I let my fingers hover over the indicated location. "Those burns are third degree, but they're smaller than the others and not on the extremities, which is good—better blood flow, smaller chance of infection."

I took a ragged breath and returned to Jackson's question. *What do I need?*

"Gauze, cloths, cool water. Any and all pain medication you have." I wracked my brain. *What else?* "If we were in a hospital, I'd start an IV—fluids first, then antibiotics."

Jackson left the shack without a word, and just like that, I was alone with an unconscious Toby Hawthorne.

H-A-N-N-A-H. I could hear him spelling out my name in my memory. *If you're a* Hanna *without the* h *on the end, I don't want to know.*

It had been easier when I wasn't thinking of the body on the floor as anything other than a patient, a collection of wounds, because the second I started thinking of him as someone I'd met, the second I thought about the bar, I flashed back to the way Kaylie had smiled that night.

Dance with me, you beautiful bitch.

I hadn't. I hadn't danced with her. I hadn't walked her all the way home. I hadn't made sure she didn't go back out. *Your loss, you glorious thing, you.*

The door to the shack slammed open, and Jackson dropped a beat-up suitcase onto the floor.

"What's this?" I asked, the words getting caught in my throat.

"I like to be prepared." Jackson's voice still sounded hoarse, and it occurred to me to wonder exactly how close to the fire on Hawthorne Island he'd gotten.

Smoke inhalation? It wasn't like I had oxygen—for either of them.

Focus on what you can *do*, I thought. With shaking hands, I unzipped the suitcase Jackson had dumped on the floor. Inside, there was a mess of medical supplies. I spotted the arthritis cream I'd bought him, but that was just the tip of the totally chaotic and disorganized iceberg. In any other circumstance, the fact that the recluse had so many medical supplies would have made him look unhinged and paranoid, but even a broken clock was right twice a day.

I started sorting through the mess, pulling the supplies I needed. *Gauze pads—three sizes, sterile. Bandages. Over-the-counter pain meds—acetaminophen and ibuprofen. Gauze rolls. Iodine wipes, alcohol wipes…*

"Saline." That surprised me enough that I said it out loud. Why would a recluse have a bag of saline—more than one, actually, with lines attached? I looked up at Jackson. "If I dig around in here, am I going to find a catheter and needle?"

"Like I said." Jackson grunted. "I like to be prepared."

He lived in a shack that probably could have qualified as a *bunker*. Was I really all that surprised? "Do you know what to do with any of it?" I queried.

Jackson threw his hands up in the air. "Would I have dragged you out here if I did?"

The boy on the floor chose that moment to suck in a frantic breath—and moan.

"Have you given him anything for the pain?" I asked Jackson.

"I was too damn busy saving his life."

I grabbed a bottle of pills and considered propping my patient up, but given the burns, I didn't want to risk lifting his upper body. Instead, I cupped a hand behind his head, gently pulling it toward me.

"I'm going to open your mouth now," I told Toby Hawthorne. I had no idea if he could hear me, no idea if I *wanted* him to be able to hear me. "I'm going to put pills in, one at a time." I looked to Jackson. "Get me some water." Unless and until I got some morphine, alternating large doses of the two over-the-counter medicines was my best bet.

I placed the first pill on Toby's tongue. His breath was warm against my hand. I brought water to his lips, then did my best to help him drink. I closed his mouth, willing him to swallow.

And that was when he opened his eyes, so dark a green I could almost imagine them black. Those eyes locked on to mine. He should have been moaning, writhing, screaming, but he was silent. He swallowed the pill.

As I placed the next one in his mouth, all I could think was that his face wasn't burned at all.

Chapter 6

oby Hawthorne passed out again before I dressed his burns, before I sheared a patch of hair on the back of his head to his scalp and bandaged his wound, before I got the IV going.

We're going to need more supplies. I didn't say that to Jackson, in large part because I told myself that there was no *we*. I'd done what I could. I'd done *no harm*. And that was more than I could say for the patient I'd treated.

Kerosene.

I stood and walked slowly out of the shack. It was only once I'd opened the door that Jackson spoke behind me. "You coming back?"

I didn't turn around as I issued a response that sounded calmer than I felt. "When the saline bag runs out, sub the second one in. You'll want to change his dressing frequently—cool water, not cold. Burn meds would help—silver cream, if you can get it."

In other words: *No, I'm not coming back.*

But in a strange way, I also didn't want to leave, because once I left, there would be nothing stopping me from making my way back to town, from finding out if Jackson had been right, if Kaylie really had been on Hawthorne Island, if she really was gone.

I didn't want to know, and that meant, on some level, that I already did.

Kaylie and I had always had a sixth sense for each other.

There wasn't a single car parked outside my mother's house. As I walked up the drive, a veritable pack of dogs threw themselves at the adjacent chain-link fence. Most were pit bulls crossbred with something larger. A final dog was leashed to a post on the front porch.

None of them had names. They weren't pets. As I approached, the dog on the porch pulled to the end of his chain, ratcheting up the warning growls. I knelt to his level, just out of range of his jaws, never blinking, and stared back at him.

"You know me," I said, even though I wasn't sure he did.

The dog went still. I'd always had a way with animals, and this time, as I stood back up, I didn't even have to work to keep my fear—and every other emotion—at bay. I felt numb as I made my way across the porch and closed my hand around the front door.

It wasn't locked. It never was.

I found my father in the kitchen. The rest of the house was silent. He stood over the stove, but there was nothing on it.

"She thought you'd come when you heard," he said without turning around.

My father's voice was lower in pitch than my mother's but less gravelly. I could remember moments in my childhood when he'd sung and she'd danced. The family business didn't mean there was no *family* here. It meant that *family* was everything—or else.

I didn't ask where my mother and her troops were. I just breathed in and out and replied to my father's statement. "Heard what?" I said, willing him to tell me, willing it not to be true.

My father turned around. "You knew your sister was running around with those boys," he accused. I didn't see the backhand coming, and it was only by the grace of God that it didn't knock me to the floor. "Did you know what those rich little bastards were playing at, Hannah?"

In my entire life, he'd never hit me. He'd been an enforcer for the family once, but when my mother had taken over, she'd made it clear that she found his brain more useful. He knew too much to be put into the line of fire these days, so his was a steadier presence, a calmer one.

I lifted a hand to my cheek. I couldn't summon up an ounce of anger or even hurt. Part of me was glad that he'd lashed out, because that meant that he'd cared. *About Kaylie.*

"I didn't know anything," I said, my voice breaking.

Suddenly, my father pulled me to him. His arms enveloped my body. He held me, the way I couldn't ever remember him holding me before.

"I should have kept a closer eye on her," my father said into my hair. "Those boys were running their mouths off all over town. They bought accelerant—and lots of it." His voice hardened. "Just a little game of arson."

A *little game of arson.* I thought about Toby Hawthorne on the floor of Jackson's shack. *A game.* My sister was dead for a rich boy's *game.*

"Are you sure—" I started to say.

"Hannah." My father put a hand under my chin. "She's ashes now." He blinked rapidly and gathered himself. "Your sister is dead, and they'll pin this on her. You just wait and see."

"*Arson,*" I realized. That was one of the charges Kaylie had been convicted of in juvenile court. She'd set the fire in question at my mother's command, a warning of money owed.

My mother. "Where is she?" I asked, my own voice hardening. My father knew based on my tone that I wasn't talking about whatever remained of my sister. I was talking about the head of the Rooney family. *"Where is she?"*

My mother sure as hell wasn't here, mourning, and something told me she wasn't out on Hawthorne Island, frantically demanding the truth, either. It had been clear the night before: She had something planned for today.

My father's arms dropped to his sides. "You a part of this family now?"

I looked away. "No."

After a long moment, he pressed a kiss to my forehead, then pulled back. "That's what I thought." I knew a good-bye when I heard one. He'd loved Kaylie. Maybe he even loved me, but it wasn't enough.

I let myself out.

I ended up on the shore, where the ocean crashed into the rocks, sending an explosion of sea spray into the air. The sky was no longer storm black. The haze over the ocean could almost have passed for fog, but I knew it for what it was. *Smoke.* I couldn't make out even the faintest outline of Hawthorne Island.

A little game of arson. I blinked into the wind, and the next thing I knew, I was *in* the ocean, up to my ankles, then my calves. It was only when the water hit my knees that I stopped.

My sister was out there. Dead or alive—and I knew at that point that she *wasn't* alive, I *knew*, but I couldn't keep from hedging my thoughts—I needed to get to her.

Even if she was *ashes*.

It was too far to swim, and I wasn't far enough gone to try, so I went back to the bar instead. I opened the door, and almost immediately, the entire place fell silent. For better or worse, I wasn't invisible now.

I was a Rooney of Rockaway Watch, and one of my family's own was *dead*.

"Someone is going to take me out there," I said.

All eyes were on me. I didn't repeat myself. I just waited for one of the men at the bar to stand.

The boat didn't get within a hundred yards of Hawthorne Island before the Coast Guard turned us back. The island was still burning—here and there, scattered flames. The rain or the Guard must have taken care of the rest.

As I stared at the charred remains of what had once been a grand mansion, the Coast Guard's voice blared over the radio once more. *"Turn back,"* it reiterated. *"There are no survivors. I repeat, no survivors."*

Chapter 7

No survivors. The words haunted me late into the night. The Coast Guard clearly wasn't looking for anyone. They weren't combing the waters for Toby Hawthorne. They thought he was dead.

Deep in my mind, a voice whispered, *Is he?*

The next morning, I had a shift at the hospital. I went, dressed in a fresh pair of scrubs, dark rings under my eyes. My supervisor pulled me aside the second she saw me.

"You don't have to be here today, Hannah." In all the time I'd shadowed her, this nurse had been about as no-nonsense as they came, but there was a gentle undertone to her words now.

She knows, I thought. *About Kaylie.* I hadn't changed my last name. Had I been kidding myself this whole time to think that I could be invisible, that everyone at this hospital didn't know exactly who my family was?

"I do need to be here," I said, my voice as even as I could make it. *"Please."*

"Go home, Hannah." That clearly wasn't a request. "Take a

week—or two. I'll talk to your advisor and make sure you aren't penalized, but I don't want to see you back here any sooner than seven days from now."

I wanted to push back, but I didn't. I left the hospital, fully intending to retreat to my apartment, but somehow, I ended up at the shack instead. I pounded three times on the metal door.

"What do you want?" That was Jackson's paranoid version of *Who's there?*

"It's me." I didn't say what I *wanted*. I wasn't even sure I knew. The door opened inward, halfway. I squeezed in, and Jackson shut it behind me. For the first time in a long time, I registered how big he was—at six foot six, the fisherman loomed over me, over just about everyone. But he'd never scared me.

I was much more afraid of what I would I see when I looked past him.

What I saw was a mattress on the floor. Toby Hawthorne was lying on his back on the mattress. His chest was still bare but for the gauze that had been used to dress his wound. There was a pile of damp rags on the floor beside the mattress.

He's alive, then. If Jackson had been tending to his wounds in my absence, Tobias Hawthorne the Second was still alive.

"Did you get the silver cream?" I asked Jackson dully.

"I dug some up." It wasn't until he handed me the jar and I saw the dirt smeared across the label that I realized he'd meant that literally.

On the bed, Toby made a noise like the creaking of a door—half-moan, half-rasp.

"You came back," Jackson noted.

I shouldn't have, but I'd had to see for myself whether Toby was still alive. Based on that moan, he definitely was. I should have turned around and walked out the door, but I couldn't shake the feeling that Kaylie wouldn't have wanted me to.

She'd never been the least bit capable of holding a grudge.

I forced my feet to move, bringing me closer to the person whose *little game of arson* had cost my sister her life. The authorities already thought there were no survivors. If Toby Hawthorne died, they would be right.

For the first time in my life, I felt like maybe I was capable of killing, like maybe I really was a Rooney. *Blood for blood.* It wouldn't have been hard. All it would have taken was a hand over Toby Hawthorne's mouth and another holding his nose.

In this state, he wouldn't have been able to fight.

I knelt beside the mattress and glared bullets at the boy who had my sister's blood on his soft, rich-boy hands. And then I swallowed, blinked back tears, and glanced back at Jackson. "I need some cool water."

Soon enough, there was a basin of it sitting beside me, though how Jackson had managed running water out here was anyone's guess. On a nearby table, I spotted a pile of clean cloths and the suitcase of medical supplies. I helped myself to more gauze with one hand and grabbed the cloths with the other, and then I got to work.

I soaked the cloths in cool water and thought, *I hate you, Tobias Hawthorne the Second.*

I peeled the dressing back from his wounds. *I hate you.*

I laid the cloths on his burns, and his chest rose with a ragged breath. His eyes never opened, not once as I repeated the process over and over and over again. Not when I unscrewed the top of the silver cream. Not when I applied it to his biceps, his collarbone, the third-degree burns on his chest and stomach.

I hate you.

I hate you.

I hate you.

My touch was gentle—far gentler than he deserved.

Pain was visible in the muscles of his chest, taut beneath the clean skin surrounding the burns. *Good*, I wanted to think. *He deserves to hurt.* But my touch was light as I continued cleaning and dressing his wounds.

And when I was done, I kept vigil. I checked on him, again and again, through the night, watching for any signs of infection.

"Hannah." Jackson said my name quietly, his voice almost but not quite soft.

"Don't," I bit out. *Don't tell me that you're sorry for my loss. Don't ask if I'm okay.*

Jackson went silent, and an hour later, the fisherman disappeared with the dawn. Left to my own devices, I went to change the dressings, wondering if Toby Hawthorne would consider this turn of events a very dark joke, like everything else.

A little game of arson, I thought viciously.

I peeled back gauze, and a hand flew up to catch my wrist. Toby's grip was shockingly strong. His lips were moving. He was saying *something*.

I pried his fingers from mine. Despite myself, I leaned down to hear what he was saying.

"*Let.*" Even that one word, said in a ragged whisper, was labored. "*Let*," he wheezed again.

I thought he was going to tell me to let him go, but he didn't.

"*Let*," he choked out a third time. "*Me.*" A breath caught in my throat. "*Die.*"

Fury rose up inside me like a beast with a life of its own. My sister was dead, and he had the gall to tell *me* to let him die?

I leaned down to whisper directly in his ear, and then I went back to work, my touch soft, hoping that what I'd said echoed in every nook and cranny of his depraved Hawthorne mind.

You don't get to die, you bastard.

Chapter 8

I stayed at Jackson's shack for three days straight. There was nothing for me anywhere else. Changing bandages, pressing pills into my patient's mouth, taking his vitals—those at least were things I could *do*. As soon as my week was up and the hospital would take me back, I'd leave, but for now, I bided my time.

There was a single piece of paper in the pocket of my scrubs. I folded it and unfolded it a hundred different ways. I'd made my decision: Toby Hawthorne was going to live if I had to drag him from the jaws of death myself. He was going to *live* with what he'd done.

"You should get some sleep." Jackson tried speaking to me at most twice a day.

"I don't need to sleep," I said. I'd gotten a few hours here and there since I'd started down this forsaken path. Jackson had fed me—with the groceries I'd bought him, no less.

"Your body will give out on you sooner or later, little Hannah."

Up until that point, I never would have pegged the town recluse, whose hobbies included firing warning shots and physically chasing people away from an abandoned lighthouse, as a mother hen.

"My body is fine," I said.

A voice, rough as sandpaper, came from the mattress: "That makes one of us."

Jackson and I were both shocked into silence. I recovered first. "You're awake."

"Unfortunately." Toby Hawthorne was smart enough to not try to sit up. He didn't even open his eyes. "If you're so set on not sleeping," he continued, the pain in his sandpaper voice matched only by its arrogance, "then perhaps you wouldn't mind shutting the hell up?"

It was like I was right back in that bar, watching him smirk and lean against the pool table, his glass balanced precariously on its edge.

Gritting my teeth, I crossed the room and started checking his vitals. *Pulse first*—my fingers on his neck. *Then breathing*—the rise and fall of his chest, breath against my palm. *Pupil reactivity.* I needed to touch his face for that one. His eyes were closed. I pried them open.

"This isn't what I meant when I told you to shut up." His voice was lower than it had been in the bar, rougher.

"You don't give me orders." I finished my check of his pupils. "Follow the light with your eyes."

"What will you give me if I do?" he quipped.

This was the first time I'd been able to do anything approximating a neurological exam, and the asshole apparently didn't intend to make it easy. "A quick and merciful death," I sniped.

He followed the light with his eyes. I tested the feeling in his fingers and toes, ran my pen lightly over the arch of his foot. His body did all the right things.

"Pay up," my patient said.

I'd promised him a quick death. "As it happens, I lied."

"You have a name, liar?" Even with smoke-damaged vocal

cords, he had a way of making questions sound like silky demands. I didn't reply. "Better yet," he continued, addressing the words to the ceiling, his eyes closing, "what's mine?"

"Your what?" I bit out.

"My name."

I stared at him, certain that he was messing with me, but my patient didn't say anything else, and a trickle of uncertainty began to snake its way through my mind.

"My name," he repeated, less demand than *command* this time.

"Harry." Jackson came to stand over the two of us. It took me a moment to realize that he'd given Toby an answer—the wrong one. Then again, I'd never had any indication that Jackson Currie actually knew who he had in this shack.

"Harry," Toby echoed. It was the arch tone with which he said the fake name Jackson had just given him that convinced me that the Hawthorne heir wasn't putting on a show.

He really *didn't* remember his own name.

"Harry what?" he asked.

"Don't know." Jackson gave a half-grunt, half-snort, which very effectively communicated that not only did he not know *Harry*'s last name—he didn't care. "I'm Jackson." His gruff voice grew gruffer. "She's Hannah."

"Hannah," the burned boy repeated, his voice smoky and hoarse. "Spelled the same backward as forward—assuming there's an *H* on the end?"

Suddenly, I was right back at the bar again. *What about you, palindrome girl? H-A-N-N-A-H. Will I see you around? We could have a little fun, set the world on fire...*

He'd known—even then, he'd already known what kind of game he'd come to Hawthorne Island to play. I had no idea why a boy with *everything* would have been angry enough, *reckless* enough to want to play with fire. All I knew was that to him, it had been a game.

"What the hell is wrong with you?" The question escaped my lips before I could stop it.

The target of my ire almost managed a smirk. "You're the doctor. You tell me."

"Nurse." My correction was automatic.

"Mendax," he replied. He gave it a moment, and then: "It's Latin, for *liar*." Pain slashed through his features, but he seemed dead set on ignoring it. "I appear to be the kind of person who recognizes lies when I hear them. You aren't a nurse, not exactly." He paused, breathing through the pain. "If I had to make an educated guess about the circumstances that brought me here—and it appears I'm the type to do that, too—I would say that I am most likely a horrible, *horrible* individual and someone wanted me dead. Am I getting warm, not-nurse Hannah?"

"You don't remember." That was Jackson, coming to the same conclusion I had.

"Amnesia." I said the word out loud and thought about his head wound. I'd been more focused on the burns, but maybe I shouldn't have been.

"Tell me, Hannah the Same Backward as Forward: Are you the one who bashed my head in?" Toby tried to sit up.

My hands went automatically to his shoulders, skirting the burns. "I'm the one who's going to," I told him, "if you don't lay back."

He gave in to my command—or to the pain. His eyes went heavy-lidded, and for a moment, I thought he might pass out again, but no such luck.

"I don't know who you or Too Much Beard over there are,"

Toby said. "Hell, I don't know who *I* am. But I have the distinct feeling that I'm the kind of person who could bring your entire world crumbling down...just...like...*that*."

He snapped his fingers without raising his hand off the bed.

You already did. I blinked back that thought—and every single memory that wanted to come. *Kaylie, at five, sitting on a fence, wearing a bathing suit and a feather boa. At seven, walking on her hands. At seventeen, throwing an arm around my shoulder.*

Toby Hawthorne had *already* stolen the world from me, but that didn't stop him from continuing. "So now would be a good time," he said, every inch the billionaire's son, "for someone to tell me what the hell is going on here."

In that moment, I came to a decision: I didn't want to think of him as *Toby Hawthorne* anymore. He could be *Harry*, for all I cared. He could be *no one*, as long as I could find a way to look at him without thinking about what I had lost.

"What happened was that an explosion threw you off a cliff into the ocean." I kept my tone detached. "*Too Much Beard* over there pulled you out of the water, and right now, the two of us are all you've got. So shut the hell up"—I reached for a bottle of pain medication—"and take *these*."

Dark green eyes opened wider once more and locked on the little white pills in my hand.

"Don't mind if I do." His lips curved slightly. "I think I might be fond of pills. But these..." He turned his head slowly to look at the bottle. "These, I seem to find disappointing."

I bet you do. My eyes narrowed to slits as I thought about the kind of drugs this rich boy was probably used to taking.

"*Do no harm*," I muttered to myself between clenched teeth. I brought the meds to his mouth. There was something that felt intentional about the way his lips brushed my palm as I fed them to him.

I wasn't particularly gentle as I poured water down his throat. "Word to the wise, Harry," I told him, my voice as close to emotionless as I could make it. "You might want to get used to being disappointed."

Chapter 9

On day four, Jackson brought me coffee. I didn't ask where he'd gotten it because I deeply suspected the tin of chocolate-brown grounds had been buried somewhere nearby. There were coffee filters in the med kit, which was about par for the course for Jackson's organization scheme. He produced an ancient coffee pot from somewhere under the sink.

I still had no idea how he'd rigged this place up with running water, let alone electricity, but he had. I didn't drink coffee, but I made it anyway, and when Jackson tossed a baggie of restaurant sugar packets onto the table, I accepted that offering, too.

Day by day and hour by hour, it was starting to look more like *Harry* would live. His burns were healing slowly, if at all, but there was no sign of infection yet. I was starting to suspect his head injury might have resulted in more than just amnesia, that there might be neurological damage that affected motor abilities in the lower half of his body. But his cognition was intact, and he was conscious at least some of the time. He could swallow and had only tempted my fury by refusing water once. He'd been in and out of lucidness, and the pain seemed to be getting worse, not better, but his vitals were strong.

He was.

"We can't keep him here forever," I told Jackson, my voice low as I dumped the sugar packets out onto the small table between us. The piece of paper from the pocket of my scrubs had long-since been worn to shreds by my folding. I needed something to occupy my hands.

"Keep him?" Jackson snorted. "Why the hell would we want to do that? Kid's a real piece of work."

That was one way of putting it. With or without his memory, *Harry*, as I continually tried to think of him, seemed to have retained the arrogance of his pedigree, the unspoken but bullet-proof certainty that the world would form itself to his liking.

I wasn't exactly prone to kissing rings.

"One of us is going to have to go into town for more supplies soon." I kept my voice low, but if the object of my loathing woke up, he'd probably hear me all the same. The bunker was six hundred square feet total, if that.

"And by *town*, I assume you mean some place other than Rockaway Watch." Jackson gave me a look.

I'd been trying not to think about the world outside of these walls, but there was no skirting that reminder of how perilous our current situation was. If my family discovered what Jackson and I were hiding out here—*who* we were hiding—it wouldn't go well.

For any of us.

"Someplace else," I agreed quietly. I picked up two sugar packets and set them on their ends, leaning the tips against each other in an inverted V, a balancing act that I just barely managed to pull off. "I'll go," I said.

I turned my head toward the mattress. Harry looked decep-tively angelic when he slept, the perfection of his face a sharp contrast to the blistered, weeping burns and blackened skin that

I knew lay underneath his gauze. His chest rose and fell as I watched, and I picked up two more sugar packets, continuing to build a makeshift, not-card castle that I knew could fall at any moment.

"I'll go," I said again. "For supplies. Tomorrow."

Chapter 10

need something stronger." Harry was fury and condescension and pain, and there was a real chance that he was plotting my demise.

I fixed him with a stare. "You need to let me work." I'd given him the maximum dose of the over-the-counter pain meds, but we were almost out. *Something stronger* wasn't an option.

I continued to tend his burns. *Strips of cloth, soaked in cool water, laid over his collarbone and arms.* The silver cream and gauze were going to be next, and we were running low on those, too.

"It feels like I'm being flayed alive." He gritted his teeth.

I knew from having been down this road with him before: The pain was going to get worse before it got better. I worked in silence for a minute or two, and then—

"Everything hurts." His voice was more animal than human. I worried that I might need Jackson to hold him still, to keep him from doing himself and his injuries irreparable harm—but then my patient's eyes made their way to mine, and his body settled.

Instead of noticing the color of his irises this time, I noticed the clarity in his gaze, the way it searched mine, like *I* was the patient, and he was something else altogether.

"Doesn't it?" he murmured. *Everything hurts. Doesn't it?*

My chest seized, the question trapping stale air in my lungs, because he was right. Everything *hurt*. That was why I was here. It was what I was hiding from.

Kaylie.

"You don't get to ask me questions," I said, and I was surprised at how animal *my* voice sounded. I was a person who'd learned from childhood to hide my emotions, to make myself small—but I couldn't hide this.

I hated him, and I was *saving* him, and the only way I could even remotely justify that was by hating him some more.

Keep going. Do the work. Gentle now. For a while, there was blessed silence.

His eyes closed. "You build little castles out of sugar packets."

I pretended I couldn't hear him—but I did. I *definitely* did.

"It's endearing, really. The sugar castles." A twist of his lips made it impossible for me to tell if that was sarcasm or if he meant it. "Do you believe in fairy tales, Hannah the Same Backward as Forward?"

There it was again—that name. Was he really so obsessed with palindromes?

I opened the jar of silver cream. "I believe in villains," I said flatly.

"Villains." He made a huffing sound, pain etched so clearly into the lines of his face—cheekbones, brow, jaw—that I couldn't look away. "It's funny," he continued. "I don't remember a damn thing about myself, but I would drink to that."

I bet you would. There was a good chance that when he'd said that he needed something stronger, he might not have just been talking about the pain. *Pills and booze.* He'd shown no signs of chills or seizures, so I didn't think he was in full-on withdrawal, not physically at least.

"The only thing you're drinking," I told him, steel in my voice, "is water."

If that made me *his* villain...*good.*

Chapter 11

When I went to leave for the supply run, Jackson followed me out. He obviously had something to say, so I waited for him to say it.

"I don't need to tell you about secrets, Hannah." It was just like him to phrase it like that, leaving the warning itself unspoken. *No one can find out.*

"It's only a secret," I replied, "if you have someone to tell." Otherwise, it was just another way of being alone.

And I was a master at that.

I took a three-mile hike and then two buses to get to a chain pharmacy in a town where I knew no one. I was wearing a massive flannel shirt of Jackson's over the same pair of scrub pants I'd been wearing for days. No one paid me a second look.

I planned to pay in cash. I'd worked from the time I was fourteen until I'd moved out, and my second-year internship had been paid. I had enough money to make rent each month, and I was Rooney enough to keep cash on me by default. No one in a family like mine put things on cards, not unless there was a reason to *want* a paper trail.

As an additional precaution, I mixed the medical supplies we needed in with other purchases—deodorant, snack food, menstrual products, and, on impulse, a spiral notebook, a pack of pens, and a deck of cards.

I got in a line with a male cashier and put the period products up first. He avoided looking too closely at anything I set on the counter after that.

Two and a half hours later, when I arrived back at Jackson's, the first thing I saw was my patient, propped up just enough to throw back a glass of whiskey.

"Miss me?" Harry said darkly.

I turned to glare at Jackson.

"We were out of meds," the fisherman grunted.

"And now we're not." I dropped the plastic bags from the pharmacy onto the floor. "Good luck with that," I told Jackson.

I'd been killing myself to save my patient's ungrateful ass, and he was well on his way to getting *drunk*.

As I turned to leave, Harry's whiskey-laden voice rolled over me from behind. "Don't worry, Beardy. She'll be back."

Chapter 12

I t had been days since I'd been to my place. If I'd been a normal person, that kind of thing probably wouldn't have gone unnoticed, but I was almost as much of a recluse as Jackson was. I stepped into my apartment assuming that no one had missed me—and then I saw the note.

My sister's name was written in all-capital letters at the top of the page. KAYLIE. The only thing below it was a time, underlined with a heavy hand: 8 PM.

I had no way of knowing who had left this message or when, but I knew it was from my mother, and I knew better than to ignore it. Best-case scenario, that 8 PM referred to tonight. Worst-case scenario, I'd missed the summons and would have to come up with a plausible explanation about where I'd been.

As eight o'clock approached, I made my way to my car. This time, when I pulled onto the dirt road that dead-ended at the Rooney compound, the number of cars parked outside made it clear: I hadn't missed anything, and I wasn't the only one who had been summoned.

This was a *family* affair.

I let myself in. A dozen people were crowded into the kitchen, including both of my parents. There was food on the stove and the countertops, lots of it. Everyone else was wearing black. I was wearing jeans and a faded gray sweatshirt. No one gave them or me a second look until my mother turned to face me. The effect was instantaneous.

When Eden Rooney took notice of something, everyone else did, too.

"Glad to see you made it to your sister's wake." My mother's tone was hard to read. "Hope the scumbag reporters didn't bother you on the way in."

Reporters? Old instincts kept me from betraying even a hint of surprise. "I didn't see any."

"Imagine that." Her lips curled slightly, and I thought about the many and varied methods my family might have used to run off unwanted visitors.

"Where are the dogs?" I asked.

"This is private property." My mother was a master at answering questions by *not* answering them. "Not my fault if someone ignores the *No Trespassing* signs."

There wasn't a single local reporter who would have taken that chance—not in this town, not anywhere close by. *This isn't just local news,* I realized. I had no idea why it hadn't occurred to me until then that the fire on Hawthorne Island had probably made national headlines.

Maybe even international.

A private island. A billionaire's tragedy. Young lives cut short. I tried not to think about the kind of media circus that would happen when Toby Hawthorne reappeared alive—and focused on the other part of what my mother had said instead.

This was my sister's wake.

Rooneys didn't do funerals. Bodies were always burned— legally or otherwise—no evidence left behind. Kaylie had already been *ashes*, so that was taken care of. There would be no official burial, no gravestone, no minister or priest.

In our family, there was only ever a wake.

"She wouldn't like so many people wearing black," I said. It was unlike me to have said anything. That was Invisibility 101.

"Think she'd approve of gray?" my mother asked me. Her voice was flat, but there was something almost human in her expression.

"I doubt it," I said, because the truth was that my sister would have *hated* my sweatshirt.

You beautiful bitch. You glorious thing, you. She'd always seen me completely differently than the way I'd seen myself.

My mother assessed me for a moment, then walked to stand right in front of me. "I know you, Hannah." I thought for a moment that she might know something, but then she continued, "You need to hear me say it." She held my gaze. "She's dead."

My mother didn't know—not about where I'd been or what I'd been doing or who I'd been doing it for. But she did know that until I'd heard *her* say it, part of me had still—*still, still, still*—refused to fully accept that Kaylie was gone.

I knew it was true. I *felt* it. But I'd been hiding from it for days.

"I know." My voice came out hoarse.

"Do you, Hannah?" She studied my face. I knew what she was looking for. *Fire. Fury.* Eden Rooney wanted to see some hint of violence in me, some desire for retribution.

I gave her nothing. It didn't matter that I'd felt those things, all of them—that I *still* felt them every time I looked at Toby Hawthorne and forgot to recast him as *Harry* in my mind.

I was not my mother's daughter.

"Eden." My father spoke from behind her, his voice uncharacteristically gentle. "Let the girl eat."

Once I left the kitchen, it was easy enough to fade into the background again. I ended up in the den, where a group of my uncles and "uncles" and cousins and "cousins" were gathered for the gnashing of teeth and the drinking of beers.

"—*fixers*. At least three of them, working for Hawthorne."

I came in, mid-teeth-gnash, to a conversation I had no context for. One after another, they one-upped each other.

"Damn cops are stonewalling us, which means they got a better offer."

"Wouldn't be an issue if state police hadn't taken over."

"Even the damn feds are circling."

I wanted no part of this conversation, but backing out of the room ran the risk of drawing attention.

"So, what?" Rory spat. "We just let them walk all over us because they've got money? We let them talk about our Kaylie like *this*?" Rory slammed a newspaper down onto the table.

I remembered what my mother had said about reporters, and then I remembered my father's words, days earlier: *They'll pin this on her. You just wait and see.*

I stepped out of the shadows, which was probably a mistake, but almost every mistake I'd ever made, I'd made for Kaylie. I reached for the paper. It took me less than a minute to read the front-page article.

The picture it drew was clear enough. *A bad girl—a drug addict with a criminal record. Three promising young men, gone too soon.*

"They're blaming Kaylie for the fire." I said it out loud. Forget the fact that those three boys had come to Hawthorne Island looking for trouble, forget *kerosene—*

"It's bullshit," Rory growled. "Eden should have let me—"

"Rory." His father cut him off just as my mother stepped into the den.

"Seems to me," my mother said slowly, "that this particular problem has taken care of itself. Those boys are dead. Trash took itself out this time."

I flashed back to tending to Toby Hawthorne's burns, again and again. *Harry.* I used the name to build a wall up in my mind. *His name is Harry. He's of no interest to anyone in this room. He's no one.*

"Cat got your tongue, Hannah?" Rory asked suddenly. I heard the seething resentment buried in his tone. I'd seen him weak and punished. He wasn't going to be forgiving that any time soon, especially when my mother had just shut him down *again.*

I didn't give myself long to debate how to respond. All I had to do was pretend that I wasn't betraying the family, every second of every day. "This is supposed to be a wake," I said. Rooneys knew how to retaliate, but they also knew how to mourn. "Kaylie was..." How could I even begin to put my sister into words? "She loved hard," I said quietly.

My sister had never managed to keep *anyone* at arm's length. She'd loved *them*, and they were monsters.

"Kaylie was born hollering at the top of her lungs." That was my mother, mourning. "Smiled for the first time when she was five weeks old and never stopped."

Rory stared at me for another second, then lifted his beer. "To Kaylie," he said sharply.

The toast caught on, and someone shoved a bottle into my hand. "To Kaylie," I whispered.

Hours later, once they were all well and truly drunk, I managed to slip out. As I walked away from the house I'd grown up in, it hit me that, without Kaylie, there was nothing holding me in Rockaway Watch anymore, nothing stopping me from getting in my car and driving east and never coming back. I could transfer to a community college a thousand miles away, far enough that it wouldn't be worth the family's effort to come after me.

With Kaylie dead, they probably wouldn't even be surprised. All I had to do was *leave*.

So why did I drive back to my apartment instead? Why did I break down in the shower instead of getting the hell out of Dodge? Why did I get out of the damn shower, get dressed, and decide to go back to the shack?

To *him*?

Chapter 13

Y ou've been drinking," I said when Jackson let me in. The fisherman smelled like a distillery.

"You didn't want Harry having it." Jackson shrugged. "It was either this or pour the bottle out." The fisherman's tone made it obvious that pouring out whiskey had never been an option.

I decided that it was just as well that Jackson had apparently drained the bottle. If he'd been sober, he probably would have noticed my blotchy skin, my bloodshot eyes.

Between my sister and me, Kaylie had always been the pretty crier.

Soon enough, Jackson was out like a light. Harry was likewise unconscious. I lowered myself to the floor next to his mattress and thought about the information I'd gleaned at Kaylie's wake. My patient's billionaire father had sent people to Rockaway Watch to do damage control. In all likelihood, that meant that all I had to do to be rid of the giant liability before me was find a way to contact one of Tobias Hawthorne's people. Within hours, if not minutes, they'd have the precious heir life-flighted to some fancy medical facility hundreds of miles away, where my family couldn't touch him.

I thought about the press and imagined what coverage of the

resurrection of Toby Hawthorne might look like. *Would anyone even question your role in the fire?* I asked him silently. *Would you pin it all on a "troubled" girl?*

I could feel the anger I'd denied myself in my mother's presence taking hold of my body. My fingers curled into my palms as the muscles in my stomach slowly knotted. I felt my rage at the way the world would remember my sister in the ache of my jaw and the clench of my teeth.

I hate you. The words grounded me, soft and velvety in my mind as I laid a hand on Harry's chest, outside the burns.

I hate you.

I hate you.

I hate you.

And then I heard the faintest of murmurs. I pulled my hand back and braced my fingers against the mattress. The room was dark, but I could hear his lips moving. I couldn't make out what he was saying, and then he started to thrash. To *writhe.*

I wondered when the last time he'd had pain medication was. I wondered why I even cared.

I grabbed the flashlight I'd left on the floor earlier and turned it on. My patient's eyes weren't open. He tossed his head violently back and forth, his whole body wracked with the force of that movement.

His burns. I did not want to hold him down. "Wake up," I said, working to hold on to my anger.

He didn't.

"*Wake up.*"

His lips moved again, the volume of his speech growing to the point that I could actually make out the words. "*The tree...*"

The villain of my life's story was more than writhing now. He was going to hurt himself.

I caught his head between my hands, my thumbs braced against his jawbone on either side. "Not on my watch, you asshole."

It took every ounce of strength I had to keep his head still, but after a moment or two, his body stopped moving, too.

"*The tree is poison.*" His eyelids flew open, and just like that, we were looking directly at each other. I'd dropped the flashlight on the mattress. Its beam did little to disturb the darkness, but somehow, I could see—or imagine—every single line and curve of Toby Hawthorne's face. *Granite jaw. Slashing cheekbones. Deep-set eyes.*

I didn't see *pain* there. I saw *fury* and *devastation* and more. For a single moment in time, it was like looking in a mirror.

And then he came fully awake. The expression on his face changed, like the surface of a lake touched by wind, and his lips moved again. "Deified," he whispered.

I thought at first that I'd imagined him saying that word, but then I heard his voice again through the darkness, through what little light came of the flashlight's beam.

"Civic. Madam. Race car." His eyes, the color of a forest at night, never left mine. "Rotator. Deed."

He was reciting *palindromes*, the smug bastard, and I was going to kill him.

Chapter 14

S oon enough, I was allowed back at the hospital. I went. I worked. I slept, occasionally.

And I kept going back to Jackson's.

I'd decided not to even try making contact with Tobias Hawthorne's *fixers*. If word got out that the Hawthorne heir was alive, the first question that everyone, including my mother, would ask was *how*. I didn't trust the billionaire's people not to land a helicopter right there on the rocks. I wasn't putting a target on Jackson's back, so that left the alternative of getting my patient to the point where he could be moved.

Nine times out of ten, I succeeded at thinking of him as *Harry*. He seemed to take special pleasure in being able to push me to the last tenth. I would have sworn the bane of my existence knew every single time his real name crossed my mind, even though he gave no sign of remembering it himself.

"Hearts or Spades?" Harry didn't even bother opening his eyes as he issued that question. His voice had fully recovered from the fire and whatever smoke he'd inhaled, and there was something liquid about the way he strung together the words, a silken but somehow pointed laziness that made him irritatingly impossible to ignore.

"Are you asking my preference?" I spread cream across his angry, red bicep. The second-degree burns were looking better. The ones on his chest, in contrast, hadn't improved. I focused on the work—not on *him* and certainly not on the feel of muscles beneath my steady, gentle hands. "Spades are more useful."

"For burying the bodies of your enemies?"

The treatment *had* to hurt, but I wouldn't have been able to tell that from the twist of Harry's lips. *You wouldn't be making jokes like that if you knew who I was and what you took from me,* I thought.

Harry had a habit of replying to my silences like they *weren't* silences. "Setting aside the questionable uses you have for a literal spade, vicious one, I was asking about the card games. You bought a deck. Makes for better castles than sugar, I suppose."

He seemed to take a very distinct pleasure in issuing reminders that, when it came to me, he saw everything, noticed everything.

"So, Hannah the Same Backward as Forward..." Harry's voice was silken despite its rasp. "What's your poison? Hearts or Spades?"

Poison. That word made me think of the phrase he'd muttered in his sleep. *The tree is poison...*

"Neither." I squashed the memory like a bug. "I have better things to do than play with you." I moved from his bicep to his collarbone—that much closer to his chest.

Harry sucked in a breath around his teeth, but the pain didn't silence him for long. "If you're so set on not playing games," he said, "then why don't you tell me why I'm still here?"

Here, as in alive? Or here meaning in this shack? I didn't ask for the clarification. "As punishment for my mortal sins," I deadpanned.

That surprised a wheeze out of him, almost a laugh. "Why am I here and not in a hospital, *mentirosa*?"

I recognized the game he was playing. "Spanish for *liar*?" I guessed.

He neither confirmed nor denied that. "Is it because of me or because of you?" he pressed.

"It's both," I said.

"And that"—his eyes finally opened—"was not a lie." There was power in Toby Hawthorne's gaze, always.

"You wouldn't be safe at a hospital." I parted with a truth and threw the wall back up in my mind, forcing myself to think of him as *Harry* again.

"You can't just say something like that and leave me hanging, Hannah the Same Backward as Forward."

Watch me, I thought, fixing gauze into place. "Done."

"Until the next time." His tone was darker now. He smiled, a switchblade smile, the kind I knew better than to trust. "It sure would be a shame if I hurt myself trying to get out of this bed and undid all that work of yours."

I folded my arms. "You'd pass out from the pain before you got very far."

"I'm feeling the need," Harry said, the barest hint of mockery in his tone as he tried another tactic, "for a bedpan."

"Jackson will be back soon."

"Maybe I want *your* assistance."

"Maybe," I told him, "you're bluffing."

"Bluffing," Harry repeated, savoring the taste of the word. "Poker, then? One round."

Something told me that if I turned him down, he'd make me pay for it—or he'd make himself pay for it. "One round," I agreed, clipping the words.

"Five-Card Draw?" There was the barest hint of a Texas drawl in his voice.

"Fine." I retrieved the deck and dealt the cards. Beating him was going to be therapeutic. After eyeing my hand, I placed two cards face down on the edge of the mattress. "I'll take two."

His eyes were only partially open as I drew two additional cards from the deck, but I knew in my gut that he saw *everything*. Each and every little tell.

"I'll hold," he murmured.

You're bluffing. I went to lay down my final hand.

He stopped me. "Nuh-uh-uh, Hannah the Same Backward as Forward. What would you like to wager?"

"With you?" I said. "Nothing."

"How about this? If I win, you give me a sheet of paper." That proposal took me by surprise. Harry was many things, but restrained and prone to modest requests were not among them.

"What do I get if I win?" I countered.

"Silence." He had an answer for everything. "Mine, for one full day."

One day without him saying a word to me sounded pretty damn nice. "Two days," I countered.

Harry accepted my terms with the slightest incline of his head. "I call."

I laid down my cards "Two pair. Kings." I named the higher of my pairs.

"Two pair," he echoed, laying his own cards beside mine on the mattress. "Jacks." He smiled a crooked little smile. "Looks like you won."

That felt a lot more ominous than it should have.

Chapter 15

I had long shifts at the hospital the next two days, which didn't leave me that much time to collect on my winnings, but true to his word, Harry didn't part with a single mocking statement as I took his vitals and checked his wounds the next night or the night after that.

Instead, he *watched* me, his eyes on mine, his focus palpable and every bit as liquid and silken as the voice he'd agreed to silence. The more deliberate he became about touching me with his gaze, the more I tried to concentrate on my work and only my work.

The head wound had closed. The hair around it was beginning to regrow. The color looked darker to me, like maybe the mahogany-red hue in the rest of his locks was courtesy of the sun. The new hair was coarse. It shouldn't have felt soft under my touch.

I shouldn't have *felt* it at all.

I didn't like the look of the third-degree burns on his chest. The others were improving, but not those. The skin was white in places, black in others. Toward the outside of the wound, where third-degree gave way to second, the skin was blistered beyond belief. Those nerve endings hadn't been destroyed, so that was where his pain was the worst, but it was the area dead center on his torso that concerned me the most—that was the area still at risk for infection, the area where the damage could go deeper than I knew.

I bandaged it and looked away, overly aware even as I did that he was still *watching* me, pain in his dark green eyes and a smirk on his lips.

After Harry's days of silence passed, he seemed intent on making up for them—on making conversation. "You work at a hospital."

"Brilliant deduction," I replied.

"You wound me, Hannah the Same Backward as Forward."

"Don't call me that."

Harry raked his gaze over my mouth and smiled slightly at whatever he saw there. "Sounds like you might be interested in another wager."

Jackson had left me alone with our patient. I had the day off, and the fisherman still had a living to make. The closer the town recluse stuck to his routine, the less likely he was to draw attention. But that meant that I couldn't just be in and out, checking on Harry. I had to stay.

I didn't trust my patient alone.

"Five-Card Draw?" I said. "If I win, you ditch the nickname forever and agree not to talk to me—and or even *look* at me—for three days."

"Steep price, not looking at you." He raked his gaze over my face—eyes, mouth, lips, jaw, then eyes again. "What will you give me in return?"

I folded my arms. "A piece of paper."

"You drive a hard bargain." He smiled, the curl of his lips deliberate and slow. "But I'll accept your terms."

I dealt the cards. Taking in my hand, I decided to play it safe, knowing he wouldn't. I placed two cards face down.

"It's always two with you." Harry seemed to find some satisfaction in that observation. Too much, really.

"Let me guess," I said. "You don't need a single card."

"Do you like being wrong?" He took two as well. I knew from the second he saw his new cards that whatever he'd drawn didn't bode well for me.

"I call," I said.

Harry laid down his cards. "Full house."

I laid down a pair of aces.

"Those are the breaks, Hannah the Same Backward as Forward. The nickname stays."

I walked over to the table and tore a page out of the notebook I'd bought at the drugstore, then returned to the mattress and dropped it, right beside his face.

"Did I do something to offend you, liar mine?"

I'm not your anything. I didn't say that. My quiet was the kind that didn't blink. Didn't flinch. "Do you want a list?"

He took his time responding, like he was rolling my question over in his mind the way I'd once seen him roll pool chalk over and under highly skilled fingers, one after another. "I get the sense," he said, his voice quiet and deep, like the calm before a storm, like still waters in the dead of night, "that I don't know how to *want* anything anymore."

Just like that, the walls in my mind came down. Just like that, I saw the boy I'd met that night at the bar, daring his glass to fall, knowing that it wouldn't. I saw the person who'd paid far too much attention to me, even then. The one who'd bought kerosene. *Toby.*

And in the next breath, I thought about my dancing, smiling, fearless sister going up in flames.

I stood and stalked away from the boy on the bed, but I couldn't leave. I was stuck there until Jackson got back. If I didn't steer the conversation, *he* would.

Harry. Think of him as Harry. "What tree?" I said, my voice quiet, even, everything he'd probably come to expect of me.

"Is that a riddle?" Harry's tone made it clear: He liked riddles.

"You talk in your sleep." I wondered if he could hear, in those calm words, the fury I still felt every time I came even close to thinking my sister's name.

"I talk in my sleep." Harry's voice was every bit as dry as mine. "About a tree?"

"Apparently, it's poisoned," I said.

Harry's reply was immediate, his tone as quiet and deep as it had been when he'd talked about *wanting*: "Aren't we all?"

Chapter 16

On my next day off, I didn't go back to the shack until well after sunset. When I got there, the metal door was slightly ajar.

It's never open. My pulse pounded in my throat as I pushed the door inward to find Jackson trying to get Harry off the floor—*trying*, because Harry was wild-eyed and fighting.

The burns—he was going to tear through brittle, paper-thin flesh. *Like hell you are, you bastard.* "Stop." The word burst from my lips. *"Now."*

The prince of agony went suddenly, eerily still. "Do people always listen to you, not-nurse Hannah?"

Jackson looked like he was considering homicide. He wasn't the only one. My heart was still jackhammering my rib cage. When I'd seen that open door, my first, subconscious thought had been that my family had found them.

Found *him*. "I don't know." I fixed my gaze on Harry. "I try not to say much."

"How's that working out for you?" Why was it that his damn lips seemed to have about a thousand different ways of twisting?

"Just fine," I said. *Until you.* "Get in bed." I crossed the room to help Jackson, and together, we managed to get Harry back on the mattress.

"Far be it from me," Harry quipped darkly, "to turn down an invitation from a pretty woman, especially when it involves a bed."

I didn't know which was worse: the fact that he was acting like I'd *invited him to bed* or the way he'd said *pretty*—like he meant it.

"You deal with this," Jackson growled in my direction. Before I could reply, he stormed out of the shack.

I followed the fisherman as far as the threshold. "What happened?" I called, as Jackson Currie did his best to disappear into the night.

"Stubborn son of a bitch thought he could stand. And walk. He fell." The outline of Jackson's body was just barely visible in the moonlight. "And then he lost his damn mind."

Somehow, it didn't surprise me that Toby Hawthorne didn't take failure well.

I stepped onto the porch, knowing I couldn't go any farther, knowing that I couldn't leave Toby—*Harry*, think of him as *Harry*—alone.

"Jackson, are we doing the right thing?" I hadn't meant to ask that question, hadn't meant to whisper those words into the night.

"Sometimes there's no such thing as the *right thing*. Sometimes, there's only Death and whatever you can do to hold her off."

"*Her?*" I asked.

"Yeah, well," Jackson grunted. "Death's a real bitch."

I went back in. Harry was lying perfectly still on the mattress, his long limbs marked by lines of tension, muscle after muscle. His eyes were closed. He looked like he'd been carved from stone, like a work of rage-fueled beauty called forth from granite by a master. But when I got closer, I realized that his face was wet. I watched as a new tear—just one—carved its way from the corner of his eye down his cheek, all the way to the base of his jaw.

I wasn't even sure he knew he was crying. *From pain? From failure? From being trapped here?* I didn't say a word as I went about checking the damage he'd done, and neither did he—not until I was finished.

"I guess that's it, then. I'm your captive for a little longer."

The word *captive* was barbed, and I tried for just a moment to put myself in his shoes: no memory, in agony, and at the mercy of strangers.

"Trust me," I said, "the second you're well enough for us to move you, I will very happily dump you three hundred miles away and leave you to fend for yourself."

"Oddly enough, I *do* trust you. I must be a masochist that way." There was a long silence and then: "Why three hundred miles?"

Honesty came more easily to me than it should have: "There are people who want you dead, and right now, all of them think you already are."

"I don't suppose you're going to tell me who those people are or why they want to hasten my tragic and inevitable demise?"

The tears were still coming from his eyes, a single drop at a time. It had to be the pain.

I went for the medication. "Have you *met* you?" I asked bluntly. I checked the log I'd had Jackson keeping to make sure I'd grabbed the right medication. The risks of an overdose were lower for this one, so I slipped out two extra pills.

One after another, he took them, his lips brushing the very tips of my fingers. I tried to look anywhere but at my hand and his mouth and the place where they met. On the floor beside the mattress, I saw a piece of paper with writing on it. I bent to get a better look.

Two words were written in oversized, uneven chicken-scratch on the page: *bourbon* and *lemons*.

"What's this?" I asked.

Pain was rolling off him in waves, but that didn't stop him from smirking. "My grocery list." He lifted his right hand off the bed just enough to make a little waving motion. "Hop to it."

Clearly, he *wanted* me to murder him. "I'm not buying you bourbon. Or lemons."

Why the hell did he want lemons?

"You know what they say," he murmured, "about making lemonade." He was hurting, but there was something more than pain in his voice, a deliberate, teasing *something* dancing lockstep with agony in his tone.

I stayed with him and waited until the pain meds took effect before pulling back to the table, where I tore a piece of paper out of the notebook for myself and started folding. Hours passed. Harry was barely moving and wasn't talking, but he was conscious.

It was only when we heard Jackson's footsteps outside that my patient spoke again.

"*I was angry with my friend; I told my wrath, my wrath did end.*" There was something almost musical in Harry's tone, something dark. "*I was angry with my foe: I told it not, my wrath did grow.*"

Something told me those words weren't his. "I don't understand," I said.

I *heard* his next breath. "I would wager, my little liar, that you do."

Chapter 17

I managed to hold out for a few days before looking up the words Harry had said. It was a poem—an old one. The poet's name was William Blake. The poem was about vengeance. I read it from beginning to end probably a dozen times, and true to Harry's prediction, I understood it.

I felt every single word of it.

The title of the poem was "A Poison Tree."

After my shift that night, I hit the grocery store. Since I wasn't planning to buy any medical supplies, I didn't bother with the two-bus, three-mile-hike routine and just went to the store closest to the hospital instead. It wasn't until I got in line to check out that I realized I was being watched.

A man stepped into line behind me. He wore jeans that looked too new and a plain T-shirt that fit him like he was more used to wearing suits. I could feel him studying me—not like a book but like something under a microscope.

I wondered if he worked for Tobias Hawthorne, if he was one of the infamous fixers—and if so, why he was still here. Or maybe he was a reporter who'd stuck around after the story had begun to grow cold, hoping for a different angle.

Either way, I refused to let on that I'd noticed him watching me. He waited until the cashier began ringing up my groceries to speak. "I hear you're a Rooney."

I bagged my own food, not even looking at him. "You can't believe everything you hear."

I didn't make the hike up to Jackson's until I was sure that I hadn't been followed back to my apartment, and when I did go—checking over my shoulder every ten steps across the rocks—I didn't say a word about the man at the store. I just wordlessly started unpacking the groceries.

"Where are my lemons?" Harry spoke from the mattress.

Jackson slid in beside me. "Where's the bourbon?" he asked, his voice low.

I gave a slight shake of my head. I hadn't bought bourbon.

"The pain, Hannah." Jackson was a no-frills kind of person at the best of times. This wasn't the best of times, and there wasn't an ounce of sugarcoating in his tone. "It's getting worse. A whole hell of a lot worse."

"It shouldn't be," I said quietly. *Should it?* I approached the patient, an uncharacteristic hesitation in my step.

"Don't touch me." For once, there was nothing smooth in Harry's tone, nothing dark or knowing.

I wished I'd bought the damn bourbon.

I laid the back of my hand against first his cheek, then his forehead. *Hot to the touch.* "I have no desire whatsoever to touch you," I murmured—but I did, again and again, checking his injuries.

At a certain point, it became clear to me that no touch was gentle enough.

There's something wrong. I'd examined everything but the burns on his chest. As I braced myself to do what had to be done, my gaze caught on an object sitting beside him on the mattress: a tiny, intricate paper cube. *Thirty folds, at least.*

"You folded this." I didn't phrase it as a question.

"Won the paper off Jackson," Harry said. He was looking at me now, and his eyes were a little glassy.

I touched his face again, confirming what I'd felt before. *Fever.*

"The question, Hannah the Same Backward as Forward," he said, his voice closer to a whisper than a rasp, "is whether you can unfold it without tearing the page."

I didn't touch the paper cube until he fell into a fitful sleep. By that point, I'd already looked at his chest.

It didn't look good.

Chapter 18

On my lunch break the next day, I didn't go to the hospital cafeteria. I went to the ER. There was a vending machine near intake, which was as close as I could get to the pit without drawing attention.

I needed to find a way past the double doors. I needed to talk to someone in trauma. And somehow, I needed to find a way to steal and smuggle out a healthy supply of Lactated Ringer's, an entire course of intravenous antibiotics, and, if I could manage it, some morphine.

The fact that I was even there, the fact that I was even *considering* throwing my life away like this—for *him*—was unfathomable, but it was either that or admit that Jackson and I were in over our heads. I couldn't see any other way out that didn't end with bloodshed.

I hadn't been able to save Kaylie, but I could do this. I *had* to do this.

I was on my third pack of vending machine Oreos when my supervisor sat down in the chair next to me in the waiting room.

"Did someone call you?" I asked her.

That got me a *look*. "Do you think I need someone to tell me what's going on in my own hospital?"

Most of the doctors who worked here probably would have objected to the suggestion that this hospital belonged to a single nurse from oncology, but I was smart enough not to argue.

"You going to tell me why you're lurking down here?" she said.

I looked toward the doors I hadn't yet pushed my way past.

"Thinking about emergency medicine for your next rotation?" my supervisor guessed bluntly. "Trauma?" She paused. "Maybe the burn unit?"

She doesn't know. A breath caught in my throat. *She can't.*

"You couldn't have saved her, Hannah."

Her. I realized that she thought that this was about my sister, about my grief.

"Maybe not," I said. "But maybe I could save someone like her." I swallowed, then covered. "Next time."

My supervisor considered that. "As it happens," she said finally, "someone in the burn unit owes me a favor."

Of everything I learned visiting the burn unit that day, the information that hit me the hardest was that the most painful time for most burn patients was when their dressings were being changed. I thought about Harry telling me he felt like he was being flayed alive, and then I thought about all the other times I'd changed his dressings, the times when his eyes had locked on to mine while I'd worked and he hadn't said a word.

That night, I stayed at Jackson's and did what I could. Instead of sleeping, I stayed up for hours, working to unfold that damn paper cube. I wondered how often Harry had seen *me* folding. It was like the sugar castles all over again, like he wanted me to know that there was no such thing as me fading into the background with him.

Finally, I did it, managing to undo each and every fold without tearing the paper at all. In the very center of the page, Harry had written four words in oversized, uneven scrawl:

EVERYTHING HURTS. DOESN'T IT?

I left for the hospital early the next day. *This is a mistake.* It didn't matter. I was committed.

Near the end of my shift, I managed to catch the door to the third-floor pharmacy with my foot before it locked. Morphine wasn't accessible, but I took the antibiotics and the IV solution. *I'm going to get caught. And even if I don't—neither of these will do a thing about the pain.*

As I tucked the stolen goods into my bag, I thought about "A Poison Tree." I thought about that tiny, intricate paper cube. I thought about the way my patient tossed and turned in his sleep, his agony obviously getting worse.

And then, on the way out to my car, once it had become clear that I wasn't going to get caught—not that night, at any rate—I thought about the *other* place I could go to get drugs. Not morphine but an opioid all the same.

Oxy.

Chapter 19

A man approached me," I told my mother. That was my excuse for coming. "At the grocery store near the hospital."

She chewed on that for a second or two, her eyes hard. "Describe him."

I did.

"Sounds like one of Tobias Hawthorne's men. The fix is in, but they're not letting up. What did the bastard want with you?"

That was a good question. *Do they know—or even suspect— that something is off?* At some point, would investigators realize they were one body short on Hawthorne Island?

"I don't know," I told my mother. "I didn't stick around to find out." I threw out a question before she could ask me another one. "What are they still doing here?"

My mother had ways of reminding people that she didn't exist to answer *their* questions. She grabbed my chin, lifting my face toward hers, even though I was already meeting her eyes.

"What are *you* doing here, Hannah?" she asked.

Say something true, and say it calmly. "Kaylie. Is her room still..." I let just a hint of weakness peek through—not enough for her to exploit, just enough for her to be certain that *she* was stronger. "Did you..."

"Go on up." Whatever else my mother was and wasn't, there

was very little senseless cruelty in her. Her cruelty always served a purpose, usually more than one. Her mercies did, too.

I knew that. I'd known that before coming here tonight, but there was no use in second-guessing myself now.

I walked up the stairs, my pace as measured as the breaths I took, and made it all the way to the end of the hall. I listened for footsteps, but no one was following me.

I let myself into Kaylie's room, and for a moment, I couldn't breathe. Her closet door was still open. Her clothes were still on the hangers, except for the haphazard piles of items she'd worn or discarded on the floor.

I walked slowly forward, then sank down, touching the shirt my sister had been wearing the last time I'd seen her. *Dance with me, you beautiful bitch.* The leather wasn't soft against my fingers, but the oversized sleepshirt I touched next *was.* I lifted it to my face, breathing in the smell of her. *Citrus and rose.* The scents didn't go together, but Kaylie had never cared.

Her chaos had been a beautiful kind of chaos—and remarkably consistent. Her room looked like it had been tossed, but it had always looked like that, so I just had to hope that no one else had gotten there first.

That no one else in the family would dare to steal from Eden Rooney's dead daughter.

It's not stealing when you're sisters, I could hear Kaylie saying. *It's borrowing with the intention not to return.*

For once, I didn't push away the memories. I couldn't—not here. I could almost feel her with me as I went through the pockets of the clothes she'd left on the floor and found two pills. That was something—but not enough. I tried her closet next, then inside her pillowcase, then under her sheets and between the box spring and the mattress.

The expectation in the family business was that wares were not sampled without permission. Business was business. Pleasure was pleasure. But I *knew* my sister.

Eventually, I found a loose floorboard under the bed. Beneath it, there was a hollowed-out compartment. Inside, there was a plastic baggie. Dozens of small white pills stared back at me. Beneath the baggie, I found a wallet.

Her last night on earth, my sister had only stolen one.

I flipped it open, and Toby Hawthorne's picture stared back at me from his driver's license. I would have recognized that smirk anywhere, but his eyes looked different to me in the photo—the shape of them, opened wider than I'd ever seen them. *He's not drunk or high there.*

He was smiling with his eyes, less *come hither* than *shall I let you in on the grandest joke?*

Suddenly, I heard footsteps coming down the hall.

I jammed the wallet and the bag of pills into the waistband of my scrubs, covering them with my shirt. Seven seconds later, when my father opened the door, I was crouched beside Kaylie's clothes again, her sleepshirt clasped in my hands.

Citrus and rose.

My father—*our* father—stared at me from the doorway. "I know," he said quietly.

He knew that I was mourning. He knew that I'd loved Kaylie with everything I had. *You don't know why I'm really here. You don't know what I've done—what I just did.*

"But, Hannah?"

I stood and met my father's eyes.

"If you want *out*..." His voice went down an octave. "Don't come back here again. I can only hold her off for so long."

Chapter 20

T he avenging angel returns." Those were the first words out of Harry's mouth when he saw me.

"I unfolded the paper," I told him, setting my messenger bag down on the floor. I began to unpack my pilfered supplies. "And, for the record, you're wrong."

I addressed my next words to Jackson, who stood with his back against the wall, watching the two of us. "I'm doing another IV. I need you to sanitize the needle, however you can."

I worked in silence. Thirty seconds after sliding the IV into Harry's vein, I was injecting the antibiotics into it. Then I reached into my bag again—for the oxy.

"Wrong?" Harry said. "Moi?"

"Some things don't hurt," I told him. "Some things are numb." I opened the baggie. "Some things need to stay that way."

I was talking about him, and I was talking about *me*.

"What did you do, Hannah?" Jackson's voice was low—and alarmed.

I didn't even look back at him as I gave Harry the oxy. "What I had to."

For five days, Harry and I barely said a word to each other on my nightly visits. I brought pills, and he left me offerings on the floor beside his mattress. Half of them were folded-paper marvels, each more elaborate than the last. The other half consisted of grocery lists.

Even with the oxy, he still wanted bourbon—and lemons.

Freaking lemons.

The antibiotics did the trick with whatever infection his body had been cooking up, and dosing him with the oxy let me do more than dress his burns. Using what I'd seen in the burn unit and a scalpel from Jackson's med kit, I'd started removing dead skin.

Sometimes, my patient cursed me for it. Sometimes, I ignored him. Sometimes, I cursed him right back.

Every day, Harry wanted more pills—and more and more and more. Once he'd turned a corner, I started cutting him back, and he got really charming.

"I'm guessing you're a virgin."

That didn't merit a response, so I didn't give him one.

He let his eyes rake over mine and down, his gaze settling somewhere in the vicinity of my lips. "You're too easy," he commented, but it was clear from his tone: He wasn't talking about sex anymore. He was talking about getting a rise out of me.

I'd given him nothing, and he was acting like my face had laid my every emotion bare.

"You don't like being looked at." Harry allowed his lips to curve in the subtlest of smiles. "Tasted, like wine."

If he thought I was going to drug him just to shut him up— just to get him to stop looking at me *like that*—he was going to be sorely disappointed. "Better wine than barbecue," I said. It took a moment for that comment to land.

I saw the exact moment he realized I was referencing his burns.

Harry snorted "Touché, Hannah the Same Backward as Forward." He propped himself up on his elbows, his back barely elevated off the bed. "I'm nicer when I'm high, and, coincidentally, *you* are also nicer when I'm high."

"No. I'm not."

With abs of steel and an iron will, he pulled himself the rest of the way into a sitting position.

That had to hurt, I thought, but you wouldn't have been able to tell that from his face.

"Look, Mom," Harry said, his voice dry as dirt, "no hands."

"I'm so proud," I said flatly.

He surged to his feet. Instinctively, I reached out, my hands avoiding the worst of his burns as I wedged them under his arms, catching him when he stumbled. That left the two of us far too close—close enough for him to murmur directly into my ear.

"Isn't it about time," he said softly, his breath a ghost brushing over my cheek, "for another grocery run?" I lowered him back down onto the mattress, and *damn him*, he smirked.

"You have my list."

Chapter 21

I bought him the damn lemons and dumped them on his bed. That didn't stop my patient from hitting me up for more pills. It didn't stop him from pushing every button he thought he could get away with pushing.

His burns were improving, day by day—all of them, now.

"What are your thoughts," he asked me loftily, "on scarred men?"

"Men?" I gave him a look. "If I see any, I'll let you know."

Time was measured in paper sculptures—cubes and pyramids, boxes and throwing stars, and little origami birds. He kept folding them, and despite my best efforts to resist, I kept picking up the gauntlet and *unfolding* them. Part of me was expecting another message. *Everything hurts.* But every sheet of notebook paper that I unfolded was blank.

I kept them in his stolen wallet. In his previous life, my patient hadn't carried much cash. Besides a single hundred-dollar bill, all I'd found in the larger pockets of his wallet was a small metal token, round and flat, roughly the size and shape of a quarter, with a series of concentric circles etched into the metal.

There was no logical reason for me to start carrying that

token with me in the pocket of my scrubs, but I did. Days at the hospital, nights at the shack, I carried it with me, and every time my fingers brushed the metal, every single time, I thought, *How long until we can move him?*

How long until I could forget any of this ever happened? Forget him?

And then, one night, in my apartment, as I defeated yet another one of his folded paper cubes, I smelled something. *The barest hint of lemon.*

I brought the paper closer to my face to sniff it, then crawled across my bed to hold it closer to the light—closer to my bedside lamp. At first, I saw nothing, but as the page took on heat from the bulb, words appeared.

MINIM.

MURDRUM.

AIBOHPHOBIA.

"Invisible ink," I said, the way another person might have said an obscenity. "And palindromes."

"Took you long enough." Harry somehow *knew* I'd figured it out before I ever said a word.

"Very funny," I told him.

"Lemon juice," he replied. I thought of his grocery lists, his incessant requests for *lemons.*

"Stand up," I bit out. It was something we were working on every day. He hadn't managed it without my support yet.

He never stayed *up* for long.

"*Minim,*" Harry said, relishing the word and showing no inclination whatsoever to rise, "a single drop of liquid—such as bourbon. *Murdrum*, the murder of an unknown person. Apropos, is it not?"

I glared at him. "It's about to be."

"And *aibohphobia*." He was getting way too much pleasure out of this. "A fear of palindromes."

"You made that up," I said.

"Did not." He had a good enough poker face that I couldn't tell whether he was bluffing, so I repeated my order for him to stand up.

This time, he humored me. My hands knew exactly where to lend their support. His body knew how to take it.

"Try taking a step," I ordered, all business. I prepared myself for a snappy comeback, but the palindrome lover in front of me made a surprisingly drama-free attempt to shift his weight to one foot and lift the other from the floor.

It dragged.

"Grace and beauty was he," Harry drawled. His was a subtle sarcasm, betrayed more by the words than his tone.

"It's the head injury." I didn't know what kind of damage his brain might have taken from the fall, but that was the conclusion that made the most sense. His legs weren't burned, and there was no evidence of spinal trauma.

I tried to lower him back down, but Harry resisted. The pale ring around the outside of his deep green iris was more visible some days than others.

"You can take a break," I told him.

I *saw* his pupils expand, black overtaking deepest green like a midnight wave devouring the edges of a white sand beach.

"Show me what's in your pocket," he proposed, "and I'll humble myself by trying again."

If Harry was *humble*, I was the Queen of England. "I'm not showing you what's in my pocket unless you *sit*."

He sat. After only a single moment of hesitation, I pulled out the token I'd taken from his wallet.

He stared at it. "Where did you get that?" I hadn't heard a tone like that out of him since I'd gotten him through the worst of the pain. *Brutal. Raw.*

"You recognize it," I said, looking down at the token.

"Where?" That was the kind of demand that cut through the air like a sword made of solid ice.

"Your wallet." I wasn't sure why I even told him that, or why I didn't fight it when he plucked that coin-like disk from my fingers and hurled it, full force, against the wall.

For once in my life, I flinched.

The door to the shack flew inward, and Jackson looked from me to Harry and back again.

Not Harry, a voice in my mind whispered. I couldn't shake the bone-deep awareness that this was *Toby*. "You recognized that disk," I said. "What is it? What do you remember?"

"Nothing." He wasn't lying. I knew that, the same way he always seemed to know when I was. "I don't remember a damn thing, but somehow, I *know*: You shouldn't have that."

For the longest moment, I stared at him, trying to stare *into* him, trying to tell if any subconscious part of him was starting to remember who he'd been before.

"You can have it," I said quietly, going to retrieve the token.

"No." There was that tone again—*brutal, raw, desperate,* even. "Hide it somewhere. Whatever you do, don't let anyone else see it."

That night and into the next morning, when I hid the token

beneath a loose floorboard in the shack, I found myself wondering why Toby Hawthorne had come to Rockaway Watch, drunk and high and looking for trouble. For the first time, I wondered if the billionaire's son had been running from something.

I wondered if he'd had a reason to burn that mansion down.

Chapter 22

A week or two after Harry's odd reaction to the token, he stopped leaving me paper creations to unfold, but he still asked for paper. I came in on my next day off to find that he'd written a single word on one of those pages.

"The name of the game, Hannah the Same Backward as Forward," he told me, propping himself up on the mattress, "is Two Moves. It's a simple game, really. All you have to do is make five words that aren't *sex*."

Every time I started to think that he was anything less than *impossible*...

"I can think of some words for you," I said. "Now stand up."

He could stand on his own now. I was there for balance, nothing more.

"Give me a happy pill," Harry proposed, "and you don't have to play."

He didn't *need* the oxy now, the way he had before. "Try to take a step," I countered, "and I'll let you explain to me why the name of the game is Two Moves."

He managed to do it this time without dragging his foot. I arched a brow, waiting.

With Harry, I never had to wait for long.

"All letters in this game are drawn with a combination of straight lines. An *O* looks a bit like a rectangle. An *R* has a point." He took advantage of our closeness to reach out and grab my hand. Before I could react, he was lightly tracing letters on the back.

His touch was deliberate and light. *Too deliberate. Too light.*

"A move consists of adding, subtracting, or repositioning a line," Harry murmured. "It's easy enough, for example, to turn an *E* into an *F*."

I knew with every fiber of my being and every nerve ending in my body that he was getting ready to draw on my hand again, so I freed it from his and gave him a quelling look. "You owe me two more steps."

He hadn't agreed to those terms, but he paid up anyway. His left foot was weaker than his right. I had no idea how long it would be before he could walk well enough to make it across the room—let alone handle a two-mile hike over rocky terrain. We couldn't risk loading him into my car in Rockaway Watch, and there was no way that Jackson and I could carry him for miles. He needed to be able to make it on his own.

"Five more steps," I told Harry, "and I'll play your game."

I didn't think he would be able to do it, even using me for balance. I was wrong.

"Pay up," Harry told me, using me to help lower himself to the floor. "Remember: You're looking for five words that aren't *sex*."

Five words. Two moves. One chance to wipe that smug expression right off his face. I grabbed the paper he'd left on the mattress.

I gave my brain a moment to split each letter into its respective lines, and then I picked up the pen and made my first move, rewriting the word by removing the bottom line on the *E*, then flipping it and moving it up.

"Got it in one." Harry cocked a brow at me. "Four more, Hannah the Same Backward as Forward."

I looked back up to the original word, staring at the letters Toby had written. It was so easy to see the one solution I wasn't allowed—remove the crossbar on the *A*, slid one of the remaining angled lines over. *Sex*. This was a diabolical game.

He was a diabolical boy.

On a new line, I broke the *S*, repositioning two of the bars.

Three left. I wrote the word *sea* myself this time, all lines and angles, exactly as Toby had written, hoping that the act of doing so would shake something loose in my mind. *What next?* My gaze was drawn back to the damn *A*, which could have so easily become an *X*.

Harry was officially the worst person I'd ever met.

Liar, something inside me whispered, but I ignored it. I loathed him. I despised him. The sooner I could get him healed and walking, the better.

I broke the *A*, ditching one line and moving another one up.

"The *T*'s a bit angled," Harry drawled, "but I'll allow it."

I rewrote the word *sea* again and stared bullets at the block-like letters. Turning *E* to *K* would have taken three moves. Turning *E* to *F* took only one, but *sfa* wasn't a word.

Why are you even playing? my common sense asked, but I ignored it. Kaylie hadn't been the only Rooney with a competitive streak, and somehow, I thought she probably would have approved.

Approved, I specified silently, *of me kicking this rich boy's ass at his own game.*

A to *H* was two moves. *A* to *V*, also two. Neither of those helped me. The wheels in my mind started turning faster. *A* to *W*—damn it, that one was three moves, which meant I couldn't use the word *sew*. *A* to *N* was only two, but as far as I knew, *sen* wasn't a word.

"Ticktock, Hannah the Same Backward as Forward."

And that was when I saw it: the obvious solution. "You said I could move lines, take them away, or *add* them."

Harry's poker face was excellent, but I knew in my gut that *he* knew he was beaten.

Adding an *L* to the end of the word only required two lines. Same for adding a *T*. And *seat* and *seal* were both words.

"Five words that aren't *sex*." Harry smirked. "I'm impressed."

I gave him a look. "I'm not." I stood up, then tossed down the gauntlet. "On your feet again."

I was going to get him walking if it killed me.

Chapter 23

Around the time that Harry could take five steps unassisted, we ran out of paper. The next day, he drew a circle on the back of my hand.

"And here I thought you valued your life," I said darkly.

"Come now, Hannah the Same Backward as Forward. You know that I don't." He said the words lightly, mockingly, but there was a ring of truth about them. There were times when he was *Harry* to me and times when I could hear *Toby* in his tone, no matter how much I tried to ignore it. His memories hadn't come back—I was certain of that—but I was also growing surer by the day that he could sense a darkness behind the veil of the blank spaces in his memory.

I couldn't help wondering what that darkness was, what secrets had been locked away by his amnesia. I thought sometimes about the way he'd begged me to let him die. I'd done a valiant job at thwarting him. He was alive. He was getting stronger.

And he was an *incredible* pain in my ass. "If you're going to torture me, not-nurse Hannah—or worse, try to motivate me—the least you could do is let me finish *that*." He nodded to my hand.

I looked at the circle. It was perfectly drawn—impossibly so. "Do I even want to know what you're drawing?" I asked.

Harry smiled, one of those smug, *one of us is winning this and it isn't you* smiles of his. "I don't know, lügnerin. Do you?"

I wasn't positive what language he'd just used, but I knew damn well what he'd said, and he was right: I *was* a liar. Every day, I came here and pretended that he hadn't killed my sister. Some days, I could almost believe it.

"One hour," I told him, my tone making clear that my terms weren't up for negotiation. "One full hour of grueling rehab. That's what you're going to give me if I let you finish your little drawing."

"You're going to work me hard." The edge of *that* smile pulled up slightly on one side.

"I hate you and want you out of my life," I replied. "Do we have a deal?"

He reached for my hand. "You know we do."

At the very top of the circle—from my perspective—he drew a *W.* The touch of the pen was light against my skin. The brush of his hand against mine as he wrote was anything but.

I hate you, I thought, as he moved on to write another letter.

I hate you.

I hate you.

I hate you.

The words were closer to a whisper in my mind than the seething vow they'd once been, but I held to them letter after letter, moment after moment, touch after touch.

When Harry was finished, he capped the pen. My gaze was drawn to his biceps and forearms, no longer under gauze. His second-degree burns had healed nicely. Any scarring he had from them would be light.

His chest was a different matter.

"Twenty letters." I focused on my hand. "I'm not going to ask what they mean."

"Excellent." He rose from the bed, ready to make good on *his* end of the deal. "Because I wouldn't tell you."

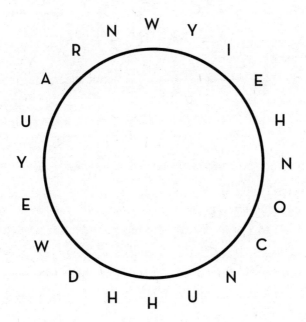

Chapter 24

That night, in my own bed, I tried to read—a retelling of *Beauty and the Beast*.

A *mansion of marvels. A stolen clockwork rose. A curse.* But it was the beast himself that kept me from reading past the first hundred pages. His habit of brutally shoving people away. His arrogance, as enduring as his curse. The fact that he *knew* what he was, knew that loving him might destroy her if, by some miracle, she was the one.

As I closed the book, a little harder than necessary, I could practically hear Harry talking about my sugar packet castles. *Do you believe in fairy tales, Hannah the Same Backward as Forward?*

I really, truly didn't. I laid back and closed my eyes, willing sleep to come, but my stubborn eyelids crept back open. *Damn it.* I looked at my hand.

I started where Harry had—with the *W*.

"*W, Y, I, E, H…*" I said under my breath. Phonetically, if I tried to pronounce that as a single word, it sounded a bit like *why?* Next was *noc*, then *nuh*.

In other words: a whole lot of nothing. Looking at all the letters, I wondered if there were any palindromes buried somewhere in the sequence. There were three *N*'s, three *H*'s, two *E*'s, two each of *U*, *W*, and *Y*.

Nun. Ewe. Eye. I really, really hated the fact that I could so vividly picture the way Harry's lips looked when he smirked. *No.* I wasn't going to waste another minute on this little game of his.

Not one.

And yet, at the hospital the next day, when the pen marks on the back of my hand began to rub off under the force of repeated hand washings, I used my break to redraw the circle and letters myself.

W, Y, I, E, H, N, O, C . . . I was vaguely annoyed by the fact that I had the entire sequence memorized—but not as annoyed as I was by the fact that I still couldn't solve it.

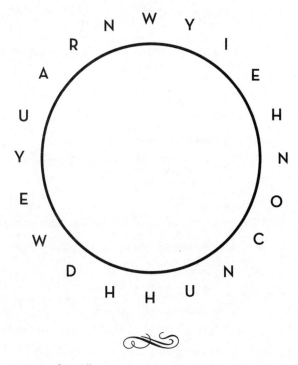

"Do you want a hint?"

I glared at Harry and his smug Harry face.

"I'll take that as a *no*, then." He winked at me as I finished rebandaging his chest. "I do hope you appreciate how magnanimous I'm being by not gloating right now."

"You *are* gloating." It always took me a moment, after I'd dressed his remaining burns, to stop thinking about the places on his chest and torso where smooth skin gave way to what I knew would someday be very heavy scars. There were days when I felt like *I* had scarred him.

I'd given him more than he ever would have had any right to ask me of me, and it wasn't enough.

"I am gloating in an *understated* manner. I assure you that, were I not, my method of gloating would be far more memorable."

I responded with a very sweet smile, which he rightly found concerning.

"Should I even ask what torture you have planned for me today?" he said dryly.

Today was my day off. "Today," I told him, "we work on uneven ground."

"Dare I hope that's a metaphor?"

"For what?" I gave him a look. "On second thought: Don't answer that. Today, we go outside."

"In the light of day?" Harry's arch question set my heart to beating in my throat. For so long, his world—*our* world—had been this shack. Going outside, where we could be seen, was a risk—but a necessary one.

"No one comes out this far," I told myself as much as him. I walked to open the metal door—first a crack to verify, then wider to prove my point. The only thing I could see was the lighthouse a hundred yards away. Nothing—and no one—else.

It took some time for Harry to make it to the threshold of the shack, but his movements were smooth. I stepped out onto rocky ground. He did the same—or tried to. If I hadn't moved in to brace his body against mine, he would have fallen. It wasn't until his fingers dug into my arm—*hard*—that I realized: He was blinded by the sun.

No windows, I thought suddenly. It had been easy for me to forget that Jackson's shack didn't have windows. *I* wasn't living there, and unless it was one of my days off, I arrived and left under cover of night.

For a month and a half, Toby Hawthorne had lived with only artificial light. *I should have taken him outside sooner.* I dismissed that thought because what I *should* have done, right from the beginning, was stay as far away from him as I could.

"What a scenic view." Harry—he had to stay *Harry* in my mind—said, still blinking. "I, for one, have always been partial to crumbling lighthouses."

I was on the verge of meeting his sarcasm with sarcasm of my own when he continued. "Call me sentimental, but there's something beautiful about anything built for one purpose that refuses to die, even once that purpose is gone."

I didn't know what it was that possessed me in that moment, but suddenly, I *had* to ask, the same way I had to breathe. "Have you remembered anything about your life before?"

Harry took a step forward, rock to rock, his jaw clenched with the effort. The sun reflected off his dark brown hair, deep red highlights shimmering in the light. "The first thing I remember, Hannah the Same Backward as Forward, is *you*."

Chapter 25

That night, I refused to sleep until I'd solved the puzzle. I'd tried reading clockwise and counterclockwise, but this time, even thinking the word *clockwise* had me looking at the circle differently.

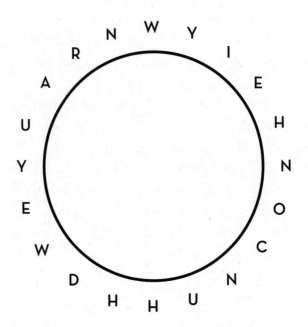

I tried placing numbers above the letters, but the spacing was off. *W* and *H* were at twelve o'clock and six o'clock. *N* and *Y* were at three and nine, but there were too many letters for the rest to fall directly on the numbers of a clock.

W, I thought, going back to the top of the circle. I traced my finger down to the bottom. *H*. That particular letter combination—*WH*—was the start of so many questions.

Who?

What?

When?

Where?

Why?

My gaze darted back to the top of the circle. Next to the W, there was a *Y*. Grabbing a pen, I drew two lines on the back of my hand—one from the *W* straight down to the *H*, and then another from the *H* up to the *Y*.

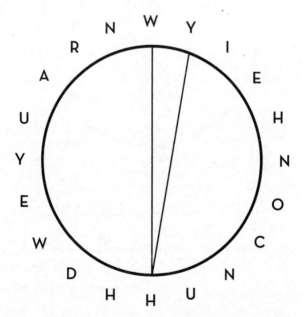

Why. I paused just for an instant. *What next?* My heart rate started beating a fraction faster, and then I trailed my finger across the circle to the letter opposite the *Y*.

"Another *H*," I noted. Unsure if I was headed down the wrong path or not, I went back up to the next letter in the upper-right quadrant, then back down to the lower left, and then I grabbed the pen, retracing those moves.

H, I, D... Up once more got me an *E*—and another complete word.

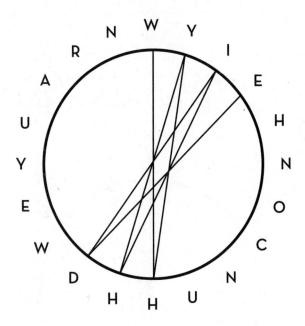

WHY HIDE...

I kept going, letter after letter, until the back of my hand looked like a spiderweb—or a starburst. The pattern was complicated enough that I couldn't help thinking about how effortlessly Harry had written out the entire sequence. He'd never even paused, like his brain was operating on another plane, like he could see the whole of the puzzle—the trap he'd laid from me, the question I'd just decoded—all at once.

WHY HIDE WHEN YOU CAN RUN

Chapter 26

I showed up to Jackson's the next night with the back of my hand washed clean and the solution to the puzzle, both diagram and words, copied onto a sticky note. I stuck it to Harry's forehead, dead center.

"And here I'd made a bet with myself that you wouldn't solve it until tomorrow." He reached up, pulled the note off his forehead, and folded it in half, not even checking my work.

"What's that supposed to mean?" I asked him, nodding to the note. *"Why hide when you can run."*

"I would think it was obvious." He got up from the mattress. "You are an expert at hiding." He cocked his head wolfishly to one side. "Behind your hair. Behind that expression that you keep oh-so-carefully blank. Behind the lies."

I could feel his gaze trying to capture mine, so I looked away, and it only belatedly occurred to me that I might be proving his point.

"I haven't lied to you since I told you I was a nurse," I said.

"You're a nursing *student*," he replied. "An excellent one. And you've lied to me many, many times, almost as frequently as you've lied to yourself. What I haven't quite figured out"—if I'd thought Harry's gaze was wolfish before, it was a thousand times more so now—"is why you try so hard to hide yourself away. I have my theories, of course."

"It's not a crime to be reserved."

"You feel things." Harry's voice was softer than it had been a moment before—not gentle, but soft in the way that silk was against skin. "Deeply." He made a study of my eyes and didn't bother to mask the fact that he was doing it. "Watching you keep your emotions locked down is like watching stormwater rise and rise behind a dam."

Everywhere I looked, there he was: dark green eyes, lighter around the rim, so focused on mine that there was no escape.

"You're grieving," Harry murmured. "And you're so angry I can taste it." He paused, daring me to tell him he was wrong, and when I didn't, he continued, "You're frightened—and not just because coming here is dangerous for you."

I raised my chin and stared him down. "You don't know what you're talking about."

"My life is four walls, this bed, a bearded fisherman with questionable survivalist tendencies and horrific taste in interior design, and *you*." He paused, just slightly. "Do you know what I've discovered about myself with all that spare time? I'm hungry, Hannah." For once he used my name. Only my name "My brain drinks in every last detail of its surroundings. Of you."

I took a step back.

He seemed to take that as an invitation—not to come after me but to tell me exactly what he saw when he drank in every last detail. "You have ways of going elsewhere in your mind. It's like you're a dreamer trapped in a cynic's body, a cynic's life. Your hands are never still but always steady. And your face—it's like you have control over every little muscle, even the ones of which most people are completely unaware."

His weight shifted slightly toward me, and there was something utterly unfamiliar—utterly new—about the set of his lips.

He's thinking about kissing me. That thought was horrible and unexpected. I told myself that I was imagining things, but...*His lips, parting. His eyes on mine.* The worst thing was that this time, I *didn't* step back.

My heart beat out a steady rhythm, and I felt it in every inch of my body. *I hate you. I hate you. I hate you.*

"Shall I tell you a story, Hannah?" His words wrapped around me. I became acutely aware of the rise and fall of his chest, of the rise and fall of mine. "A fairy tale? I think I will, and you can tell me how I do. Once upon a time..." Harry took a step back, then another, giving me room to breathe, giving himself room to take in all of me at once. "There was a princess, born to a feckless king and a wicked queen."

I thought about my father, holding my mother off—to a point and only because he'd lost Kaylie first. But I refused to let my opponent think he'd gotten anywhere close to the truth.

"Name one fairy-tale princess who was actually born to a wicked queen," I said.

"Hit a nerve, have I?" He flashed me a twisted, knowing smile. "Princess Hannah shined like a beacon in the darkness, nothing like those around her. *Selfless. Kind.*" There was an edge to the way he said those words, like they weren't entirely compliments. "But alas, the selfless never fare well in fairy tales until the very end."

"I'm not selfless," I shot back. "You said it yourself—I hide." Making myself invisible for so long had come at a cost. I'd left Kaylie in that house. I'd left her at our mother's mercy. I'd told myself that I would get her out, but I *hadn't*.

And you're the reason why, I thought, staring bullets at the person telling me the story of *my* life.

"Not selfless?" Harry said. "You're here, aren't you? I am, even by my own reckoning, a real prick, and yet, you come here, day after day. You avert your eyes. You look through me when you can. But you're here. You saved me."

"Because you *wanted* to die." The words burst out of me.

"It's possible," Harry allowed, "that the princess is capable of spite." He gave the smallest of shrugs. "Her mother is, after all, a wicked queen."

A muscle in my jaw twitched. "What has Jackson been telling you when I'm not here?"

That was the only explanation for the story my *real prick* of a patient was spinning, the only way he could have ever seen so much. No one was *that* perceptive.

"The fisherman hasn't told me a damn thing. As it turns out, Beardy is impossible to get a rise out of. But you..." He smiled. "You're like a lock with seven keys, each more complicated than the last." He gave another little shrug. "I deeply suspect that I've always been fond of picking locks."

"Start moving," I gritted out, gesturing to the door. "Walk. Use your legs, because we're getting ready to go out on the rocks." I was going to get him all the way to the lighthouse this week if it killed me.

"Always the taskmaster, never the pupil." Harry had the gall to make a tsking sound, then launched back into the fairy tale of my life, as seen through his eyes: "When she was very young, Princess Hannah learned to lock herself away. She had a secret, you see. *Magic*. And the evil queen would have sucked her dry."

My throat tightened. He was describing the wrong sister. *I* wasn't the one who'd been magic.

"So the princess locked herself away. She built towers, one inside the other inside the other, all of them invisible to everyone but her. *Locks and keys.* Alone—where no one could harm her, where her magic could be used to do no harm."

I didn't *have* any magic. I was unremarkable. I was *nothing*.

Why wouldn't he just let me be nothing?

"Is that the best you can do?" I gritted out, unsure why the words came out hoarse instead of harsh.

Harry started walking toward the door, slow and steady, his eyes never leaving mine. "I see you, Hannah the Same Backward as Forward. All of you."

This was worse, *so much worse* than being kissed—because I believed him.

"I see you, too," I said, my voice like steel, even though my heart was pounding. "I see a scared little boy who *runs*."

I was sure now: That was what he'd been doing when he came to Rockaway Watch. I didn't know exactly why—*the poison tree, the metal token*—but he had sure as hell been running away from something.

"I see a coward," I continued mercilessly, "who only fights the battles that don't matter because facing down the ones that do would be too damn hard." I pinned him with a look. "Has it ever occurred to you, *Harry*, that you don't remember who you are because you don't want to remember?"

The next thing I knew, he was directly in front of me. "Then *tell me.* Who am I, Hannah?"

I realized suddenly that this might have been his endgame with this whole conversation. Maybe he'd pushed and pushed and pushed with the sole intention of making me push back.

"In fairy tales," Harry said, "there's a power in names."

He was so close—and I was suddenly certain: He was thinking about kissing me again.

He won't do it, I told myself. *I won't let him.* If he was so damn set on telling stories, I'd tell him one. I would give him exactly what he was asking for. His name. His background. The truth about the fire—and the blood on his hands.

I opened my mouth. The instant I did, he stepped back and sucked in a breath. It was like I'd just taken a knife and sliced open his skin.

The change in him was so sudden and absolute that my mind went immediately to the way he'd reacted when he'd seen the metal token.

"On second thought," he rasped out, "don't tell me."

He was the one who'd opened Pandora's box here, the one who'd laid me bare. He had pushed and pushed and pushed, and he could damn well deal with the consequences. "Your name is—"

"*Please.*"

I hadn't expected that.

This time, *he* was the one who looked away. "As it turns out, Hannah the Same Backward as Forward, apparently, I'd rather stay *Harry* to you."

Chapter 27

I didn't say a word to him for three days. Remarkably, he didn't say anything to me, either. On the fourth day, I realized he was barely eating. I hadn't gone to the trouble of nursing his ass back to life to watch him wither way now.

I set a plate of food roughly down on the mattress beside him and waited.

His gaze slid toward mine. "I've read enough fairy tales to know that one should be wary of magical beings bearing food."

I wasn't going to go down the fairy-tale path with him again. "Eat, and I'll play," I said flatly. "A game of your choosing—within reason."

"And you claim that you aren't selfless." Harry picked up the plastic fork I'd provided, twisting it between his fingers. "That you have no magic. That you aren't a ray of uncompromising, unbroken light."

"Eat," I told him, "and shut up."

"And here I thought the last few days had established that I'm only capable of doing one of those things at a time."

I had the sense that might be one of the truest things he'd ever said to me, that he could shut the world out and lose interest in even food—or let it all in.

"*Eat*," I said again. "We'll never make it to the lighthouse if you don't."

The lighthouse and then farther and then far enough that he could *leave*.

Harry began to eat. "Hangman," he told me.

"Hangman?" I repeated.

"That's the game. But to make it interesting, there'll be a wager. I have the sense that my people—whoever they are—are very fond of wagers, risky ones in particular."

It was on the tip of my tongue to tell him exactly who his people were, but I *knew*—he didn't want to know.

His brain wouldn't *let him* know.

"What's the bet?" I asked.

"I propose the following terms..." Harry took his damn time spelling it out between bites. "You have three days and unlimited chances to guess my word. Instead of drawing bits and pieces of a stick figure with each wrong guess, I'll draw the hairs on your head one at a time, if I have to. But if, after the third day, you cannot guess my word, you have to tell me all about the wicked queen."

My mother.

He must have seen refusal in my expression, because he gave me a second option. "Either that or you can tell me about your lost one."

"Lost one?" I repeated.

"The person you're grieving. The one you loved so fiercely." He caught my gaze again. "No one has eyes like yours, Hannah the Same Backward as Forward, unless they've lost."

Eyes like mine? They were a muddy hazel, unremarkable, guarded. "And what will you give me when I win?" I said.

"*When?* I admire your confidence, misplaced though it might be."

"I've solved your last two puzzles, haven't I?" I shot back. I'd also unfolded every single one of his paper creations without ever tearing them. Every challenge he'd set out, I'd met.

"What do you want if you win, liar mine?"

I want... I couldn't make myself finish that sentence, not even to say, *I want you to make it all the way to the lighthouse. Now.* "I don't know."

"An unspecified boon?" Harry raised both brows. "How very fairy tale of you, Hannah the Same Backward as Forward."

"Frightened?" I taunted. I preferred this Harry to the one of the last few days.

"Terrified," he replied with a smile. "You have a deal."

Chapter 28

We were still out of paper, so Harry drew his puzzle on a napkin.

— —— — —— — —— — —— — —— — —— — —

I eyed the spacing between those letters. "Is that all one word?"

"Why, yes, it is."

I narrowed my eyes at him. There had to be a catch to the fact that he'd given me unlimited guesses. There were only twenty-six letters in the alphabet. "*E*," I said.

Harry helped himself to another napkin. I expected him to draw the typical hangman frame, but all he drew was an oval.

"*A.*"

A single, arcing line, in the vicinity of what I had to assume would eventually be my eye.

Someone was feeling overly confident here, and it wasn't me. Narrowing my eyes, I went through the rest of the vowels, including *Y*.

That lone eye was starting to take shape, and I realized: Harry could *draw*. This was definitely no stick figure. It was the beginnings of a very detailed sketch, and I remembered the way he'd said that he would draw my hair one strand at a time if he had to.

"There's no such thing as a word without vowels," I told him.

Harry shrugged. "I never promised to spell my word with letters."

"Then what else would you—" I cut myself off. "Numbers. We're playing Hangman in *code*?"

"As fond as my people are of wagers, I believe we're also very fond of skewing the game." Harry twirled the pen in his fingers like a miniature baton. "In my defense, you have as many guesses as the hairs on your head, the stars in the sky, and the number of ways you've imagined wiping this smug expression right off of my classically handsome face."

"You're not that handsome," I said darkly.

He smiled. "Did you know that *bugiarda* is Italian for 'liar'?"

After guessing the numbers one through twenty-six, it was apparent that this wasn't going to be an easy code to break. Only four numbers had resulted in him *not* adding a stroke to his drawing of my face: 5, 3, 7, and 2. Each number was used only once, the remaining spaces blank.

"Hypothetically speaking..." I fixed Harry with a look. "What's the range of numbers in your code?"

"Hypothetically? It might range from two to three hundred and ten."

Three hundred and ten? There *had* to be some significance to that.

"Care to guess again?" Harry taunted, and I tried not to think about what his sketch might look like once I'd guessed all of the numbers left up to three hundred and ten.

I stared at the puzzle, ignoring the second napkin altogether.

_ _ _ _ _ _ _ _ **5** _ _ **3** **7** **2** _

I needed to take my time, to look at this from every angle before I gave him a chance to send me wandering off down a path of *his* choosing. "Put the pen down and get up," I ordered. "We're done for today."

Chapter 29

After a long shift the next day, I came back and guessed every single number between twenty-seven and three hundred and ten. In my hours away, I hadn't come up with any better strategy.

As the numbers were filled in on the puzzle, my face took shape on the other napkin. I'd been wrong when I'd inferred that Harry was an excellent artist.

He was a *remarkable* one.

It wasn't just that he'd captured my features. It was the *way* he'd done it. My wide-set eyes looked like they were fixed on something in the distance. There was an almost dreamy look in them that was completely at odds with the hardness he'd captured in my jaw. He'd drawn my lips slightly parted and twin lines between my brows—not quite a *furrow*. My cheekbones were sharp, but he'd somehow managed to make my cheeks look soft. He'd drawn my neck long, my hair loose and a little wild, like I was standing on a cliff, staring into the wind.

Somehow, the overall effect wasn't soft or hard or sharp or dreamy or wild or any of the descriptors that fit its individual components. I just looked...*alive*.

I had no idea how he'd managed to make me look like *that*

without exaggerating a single one of my features or forcing emotion onto them in a way that would have at least told me he'd taken some artistic license. But he hadn't. There wasn't a single part of his sketch that I could look at and think, *that's not me*, and yet, there was absolutely *nothing* nondescript about the person he'd drawn.

"Thoughts?" His voice broke into my mind.

I told myself that he wasn't asking about the drawing and looked at the puzzle instead.

39 38 32 44 45 310 53 35 5 34 22 3 7 2 42

I'd hoped for some repeat numbers—or better yet, repeated combinations of numbers—but every single number in the code was unique.

This was impossible. Literally. There was no way for me to figure out what any of those numbers stood for.

"You could start by writing out the letters of the alphabet." Harry was beyond *smug*. "See if anything jumps out to you."

Was that a hint or just gloating? With him, there was no way to tell, but on the bright side, the more annoyed I became with the puzzle, the closer I came to being able to forget that drawing and the way I looked through his eyes.

Ignoring his suggestion to write down the letters of the alphabet, I focused on looking at the numbers themselves. *Four single-digit numbers. Only one three-digit number.* I set all four of those aside for a moment. Of the ten two-digit numbers, five started with a three; three started with a four; and there was one each starting with a two and a five.

"I really would recommend writing out the alphabet," Harry drawled, altogether too pleased with himself.

That was definitely a clue, and I wasn't going to give him the satisfaction of seeing me take it.

"Enough playing around," I said. "I still have one more day, and we have work to do."

He reached for the other napkin, the one on which he'd drawn me, stroke by stroke and line by line. He looked from the sketch to the expression on my face now. "And there you are," he murmured, his voice rolling over me like a summer storm rolling in. "There," he repeated, a rumble in his quiet voice, "you are."

The next day, I had the kind of shift where breaks were few and far between. I'd heard nurses in labor and delivery say that the maternity ward always got crowded when there was a full moon. It made no sense whatsoever, but oncology was the same way—at least today.

By the time I actually got a moment to myself, I was less concerned with eating than I was with the fact that tonight would mark day three. Losing this bet would mean telling Harry about either my mother or Kaylie.

I am not going to lose. On my way to the cafeteria, I grabbed a piece of paper out of the printer and a pen off the desk in the nurse's station. Mentally cursing Harry the entire time, I finally took his suggestion and wrote down every letter of the alphabet. I stared at the letters.

A large percentage of the numbers in the code start with three, I reminded myself. *And there are more numbers with two digits than with one.* I had no idea what to make of the fact that three hundred and ten was the only three-digit number in play.

Why? I stared at the letters that I'd written out. *Damn him.* Would one repeated number/letter really have been too much to ask?

Harry's voice answered in my mind: *As fond as my people are of wagers, I believe we're also very fond of skewing the game.*

And that was when I realized: *not a single repeat letter.* I scarfed down a single apple, then made my way back to the nurses' station on the third floor. Keeping my eye out for my supervisor, I slid around the desk and took a seat at the computer.

Thankfully, the hospital computers had internet, because I had a question, and Ask Jeeves at least purported to have all the answers.

I plugged in my question. Glancing up from the keyboard, I saw my supervisor coming my way. I looked back down at the results and...

Got it. I closed the browser but didn't make it around to the front of the station before she spotted me.

"Hannah." Her tone wasn't sharp, not exactly.

"I was just—" I started to make excuses, but she didn't let me finish.

"You should go, Hannah. *Now.*" She glanced back over her shoulder, and I realized suddenly that I wasn't being sent away because she'd caught me using the computer.

What's going on? My heart skipped a beat as I looked past her to the hall. It was empty, but it didn't stay empty for long. Double doors swung inward, and a patient was wheeled in. It was clear she'd come in through emergency, but she was being admitted here.

To oncology.

And the patient in question was my mother.

I didn't leave. I *couldn't,* because that would have been an invitation for her to come after me. If there was one thing that I knew for sure, it was that Eden Rooney didn't allow anyone in the family to see her weak and walk away.

Why hide when you can run? Right now, I couldn't afford to do either, so I bided my time, and I donned my poker face, and then I let myself into her room.

She was in the bed. She looked small. But I wasn't fooled.

My mother stared me down. "You don't know anything, girl." *Gravelly voice, measured tone.*

I refused to feel any of the trepidation I should have felt at that combination. "I don't want to know anything," I said.

"Can't always get what we want, can we?" Eden Rooney wielded pauses like thrusts of a knife. This one was long—tortuously so. "I had plans for your sister," she said finally. "And you haven't left Rockaway Watch."

In other words: She'd had plans that required either a daughter or a young woman, and *I* was fair game.

"I'm just here until I finish school," I said—neutral tone, neutral expression.

"I suppose we have that much in common, finishing what we start."

The muscles in my throat tightened as I remembered pushing the needle through Rory's skin. I'd known when she left that night that she would be back, but then Kaylie had died, and my father had somehow been able to hold her back.

Until now. "I'm not going to say anything to anyone." My voice was as quiet as ever.

"About what?" my mother spat.

I couldn't say *that you're sick.* I couldn't utter the word *cancer* or so much as mention medical privacy law. I sure as hell wasn't going to say, *I'm not going to tell anyone I saw you weak.*

"Exactly." My mother's tone was deadly. "I can get to you. Anytime. Anywhere."

Before I could reply, she started coughing.

Is it lung cancer? I swallowed the question back. When I did speak, my voice came out tight. "Are you going to be okay?" I felt like a child, asking that question. I sounded like one, too. I didn't want to care about the answer. I should have been looking out for myself—not her. *Never* her.

Shrewd eyes took me apart, piece by piece. "You loved your sister. Never would have guessed you felt a damn thing for me."

I don't want to.

She stared at me for the longest time. "You're smart, Hannah." There was no logical reason for *that* to be the sentence that sent a chill down my spine. "You're my daughter, truly."

No. I wasn't. Not in any way that mattered. "You don't want me back," I said.

"Is that a threat?"

I'd seen her here. I knew her secret. There were people in the Rooney family who'd never been happy with a woman running things, people who would absolutely take advantage of any weakness she showed.

It is to your benefit to keep me away from them. I didn't say that. What I said was: "Am I smart or am I a person who would threaten you?"

She let out a little snort. "You look like me, you know. People have said so since you were a child."

I thought about Harry's drawing, about the way he'd made me look—not *soft* or *hard* or *sharp* or *dreamy* or *wild* but *alive.* My mother and I didn't look a thing alike.

I was nothing like her.

I turned to leave, but as I hit the threshold, I paused. I *knew* not to hesitate, but I did it anyway, because for better or worse, she was my *mother.*

"Does Dad know?" I asked without turning around.

"What do you think?"

I shook my head. "I think I should go."

I made it all the way out the door before she spoke again "Hannah?" I didn't turn around, but I stopped long enough for her to issue one parting shot. "I miss her, too."

Chapter 30

For as long as I could remember, I'd only ever cried in the shower. The one in my apartment was tiny, but that didn't stop me from latching my hand around the shower curtain and slamming it back into the wall.

Tears were weak, but crying in the shower didn't count.

I turned on the spray. Every muscle in my body felt like a rubber band pulled to the breaking point. Not even giving the shower time to warm up, I stepped into the tub.

I shuddered.

I let go.

I'm not crying. When my tears mixed with the spray, I could tell myself they didn't exist. And why *would* I have been crying, really? If anyone on this planet deserved cancer, it was my mother. If she died, what was it to me?

Seriously, what was it to me that she'd claimed to miss Kaylie?

What did it matter that I knew my sister had loved her, too?

What did any of it matter?

My breaths were ragged now. But I *wasn't crying*, and I refused to hurt. Slowly, my breathing evened out, one thought rising up over all the rest, one thought allowing me to turn off the spray: *I have a wager to win tonight.*

"You're late." Harry was the one who opened the door when I got to the shack. There wasn't a single light on inside.

"You're still up," I said.

"I'm always up." Harry gave a little shrug. "Sleep is for mortals." I could feel him peering at me through the darkness. "You've been crying."

The moon was full overhead, but there was still no way he should have been able to tell that.

"You're delusional," I replied. "And the answer is *uncopy-rightable*." It was the longest word in the English language—discounting medical jargon—that contained no repeat letters. *That* was what I'd looked up on the computer, right before my mother's appearance at the hospital had shaken me to my core. "Where's Jackson?" I demanded.

I didn't want to be alone with Harry right now, and I didn't even know why—or maybe I *did* know and didn't want to admit it.

"Beardy leaves me alone more now, when he thinks I'm sleeping." Harry imparted that information in a tone I couldn't quite read.

"I thought sleep was for mortals," I replied.

I could practically hear him smile that twisted little smile of his. "You got the right answer, Hannah the Same Backward as Forward, but what's the code?"

I stepped over the threshold and flipped the light on, tired of listening to the sound of his voice through the darkness. "Why does it matter?" I retorted. "I won the wager either way."

"Haven't you learned by now?" Harry asked me. "Everything matters—either that, or nothing does."

There is no in between. I suddenly knew that coming here tonight had been a mistake, just like I knew that I wasn't leaving.

Harry was wearing an old shirt of Jackson's that was so ratty and thin I could see the outline of bandages beneath the fabric. I didn't want to tend to him right now.

I also didn't want to be alone. Being alone was perhaps my greatest skill in life, and *I didn't want to be alone.*

"You asked me about my lost one." My voice came out hoarse. I needed to talk to someone, and he was there.

He was *right there.*

"As much as it pains me to admit it, I didn't win this wager, Hannah the Same Backward as Forward." In other words: I didn't have to tell him a damn thing.

"I have a sister." The words tasted like dust in my mouth—another lie. "I had a sister."

Seeing my mother had dredged up all the mourning I hadn't let myself do, all the grief I'd never fully let myself feel. And he was there. *Right there.*

"I'm sorry."

I could hear it in his voice: He was. Harry was sorry I was hurting. He was sorry my sister was gone—but he didn't know that he was the reason why.

"You don't get to be sorry," I said fiercely, and then before he could even think about asking me why, I turned back toward the still-open door, toward the full moon outside. "The lighthouse," I gritted out.

"What about it?" Harry asked, his tone far too gentle for my comfort.

"That's what I want," I said, clipping the words. "For winning our wager. We're going across the rocks to the lighthouse. We're doing it in under five minutes, and you're making it all the way there."

He didn't respond immediately. "As boons go, this is something of a disappointment."

"Don't you remember me telling you that you should get used to being disappointed?" I shot back, stepping out of the shack and down onto the rocks.

"Sounds vaguely familiar," Harry said. He followed me. I didn't hold an arm out to help him keep his balance. He could keep his own damn balance. "But, Hannah?"

I was already moving through the moonlit darkness.

"I have never," Harry said, following in my tracks, pacing me no matter how much pain it caused him, "been disappointed in *you*."

I thought about him telling me that first thing he could remember—his *beginning*—was me. *I have never been disappointed in* you. What right did he have to say things like that to me, to say *anything* to me, when he was the reason my world had fallen apart?

What right did I have to listen? To think about that picture he'd drawn of me, when the only thing I should have been thinking about was how much I hated him?

"What was her name?" Harry's voice was quiet behind me, but I couldn't shake the feeling that I would have been able to hear him from a mile away. We were maybe ten yards into the hike to the lighthouse now, and he hadn't reached for me once. "Your sister."

"Kaylie," I said.

Harry didn't reply immediately. I wasn't sure if he was struggling over the rocks or respecting the weight my sister's name held for me. For the first time since we'd stepped outside, I turned around.

Even in the moonlight, I could see the strain along the muscles of his neck. This wasn't easy, but he was doing it.

"How did she die?" Harry asked me. His tone was neither harsh nor gentle. It simply was.

You killed her. I turned back toward the lighthouse and kept going, taking my speed up a notch. "You didn't win our wager," I said. "I don't have to answer your questions."

The next thing I knew, he was beside me, matching my speed, which was the last thing he should have been doing. *I need to slow down.* It wouldn't do either of us any good if I injured him further. But somehow, I couldn't bear to pull back.

And somehow, his own movements a little jagged, he kept up. "Have I ever given you the impression that I actually know how to lose?"

He hadn't. Of course he hadn't. He was *Toby Hawthorne.* But to me, he was Harry, and he was *right there*, and I didn't want to be alone.

"You don't have to tell me a damn thing, Hannah the Same Backward as Forward. But whatever you want to give me, I'll take."

I have never been disappointed in you.

Whatever you want to give me, I'll take.

This was a mistake—coming to see him tonight when I was so raw; dragging him out here; forcing him to push himself this hard. It was all a mistake, one I just couldn't stop making.

Beside me, Harry stumbled. I caught him. My hands latched on to his arms, just above the elbows. I held him up with strength I hadn't even realized I had. After a breath or two, he regained his footing, and the tension against my hands subsided, leaving the two of us staring at each other through the moonlight.

Me and the rich boy who'd killed my sister and didn't even know it.

I felt his gaze like the lightest of touches, like the wind that caught my hair, just like in his sketch.

"You're an ugly crier," he told me softly, "for what it's worth."

I shook my head at the sheer audacity of him—*always*. "How's your pain?" I asked, dropping my hold on him.

"Irrelevant," he replied. "How's yours?"

"Can you do this?" I pressed, refusing to tell him a single damn thing about *my* pain.

Harry smiled a small and crooked smile. "Agony only matters if you let it." He took a step—and then another.

We hiked in silence, the two of us across those rocks. The silence held until we were well over halfway to the lighthouse. For reasons that I couldn't even begin to pinpoint, I was the one who broke it. "My mother has cancer. I'm not supposed to know, but I do."

"I take it you're also not supposed to care?" His tone made me think of the fairy-tale version he'd spun of my life, the way he'd described me.

"Stop it," I said. "Stop acting like I'm…" *Selfless. Kind. Here tonight for any reason other than a masochistic need to self-destruct.*

"Like you're *you*?" Harry said, his voice echoing over the rocks toward the ocean.

"You don't know me," I told him harshly.

"You don't believe that."

The problem was that he was right: I didn't. "My mother's a murderer," I said, hoping to shock him. "Many times over."

"Has she ever hurt you?" Harry's voice sounded different: low and almost too controlled. That was the voice of someone who wanted to hurt anyone who'd hurt me.

This is a mistake. Every part of it. Every damn moment. It was a mistake, but we were getting closer and closer to the lighthouse, and there was no turning back. There had been no turning back from the moment he'd opened the door.

"My mother has never laid a hand on me," I said quietly. "She's never had to."

"I think...I think I might know what that's like." Beside me, Harry stopped walking. His hair was long enough now to almost fall into his eyes. In moonlight, it looked closer to black than dark reddish-brown. After a long moment, he started moving again, taking one step, then another. I forced myself to walk on, too.

Seventy percent of the way there.

Eighty percent.

"Sometimes, when I look at you," Harry said, his voice rougher now, as it echoed through the night, "I feel you, like a hum in my bones, whispering that we are the same."

We're not. We can't be. But every puzzle he gave me, I solved. *I have to stop.* We had to. But damn it all the way to hell—I kept walking.

And so did he. "But then you do something, Hannah the Same Backward as Forward, something *selfless*, something *kind*, and I know—*I know*—that you're different. Different than me. Different than the whole damn world."

"Stop talking." My voice shook. Maybe my body did, too. In the back of my mind, I could hear Harry describing my emotions: *It's like watching stormwater rise and rise behind a dam.* "Just stop."

We were close now—ten yards away, if that.

"I don't know how to stop," Harry said quietly. "I'm not sure I ever did."

I thought about the boy I'd met in the bar. About *kerosene.* About every single *impossible* moment with him since.

I hated him.

I *did.*

But as he reached the lighthouse and slapped a hand against its crumbling stone wall like a swimmer finishing a race, I also believed him: He didn't know how to stop. He was *right there*.

And I didn't want to be alone.

The bane of my existence stared at me through the darkness like it wasn't dark at all. "I don't know how to quit this," he told me. "Quit *you*."

What's there to quit? I thought, but I couldn't say those words out loud, because I couldn't stop thinking about bits of folded paper and lemons, about palindromes and puzzles—

"But I'm a selfish bastard, aren't I? I probably wouldn't quit you even if I could."

I placed my hand on the crumbling stone, next to his. "You are a selfish bastard," I breathed. "And there's nothing to quit."

"Liar," he murmured, and when he brought his hands to my face, when he buried his fingers in my hair, I didn't fight it.

But *not fighting* wasn't enough for him. He brought his lips to just almost touch mine. *Almost.* And then, damn him to hell and back, he waited.

For me.

Forgive me, Kaylie. I closed the gap. The moment my lips touched his, he shifted his body and mine, and suddenly, my back was up against the lighthouse and nothing else in the world existed except *this*.

Moonlight and him and *this*.

I'd never kissed anyone before. Twenty years old, and I'd never even *imagined* that it could—

"This is a mistake," I gasped, barely pulling back. "You're..."

"Horrible," he filled in, and then his lips crashed down on mine.

Horrible. "Yes," I said.

"I have no redeeming qualities," he murmured, as I turned and pressed *him* back against the lighthouse.

"None," I said.

His hands still in my hair, he tilted my head back, trailing kisses along my jaw and down my neck. "You hate me."

I hate you, I thought, my back arching.

I hate you.

I hate you.

I hate you.

Chapter 31

I woke up with my legs intertwined with his—*inside* the lighthouse. It wasn't until I'd extracted myself and felt my way through the darkness to step back outside that I realized: It was still nighttime. The moon was high in the sky.

The lighthouse had been built on a jut of rocky land that hung out over the ocean. Coming to stand on the point, I could hear waves crashing against the rocks below. If it had been high tide, I might have felt the spray, but as it was, all I felt was the weight of what I'd done with Harry and the fact that I couldn't banish the image of his face, his body, his scars from my mind.

Had I hurt him?

Did I care?

I leaned back against the aging lighthouse, letting out a shudder of a breath and taking in the moon and the stars and the darkness and the cost of not being alone. In the sky, one star glowed brighter than all the rest.

"Well, well, well," a voice said behind me. "Who's doing the walk of shame now?"

That wasn't Harry. It wasn't Jackson. It was a voice I knew as well as I knew my own, and she sounded like she was enjoying herself.

"Kaylie?" That wasn't possible. I didn't turn around, because it wasn't *possible*.

"I'm so proud, you beautiful, saucy, audacious little minx, you."

I turned. I couldn't help it. And there she was. *Kaylie*.

She's here. The fire. She didn't—I reached for her, and my hand passed straight through her body.

"Neat party trick, huh?" she said, smiling like there was no tomorrow.

My throat stung. "You're..."

"Everything I ever was," she told me.

Not possible. "This isn't possible," I said, the words ripping their way out of me like a beast from a cage.

"Anything is possible," Kaylie said, "when you love someone with no regrets."

She's not really here. This isn't happening. I was imagining this, imagining her—or else it was a dream, but I didn't care. I couldn't, because she looked so real.

She looked like my Kaylie. "I am nothing but regrets," I said.

"I am Kaylie Rooney," my sister replied, putting her hands on her hips, "and I do not approve that message." She was so very... *Kaylie.* "You're my sister, bitch. No regrets." Her smile was infectious now, an *on top of a pool table, on top of the world* kind of smile. "Dance with me, Hannah."

I hadn't, the night before she died. She'd wanted me to dance, but I hadn't.

I wasn't going to make that mistake twice.

"You call that dancing?" Kaylie tossed her head back, lifting her arms over her head, the movement of her hips so natural it made it seem like dancing was her default state. "Just let go. Feel the music."

"There is no music." I was the logical one. The rational one. Our dynamic, so familiar I ached with it, brought tears to my eyes. I wasn't in the shower, and I only ever cried in the shower—but I couldn't help it.

"Less crying," Kaylie ordered imperiously. "More wild abandon."

Let go, I told myself. *Feel the music.* In my heart I knew: *She* was the music. This wasn't real. It couldn't be, but I danced the way she did, like I'd been born shouting my joy and my fury to the moon.

"Now say it," Kaylie told me. *"No regrets."*

Anything is possible when you love someone with no regrets. I couldn't say a damn thing.

"No regrets, Hannah. Not about me. Not about him. Not about finally letting go. I need you to say it."

My throat closed in around the words. "I can't."

"Don't stop dancing, okay?"

I didn't want to stop. What if I stopped, and she disappeared? "I'm not going to stop."

"I'm going to hold you to that, you glorious thing, you—and not just about the dancing." Her hair was going wild in the wind. How was it that the wind could touch her, but I couldn't?

How was any of this possible?

"Don't stop," Kaylie told me fiercely. "Living. Loving. Dancing. Don't you dare stop for me."

I thought about Harry. About the lighthouse. About his lips on mine, the touch of our skin. "He killed you."

"It was an accident."

I felt the dam inside me break. I couldn't stop dancing, couldn't risk losing her again, so I let everything I felt—everything I'd been trying so hard not to feel—out into the dance.

"I always knew," Kaylie said. Her movements were slowing, like gravity couldn't touch her quite so much, like she was dancing on a different plane. "I knew that I was going to burn bright and fast. And, Hannah? If you loved me, you won't waste a second of your life regretting a damn thing."

I love you, I thought, *present tense*.

"No regrets," Kaylie told me, her voice rising over the wind. "And, for the record, I like him."

Him. Harry. "You would," I scoffed.

"He sees you." My sister had absolutely no mercy. "He makes you feel."

I couldn't form a single word, and the ghost of my sister went silent in a way that made me afraid that she was fading.

"Promise me," she said, her voice fainter, "that you'll keep dancing."

Tears were streaming down my face. "Every day."

"I'm sure you'll get better at it eventually," Kaylie said with faux seriousness, her voice solid again for the moment. "And don't miss me too much, okay?"

This felt like good-bye. *No.*

"Absolutely no naming your children after me," Kaylie continued, twirling, her arms held wide. "I mean, I guess a middle name would be okay—an homage, not *Kaylie* exactly."

I couldn't bear to lose her again.

"No regrets," Kaylie whispered. I could nearly see *through* her now.

I repeated her words back to her, hoping to pull her back to me: "No regrets."

And just like that, she was gone. Just like that, I was alone, looking up at a sky where one star shined brighter than all the rest.

And just like that, I woke up.

Chapter 32

My legs weren't entangled with Harry's, the way they had been in my dream. I was lying on my side, and he was on his, my body curled slightly inward and his curved around it. My head was nestled against the spot where his shoulder met his chest.

I wondered if I was hurting him, and the sense of déjà vu that hit me then was almost as palpable as my memory of Kaylie dancing. *No regrets.*

Light seeped through the cracks in the lighthouse walls. It was morning. I extracted myself as carefully as I could from the arms wrapped around me.

This was real. *This* wasn't a dream. I grounded myself in that knowledge, in the sound of Harry's breath and the lingering feel of his warmth on my skin, and then I left in absolute silence and stepped outside to a morning utterly devoid of wind.

I walked to stand exactly where I had in my dream, but my sister never came. Ghosts weren't real. Dreams weren't, either. But the specter my mind had conjured up—it had felt like Kaylie, felt *so much* like her that the promise she'd forced out of me felt real.

No regrets. Those two words summarized my sister better

than any others possibly could. If she'd been more capable of regret, maybe she would have been more capable of caution, of holding grudges, of looking backward or forward or anywhere but the *now*.

Promise me...I could hear her in my mind, and even though my instinct was to bow my head the second my eyes started to sting, I bent my neck backward instead, tilting my face up to the morning sky. *Don't stop. Living. Loving. Dancing.*

My breathing went ragged as tears began to slowly carve their way down my face, one after another. And then I heard the sound of footsteps behind me.

I turned to find *him* walking slowly toward me.

"Are you trying to kill me, Hannah the Same Backward as Forward?"

I thought at first that Harry was referring to what had passed between us the night before, but then he brought his hand to my face and wiped a tear away with his thumb.

"I take back what I said before about you being an ugly crier," he murmured. My body, traitor that it was, listed toward his. "You're a *hideous* crier." His lips slanted upward on one side. "A blight on my tender eyes."

"Nothing about you is tender," I said.

"Liar." Harry let that word hang in the air for a moment. "If *this*"—the pad of his thumb slowly rid my face of another tear— "is about me..."

"It's not," I said.

Harry took me at my word. "In that case, and assuming you *don't* want to talk about it..."

"Good assumption."

"Care to tell me how horrible I am again?" He arched a brow. That was clearly an invitation. In the light of day, I wasn't quite so desperate for the touch of another human being. I didn't *need* him, the way I had before.

I needed to dance. *Every day.* I needed to *feel*—the way Kaylie had always felt everything. She'd spent a lifetime trying to drag me into the sun, into trouble—and there *trouble* was, standing far too close to me.

I knew exactly what my sister would have told me to do.

"I would love to outline your flaws," I told Harry, emphasizing each and every word. "In detail."

Something flashed in his eyes, white-hot and hard to describe.

"But," I continued, "I have to go to work, and you have to make it back to the shack—without stumbling this time, even once."

"Always the taskmaster," Harry drawled.

I inhaled, then exhaled, then inhaled again. "No regrets."

Chapter 33

I made it through my entire shift without seeing my mother. I wondered if she'd checked out—and if so, if she'd done it against medical advice. I wondered what her prognosis was.

I wondered how much time I'd bought myself.

And I decided: The day I got Toby Hawthorne out of Rockaway Watch, I was leaving, too—not *with* him. I hadn't completely lost my senses, and I wasn't that naive. The second *Harry* found out who he really was, the second I tipped his billionaire father's men off about his location, he would be gone.

The two of us would, in all likelihood, never see each other again. He would go on his way, and I would go on mine.

Soon—but not yet. He wasn't ready yet. We had time.

I came back to the shack under the cover of darkness that night knowing that I had the next two days off, knowing that I wasn't going to leave until I had to.

"We're going back to the lighthouse." That was the way I greeted Harry the moment he opened the metal door. This time, I could see Jackson seated at the table in the background, but the fisherman didn't say a word to either of us.

"Your wish is my command," Harry drawled, stepping out into the night.

I'd made sure I wasn't followed on the way here. I'd scanned the surrounding area. We were alone.

"Anyone who knows anything about fairy tales," I said, "knows not to trust a statement like that."

Harry walked past me, over rocky ground, and this time, he didn't stumble. Something about the way he moved told me he was still in pain, but that pain didn't matter—not to him.

"It's a good thing," he called back to me, "that I've never pretended to be trustworthy."

The first time a person made a mistake, it could be just that: a mistake, a one-off, a blip. The second time, it was a pattern. It was *intentional*.

It was devastating in the best possible way.

Still a mistake. I knew that, and I had no excuses. I couldn't pin this on a dream. This was me. This was what happened when I let someone *see* me, when I let myself imagine what it would be like not to be alone.

I never *decided* to let him in. I just stopped lying to myself, and there he was—past my shields, under my skin, this horrible boy, this person I'd *hated* and *hated* and *hated* and somehow didn't hate anymore.

On our second night at the lighthouse, I slept without dreaming, my body tangled with his, and I woke up alone.

He was gone. *What if he took off?* My entire body seized with that thought. He'd been strong enough to get to the lighthouse. What if he'd thought he was strong enough to go farther? *What if he's done—with this, with me, with waiting for his escape?*

What if he'd gone into town?

I burst out of the lighthouse into the night—and then I saw him.

Past the jut of land on which the lighthouse stood, down below, there was a small bit of beach. Harry must have climbed down—*reckless*—to reach it. I could make out his silhouette in the moonlight.

He was on his knees, drawing something in the sand.

Someone could see you, I thought. *See us*, I corrected myself, as I looked for a path to join him. I knew that the risk was probably small. It was the middle of the night. From a distance, he wouldn't have been visible, even with the moonlight.

I wasn't sure that *I* would have seen him, if he'd been anyone else.

Drawing closer, I realized that Harry wasn't drawing on the sand. He was *writing*—letters. Large ones. An entire alphabet's worth.

That was when I remembered: I'd won our game of hangman, but I'd never broken his code. *You could start by writing out the letters of the alphabet.* That had been his smug little hint. *See if anything jumps out to you.*

He spotted me as he was finishing the *Y*. "You thought I left, didn't you, Hannah the Same Backward as Forward?"

The waves crashed behind us and rolled up onto the beach, stopping maybe five feet from where he was writing, a natural soundtrack with valleys and peaks.

"Leaving the wrong way could get you killed," I said as he drew the *Z* with a flourish. Another wave crashed behind us. "It could get me killed, too."

It was the first time I'd ever put that thought into words: If the world found out what I'd done, if my family did, if letting me live would be read by others as a sign of weakness...

"Tell me." Harry stood.

I looked down at his alphabet—what I could see of it in the

moonlight. "The answer or the truth?" I asked. *The code—or why we have to be so careful?*

"Dealer's choice."

I knelt in the sand, getting a better look at the letters he'd written, attending to them one by one. There was nothing remarkable about the *Z*, the *Y*, the *X*, the *W*...

"People who cross my family end up dead." I kept my explanation short and to the point.

"Drugs?" Harry saw the answer to that on my face, even with nothing but the moon for light. "But with me..." Harry took his time with the next bit. "It's not business. It's personal."

He was getting too close to something I wasn't sure either one of us could handle.

"That wasn't a question," I noted.

"Games are easier than questions for me. *Puzzles. Riddles. Codes.*" Harry looked down at the alphabet he'd drawn in the sand. "My memory is a blank slate, but there are a surprising number of things I haven't forgotten. I know how to tie my shoes. I know how to breathe through pain and wrap it in an imaginary iron box in my mind. And I know that there wasn't anyone who could solve *this* before you."

I wasn't sure, when he said *this*, if he was talking about the code—or himself. All I knew for certain was that the way he said the words *before you* made me think about *him*—his breath on my skin, my breath on his.

Once upon a time, hating him had been the easiest thing in the world.

"The way you wrote the letters is boxy and angled." I moved my way down the beach, bringing my fingers to touch the *U*, then the *S*.

"Drawn only with straight lines," I continued, "just like they were in Two Moves."

"And what does that tell you?" Harry challenged.

"It's all connected." My answer was automatic, and so was the way that *I* started drawing in the sand. He'd taken up most of the dry canvas, so I went to where the sand was barely damp and dragged my finger through its surface, writing out the code from our game of hangman by memory.

39 38 32 44 45 310 53 35 5 34 22 3 7 2 42

My lips starting to curve, I wrote the answer above the numbers—*UNCOPYRIGHTABLE*—and then I turned my attention back to Harry's alphabet, walking down the beach, all the way to the start.

To the letter *A*.

I wrote a 3 next to it—the correct digit, based on the code. "A lot of the numbers in the code start with a three," I noted out loud. I looked back toward the encrypted string of numbers and the word I'd written on top of them. "Only two of them start with a two."

L and *T*.

"You see it, don't you?" Harry asked.

I scowled at him. "*B* shouldn't be seven."

He shrugged. "Depends on how you draw it." I looked back to his *B*. He'd drawn it with no angles, only parallel and perpendicular lines.

Seven lines. "*A* is *three*—it takes three lines to make the letter. *B*, the absurd way you've drawn it, takes seven. If you'd used angled lines, the way you did for the *R* in our last game, it only would have taken five."

"Six if you break the long line into two smaller ones." Harry had absolutely no remorse for playing dirty. "I warned you before: I learned to skew games in my favor from the master."

That wasn't what he'd said before, not exactly. My gut said that, whether he knew it or not, he was talking about his father. The billionaire. A person didn't amass a fortune like that without skewing the game.

"Do you know," I asked Harry quietly, "who you're talking about?"

I saw a muscle ripple over his jaw, and for the longest time, he said nothing.

"Your mother never hurt you." When Harry finally did speak, his voice was perfectly even, perfectly calm, and far too much like my own. "She never had to. That's what you said last night."

His reply had been that he thought he might know what that was like.

"When I was nine…" I swallowed and fixed my gaze in the direction of the seemingly endless ocean, dark as the night. "I heard her throw a man to the dogs. They were starving, and he was bleeding. That was the day I realized she kept them hungry and mean for a reason."

I was fairly certain my mother hadn't realized that I was at home that night. I'd always been grateful that Kaylie hadn't been.

"You were right before," Harry said suddenly, "when you called me a coward."

I wondered what slivers of memory, what secrets my own had shaken loose in his head.

"I know I was running," he told me, his voice low. "I just don't know from what—or who." His eyes opened and found their way to mine. "I'm coming around to your perspective on hiding. It's not so bad, being hidden." He took a step toward me, into damp sand. "I don't mind being someone's dirty little secret, as long as it's yours."

For the longest time, neither of us said another word, and then I turned back to the letters in the sand, the ones he'd written. Next to the A, I'd already written a 3. Next to the B, I wrote a 7. A C, when drawn with only straight lines, required three lines, and in the code, the letter C had corresponded to the number thirty-two.

I wrote that in the sand. "Thirty-two," I said. "As in, three dash two. It's the second letter written with three lines."

"There are a lot of letters," Harry told me, "that can be written with only three lines."

I'd broken his code. I felt his presence like breath on my skin and wondered if he could feel mine the same way. I wondered what the hell we were doing, what the hell *I* was doing.

No regrets.

"I read the poem." I wasn't even sure where that came from. "The one you quoted to me, weeks ago. 'A Poison Tree' by William Blake."

Harry took a step toward me, then another, leaving him standing maybe a foot away. "Say that again."

"'A Poison—'"

"The poet's name," he cut in, and the intensity in his voice was like nothing I'd ever heard.

"William Blake," I said. I stared at him through the dark, wondering what he'd remembered—or what he was on the verge of remembering.

"It's right there," Harry said hoarsely. "Just out of reach."

"What is?"

"*Something.*" He turned his back on me and started pacing—except *pacing* wasn't even the right word. It was closer to *prowling.* "*The tree is poison, don't you see?*" His voice was low, but I heard every word. "*It poisoned S and Z and me.*"

He was remembering, and it hit me just how badly I didn't want him to. But I couldn't hold him back. "What does that mean?" I asked. "*The tree is poison...*"

"I don't know." He gritted out the words.

"*S* and *Z,*" I said quietly. "You have sisters." I'd read that much in those news articles that had been so quick to pin the Hawthorne Island tragedy on *my* sister. "One named Skye, one named Zara."

"Did I love them?" Harry asked roughly. "*My sisters.* Did I love them the way you love Kaylie?"

He said Kaylie's name like it mattered, like *she* did. He'd described my love for Kaylie in the present tense, but when he'd asked about his own sisters, he'd used past tense: Did *I love them?*

Like the person he'd been was already dead and gone.

"I don't know." I went with honesty, knowing he would hear it if I didn't. "They must be missing you, the way I miss Kaylie."

He angled his eyes sideways toward mine. "Come now, Hannah the Same Backward as Forward, why would anyone miss me?"

My hand caught his as he prowled past. He stilled and looked down at our hands, and then his fingers curved around mine, and he pulled me toward the water.

Sometimes, I could hear him saying, *when I look at you, I feel you, like a hum in my bones, whispering that we are the same.*

I tried to banish the memory of his voice and ended up hearing another voice in my mind instead. *Promise me…*

I looked up, my eyes searching the night sky. Overhead, one star glowed brighter than all the rest.

Kaylie.

I'd made her a promise. Whether it had been real or not, I sure as hell wasn't breaking it. Waves lapped at my feet as I pulled my hand from Harry's and raised it over my head.

"What are you doing?" He stared at me through the darkness.

"Dancing," I said, remembering my sister telling me to *feel the music.*

Harry arched a brow. "You call that dancing?" A slow smile commanded his lips.

The next thing I knew, he was dancing, too. His body knew exactly how to move. I kept dancing, and he danced toward me, until there was no space left between us at all. *Damp sand. Night sky. The breeze off the ocean.* I felt it all, the same way I felt him. The two of us moved in rhythm with each other for the longest time, and then, without warning, we were kissing in the moonlight, and there was nothing frantic about it this time, nothing angry or brutal. He kissed me like the tide comes in, little by little by little.

No regrets.

"What are we doing?" My lips brushed his with every word.

Harry murmured his answer directly into my skin: "Nothing— or everything."

For him—and maybe for me—there was nothing in between.

Chapter 34

Within the week, I could see: He was getting stronger. A week after that, and I knew: It wouldn't be long until Harry was ready to make the trek across the rocks.

When he leaves, I promised myself again and again and again, *this is over. When he leaves, I'm leaving, too.*

And then, one morning after yet another lighthouse night, we both woke with the dawn, and I knew with sudden clarity that I wasn't going to work that day—and maybe not ever again.

My supervisor would understand. She'd been on pins and needles since my mother's appearance at the hospital. As for the school, anyone who knew I was a Rooney, anyone who knew what that meant, would understand why I might need to disappear.

And I wanted every minute that I could get.

"What have you been doing all day, every day to pass the time?" I murmured. Harry and I were alone in Jackson's shack. Jackson was, as was typical for the daytime and more and more nights, out on his boat.

"Well," Harry told me, "when I get bored, I build castles out of sugar."

I gave him a look.

"Anything can be a game, Hannah the Same Backward as Forward, if you know how to play."

And from then on, day after day, the two of us played.

The Cracks On The Wall Game. We played it lying on our backs on the floor of the shack. One of us chose a specific crack on the wall and challenged the other to guess which one it was—with delightful *penalties* for every incorrect guess.

The Boards On The Floor Game. Some boards you could step on. Some you couldn't. It was a way for him to work on his balance, precision, and control, and it reminded me a bit of The Floor Is Lava... but with *penalties* for every misstep.

Neither one of us ever touched the loose board, the one beneath which I'd hidden that metal token from his life before. I took that to mean that Harry knew exactly where it was and that both of us wanted it and everything it represented to stay buried at least a little longer.

The Not A Single Glare Game was one of Harry's favorites. He tried—expertly—to get under my skin, and I did my best to keep my face perfectly blank. As he ratcheted up his *impressive* efforts, I found increasingly creative ways of putting him in his place... without a single glare.

Checkers. We found an old set of Jackson's. Harry cheated. I cheated right back.

The Close Your Eyes Game was another test of Harry's balance and limitations, of his body's ability to react to the unexpected. I hid somewhere in the room, standing perfectly still, and he had to find me with his eyes closed, walking over and around obstacles, listening for me with every breath.

There was something about watching him move slowly toward me with his eyes closed, something about trying to breathe as quietly as I could, knowing he could hear me anyway. Whenever Harry managed to catch me, he relished saying four words and *only* four words.

"Turnabout is fair play."

When it was my turn to find him, Harry went all out. He never just *stood* anywhere. He climbed or he knelt, twisting himself into an impossible position to lay in wait for me. With my eyes closed, I would listen for the sound of his breathing, his heartbeat, the slightest of movements. And any time I got close, *he* would move—silently, close enough to me sometimes that I could feel his movements in the air.

There were times when I paced after him—my eyes closed, listening for him, *feeling* him—that I thought about fairy tales, about the little mermaid without her voice, Rapunzel with her hair shorn. Sometimes, the absence of something you'd come to rely on could be a gift. Tamping down one sense could send the others into overdrive.

On a particular day—what I knew was probably going to be one of our last days—I went very still, sure that he was close. I *listened*, and when my target silenced even his breath, I inhaled through my nose. We'd both been using the same cheap soap, but somehow, Harry smelled to me of saltwater and the ocean breeze and something earthy, like summer grass.

I turned, then sidestepped. "Found you." My fingers made their way to the side of his face, then to the back of his head as my eyes opened.

"Cheater," he murmured.

I hadn't cheated. "You are a horrible loser."

He shrugged, then began lowering his lips toward mine. "I've never claimed to know how to lose."

Chapter 35

The Don't Look Down Game. It was past midnight two days later, and I was running out of excuses to delay leaving any longer. The two of us were standing at the very edge of the lighthouse point, the tips of our feet hanging over the drop-off, like a glass of whiskey balanced precariously on a pool table.

"We're standing on the edge of the Eiffel Tower," Harry said. Between the two of us, *he* was clearly the more accomplished liar. He had a gift of making every word out of his mouth sound and feel true. "We're at the very top," he continued as the wind picked up. "It's a thousand-foot drop. *Don't look down.*"

I didn't look down; I edged forward—just a little more—well aware that the old Hannah wouldn't have ever taken the risk and equally aware that Harry would never let me fall.

"Why would I look down," I retorted, "when we're so close to falling off a tower spire?" I could picture it so vividly in my mind—the two of us, elsewhere.

"A tower?" Harry murmured. "One of yours?"

In his fairy-tale version of my life story, I'd locked myself in tower after tower after tower. There were no walls between us now, no boundaries between my body and his, nothing between us except the reality I kept putting off.

"Don't look down," I whispered. I swallowed as the ground shifted slightly beneath our feet, a rock audibly falling away from the edge.

I could hear the waves, angry and rough, down below, but I couldn't see them.

Don't look down.

Don't look down.

Don't look down.

Harry squatted, picking up a rock without ever lowering his chin or his eyes, then stood again, the smooth movement a testament to just how far he'd come. Without a word, he hurled the rock into the distance, into the ocean.

Don't look down. I thought about the day he'd thrown the metal token against the wall, so hard it had sounded like a gunshot. Within seconds, I had a rock in my hand.

The wind picked up, and with no warning, lightning flashed somewhere in the distance. I was taken back to that day at the hospital, to the moment flames had shot into the sky.

"There's a storm coming," Harry said beside me. I wondered if any part of him remembered.

"Looks like it could be a big one." I picked up my own rock and hurled it into the waves, keeping my eyes trained on the velvety darkness of the horizon.

The storm was coming, and neither one of us looked down.

Harry took a step back from the edge. His arms wrapped around me from behind, and he lowered his head, breathing me in. "As far as I'm concerned, Hannah the Same Backward as Forward, you're the storm."

He never called me *liar* anymore, not in any language, not since I'd given in, fully and completely, to this thing between us. *Nothing—or everything.*

I closed my eyes and leaned back against him. I could smell rain on the wind, and some prescient part of me said that the storm was a sign. I knew in the pit of my stomach that I couldn't put it off any longer.

He was ready. Once the weather cleared, he could make it across the rocks. *We* could.

This had started with a storm, and now, it was ending.

We stayed out long enough that we got caught in the rain. It rolled in off the ocean like a sheet of solid water. We saw it coming, and neither one of us made a single move to back away.

Deep down, I thought he probably knew, too: This was our last night.

The rain was the kind that battered you from all sides. Within seconds, we were drenched, and still, neither one of us could take a single step toward the lighthouse, let alone the shack.

"You look like a wet cat." Harry had to yell to be heard over the roar of the downpour.

"You look like a wet dog," I told him, and he proved my point, shaking off the water. His hair was long enough now that it was almost always in his face. My fingers itched to push it back, but he beat me to moving first, burying his fingers in my wet hair, pushing it back and away from my soaked face.

"You look like a fairy tale," he murmured. He stared at me then, like he was preparing to draw me again or committing this moment to memory, the way I was. "Come with me, Hannah the Same Backward as Forward." He paused. "When I leave, come with me."

Those words, sudden and real, took my breath away. My mouth went unbearably dry. "I am coming," I told him. "Across the rocks. I'll get you to where you can call for help, and—"

"No." He ran his hands back through my hair, and then they were cupping my jaw, lifting my face toward his. "Come with me, Hannah."

It was so dark, I could barely see him, but I didn't need to. We might as well have been playing The Close Your Eyes Game, because I could *feel* his presence, his body, *him*.

"I can't go with you," I said. The words were almost lost to the wind, but nothing was ever lost on him.

"Why not?" he demanded. He kissed me to punctuate that question, but there was nothing *demanding* about the way he kissed. Every one of his kisses was an invitation, a love song, a beckoning to something more.

I was going to miss this—like a drowning person misses air, like I'd miss the sun if it went black. *No regrets.*

I didn't answer his question. Back in the real world, he was a billionaire's son. He was presumed dead. He was responsible for a tragedy that I didn't even want him to *know* about, one I couldn't bear thinking about myself.

Soaked and freezing, I shivered as he traced the lines of my jaw with his thumb. He nuzzled me, then took my hand and began pulling me back up the rocks, toward the lighthouse.

"What are you doing?" I asked him. *What am I doing?* What *had* I been doing all this time?

"For once," Harry told me, his voice cutting through the downpour and to my core, "you get to be the patient."

We made it to the lighthouse door.

"For once," Harry said, pulling me through that door, out of the wind and out of the rain, "let me be the one who takes care of you."

Chapter 36

There wasn't much he could do inside the lighthouse, where there was no light, no heat, no blankets.

Nothing but Harry and me.

He started by wringing out my hair, then his fingers worked their way gently through it, ridding it of tangles one by one. His own soaking shirt came off next, and he pulled me back against him, the heat of his body spreading to mine as he gathered the fabric of my shirt and began wringing it out, too.

Water trailed down my neck, down my back, and his fingers traced the same path.

I wasn't shivering anymore.

"You don't have to do this," I told him.

He didn't have to speak for me to hear his response. *Don't you know, Hannah the Same Backward as Forward? I would do anything for you.*

We made it back to the shack just before dawn. Jackson was there—and awake. The fisherman took one look at the two of us and grunted. Then he went to make himself scarce. "Damn kids."

Giving Harry a warning look, I went after the man who'd pulled him from the water, all those weeks ago. "Jackson—"

"None of my business," Jackson growled. He had to have noticed that I'd stopped leaving, had to have noticed the way Harry and I disappeared at night, but he hadn't said a word about any of it to me.

"It *is* your business," I said, and when Jackson didn't reply, I forced myself to say something that I really didn't want to be saying. "He's better now. Not completely healed, but well enough to make it across the rocks."

I wasn't sure if Harry would ever be *completely* healed. He'd certainly always have the scars.

"He's leaving." I looked away before I elaborated. "And so am I." That was the first time I'd spoken the words out loud. "I'm leaving Rockaway Watch, Jackson—not with him, I *know* I can't go with him. But once I get him far enough away that we can make the call without it being tied back to you, once his father's people come to get him, I'm leaving, too."

Jackson stared at me, hard. For a moment, he seemed like the old Jackson Currie, like he might be considering shooting me, just for the hell of it.

"What are you doing, little Hannah?"

I knew somehow that he wasn't talking about me leaving. He was talking about the rest of it. *Harry and me.*

I shook my head, refusing to even try to give him an answer to that question when I didn't have one myself. I couldn't tell him that I was dancing, living, letting go. I couldn't begin to describe what it was like, for once in my life, to be seen, to *feel*.

"I don't know." I could admit that. I had to. "But he's ready."

Jackson gave me a hard look. "Are you?"

I looked away. I'd known from the beginning that each day that Toby Hawthorne was here, Jackson and I were both in danger.

Harry just hadn't felt like *Toby Hawthorne* to me for a very long time.

"I need to go back to my apartment," I said. It was paid up through the end of the month, but I was betting my landlord would start throwing my things away the very next day after that, legalities be damned. There wasn't much I wanted.

Some clothes.

My important papers.

My emergency stash of cash.

Ideally, I would have taken my car, too, but that would have required coming back after getting Harry to safety, and I didn't think I could risk it. Better for Hannah Rooney to have disappeared a couple of weeks *before* the miraculous reappearance of Toby Hawthorne than after.

Jackson grunted at me again, and I thought that was the end of the conversation, but then he proved me wrong. "You always were the damnedest Rooney."

Chapter 37

I'd only been back to my apartment once since I stopped going into work, for clothes. If I'd been thinking straight, I would have packed up everything I needed then, but I hadn't.

Hadn't been thinking straight.

Hadn't packed.

I let myself in and got straight to work. Fifteen minutes later, I was almost done. Sixteen minutes in, my front door opened, even though I'd locked it behind me.

"Look what the tide dragged in." Rory took up nearly the entire doorframe, and I was smart enough to know that was intentional. He wanted me to be keenly, viscerally aware of the difference in our sizes.

He wanted me thinking about the fact that my exit was blocked.

"I don't know what you mean." Neutral tone, neutral expression—old habits kicked back in fast.

"Don't you, Hannah?" Rory's smile was the furthest thing from comforting. "I'm surprised. Eden's always saying you're so smart."

I thought about the way I'd shown my cousin up that night, when my mother had dragged him here to teach him a lesson.

Rory hadn't known that he'd gotten into a fight with a Hawthorne. I'd figured it out.

I told myself that was all this was. I told myself that he didn't *know*. He couldn't.

If he'd known what I'd really been up to these past few months, I probably would have been bleeding by now.

"What do you want, Rory?" I said flatly.

"We all thought you skipped town." He stared at me for a moment, then his expression turned self-congratulatory. "I had someone keeping an eye on this place, just in case."

"That's not an answer to my question," I pointed out. My voice was calm, but on the inside, I was saying every prayer I knew that whoever my cousin had paid to tell him if I came back to my apartment hadn't realized what direction I'd come from.

Where I'd been.

"What makes you think I'm here to answer *your* questions?" Rory's beady eyes narrowed. "Where have you been, Hannah?"

I channeled my inner Jackson: "None of your business."

"That's what you've never understood." My cousin pointed a finger at me. "Our family *is* business. Business is family." He nodded toward the bag in my hand. "Looks like you're running away. I have to ask myself why—and what you might know."

That tipped me off to the fact that he was here on his own behalf, not my mother's. Maybe he suspected there was something off with her.

Maybe he thought I'd disappeared because I knew what it was.

"You know, Rory," I said slowly, "you should ask yourself if my mother would want you here." I nodded toward the scar along his cheekbone. "It's healed up nicely, by the way."

"You're up to something," he spat.

That's an understatement. "Look on the bright side," I told him. "Once I'm gone, she's going to need an heir."

"It was never going to be *you*." His lip curled. "Or Kaylie."

"Don't you say her name," I said, my voice low.

Rory shook his head, his eyes narrowed. "Who do you think watched over her after you left, huh?"

That was the only kind of blow he felt confident issuing. *He doesn't know a damn thing, and he's not suicidal enough to lay a finger on me without permission.*

All I had to do was to buy myself some time. I just needed him to leave, so I could do the same. Permanently. Considering my options, I let my control falter visibly, let him take that as a victory.

"I don't want to fight with you, Rory." My voice was mostly steady, but it was higher now. "I'm messed up, okay? Is that what you want to hear?"

It was *exactly* what he wanted to hear, so I gave him more.

"I am in pieces," I said. "I am *nothing*. And all I want is to disappear."

I wasn't in pieces. I wasn't nothing. And there was something I wanted much more than to disappear—something impossible, something *real*. But he didn't know that.

If I played this right, none of them would ever know that.

"Why do you care if I leave town?" I continued brokenly. "I was never really one of you. I don't know anything. I'm not a threat to anyone." I told him the kind of lie he was wired to believe: "I'm just a girl."

Rory looked down at me as he stepped from the doorway. "Not so smart now, are you, Hannah?"

I let him have the last word.

Once he was gone—once I'd verified that he was gone—I

took my lone bag and got in my car, and I drove. Going straight back to Jackson's wasn't an option, not anymore. I hadn't wanted to risk stashing my car anywhere before, but that choice had been made for me now. I couldn't go to Jackson's from Rockaway Watch.

I'd have to take the back way in.

So I drove—out of town, onto the highway. I kept driving until I was sure no one had followed.

And then, I had to get back.

It was dark—and then some—when I knocked on the metal door of the shack. I'd walked miles, taken multiple buses, walked miles more. And still, my body was flooded with adrenaline. Harry and I—we had to get out of here.

Tonight.

"What do you want?" Jackson practically snarled his customary greeting.

"It's me," I answered.

A long time passed before he opened the door. When he did, I looked automatically past him—but Harry wasn't there.

My heart leapt into my throat.

"He's waiting for you," Jackson said, putting me out of my misery. "At the lighthouse." The fisherman must have gotten a better look at me then, because his eyes narrowed. "What the hell happened to you?"

"Harry has to go," I said. "Tonight. My cousin Rory is sniffing around. He doesn't know anything—yet—and I'm certain I wasn't followed here, but—"

Jackson cut me off: "I don't need to know."

I stared at him for a moment longer, this man who had pulled a dying boy from the ocean and given him to me. And then, wordlessly, I turned and made my way across the rocks to the lighthouse.

To Harry.

My body knew the path by heart. I could have hiked the rocky trail in my sleep, but I was beyond awake—heart-pounding, breath-a-little-shallow, body-on-high-alert, might-never-sleep-again *awake*.

I opened the lighthouse door expecting it to be dark inside and was greeted with light. Candles, at least a dozen of them, had been scattered around the perimeter of the room. I had no idea where Harry had even gotten them.

In the middle of the floor, there was a light-blue blanket. Harry was sprawled out on it, waiting for me. In front of him, there was checkerboard—but not *just* a checkerboard. It looked like he'd cut out the individual squares with one of Jackson's knives and rebuilt it from scratch. Some marvel of ingenuity and engineering made it look like most of those squares were hovering midair.

"Three-dimensional checkers." Coming from Harry, that was equal parts invitation and challenge.

I stood for a moment in the doorway, taking in the candles and the blanket and the *game*, and something in me broke a little. "We have to go." My voice came out hoarse. "Tonight." I closed my eyes, a phantom hand locking around my heart. "Now."

I heard Harry get up. I heard him coming closer. The Close Your Eyes Game. I felt each and every step he took.

"We don't have to do anything." His voice started soft, then grew in strength and volume, in intensity. "I don't need anything, Hannah, except this."

His voice surrounded me. He was right in front of me now, and I couldn't bear to open my eyes.

"Except you," he whispered.

I couldn't keep my eyes closed any longer, and when I opened them, dark green eyes, shining with the light of bad ideas and worse ones, met mine.

"If who I am is a problem, Hannah the Same Backward as Forward, then *to hell* with who I am." His voice was everywhere. *He* was everywhere I looked, and I could tell: He meant it. "I don't care about who I was before. I don't care about that life. I care about this one, about *you*. We can stay here or we can go, we can run or we can hide, but anything I do—I am doing it *with you*."

A breath caught in my throat, and I forced myself to keep breathing, the way he always had, through the pain. "You don't understand," I said. "You don't know what you would be giving up."

From the very beginning, I'd known that someday he would go back to being Tobias Hawthorne the Second, the only son of a billionaire, with the world at the tips of his fingers. I had assumed from the beginning that someday he would find out about Hawthorne Island, about Kaylie, about all of it.

But what if he didn't have to?

He'd been running from something. What if he *didn't* go back? What if he stayed *Harry* and Toby Hawthorne stayed dead?

What if, this time, we ran together?

"I know what I won't give up, Hannah the Same Backward as Forward." Harry's hands made their way to my face. "I won't give up the person I am with you. For you. *This*..." His fingers explored the contours of my jaw, my cheekbones, my temples, like he was attempting to see me with all of his senses at the same time. "*This* is real. My life before can stay a bad dream, and you can tell me, *Hannah, O Hannah*—who made you look like this?"

Hannah, O Hannah. Another palindrome. I might have responded to that, if it wasn't for his question. *Who made you look like this?*

I'd almost forgotten about Rory, about the reason that tonight was it, the reason we *had* to go. Now.

"One of my cousins." I wasn't going to lie to him—not about this, not when I was considering spending the rest of my life lying to him by omission so we could live a fairy tale. Together.

"Did he threaten you?" Harry clipped the words, and the lines of *his* face hardened. "Touch you? I'll kill him."

"No." That was the last thing we needed. "You won't. We're running."

"*We*," Harry repeated, and just like that, with one word, my decision was made.

"We'll start over," I whispered, "far, far away."

That had always been a part of my plan—leaving this world behind, leaving my family behind. And from the time I was a child, I'd never planned on going alone.

"Far, far away," Harry repeated. He pulled me toward him, his lips coming down on mine little by little by little. "Once upon a time…"

I kissed him back, kissed him like we were caught in the rain, like we were standing at the edge of the Eiffel Tower, like I'd just found him in the dark, like if I kissed him hard enough and long enough, nothing in this world would exist except the two of us.

Once upon a time…far, far away…

"Sagas," I whispered, kissing the exact spot on his neck where I could feel his pulse. "Level. Aha." *Palindromes.*

He grinned and pushed me lightly back against the light-house wall, pulling off his own shirt and offering up an aching, whispered palindrome of his own. "*Wow.*"

I'd hated him until I'd loved him, and now, I would love him until the end.

"Once upon a time…" I whispered, trailing kisses down his

jaw, his neck, along his collarbone, and down to his scars. "There was a girl..."

"And a boy..." he murmured into my skin. "And pain and wonder and darkness and light and *this*."

Once upon a time, I thought, *there was us*.

The next thing I knew, neither one of us was standing up. He was on the ground, and I was on top of him.

Three seconds later, we'd knocked over a candle.

The floor of the lighthouse was made of old, rotting wood. The flame caught, spreading from board to board. Beneath me, Harry froze, his limbs motionless, his chest still, like he wasn't even breathing. I snapped out of it first and moved—fast. I grabbed the blanket, threw it on top of the flames, stamped on it.

Even once the fire was out, Harry remained motionless.

The smell of smoke was unmistakable. I knelt, reaching for him. "Harry?"

After a long moment, he took my hand in his. He held it tightly for a second or two, and then, as he closed his eyes, he placed my hand gently on the floor beside him. He let go.

"Harry—"

"That isn't my name." His voice sounded the same. The ache in it, the darkness, the emotion rising up like stormwater behind a dam—it was all familiar, but still, I *knew*.

The fire. The flames. He *remembered*. I wasn't sure how much. An instant later, he was on his feet, prowling the room from candle to candle. He snuffed one flame out, then another, pinching the candles' wicks between his forefinger and his thumb.

He was going to burn himself.

"Stop." I caught him before he could make it to the last candle. He broke out of my grip, and this time, when he snuffed the flame out, he did it slow, like he wanted it to hurt.

"*Stop*," I said hoarsely. I hadn't healed his burns for him to scorch himself now.

With the last flame extinguished, Harry let his hand drop to his side. I let myself think of him that way, as *Harry*, one last time, even though I knew: He wasn't *Harry* anymore.

"I never did know how to stop." Toby Hawthorne said those words in an unnaturally calm voice. Not even half a second later, he drove his fist into the wall. I *heard* the impact of his knuckles against the stone, *heard* the wall of the lighthouse creak, like it might come down around us.

"Stop," I said again, my voice quiet and just as calm as his. "Toby." That was the first time—ever—that I'd used his real name out loud. "*Stop*."

He looked at me like I was an angel—and not the sweet kind with clouds and a harp but the terrifying kind, otherworldly and too bright to behold.

He looked at me like I was his world—and like that world was ending.

"You knew." He stared at me, the muscles in his throat visibly taut. "You know."

"You need to breathe," I told him.

"Kaylie." He said her name, and then he said it again and again and again. "Kaylie. *Your* Kaylie. I killed her, Hannah. I killed all of them. The fire—I was so damn angry, and at first, it was just supposed to be the dock. But I hated my father so much, hated everyone so much, it didn't seem like enough. And when Colin suggested we go for the house—"

He didn't finish. When I tried to reach for him, he tore himself away from me like my touch scalded his skin more than any flame could have. He stumbled out of the building, into the night, gaining traction and speed as he went. I ran after him as he ran for the lighthouse point.

I saw then what he intended. He was going to hurl himself off the point—into the water, into the rocks. Adrenaline flooded my veins, and I made it to him before he could do a damn thing. I latched my arms around him, holding him back with everything I had.

He fought me. Toby Hawthorne *fought* to die, and I fought back harder. In the end, I won, because he wouldn't hurt me, and I had no such compunctions.

If I had to hurt him to save him, then that was too damn bad.

"You told me . . ." He was wheezing now, like he was right back in the fire on Hawthorne Island. "You told me I didn't *get* to die."

"You don't." I caught his head in my hands and forced his eyes to mine. "Not now, not ever until you're old and gray. Do you hear me, Toby Hawthorne?" I said his full name like he'd been *Toby* to me this whole time, because suddenly, it didn't matter—*Harry. Toby.* He was the same.

He was mine.

"You don't get die on me," I said, my voice low and fierce. "You don't get to make me *love you* and then destroy yourself."

He looked me right in the eyes. "You don't love me. You can't. I killed her."

"It was an accident." I'd never said those words before. He shook his head, and I said them again. *"It was an accident, Toby."*

"You hated me." He understood now, so many things he hadn't before, and I heard it in his voice: If it wasn't this cliff, it would be another.

"I hated you until I loved you," I said. "And I'll love you until the end."

This wasn't the end. I wouldn't *let it* be the end of him or me or *us*.

"So whatever you're thinking right now," I told him ferociously, my voice shaking, my body threatening to do the same, "get it out of your mind. I have lost enough, Toby. I am not going to lose you, too. *Do you understand me?*"

Did he? Did he understand that I didn't know how to breathe without him anymore? I'd spent weeks knowing that I was going to lose him—but not like this, not when we'd been so close to *everything*.

Once upon a time . . .

Far, far away . . .

"Promise me." I did to him what Kaylie had done to me in my dream, because what choice did he have except to make this promise? I'd lived with the reality of his role in my sister's death for months, but it was brand-new to him.

There was nothing he would deny me right now.

"Promise me," I said again, "that you will live." *Promise me, you bastard.*

He promised.

Chapter 38

We didn't leave that night, the way I'd intended for us to, the way we *needed* to. Instead, Harry walked wordlessly back to Jackson's shack. Jackson was gone when we got there. I wondered where he was. I wondered if he'd heard us.

We'd been shouting, Toby and me. There'd been wind.

"If you want to go back," I said, once Toby and I were inside the shack, alone, "now that you know who you are, if you want to stop running—I understand."

"Is that what you think this is?" Toby stopped right next to the loose floorboard, the one we'd avoided in all those rounds of The Boards On The Floor Game. "You think," he continued tersely, "that now that I know who I am, who my father is, I want to go *back*?"

"I don't know," I whispered.

Toby looked at me like looking at me *hurt*. "I meant what I said before, *Hannah, O Hannah*. Every word of it. *This*—you, me—it's the only thing that's real. It is the only thing that matters to me. If I could snap my fingers and make my last name anything other than Hawthorne, I would." He closed his eyes. "If I could take it all back—"

The fire. Kaylie. All of it.

"I'm a murderer."

"You're not," I insisted, closing the space between us. "You didn't start the fire. You never lit a single match. None of you did. And Toby? I don't think you would have, not unless you knew for a *fact* that everyone was clear of the flames."

Kerosene. Lightning. A tragedy in two words.

"I'm the reason your sister is dead, Hannah. She's your lost one, and *I'm the reason you lost her.*" He was almost shaking now. "I have to turn myself in."

I swore at him, every single curse word I knew. "They'll kill you. Do you understand that? My family will *kill you*, and you promised me that you would live."

I grabbed him by the shoulders, trying to *make* him look at me, but he closed his eyes, and when he finally opened them again, he fell to his knees in front of me, his head bowed.

Toby Hawthorne knelt at my feet, like a sinner in confession. He stayed there, his body shuddering, refusing to let me touch him, and then he lifted the loose floorboard. He reached into the hole and locked his hand around the metal token.

"The tree is poison, don't you see?" he said, his voice hoarse. *"It poisoned S and Z and me."* He looked up at me, tears in his eyes. "I remember. All of it. The whole, sordid truth."

The story of his life came in bits and pieces through the night. He forced himself to tell me, to relive it, a form of penance that I hadn't asked for. But I listened, recasting his story as a fairy tale in my mind, the way he once had mine.

The prince had discovered that he was adopted when he was fourteen. His father's subjects didn't know. His sisters, the princesses, didn't know. His mother, the queen, had faked a pregnancy, and even once he'd discovered that much, the young prince hadn't realized why—not at first. He'd spent years wondering why the brilliant king and the sparkling, joyful queen had gone to such lengths to hide the truth about their only son.

And then, one day, the prince had found the corpse.

I tried to imagine what it had been like for Toby to see human remains and to realize, as he had eventually realized, that it had once been his biological father, a man named William Blake.

William Blake. I had no idea how a nineteen-year-old had even pieced it all together. He didn't say. And the entire time, as the boy I loved laid himself bare to me, I just kept thinking the words he'd once said: *Sometimes, when I look at you, I feel you, like a hum in my bones, whispering that we are the same.*

My mother was a murderer, too.

The metal token—the one he'd reacted so violently toward—had belonged to William Blake, and, along with Blake's remains, it served as proof of Toby's biological father's death at his adoptive father's hands. It was proof of *Toby's* identity as the grandson of another very powerful—and even more dangerous—man.

Another king . . .

He told me every last detail about his grand good-bye to the life he'd lived before: moving his father's remains, fleeing the palatial Texas estate where he'd been raised, leaving messages—more than one, encrypted of course—to make it clear exactly what he knew. Spiraling, he'd partied his way across the country and ended up *here.*

The one thing he didn't seem to remember was meeting me in the bar.

"The kerosene—it wasn't my idea." He closed his eyes when he said that. We were lying on the floor of the shack now, and I laid on his ruined chest, where I could hear his heartbeat and know that he was still there, that he was alive.

He'd *promised* me that he would stay that way, no matter what.

"It wasn't my idea, but I agreed, because I'm *poison*." He made an attempt to roll out from underneath me, but I didn't let him. "No matter who gave birth to me or what blood runs in my veins, I'm a Hawthorne, everything my *father* raised me to be. I won't poison you, too, Hannah. You deserve—"

"*You*," I bit out. I pushed myself up into a sitting position and locked my eyes on to his. "I deserve *you*. I deserve to be happy, and you make me happy, you impossible, arrogant, self-destructive, infuriating, brilliant, *wonderful* son of a bitch."

He lifted his hand to my face, and in my mind, I could see the way he'd drawn me, could hear him murmuring, *There you are.*

"If I know one thing about my sister," I continued fiercely, "it's that Kaylie would want me to be happy, too." I wasn't going to avoid saying her name. He needed to know that I didn't have to pretend my sister away to look at him, to see him, to want him.

Anything is possible when you love someone with no regrets.

"I liked her." Toby breathed—in and out, and I tried to do for him what I'd done so many times, back when I'd hated him and he was half out of his mind with pain. I held his gaze, breathing through it with him.

"Your sister was worth ten of me and my friends," he said quietly, "and she knew it."

My throat tightened. My eyes stung. I laid my head back down on his chest, a physical, tangible sign to him that he wasn't going anywhere, and I told him about the dream. "*No regrets*," I reiterated when I was done. "She made me promise."

"God, Hannah, I'm so—"

"Don't tell me you're sorry." I put my hand to his mouth.

Words could never be enough, but *he* was. *We* were. "I don't want you to be *sorry*."

I wanted him to be mine.

He kissed me—just once, lightly, a ghost of a kiss, before we fell asleep. It wasn't until I woke up the next morning and found a letter where he should been that I realized...

That kiss had been *good-bye*.

Chapter 39

Dear Hannah, the same backward as forward…

I didn't read past the salutation on the letter. I ran to the lighthouse. He wasn't there. I ran across the rocks, miles across them, to the town where I'd planned to take him, where *we* were supposed to run.

Nothing. I couldn't find him. I looked, and I looked, and I looked, but he was gone.

Why hide, I thought, feeling like the sky was crashing down on me, like my body was folding in on itself until I couldn't breathe, *when you can run?*

Toby Hawthorne excelled at running, and deep inside, I *knew,* the way I knew his body and his scars and the way he smelled, that I wasn't going to find him. I *knew* that he wasn't coming back, knew it the way I knew how he felt through the darkness and what I looked like through his eyes.

I knew it the way I *knew* that we could have had something beautiful, if he'd let us.

I went back to Jackson's, and I read the whole damn letter, cursing Tobias Hawthorne the Second with every breath, aching for him like my body might never *stop* aching for him. He opened by begging me not to hate him—not for leaving, at least. If I was going to hate him, he wanted it to be for the right reasons.

> *You can tell me over and over again that I never would have struck the match. You can believe that. On good days, maybe I will, too. But three people are still dead because of me.*

I breathed through the pain, the way he had, back when his world had been fire and I'd hated him with everything I had.

I breathed through the pain, knowing that I couldn't hate him anymore, not even when I read the words: *I can't stay here. I can't stay with you.*

He could have. He *could* have stayed.

I couldn't stop reading.

> *I don't deserve to. I won't go home, either. I won't let my father pretend this away.*

Most of the rest of the letter was spent warning me that his father *would* come, that eventually, the billionaire with his many fixers would figure out that his son had survived. Toby didn't want me in Rockaway Watch when that happened. He wanted me to leave, just like we'd planned.

But alone.

> *Change your name. Start anew. You love fairy tales, I know, but I can't be your happily ever after. We can't stay here in our little castle forever. You have to find a new castle. You have to move on. You have to live, for me.*

He wasn't playing fair—not when I'd told him about the promise *I* had made, not when he knew that I had to keep living and keep dancing and keep feeling, no matter what.

If you ever need anything, go to Jackson.

My jaw hardened when I read that part, because I was pretty damn sure it meant that *he* had gone to Jackson on his way out. The next words confirmed it for me.

You know what the circle is worth. You know why. You know everything.

It was just like the boy who loved codes to use the vague descriptor—*the circle*. Let anyone who read this letter even *try* to figure out what that meant. But it was the next sentence that stole my breath:

You might be the only person on this planet who knows the real me.

I knew that he loved puzzles and riddles and games and being a pain in my ass. I knew that he was the kind of person who, when you asked how his pain was, answered *irrelevant*. He was an artist. He was brilliant. He was *hungry*. He was gentle. And he never missed picking up on a damn thing, especially when it involved me. He played three-dimensional checkers and quoted poetry, and I wasn't even sure he knew what a person could actually buy at a grocery store, other than bourbon and lemons. He loved palindromes.

He loved me.

I forced myself to read the last two lines of the letter:

Hate me, if you can, for all the reasons I deserve it. But don't hate me for leaving while you sleep. I knew you wouldn't let me go, and I cannot bear to say good-bye.

He'd signed it *Harry*.

There were no words for what I felt, reading that signature, thinking of him. My insides felt hollow, like a black hole. I couldn't even remember how to breathe.

But suddenly, there were arms around me. *Jackson*.

"You *let* him go." I pushed against the fisherman, hard, but he held tight to me. That crusty, cranky, gun-toting recluse held me until the dam inside me gave. I clung to him then—the closest thing I had in this world to a friend.

"Some people are like the ocean, little Hannah," Jackson told me, his voice as gruff as ever. "You can't let or not let them do a damn thing."

"Like the ocean," I repeated. I thought back to what he'd said about Death and made an educated guess. "A real bitch?"

"A force."

I wanted to sob, but I couldn't, because he was right. Toby Hawthorne was the damn ocean. He was a force. He was awful and wonderful and whether he was here or not, whether I ever saw him again or not—he was never going to be *nothing* to me.

I looked up at Jackson. "He says his father will come looking for him. The *item* that Toby gave you? It could be dangerous to hold on to it."

Jackson snorted. "I'm not afraid of billionaires. I don't even use banks. And that *item*? Harry asked me to hold on to it for you, so I'm thinking that's what I'll do."

There was no arguing with that, not unless I wanted him to go for his rifle.

"My family." I doubted this would go any better than trying to warn Jackson about Tobias Hawthorne had, but I had to try. "If the billionaire comes sniffing around, it could tip them off, too. My cousin Rory's already suspicious about what I've been up to. If he passes those suspicions on to my mother, if she figures out you helped Toby, helped *me*—"

"Who says I'm helping anyone?" Jackson chose that moment to press a wad of cash into my hand—a very large wad.

"Jackson," I said, "you can't—"

"Change your name," he told me sternly. "Don't look back. Sooner or later, Eden will go looking for you. Make sure she can't find a damn thing."

"How would you know what my mother would or wouldn't do?" I asked. He'd used her first name. I thought suddenly about the way he'd told me that I was the damnedest Rooney, like I wasn't the only one he knew. Personally. "Jackson—"

He cut me off: "None of your business."

I really should have seen that coming. "I'll go," I said. It was what Toby had asked of me. *You have to move on. You have to live, for me.* "I'll disappear," I told Jackson. "But what about you?"

"Someone's gotta look after the lighthouse."

I hugged him again. "You're a good man.

He narrowed his eyes at me. "I oughtta shoot you."

I almost smiled. "Please don't."

Chapter 40

Three months and a lot of covering my tracks later, I ended up in a town called New Castle, Connecticut, just about as far away from Rockaway Watch as I could get. I chose *Sarah* as my first name—not a palindrome. There were weeks at a time when I didn't want the reminder and weeks when all I could think about was puzzles and games and codes and *him*.

I danced every day.

I worked in a diner. I made friends with my coworkers. I thought now and then about going back to school, even if I had to start over, but at the end of the day, I didn't want to risk any connection to my old life, not even becoming a nurse.

I couldn't risk being found—not by my family and not by Toby's.

As the years went by, I slowly stopped expecting the tragedy on Hawthorne Island to end up back in the news, stopped expecting anyone else to discover what I knew: Somewhere out there, Toby Hawthorne was alive.

I loved him.

I loved him.

I loved him—and hated him, too. I tried to forget him—one

night with one man, and I ended up pregnant as a result. Almost from the beginning, in my mind, the baby was ours.

Toby's and mine.

I told myself that it was wrong. My baby had a father, though he was certainly no prince. I promised myself that when she was born, I was going to give her the actual father's last name. But in my heart, *she* was the fairy-tale ending Toby and I had been denied. She was my new beginning, and I swore that I would be her everything, that I would teach her how to play, how to make everything a game, how to find joy. *Every day.*

I swore that she would grow up dancing. She would never be invisible. She would always be loved. And someday, I'd tell her— all of it. My story. *Our* story.

Her due date came and went, but my baby showed no signs of making her appearance until the storm of the century rolled in. It was the worst I'd ever seen, worse even than the night of the fire, and I heard a whisper somewhere in my mind.

As far as I'm concerned, Hannah the Same Backward as Forward, you're the storm.

Hurricane-strength winds knocked out power lines and blew out windows. My apartment lost electricity—and that was when my water broke. There was no way I could drive. Streets were flooding. I tried calling 911 but couldn't even get through.

I told myself that I had time, that babies, especially first babies, didn't come *that* quickly, but each contraction hit me like my body was being split in two. I tried to make it to the door, feeling my way through the darkness, and suddenly, there he was.

"Harry." That name came first, then the other one, the true one. *"Toby."*

"I've got you, Hannah." He lifted me off the ground, and my head lolled against his chest as he continued. "The Same Backward as Forward."

The next contraction hit, the worst yet, but I didn't scream, the same way he hadn't, as I'd nursed him through agony all those nights.

He was here.

He was here.

He was here.

And she was coming.

Somehow, he got me into my bedroom and onto my bed. I could feel myself on the verge of losing consciousness, but his voice brought me back.

"I wrote to you."

The lights flickered, and suddenly, I could *see* him. All I wanted was to see him. "I hate you," I said, but the words came out tender—a love song. *Our* love song.

"I know." He pushed my knees up, put two pillows beneath my head, pressed sweat-drenched hair back from my face.

"For leaving," I clarified, thinking of that damn letter. "I hate you for leaving and *only* for leaving, and, for the record? I love you, too."

My voice gave way to a scream, and his hand slipped into mine. I held on so tightly I half expected the bones in his fingers to break, but he never even flinched.

I love you.

I love you.

I love you.

"You son of a bitch," I said, breathing the words the moment I could. "I love you, *you bastard.*"

"You're almost there."

I glared at him. "I want the letters you wrote me."

My glare triggered his smirk, like not even the years and the miles he'd put between us could circumvent that reaction. "They're postcards, actually."

He looked years older than he had the last time I'd seen him—harder, sun-worn. His tan wasn't even. His shirt was threadbare. Facial hair marked his jawline, and still, I knew every line of his face.

"I want," I said, my body seizing with pain, "my *postcards*."

"One more push," he told me, "and you can have them."

I love you.

I love you.

I love you.

I didn't realize I'd said a damn thing until he said it back.

"I love you," Toby Hawthorne told me. "I have loved you from the moment you dumped a half-dozen lemons on my bed. From before that, even. From the moment I saw you folding paper, from the first sugar castle, from the instant you promised me a merciful death and *lied*."

I couldn't do this, but I had to. For the baby, I had to. I pushed, and I screamed.

"I loved you," he whispered, "when the world was pain and the only thing that made sense was your eyes. I loved you before I knew to hate myself, and I have loved you every day since."

I love you.

I love you.

I love you.

And then he had her. She was real, and she was there, and for a single moment in time, she was *ours*. And then the ambulance arrived. I didn't even remember him calling it. I had no idea how he'd gotten through.

The love of my life tucked my brand-new baby onto my chest, and just like that, he was gone.

Like the wind.

Like a dream.

Chapter 41

He came to me hours later in the hospital. My daughter—*precious, precious girl*—was asleep on my chest. The birth certificate sat on the table next to my bed. I'd filled out the last name—her biological father's, *Grambs*—and the middle name.

"Kylie." Toby's voice was quiet and low. "Like Kaylie, minus one letter."

"An homage," I said. "I was forbidden from anything else."

Toby stared at me for the longest time, and I knew that he was thinking about everything I'd told him about the dream. *No regrets.*

Eventually, he turned his attention to the bedside table and the birth certificate. He picked up a pen.

"What are you doing?" I asked.

"Signing." He never had been held back by little things like decency or rules. "For him."

I didn't question how he knew the father's name or why he was signing. I wanted him to. In my heart, she was *his.*

"Stay," I said softly.

"I can't, Hannah. My father—he knows I'm alive. Everywhere I go, he's never far behind. He wants me or what I took or both. I won't let him near you." He looked down at the baby, sleeping on my chest. "I won't let him anywhere near *her.*"

Given what I knew, I couldn't argue with that. Seeing Toby holding my daughter, I finally let myself think that maybe my happily ever after wasn't ever meant to be with him.

Maybe it was always *her*, this perfect little girl.

"Take her," I told him. "Hold her, just this once."

I expected him to fight me on it, but he didn't. He held my baby girl like she was ours, and *our* girl looked so tiny in his arms. He cradled her against his chest.

"Are there scars?" I asked him.

"Numerous scars," he told me, and something about the way he said it made me think that he cherished them—every single one. He lowered his head, nuzzling the top of hers, and my daughter opened her eyes and looked straight at the man I loved.

"Avery," Toby murmured. It took me a moment to realize that he'd just suggested a name. "Avery Kylie Grambs." Toby looked from the baby to me with a crooked little smile. "Rearrange the letters."

We wouldn't have been *us* without one last challenge, one last game.

"Avery Kylie Grambs," I said slowly, "rearranged..." My eyes met his. He handed the baby—handed *Avery*—back to me. "A Very Risky Gamble," I murmured.

"I knew you'd solve it." He lowered himself to his knees beside my hospital bed. "You always do."

I didn't want to put her in her bassinet. I didn't want to fall asleep. I didn't want to blink. I didn't want him to go.

But he did.

He left me a stack of postcards—written in invisible ink.

Epilogue

Careful," I told Avery. At the ripe old age of eighteen months, she was getting bolder about climbing the booths in the diner. She'd been a serious baby, but as a toddler, she was pure, undiluted chaos.

Pure joy.

She was *ours*. Ricky Grambs had only seen her twice. I didn't care. Avery didn't seem to, either. We were a world unto ourselves. Soon enough, I'd be teaching her to build castles out of sugar.

But for now, my shift was over, and it was getting closer to dancing o'clock. Sweeping her up on my hip, I headed for the door—but didn't make it all the way there.

"Pardon me."

A *customer*. I could have directed her to someone else, but some customers didn't really appreciate the idea of a waitress ever going off shift.

"Do you need a table?" I asked.

The woman's age was hard to peg—older than me, but beneath the red kerchief she wore tied under her chin, her hair didn't seem to have a single strand of gray.

"Why don't we sit?" she said. Her tone very much implied that was not a suggestion.

My survival instincts kicked into gear. *Why would we—*

She reached up to untie her red scarf, then held it out to Avery, who immediately locked it in a little toddler death grip.

"I believe you may have been expecting my husband." The woman stepped around me—toward a booth. "Toby's father will find you eventually, I'm sure."

Toby. Mine was the kind of quiet that didn't blink. Didn't flinch. *Her husband?* Based on everything I'd read, Toby's mother had died less than a year after the fire on Hawthorne Island.

And yet...

And yet...

And yet...

"But for now," the woman said, taking a seat in the booth and nodding for me to do the same, "you'll deal with me."

That night, I couldn't sleep. I invented a new game to play with Avery, one she'd need to be a little older to join in on. I smoothed a hand over her baby-fine hair as she slept, unwilling to let her out of my sight, unwilling to so much as put her down.

I'd been given an offer.

I'd turned it down.

That was supposed to be the end of it.

But still, I couldn't sleep. I sat in the rocking chair I'd bought at Goodwill, and I rocked my sleeping baby, and I played our new game, whispering into the night.

"I have a secret..."

THE COWBOY AND THE GOTH

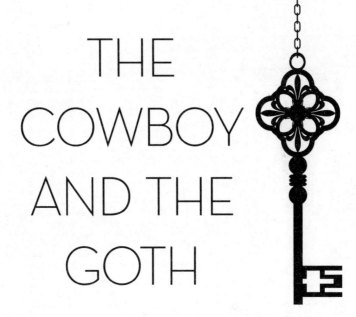

He brings his lips to just almost
touch mine, a silent reminder that
I don't have to say a word, that
he has never and will never
demand from me anything that
I don't want to give.

Now

I've never really excelled at taking tests, but even I can pee on a stick. Once the deed is accomplished, I take a deep and cleansing breath and set the test on the counter, resisting the urge to nibble my chipped, neon-blue thumbnail as I wait.

And wait.

And wait.

As bad as I am at tests, I'm usually pretty good at waiting. Some optimists see a glass filled partway and call it half full; I've always been the kind of optimist who can look at a cup that contains a single drop of water and imagine that cup overflowing—with Mountain Dew. I am practically a professional at daydreaming a bright side into existence when really there is none.

But now? Standing in an enormous, sparkling marble bathroom bigger than my first apartment, waiting to see if a second pink line appears on that stick, I look from the pregnancy test to the ring on my left ring finger: a deep red stone that glows almost black in some lights. It's a garnet, not a ruby, and he cut the stone himself.

It's perfect.

I think about the man who put this ring on my finger, and for once in my life, I don't daydream anything. I remember.

And remember.

And *remember*.

Then

The cowboy is looking at me. It's not a fleeting kind of look. Nash Hawthorne's gaze is like a gentle, calloused thumb brushing lightly over my cheekbone, just under my blackened eye.

"What happened here?" His voice is a low and even murmur. No machismo. No swagger. No pity, either. But it's clear that I have Nash's attention. *All* of it.

I raise my chin. "I'm fine."

"I can see that." His voice is whiskey-smooth and steady in a way that makes me think that he could walk through fire and not even blink. "But if you decide you'd like to give me a name?" There it is again—the *feel* of his gaze, the lightest of touches. "I'd take it."

His eyes are brown, darker around the outside and center of his irises and almost amber in between. The expression in those eyes is measured—but deep. This cowboy would very much like the name of the man who gave me a black eye, but somehow, Nash doesn't feel angry to me. Every instinct I have says he isn't the stormy type.

Nash Hawthorne is pale blue skies. He's grass and mud. He's *steady*.

And I probably shouldn't even be looking at those amber-and-mahogany eyes of his, because even the daydreamer in me knows that *steady* and *gentle* and *good* would never be interested in me.

Then

W ord of advice, darlin'—might be you'll want to keep a closer eye on that kid sister of yours."

I've been at Hawthorne House for a few days, which is long enough to realize that, while Nash Hawthorne might not be the type to order me around, he isn't above making *suggestions*, in that slow-talking, casual, *we're just having a little chat over a game of pool* kind of way.

Casual suggestion, my ass.

"Avery is fine," I tell him. I'm not usually prone to arguing with people, but (a) he's wrong about my sister, who wants to major in something called *actuarial science* and who wouldn't know teenage rebellion if it bopped her on the nose, and (b) I kind of like arguing with Nash Hawthorne.

He lines up his next shot and gives every appearance of being casual about that, too, but I'm not fooled. The cowboy might take his time with things—*and people*—but we both know damn well, before he ever takes the shot, that he's going to sink it.

I'm pretty sure he could do it with his eyes closed.

Within a minute, two more balls have gone down, too, and his cowboy hat comes off.

"Avery," Nash Hawthorne drawls, going around to the far side of the pool table, "is trouble." His gaze flicks up toward mine. "That's not a criticism, by the way. My brothers and I—we're trouble, too."

That is an understatement.

As Nash casually lines up another shot, I try not to notice the way the muscles in his shoulders and back pull at his white T-shirt, the kind of shirt that looks like it's been worn a thousand times.

"Avery has never been any trouble," I insist. "She takes care of herself." What I don't say is that I *wish* my little sister was more trouble. I wish I was the strong one. Or the smart one. The sister with a plan.

"You take care of her." There's something soft and deep in Nash's voice when he says that.

I look away. "When she lets me." My eyes find their way back to his.

Down, girl, I tell myself. Even playing pool with Nash Hawthorne is probably a mistake—see also: muscles beneath that white T-shirt. But my life has been turned upside down, and Nash is pretty much the only one I have to talk to in the grand mansion that is Hawthorne House. This place is a forty-thousand-square-foot Wonderland with a basketball court and a bowling alley and two theaters and a spa, and left to my own devices, I am almost certainly going to get lost or break something or sneeze on some priceless artifact that's just lying around.

Nash Hawthorne is the lesser of two evils. He stays on his side of the pool table, and I stay on mine—but he sure doesn't seem to be in any hurry to look away from me.

He sinks his next shot without ever looking down.

"Show-off," I mutter.

Nash straightens and lets the end of his pool cue rest on the ground. "There's a difference," he says in that Texas drawl of his, unhurried and smooth, "between showin' off and deciding you're done giving a damn about people who expect you to dim your light so they can feel more like the sun."

It sure doesn't feel like he's talking about *himself*.

Wordlessly, he passes his pool stick over the table to me. "Your turn."

It has not escaped my attention that he never missed a shot, but I don't argue—about that. "You're wrong about Avery," I say, as I sink my own shot, determined to change the subject back to the one thing that feels safe, the reason I'm here at all. "My sister isn't trouble. She's like a miniature adult." A strand of blue hair falls into my face, and I blow it out of the way. "She's better at being a grown-up than I am."

"That so?" Nash saunters around the table from his side to mine, and there's just something about the way he moves, like he would approach a herd of wild horses the same way he's walking toward me now. "Because from where I'm standing, sure looks like you're giving up everything for the kid."

"Yeah, well..." I look down *"Everything* wasn't much."

"Some of us don't need much." Nash's voice is quiet now. "Just something small to call our own and the feeling that we're doing something—anything—*right*."

Yes, something in me whispers—and I stop myself right there. Right freaking there! *Do not pass go, Libby! Do not collect two hundred dollars!* Nash Hawthorne is the grandson of a billionaire. He grew up *here*, in this mansion of mansions, the world at his fingertips.

What does he know about small dreams?

The cowboy responds like he's literally read my mind. "Never was too fond of all this." Nash looks up at the soaring ceilings and shrugs. "Give me a one-bedroom apartment on top of a dive bar any day—preferably with a few things that need fixing. Maybe some books the previous resident left behind." Nash leans against the pool table. "A place I can go to see the sky."

"You have all of this, and you don't even want it?" I can't help the question, can't help wanting to understand him, even though I know exactly how dangerous that desire is.

I have a history of bad decision-making—*VERY BAD DECISION-MAKING*—when it comes to men. And he's a Hawthorne.

"I want other things." Nash shrugs again. "But this is where I'm needed, and no matter how often I take off for parts unknown, I always come back."

"For your brothers." I don't phrase that as a question, because it's not one. *You take care of people, too.* I miss my next shot and pass the pool cue back to him.

The cowboy beside me has the audacity to *wink* as he lines up his next shot with the cue behind his back. "Now," Nash drawls, "I'm showing off."

I roll my eyes, but I'm also grinning—not a good sign, but I need a friend right now. *Just à friend*, I tell myself sternly.

A friend who takes care of his little brothers.

A friend who's watching out for my sister.

A friend who wears worn white T-shirts that look *soft* and *thin*.

"I'll make you a bet, Libby Grambs." Nash nods to the pocket in which he's getting ready to sink the eight ball, does the deed, and sets the pool cue down. "If that sister of yours proves me wrong on the *trouble* front, I'll stop showing off."

I shouldn't bite, but I do. "What happens if Avery proves you right?"

"If I win..." Nash's smile is slow and steady, a match for the pace of his words. "You promise to *start* showing off." He picks his cowboy hat up off the side of the pool table. "And I'm buyin' you a hat."

Then

Objectively, there are worse places to be than on a private jet with Nash Hawthorne. He sits on one side of the aisle, and I sit on the other. We are grown-ups on a mission. That mission just took us to my hometown, and it's getting ready to take us to Costa Rica.

Costa Rica. I don't know whose life I'm living, but it's definitely not mine.

Across the aisle of the *private jet*, Nash is looking out a window into open sky, and I'm reminded that Nash Hawthorne *is* wide open spaces and barely damp dirt, the smell of leather and the heat of the sun. Right now, he needs to shave.

I hope he doesn't.

"You'll want to keep ahold of that letter." Nash's voice rolls over me like wind through wheat. "And the envelope," he adds. "Hawthornes are awfully fond of invisible ink."

We are on a Hawthorne hunt. The homeless man who used to play chess in the park with my sister is a secret, not-actually-dead Hawthorne, and honestly? That is not the strangest thing about my life right now.

My hair is brown. Just...brown. I'm wearing it braided back from my face, but unfortunately, I suck at braiding. Being respectable doesn't come easily to me. I can't even sit with my legs on the floor. They're tucked up under my body in this oversized, leather, *private jet* seat.

I'm trying my best to be something I'm not—for Avery's sake. I keep looking out the window, and then looking at Nash, and I *really, really* hope he doesn't have time to shave any time soon.

"Don't take this the wrong way," I say, as his eyes settle comfortably on mine. "But your family is weird. And that's coming from *me*."

The difference is that Hawthornes are weird the way that Stonehenge is weird—magnificent and inexplicable. Hawthornes are invisible-ink weird. Hidden-passageways and secret-traditions weird. They are—and this is an actual example—I-dare-you-to-lick-that-Picasso weird.

"I don't know," Nash says. "You never struck me as all that odd."

I am blue hair and black nails, skulls and sparkles—or at least, I was. "You're just saying that because I'm playing normal now."

Nash Hawthorne's shrugs should be considered deadly weapons. The man shrugs, and it is impossible *not* to imagine him shirtless. "You seemed normal enough before," he tells me.

I have spent my entire life wanting to be *normal* and *special*, wanting to be both of those things at the exact same time, even though they are pretty much opposites.

"I guess no matter what," I say softly, "I'm still me."

"Don't say that like it's a bad thing, darlin'." Nash leans across the aisle, catching my gaze and holding it.

"Don't call me darling," I tell him, like I'm not counting the rings in his eyes.

"My apologies." Nash does not sound sorry. I get the sense

that he'd rather I be glaring at him than be sad. "Is Libby short for Elizabeth?"

"No." I mean to stop there. I really do. "I'm pretty sure my mom thought it was short for Little Bitch." This is exactly why I am an optimist. I've always *had* to be one. Sometimes, believing the best in people who don't deserve it, believing that they love you even if they don't—sometimes, that's all a person can do to survive. "Sorry," I say. "I guess going back home got to me more than I thought."

Nash moves across the aisle to sit next to me. He puts his hand under my chin and raises my eyes to meet his. "Don't you ever apologize for the things you've survived."

There are moments in life when time slows down, when the world fades away until the only thing that exists is two people, looking at each other. *Nash. Me.*

After an eternity and then some—but not nearly long enough—he leans across me to flip up the shade on my window. "Look out there."

I turn and stare at the brilliant green-blue ocean below, even though all I really want to be looking at is him. All my hands want to do is touch his face, feel the grit of his more-than-just-five-o'clock-shadow beneath my fingers.

Whoa there, Libby!

I reel it back in. Outside the plane window, I can see land. Trees, mostly, and the very top of a beautiful, ancient, work-of-art kind of building coming into view.

"What's that?" I ask when what I'm really thinking is that Nash Hawthorne *isn't* weird—not my kind of weird and not the Hawthorne kind, either. Mr. Motorcycle Cowboy has never worried about being normal or tried to be special. Unlike his brothers, this man has never in his life dared someone to lick a Picasso.

Nash Hawthorne just *is*. He's wide-open spaces and barely damp dirt and *here*. His hand finds its way to the back of my neck, beneath my messy, messy braid, and he answers my question like it's the most natural thing in the world.

What's that?

"Cartago."

Then

Finding the Cartago house—one of many, many vacation homes owned by Tobias Hawthorne and left to my sister— is not the hard part. Getting to it is.

"There were few things the old man loved more than a house built into a cliff." Nash doesn't seem too fussed about that. "There's a path somewhere." His gaze rolls over the thick, lush vegetation that seems to cover every possible route up. "What do you think, Lib? Do we look for the hidden path or borrow a machete and make our own?"

I give him a look. "Who's going to loan you a machete?"

Nash executes one of those shrugs of his, as if to say *Who wouldn't loan me a machete?* And honestly? He's probably right. Nash Hawthorne has a way with people.

I look up at the wild, green, practically vertical stretch of land separating us from the house at the top of the cliff. "I don't want to cut anything down if we don't have to."

It's beautiful here. It's real.

Nash takes in the view. "The hidden path it is," he says.

"Let's try…" I take a deep breath, then point. "This way!"

"Lead on, darlin'. I trust your instincts."

"Oh, my instincts should definitely not be trusted," I say. "Pretty much ever."

Nash looks at me for a moment, then shifts his gaze back to the tangle of tropical plants standing between us and our destination. "It's funny," he says.

"What is?"

"The old man had a way of planning for everything." Nash starts walking in the direction I indicated. "But I'm bettin' he didn't plan on you."

I make a face. "Why would he?" In the world of billionaire Tobias Hawthorne, what was I?

"I'm not sayin' he didn't realize you would come with Avery." Nash keeps right on walking. "Of course he did."

"Then what are you saying?" I probably shouldn't even be asking, but I want to know. I really, really want to know.

"I'm saying"—Nash doesn't drop the *g* this time—"that I trust your instincts, and I'm almost positive the old man never planned on that. He didn't realize that you would be . . . you."

Me. At the exact same time, Nash and I both see a break in the brush. I push past low-hanging limbs on green, green trees. Nash is right on my heels, and like magic, the path—practically a tunnel through the vegetation—reveals itself, winding up, up, up.

"How's your endurance?" Nash asks.

"Relentlessly optimistic and also stubborn." I grin. "How's yours?"

Brown eyes linger on mine. "I was built for the long haul."

For the longest time, the two of us just climb. I've never been this comfortable with silence before. But eventually, my brain starts to play a little game called What If He Takes Off His Shirt?

I break the silence. "Have you ever been here?"

"To this house or Costa Rica?" Nash looks over at me, but neither one of us stops climbing.

"Either." I'm breathing hard, but it feels good. "Both."

"Yes on the country, no on the house. I don't exactly like to travel in style." Before I can ask why, he elaborates. "I like to sweat. I like going to sleep at night with aching muscles, my body spent, knowing that I did something real. I like having to find my own way, and I like meeting folks where they are—on their terms, not mine."

This man. I don't let myself think anything other than that. "Meeting folks," I echo. "And borrowing their machetes."

Nash grins—and both of us keep hiking.

"Your grandfather." Again, I'm the one who breaks the silence. "You always refer to him as *the old man.*"

This is almost certainly none of my business, but it's something I've been wondering about for a while.

Nash doesn't seem to take umbrage at the question. "Makes him sound mortal, I suppose."

"Mortal," I repeat. "As opposed to...Zeus?"

In front of us, a branch blocks the path. Nash lifts it for me to duck under. "He liked to think so, but if you ask me, he was closer to Daedalus, always making labyrinths, hiding monsters, pushing all of us to fly too close to the sun."

He lifts another branch, and we come to a clearing—just enough of one to see the wildflowers and vines growing into the very walls of a small but stunning house, one that looks like it's always been here, like it wasn't *built* so much as called forth from the earth.

"And there she is," Nash says. He nods to the doorframe. "See the upper-left corner? It looks like it's coming apart, but..." He heads that way and stretches one hand overhead, and the next thing I know, he has a key.

The head of the key is ornate, its design complicated and in no way a match for the house. It's a very *Hawthorne* kind of key.

"Could be a decoy," Nash tells me. Instead of trying it on the house, he holds it out to me. "You feelin' lucky, Lib?"

I take the key from him. "I always *feel* lucky. Reality just doesn't always get the memo." But this time is different. When I try the key, the door opens.

We step straight into a living area. Beyond it, I can see a small kitchen and a twisting metal staircase going up to the second floor. "What now?" I say. "What are we looking for?"

This house is part of a trail laid by the dead billionaire—a puzzle, a game. I take another step forward—or at least, I try to, but suddenly, Nash's hand is on my arm.

Suddenly, his body is right in front of mine.

"There's food cooking on the stove." Nash's voice is low. There's not a single hint of tension in his muscles, but that doesn't mean there's no *danger* here.

Overhead, a floorboard creaks. Nash shifts, his movement liquid, his body a shield for mine. I peek around him to see someone descending the stairs. At first, all I can make out is shoes. Men's shoes.

I think about why we're here—our Hawthorne hunt. "Do you think it's him?" I whisper. *Toby Hawthorne.*

"Could be," Nash says under his breath. "Either that, or we're in a labyrinth, and that's the Minotaur." I don't have time to read much into that before he raises his voice. "We're not intruders," he calls out. "We're Hawthornes."

"I'm not," I whisper behind him, keeping my voice too low for anyone but Nash to hear.

"You're one of ours," he murmurs back, his eyes staying locked on the stairs. "Close enough."

One of ours. The words linger as the possible-Minotaur—who is definitely not Toby Hawthorne—steps into view. There's something familiar about the man, but I can't put my finger on what.

It might be the way he moves.

"Hi," I say brightly, taking the bull by the horns—no Minotaur pun intended. "I'm Libby, and this is—"

The man across from us gives a little nod. "Nash."

I look from the man to Nash. "You two know each other?"

"He wasn't saying my name." Nash never takes his eyes off the man. "He was introducing himself."

And suddenly, I realize: This man's last name is *Nash*. He doesn't seem overly fussed with our sudden appearance here, doesn't so much as bat an eye.

Like father, like son.

Then

An hour later, Nash and I have what we came for, and we find a bar. I don't feel the least bit guilty about not heading straight for the jet. Nash just met *his father*. Libations are needed.

I also try to offer up a distraction. "What do you think is in here?" I pick up the small glass vial that Tobias Hawthorne gave Jake Nash years earlier—the one Jake was instructed to give any Hawthorne who came looking. Inside the vial, there's some kind of purple powder.

Nash says something in Spanish to the bartender, then takes up position on a barstool and answers my question. "Just another part of the old man's game."

Shot glasses are placed in front of us. Nash takes one and hands me the other.

"Cheers." I down my shot, no hesitation. It burns all the way down. "So." I give Nash a look. "Your father."

"Seems like a nice enough guy."

I reach for him, my fingers curling around his. Nash is used to being the protector. He's not used to being protected, but right now, that's too damn bad. I give his hand a squeeze.

Nash squeezes back, then takes his own shot. "I shouldn't be surprised. Money talks."

Jake Nash has spent twenty years in Cartago, living high and free—and far, far away from his son.

"Hypothetically," I say cheerfully, "what are your thoughts on laying a curse on the bones of a man who is already dead? Because I know people."

"Of course you do." Nash grins and then he picks up his empty shot glass. "The old man was a real bastard." Those words are said with no heat. "But he mostly ignored me. I was more of what you might call a group effort—Zara, the Laughlins, Nan, my grandmother Alice..."

"No one ever talks about her," I note.

"She drank jasmine tea and loved to throw parties." Nash smiles slightly. "I can remember her dressing me up in little suits. And if I happened to make a mud pie while wearing one of them, her response was usually to compliment my recipe." He shook his head. "I don't remember much more than that. She died before Grayson was born. Once Alice was gone, the old man's focus shifted. Gray, Jamie, and Xan—they were Tobias Hawthorne's from the cradle. The old man tried stepping in with me, too, but I wasn't exactly obliging." He nods to the bartender, and the next thing I know, we have a second round of shots.

Nash lifts his eyes and meets my mine. "To us," he says. "To being better than *they* were."

They. His grandfather. His father. His mother. And *my* parents, too. I think about Nash back on the plane, telling me not to apologize for the things I've survived.

To us. I take the shot, and then I decide that I am done being sad—for either of us. I point a finger at Nash. "You," I say emphatically, "need a Magic 8 Ball."

He cocks a brow. "That a kind of shot?"

From his expression, it is impossible to tell if that's a joke. I smile slightly and give him an earnest reply. "It's a toy. You know—you ask it a question, give it a shake, it gives you an answer?" My body is still burning from the second shot. It's a good kind of heat. "I used to lay in bed at night," I tell Nash, "and find a million different ways of asking the Magic 8 Ball if things would get better."

I've never told anyone that before.

"And most of the time, it told you it would." Nash gets it immediately.

"It's possible," I say loftily, "that I allotted myself a generous number of redos if I didn't like the answer." I point my finger at him again. Two shots in, and I am super pointy. "Come on, cowboy. I'm the Magic 8 Ball. You're the one with the question."

Is this a mistake? Probably. But I'm starting to think that everyone deserves at least one mistake in this life that they wouldn't take back, even if they could.

"Okay, Magic 8 Ball." Nash, as always, takes his time. "Am I going to be able to talk the indomitable Miss Libby here into a third shot before we head back to the jet?"

I take a moment to commune with the universe and consider my answer. "Ask again later."

Nash is, as ever, undaunted. "Am I ever gonna get to see you with blue hair again?"

I push down the urge to touch the tips of my hair. I dyed it for Avery. To be respectable. To stop being *me*. "You don't like the brown?" The question slips out.

Nash turns on his barstool to face me. "I like that *you* like the blue." He cocks a brow. "So...?" he prompts.

I swallow. "Signs point to yes."

Nash's next question surprises me. "Will I ever see Jake Nash again?" Asking that question is as close as he's come to admitting that he's hurting, that he wants more from the man responsible for half of his DNA.

No matter how much I want to, I can't lie to Nash. "My sources say no."

He chews on that for a moment, and then he moves on. "Will I ever get to see you in a cowboy hat?"

I narrow my eyes at him. "Don't count on it."

"That sounds like a challenge. And for the record, darlin', I'm pretty sure I'm winning that *trouble* bet we made about your sister."

Given the number of secrets Avery has been keeping, I'm not sure I can argue. But I'm also not about to tell him there's even the slightest chance that he's right.

"One more question," I tell him instead.

"What are your thoughts on going ax throwing?" Nash smiles what I think of as his cowboy smile, understated and slow. "With me."

This is definitely a mistake. *We* are. But I can't help myself. "Outlook good."

Maybe it's the alcohol. Maybe it's Cartago. Maybe it's the fact that Nash Hawthorne has never even seemed to realize that the two of us don't make any sense at all.

"My turn." Nash is still smiling that same cowboy smile. "Ask me something."

What do you see when you look at me? That isn't a yes or no question. *Am I just another person for you to save?* Nope. I'm not asking that, either. But there is something I want to know, something I would ask the Magic 8 Ball if I had one with me now.

"Would Avery's mom be proud of me?"

It's probably a silly question, but Avery's mother was the only person, when I was a kid, who ever made me feel special. And normal. She made me feel like I was both of those things at the same time, even though they weren't the same at all.

Nash, in the role of Magic 8 Ball, considers my question, communes with the universe—and then he lifts his hand to my face, pushing his fingers back into my thoroughly demolished braid. "It is decidedly so."

That's a real Magic 8 Ball answer. *You knew exactly what I was talking about the whole time, cowboy.*

"How about that drink?" Nash murmurs.

One last drink, and then we'll have to go back. To my sister. To his brothers. To reality.

I put my hand on the back of *his* neck. "Outlook good."

Then

"You can never have too many cupcakes," I announce—for my own benefit—as I pull my sixth dozen for the day out of the oven.

I am not avoiding Nash Hawthorne.

Really. Truly. I am not—

And here he is. The moment he steps foot in the kitchen, I try to act normal, like Cartago never happened. "Choose your poison," I tell the cowboy. "You're probably going to want a napkin."

There is a slight chance that I may have been going overboard on the frosting.

"Lib."

One word—my name, shortened in that very Nash Hawthorne way. But it's enough for me to know: *Something is wrong.*

"What is it?" I start across the kitchen toward him. He's wearing yet another T-shirt that's seen better days. This one is a deep, mossy green.

Every muscle in his body is taut.

"It's Avery." Two words—just two, but they have me coming to a complete and utter halt. Nash Hawthorne could walk through fire without batting an eye. If an earthquake hit, and the ground beneath him cracked, he'd just shift his weight and wait for the aftershock to pass. But right now, there is *nothing* casual about Nash Hawthorne.

"What about Avery?" I barely get the words out.

"I need you to breathe for me." Nash closes what little space remains between us in a single breath. His arms wrap around me.

He's got me.

"I am breathing," I lie.

"Breathe, Lib." He pulls me against him. My head on his chest, I breathe in Nash Hawthorne.

"What happened?" I whisper. His T-shirt is soft against my cheek.

"First thing you need to know is that she's alive." Nash's voice isn't any gentler than usual, and I am so damn grateful for that. He keeps one arm curved around me, and the other makes its way to the back of my head. "Second thing you need to know is that there was a bomb."

What? No. "What kind of bomb?" The instant I force out the question, the self-protective part of my brain clicks on. "Like a metaphorical bomb? A little, totally legal, firework-style not-really-a-bomb bomb?"

I see Nash's chest rise and fall, and I realize that the only reason I am breathing is because my chest is rising and falling in unison with his.

"Tell me Avery made a movie that did really bad at the box office." I'm practically begging now.

His hands come to the side of my face, his thumbs cupping my jaw, his fingers curving back around my neck.

This is bad. This is very bad.

"Her plane exploded." His chest rises and falls. Mine rises and falls. I'm still breathing. I'm still just barely breathing. "The jet was on the ground at the time," Nash continues quietly. "Avery wasn't in it, but she was close enough to get caught in the blast."

"No." I will not let this be true.

"Libby—"

"Absolutely, positively *not*." I wrench my head from his hands—or at least, I try to, but he won't let me go.

"Ask me if she's going to be okay."

My mouth is so dry, it feels like my tongue might crack. "Is she going to be okay?"

"She's trouble." Nash leans his forehead down to touch mine. "We're gonna have to keep an eye on that one, Lib. You and me."

My heart feels like it's tearing in two, but I won't let it. "We're going to take care of her," I say, because that's what we do, Nash and me. We take care of people.

"Damn right we are," the cowboy says. "And she is going to be just fine."

I hear what he isn't saying: "She has to be." She might not be, but she *has to be*—and Nash Hawthorne and I are damn well going to make it so.

Then

've barely left Avery's side, except to talk to the doctors. So many doctors. My head is spinning—though that might be the fact that I haven't really been eating, which is why Nash just forced me to go to the cafeteria.

He promised he'd watch Avery while I was gone.

Coming back down the hall toward Avery's room, I can hear Nash's low, steady voice—far more familiar than it should be—talking to my sister.

"Far be it from me to issue threats here, kid, but if you think for even a second that you're gonna stop fightin'? You've got another thing coming." Nash is using the same tone I've heard him use to pull rank on his brothers. "You don't get to give up, Avery Grambs."

I step into the room to see the cowboy holding my sister's hand in his.

"That's the thing about being loved, kid. It ties you to people." Nash sees me then, but he doesn't let go of Avery's hand. "And once you're tied to one of us, you're tied to all of us. And the thing about Hawthornes is . . ."

I sit down next to him, take her hand *with* him.

"Hawthornes never," Nash Hawthorne tells my comatose sister, "let go."

There's a person that Nash hasn't let go of—not completely. She was his fiancée once. They grew up together. She is everything I am not, and I just found out that she's playing games with Avery's life, the kind of games that involved smuggling my comatose sister out of the hospital *while I was asleep in the room.*

"Have you lost your pantsuit-loving mind?" I am yelling—*really* yelling.

"Calm down," Alisa Ortega says, all business.

"You don't get to tell me to calm down!" I have never bellowed in my life before, but I sure as hell am now. We're back at Hawthorne House, which has always felt like Alisa's home turf far more than mine, but I'm not about to back down. "Avery's in critical condition, and *you had her moved.*"

I am shaking. Literally shaking. Legally, Alisa Ortega shouldn't have been able to do a damn thing. I'm Avery's guardian. Not her. *Me.* And I know she hates that. I know that she has looked at me and, from day one, seen a liability.

"I did what needed to be done." There's emotion in Alisa's tone now, more of it than makes sense—until I realize that Nash just walked into the hall.

"For the money." Nash Hawthorne walks toward us—toward her—step after slowly considered step. "You did what needed to be done *for the money.*"

If Avery had stayed at the hospital any longer, she would have lost her inheritance. That's why Alisa brought her back to Hawthorne House, why the lawyer risked my sister's life to make it so.

"She's fine." Alisa raises her chin. She's looking at Nash and only Nash, and I'm struck by all the ways they fit and don't fit. He's dirt and warm wind. She's boardrooms and heels clicking onto tile. But there's history there, something between them that's not cool or warm.

Something that burned hot once.

"Avery," Alisa says, the slightest catch in her voice, "is going to *thank me*."

"If it were up to me..." Nash never raises his voice. "You'd never step foot near the kid again."

For all her poise, the great Alisa Ortega looks like he just knocked the wind from her lungs. "Nash."

Just from the way she says his name, I feel like I shouldn't be here—not watching the two of them and not with him, either.

"You don't mean that," Alisa continues, every inch the lawyer laying out her conditions and terms.

"You don't get to tell me what I mean, Lee-Lee." Nash turns away from her then. "You never did."

Before he can say a single thing to me, I flee.

That night, Nash comes to Avery's room. It's right across from mine, but I haven't even so much as laid down on my own bed.

My sister is going to wake up.

She is going to be fine.

She is going to kiss Jameson Hawthorne, who comes to see her every day. I am going to have to keep an eye on those two when she wakes up, which she is going to do, because *everything will be fine*.

"I brought you something." Nash sits down beside me, next to Avery's bed.

"It had better not be a cowboy hat," I say. I can't quite bring myself to look at Nash—not after being the third wheel in his fight with Alisa. "Is it soup?"

"It's not soup." Nash sets a plastic bag at my feet.

I lean down to inspect the contents, and my heart jumps into my throat. "What's this?"

I'm not asking what it actually is, because I have eyes, and I can see that's he bought me a veritable rainbow of hair dyes. Bright colors, all of them.

"Your sister needs you," Nash tells me, and then his hands find their way to my face—*again*. I can't help remembering the other times, can't help remembering *Cartago*. "She needs *you*, Lib."

The real me. That's what he's saying. I am dyed-neon hair and dark nails and way too much kohl rimming my eyes. I'm thigh-high boots and black velvet chokers. I'm not normal. I'm not special.

I'm *me*. "I can't, Nash," I whisper.

Jameson appears in the doorway, and I vacate the spot beside Avery's bed so he can take it. I make my way out into the hall, and Nash does the same.

"I can't," I tell him again. I don't know if I'm talking about the hair dye or *him* or *us* or the fact that I can't keep doing nothing when my sister is in a medically induced coma, when she might never wake up.

Nash takes the bag of dyes from my hand. "I can," he says. "If you let me."

Then

My hair is a half-dozen different colors. My sister is awake. The world is as it should be...except for the fact that I let Nash Hawthorne wash my hair.

I let him dye it for me.

I've never been to his room before, but I manage to find my way there now.

The door is open. To one side of his bedroom, there's a large wooden workbench with a steel stool. Nash's clothes—not that many, which explains how worn his shirts are—are folded on one side. The other is covered with wood, not the kind you buy but the kind you find.

"Lib?" Nash looks up from a bed made of exactly that kind of wood. His legs are stretched out, a beat-up six-string guitar in his lap. The moment our eyes meet, he puts the guitar to the side and stands.

"She's awake," I say.

Tension melts off Nash's body. I see it—see the difference in him—immediately. This is the Nash Hawthorne version of a hallelujah.

"She's *trouble*," he counters, softening the words with that cowboy smile of his.

This is the man who, when we barely knew each other, spent the night in a chair beside my bed so I could sleep without bad dreams; the man who played Magic 8 Ball with me in Cartago; the one who eats cupcakes like they're apples; the one who needs to shave again but hasn't.

Trouble. I recognize his reference to our bet, but I'm not going down without a fight. "She's alive."

"Your sister," Nash says, the smile slowly spreading across his face as he saunters toward me, "is never-met-a-loose-thread-she-didn't-want-to-pull-at, risking-everything-for-answers, in-over-her-head-with-my-brothers *trouble*, and you know it, darlin'."

I take a step forward. Nash casually kicks his bedroom door closed behind me. He's smiling like a Cheshire cat now, and I don't know why—not until I look at the back of his bedroom door.

Hanging there is a cowboy hat, just my size.

Then

There is a cowboy hat in the oven. There is a black ribbon around the base of the hat. There are hot pink skulls on the ribbon.

"Nash!" I holler. It's been months, and I don't know how many hats. At first, he was subtle about it, but for a full two months now, every single person in Hawthorne House has cued into his game.

The man is, in a word, persistent. "Behind you, Lib."

I turn and see him sitting on the counter, his long legs dangling.

Look at him, I tell myself. *And look at me.* Nash Hawthorne is scuffed cowboy boots and wild horses, subtle smiles and dirt beneath his nails. He's the things he builds with his hands, the guitar he plays.

He has to know this is never going to work. *Look at him looking at me.*

Nash Hawthorne and I are not dating. In fact, we have not-date night weekly. My ax-throwing skills are rapidly improving. He's teaching me to play guitar.

But I'm still not wearing his hats.

I know myself. I know that if, in a moment of weakness, I put on one of the many, *many* cowboy hats he's given me, the moment I let myself dream the most beautiful dream of *us*—

I can't.

"Do you ever think," Nash says, helping himself to one of *my* cupcakes with a slow, sly smile, "about Cartago?"

Then

I am not waiting up for Nash Hawthorne. The fact that he is out doing who knows what and the fact that I am up examining the age-old question of *How much chocolate is too much chocolate in one cupcake?* are completely unrelated.

I'm not worried. Nash Hawthorne is not the type of person you worry about.

He's the type who comes home bleeding at two in the morning with a puppy in his shirt.

His lower lip is busted right down the center. There's a cut on his jaw, a split in the skin directly over his left cheekbone. And as much as I want to be mad at him for fighting, I can't be.

It is literally impossible to be mad at a man who is wearing a sleeping puppy like it's a baby, snuggled up against his bare chest.

"You're bleeding," I say. His lips are swollen, smeared with blood—and that's not even touching the jaw or his cheek.

Nash does a good impression of someone who doesn't feel a thing. His bleeding lips have the audacity to curve. "She's worth it."

She. He's talking about the puppy. Coming closer, I resist the urge to reach out and touch her velvety soft ears.

"You were looking for a fight." That's why I'm up, why the well-stocked Hawthorne House chef's kitchen is now out of every ingredient that in any way involves chocolate. Nash and his brothers are hurting—the boys because they just found out their grandfather wasn't who they thought he was, and Nash because he knew the whole damn time.

"I'm never lookin' for a fight, Lib." He lifts a hand to caress the pup's tiny head. *Gentle* doesn't even begin to describe Nash Hawthorne. "I found her in an alley behind a college bar. Bunch of drunk frat boys had a stick."

Nash is not one to overshare, but I can imagine what happened the second he heard so much as a single puppy whimper.

"Now would be a good time to tell me that you did not do a murder. Or five." I study his swollen lips, his jaw, the cut on his cheekbone.

Nash shrugs. "They saw the error of their ways pretty quick."

The puppy makes a little whuffing sound in her sleep, and all my best-laid plans are rendered obsolete. *Nash Hawthorne. Bare chest. Puppy.* This is the very definition of a red alert.

I come to stand close enough to touch him—and her. "Is she okay?" I ask softly.

"She's warm." Even when he's tender, Nash is matter-of-fact. "She's safe." He lifts his gaze from the puppy to me. "She's ours."

"*Ours*," I repeat, "as in yours and your brothers'." I am fighting a losing battle, but at least I'm an optimist. "This is a Hawthorne dog." I lift my hand to her head, stroking her baby-soft fur.

"Got any thoughts on a name?" Nash asks me. The pup stirs in her sleep, nuzzling me right back.

I *cannot* name this puppy. Just like I can't move my hand from her head to his warm chest. From his chest to his bleeding lips.

For the first time pretty much ever, it occurs to me that Nash Hawthorne might actually need someone to take care of him.

"I am not naming this dog," I tell him. "But if I did, I'd call her Trouble."

Then

I'm wearing a cowboy hat and painting Nash Hawthorne's nails a very fetching shade of black.

His fingernails.

His thumbnails.

And then I make him wait until those nails are dry.

"You're killing me, Lib."

I smile a cowboy kind of smile to go with the hat. "I've always been good at waiting." At dreaming. At hoping. And I am done punishing myself for that.

Nash's eyes are brown, darker around the outside and center of his iris and almost amber in between. Right now, the expression in those eyes isn't measured in the least.

The black velvet cowboy hat on my head goes surprisingly well with my corset.

When his nails are dry, he lifts first my right wrist and then my left to his mouth, his lips brushing over my pulse, over the words I've tattooed there, reminders that I'm a survivor, that I can trust myself.

And him.

My hands make their way to his neck and jaw. He needs to shave, and I really hope he doesn't.

I hope.

And I hope.

And I hope.

Then

I used to wake up from bad dreams and bounce out of bed and smile and think about all the good things that *could* happen that day, a surefire recipe for chasing the darkness away. Now there is no darkness, no nightmares.

Now I wake up and roll into him.

Even in sleep, Nash's arm curls protectively around me. We're in London. I've never been before, but I would be content to stay here in bed with him all day. There's something about being held, something about *letting* myself be held, about the way my head fits under his chin and the warmth of his body against mine.

There's something about knowing that he is content to just hold me.

"Mornin'." Nash's chest rises and falls with a breath that tells me he's awake but not opening his amber-and-mahogany eyes any time soon.

I lean my head back, my neon hair a veritable rainbow on *his* pillow. "Mornin', darlin'," I drawl in the lowest voice I can muster. I am pretty sure his brothers would agree: My impression is spot-on.

"Waffles or pancakes?" Nash asks me. "I'm cooking."

Nash is an excellent cook. "Both," I tell him.

"Correct answer." Nash rolls over onto his side. "Hey, Lib?"

I close my own eyes, warm and snug, feeling the rise and fall of my own chest. "Yeah-huh?"

"I got you something."

There's something in Nash's voice that makes me open my eyes. He sits up and reaches for the nightstand, and all I can think is that he's perfect. This is perfect. We are.

I might not be, but *we* are.

I sit up, just as Nash holds out his *something*. I smile. "A Magic 8 Ball." I think about Cartago—and everything since. "You are *very* lucky that isn't another cowboy hat."

I have it on good authority that I wear them well.

"I am." There it is again—a low, almost heady tone in his voice. "Lucky."

I look down at the Magic 8 Ball in my hands and slowly turn it over. The blue triangle clearly visible in the window bears four words.

WILL YOU MARRY ME?

I look up at Nash.

"That question—it doesn't have an expiration date." He is, even now, so damn steady. "You don't have to say a word, Libby Grambs. Today, tomorrow, five years from now—if and when you want to answer, all you have to do is give that ball a shake until whatever feels right to *you* comes up." His hands find their way to mine.

I know every single callus on his fingers, on his palms. I know every scar.

"And if that answer is *Ask Again Later* or *Very Doubtful* or *Yes*, you just bring me that ball, knowing that everything is going to be just fine. *We* are."

My mouth is dry. "Nash..."

He brings his lips to just almost touch mine, a silent reminder that I don't have to say a word, that he has never and will never demand from me anything that I don't want to give. I've spent my life tiptoeing around glass and walking through minefields, but Nash is steady. Nash is pale blue skies. Nash is grass and mud, wide-open spaces, worn leather.

Nash is mine.

"Pancakes," he says, drawing my lips into a kiss. "Waffles." And another. "London." And another.

He kisses me until I believe him with every fiber of my being: Whatever my answer, everything is going to be fine.

Whatever my answer, *we* are.

And that's why I'm ready. That's why I *keep* kissing him and shake the Magic 8 Ball. That's why I pull back and keep shaking it, until the answer I want pops up.

One word. Just one. **YES.**

Now

've waited long enough now. The answer is *right there*, but I can't look at the pregnancy test. Because all of a sudden, I'm not remembering anymore. All of a sudden, I am dreaming—about a little boy with muddy-brown hair or a little girl with amber eyes who's stubborn as a mule. I'm dreaming about being the kind of mom I always wanted—about impromptu dance parties and wiping flour off of little noses and rolling down grassy hills just because we can.

"You're crying." Nash is on the other side of the bathroom door. I'm a silent crier. There's no way he can actually know that there are tears streaming down my cheeks.

And yet, he does.

I open the door. His hands are gentle, calluses lightly skimming my cheek as he wipes away my tears.

"If you've got a name," he tells me, "I'd take it." He's asking for the name of the person who made me cry.

I take a deep breath and look past him, toward the counter and the object laying on the counter, and I give him something else. "Hannah," I say, and then I swallow. "For a girl, I was thinking Hannah."

I see the shift in his expression, and suddenly, there's nothing steady or understated about what I see in his eyes, and I know—

He's dreaming, too.

And it's beautiful.

"It might not be positive," I told him. "It probably isn't. But—"

"We look together," he told me, taking my hands in his. "On three."

"One." I start off the count.

"Two." He smiles, and then I do.

"Three."

FIVE TIMES XANDER TACKLED SOMEONE (& ONE TIME HE DIDN'T)

"I tackle with love."

The Time with the Sloth

Dangling upside down off the front of an airplane, two-year-old Xander Hawthorne, who was currently a sloth, had an excellent vantage point for the drama unfolding below. The Cessna to which toddler Xander clung was a new addition to the playroom, but the fact that he and his brothers had been given an *actual* airplane to play on did not strike Xander as strange in the least.

To be fair, he was two, and he was a sloth. Not much struck him as strange.

Down below, his brothers Jameson and Grayson waged an epic battle—or rather, *Super Jameson* was in hot pursuit of *the Graysonater*. Xander, who was not a superhero because he was a sloth, assessed the situation with great interest.

Grayson was bigger than Jameson.

Grayson was faster than Jameson.

Grayson was *probably* going to win…unless Jameson used his head. That was something their grandfather was always saying. *Use your head, boys.* And…yes! Jameson was using his head! As a battering ram! *Wa-pow!* Super Jameson and the Graysonater both went flying.

Xander was fascinated. *Innnnnterrressstttttting*, he thought, dragging the word out super slowly, so committed was he to being a sloth—a sloth who really hoped that Jameson would do that awesome head thing again.

Down below, the Graysonater recovered quickly. Xander watched, captivated, as his brothers wrestled. Grayson was on top! No, Jameson! No, Grayson! The next thing Xander knew, Grayson had Jameson pinned.

Unable to move his arms or legs, Jameson fell back on a move of last resorts, one that two-year-old Xander knew all too well. "Beware the tongue of doom!" Jameson yelled.

Grayson was mortally offended. "No licking!"

Jameson bent his neck upward. He extended his tongue. He went in for the lick, and the Graysonater reared back. Super Jameson surged and—

"Boys." With a single word, Tobias Hawthorne brought the battle to a complete and utter standstill.

Jameson's tongue was still hanging out.

"You're Hawthornes," the old man said. "If you're going to do something—and I do consider wrestling to be *something*—then do it well. Do it *right*."

Grayson and Jameson scrambled to their feet.

Their grandfather raised a brow. "Where is Xander?"

"Not up here!" Xander yelled down. Their grandfather angled his eyes up to the Cessna. "I'm a sloth," Xander declared loftily. "Look at my toes!"

Billionaire Tobias Hawthorne *almost* smiled. "They are very nice toes, Xander." Then the old man turned back to Jameson and Grayson. "Now, you two. Show me how to wrestle with *proper* form."

"Oh, c'mon." A new voice entered the fray. "They're just playin'."

Xander, still hanging upside down, beamed at his oldest brother as said oldest brother stepped into the playroom. Nash was Xander's favorite! Nash was ten! Nash was making a funny face at their grandfather!

The old man looked from Nash to Jameson and Grayson. "Boys," he said to the younger two, "I believe your brother has just volunteered."

For what? Xander wondered.

Down below, Jameson grinned. Grayson took one step forward. And suddenly, Xander understood: Nash had volunteered to *wrestle*!

Super Jameson and the Graysonater were teaming up against Doctor Nashtopus.

Swinging himself back and forth on the nose of the Cessna, Xander contemplated the universe. Perhaps...perhaps he was not a sloth anymore? Perhaps he was a boy? A boy who could play wrestle, too?

"Watch your stance, Grayson," their grandfather called out. "Jamie, you're advertising your next move. Eyes on your target, both of you." Xander barely heard the string of corrections his billionaire grandfather offered his brothers. He was too busy being sneaky.

Sneaky.

Sneaky.

Sneaky.

Grayson went low. Nash absorbed the hit. Jameson twisted and threw his weight forward. Nash sidestepped. Grayson surged and—

Wa-pow! Xander used his head! Grayson fell backward. Xander landed on his chest, then bounced. "That was fun! Can we do it again? And again? And again?"

"Definitely," Jameson told him with a wicked little smile.

"No," Grayson said, removing the bouncing toddler from his chest.

The old man really did smile this time. "Let that be a lesson to you, boys," he told the older three. "Never take your eyes off the sloth."

The Time with Go Fish

Some situations required finesse. This was not one of those situations. Eleven-year-old Xander brandished his sword. "Go fish."

Across the table, Grayson's eyes narrowed ever so slightly. It was a look Grayson had borrowed from their grandfather and one to which Xander was—luckily—completely immune.

After a long, drawn-out moment, Grayson finally made his intentions clear: Instead of reaching for *his* sword, he drew a card.

"Please tell me you drew a seven," Jameson said wickedly.

"I did not." Grayson flicked his pale eyes toward Xander. "I am, in fact, fairly certain that Xander was bluffing and that he has the final seven."

Xander, like all Hawthornes, was an excellent bluffer. "If you were certain of that, my very blond, very lethal brother, you would have drawn your sword."

Thus were the rules of Hawthorne Go Fish. Bluffing was allowed. Any time you said *Go fish*, you drew your sword. If the other player thought you were lying about the contents of your hand, all they had to do was respond in kind, at which point, a duel commenced.

Blade against blade! Brother against brother! What was a

laid-back Sunday morning card game without the occasional sword fight?

Of course, there *was* a penalty involved for calling a bluff when the other person *wasn't* bluffing. A penalty that involved permanent markers. Xander was already mustachioed. Grayson was not.

And that had made it a little bit easier for Xander to get away with bluffing.

He set his sword down and grinned. "Hand over those sevens, Gray."

Grayson groaned. Xander pretended to twirl the evil mustache that Jameson had drawn on his face earlier in the game.

"Jameson..." Xander adopted what he thought of as his James Bond voice. "Give me your aces."

Jameson leaned back in his chair, running his index finger lightly over the edge of his sword's blade before taking hold of the handle. "Go. Fish."

Those words were *clearly* a dare.

Xander arched a brow. "Think you that I am afraid of a little beard, brother?"

"I think," Jameson said lightly, his expression giving away nothing, "that Grayson has the ace you're looking for." Jameson paused. "And for the record, it definitely won't be a *little* beard, Xan."

Xander stroked his chin, considering his options. If Jamie did have the ace, Xander would have to fight him for it, and although Grayson was the best swordsman among them, Jameson was a close second.

Xander's talents lay elsewhere. "Maybe Gray does have the last ace," Xander said amiably. "Or maybe..." He reached for a card from the pile. "That ace is *right here*."

With a dramatic flourish, Xander flipped the card. To his absolute delight, it *was* the ace, an enchanting turn of events for two reasons: First, it meant that now Xander had all four aces— on top of all four sevens—and world domination was that much closer to his grasp.

And second, it meant that *it was on!*

No swords.

No duels.

No holds barred.

Just, per the rules of Hawthorne Go Fish, a good, old-fashioned brotherly brawl!

"I want you both to know," Xander announced five minutes later, as he climbed on top of the antique card table, preparing to hurl himself off it, "that I tackle with love!"

He aimed the warning at Jameson—then flying-tackled *Grayson*.

The Time with Rebecca

Rebecca was Xander's person. She was quiet. He was not. She was sensible. He was ... not. But for years, the two of them had shared a never-spoken understanding of what it was like to be the youngest, to live in the oversized shadows of older siblings who *wanted* things and went after the things they wanted—the win, the world, each other.

It wasn't like that with Xander and Bex. Nothing had changed between them when they had become teenagers. At fifteen, they *knew* each other, which is how Xander knew...

"Something's different about you." Xander punctuated that statement by jumping from the arm of one giant leather sofa to the next. "My Xander sense is tingling."

"Not a fan of the word *tingling*," Rebecca told him, walking along the back of the sofa with the same understated grace with which she would have balanced on a log in the Black Wood.

"So noted," Xander replied. He executed a flying-squirrel leap toward the fireplace, caught the edge of the stone mantel, and pulled himself up to sit on it, his endlessly long legs dangling down. "My Xander sense is *buzzing*, and the source of that disturbance is..." Xander deployed a finger gun with expert precision, pointing his index finger directly at her. "You."

He'd noticed it a few days earlier: a subtle, automatic curve to Rebecca's lips, a secret smile Xander wasn't used to seeing on her classically beautiful face. That smile, paired with the completely uncharacteristic and almost dreamy look now discernible in her emerald eyes, could only mean one thing.

Xander grinned. "There's a girl."

"There is not," Rebecca said a little too quickly.

"There is!" Xander was delighted by this turn of events. "Is she broody with hidden depths or sunshine in human form—or, ooohhh, is she a Sagittarius?"

Rebecca opened her mouth, presumably to deny again that there *was* a girl, but Xander preempted any such denial.

"If you lie to me again, I am going to stand up on this mantel and dramatically throw myself into the magma below, meeting my tragic, untimely, and exceptionally well-acted death with Xander-like aplomb."

Rebecca said nothing at first, as she hopped from the back of the couch to a chair and then eyed the space between the chair and the fireplace.

"You can do it," Xander said encouragingly—and he wasn't just talking about the jump.

Rebecca threw a pillow onto the floor, then leapt onto that.

"Pillow is toast," Xander, the rule-keeper for The Floor Is Magma, announced gravely, "in three, two, one..."

Rebecca jumped, grabbed the mantel, and pulled herself up.

"Your Floor Is Magma technique is, as ever, *flawless*," Xander told her. "But you know the rules. A pillow assist enti-tles me to one question." He lifted his hand and poked Rebecca's shoulder gently with his index finger. "There's a girl..." he prompted.

On top of the mantel, Rebecca pulled her knees to her chest

and rested her chin on her knees. "There's a girl," she admitted. "And she's . . . complicated."

"Good complicated or bad complicated?" Xander's tone made it clear: He found those prospects equally appealing.

Rebecca smiled helplessly. "Both?"

Something about the way Rebecca said that word set Xander's Xander sense to *buzzing* once more. "Theoretically speaking," Xander said thoughtfully, "how long has there been a good-complicated, bad-complicated girl in the life of my very best Rebecca buddy?"

Rebecca directed her answer to her kneecaps. "Hard to say. It's . . ."

"Complicated?" Xander offered. The wheels in his Hawthorne brain started turning. Rebecca mostly kept to herself at school. Emily—Rebecca's sister and admittedly not one of Xander's favorite people—had a habit of *needing* Rebecca any time she showed the slightest sign of making friends. Xander was well aware that the only reason Emily didn't try pulling the same thing when Rebecca was with him was the infamous Lederhosen Incident from the summer he and Rebecca were nine.

For all her faults, Emily Laughlin knew better than to mess with Xander Hawthorne.

"Hypothetically speaking," Xander said, "*where* did you meet this—"

"Hello?" A demanding voice echoed through the foyer. Xander recognize it immediately: two-thirds *Impress Me*, one-third *I Am Not Impressed*. Thea Calligaris. Her uncle was married to Xander's aunt, and Thea was one of Xander's very favorite people to annoy.

His eyes widened suddenly.

Thea was a frequent visitor to Hawthorne House. She was Emily's best friend. She was a *Sagittarius*.

"Rebecca Laughlin," Xander said in awe, "you lovable, rascally minx."

Rebecca shot laser eyes at him. "Not a *word*, Xander. Not. A. Single. Word."

In that moment, Xander heard everything that Rebecca *wasn't* saying. Her entire life revolved around—and had always revolved around—what *Emily* wanted.

Emily, who had a heart condition.

Emily, who their mother obsessed over.

Emily, who had always, always been given her way.

Emily Laughlin didn't allow anyone to put her second. Not her sister. Not her best friend.

"I'll help you," Xander said fiercely. "Double-O-Xander, at your service. You have no idea how sneaky I can be."

Before Rebecca could reply, Thea appeared in the archway into the Grand Parlor. Her eyes came to rest on Rebecca's for just a second, just an *instant*, but that was enough for Xander to confirm: Beneath the mean girl facade—which maybe, possibly, probably wasn't entirely a facade—Thea felt it, too.

"Do I want to know what you two are doing?" Thea Calligaris really knew how to sell an eye roll.

"The floor is magma," Xander told her seriously. "Quick! Jump on the couch!"

"Xander," Rebecca warned.

Xander did not heed her warning. How could he? Thea was *right there*, and she was complicated, and they needed him, in all of his Xander glory.

"Don't worry," Xander told Rebecca seriously, as he pulled his feet up on top of the mantel and crouched. "I'll save her!"

Thea did not see the tackle coming. No one ever expected a Xander Inquisition.

"What the—"

Expert tackler that he was, Xander ensured that they landed safely—and more or less gently—on the couch. "And thus," he said dramatically, "the damsel was saved. And thus..." He grinned. "An alliance was born."

"Alliance?" Thea looked at him like he'd just sprouted a few extra heads and possibly a second butt. "Have you lost your mind?"

Up on the mantel, Rebecca sighed. "He knows," she told Thea.

Thea's eyes cheated to Rebecca's.

"I know," Xander reiterated helpfully. "And I am pleased to inform you that I make an excellent accomplice."

The Time with the Motorcycle

Xander was no stranger to bad ideas. Or unusual ideas. Or the occasional this-is-either-brilliant-or-an-offense-against-common-sense-and-gravity idea. He was, in fact, a *connoisseur* of ideas, swishing even the most outlandish possibilities around in his mind and taking a delicate little taste.

But even Xander recognized that stealing Nash's motorcycle was a very, very, extremely, definitely, *entirely* bad idea. If Jameson succeeded at stealing their oldest brother's bike, Nash was going to *do a murder*—in a mostly nonviolent, no-Jamesons-were-irrevocably-harmed-in-this-ass-kicking kind of way.

Xander's common sense, discretion, and desire for self-preservation were all in agreement: He wanted no part of this.

So of course he had to intervene.

"If not me," Xander said to himself as he leapt over the railing on his balcony and began scaling down the side of Hawthorne House, "then who?"

He was aided in his climb by two suction cups, an expandable grappling hook he kept on his person for just such occasions, and a blueberry scone. God bless pockets!

Xander landed on the front lawn, polished off the scone in two bites, and started sprinting. Jameson was already straddling the bike. Luckily, Xander's legs were long, and his post-scone speed was a thing to behold.

The bike roared to life and—*wa-bam!*

It was a top-three tackle, if Xander did say so himself. They hit the ground rolling, then sprang to their feet in unison. Xander was bigger. Jameson had a habit of fighting dirty. And right now? Jamie was fighting like a person who had nothing to lose.

"Whoa there, Captain Big Feels!" Xander put some space between them and held his hands up in a mea culpa that also—conveniently—doubled as a ready stance. "It's just your friendly neighborhood Xander looking out for the longevity of one of his top-three favorite brothers!"

"Back. Off."

Xander did not back off. "You don't want to do this."

"*This?*" Jameson challenged. There was something dangerous in his tone, something wild but contained, unstoppable.

Good thing all Xander had to do was try to stop him!

"*This*, as in stealing Nash's motorcycle," Xander specified helpfully. "Presumably to take off for parts unknown. And it seems you have forgotten your helmet?"

"I haven't forgotten anything." Jameson took an ominous step toward Xander.

And there it is, Xander thought. His brother had as good as admitted that the danger—the lack of helmet, Nash's wrath—was the point.

Jameson was hurting. Just like Rebecca was hurting. Just like Grayson was. Emily's death the month before was like a black hole, sucking in entire universes around it. But the difference between Jameson and Grayson, between Jameson and Rebecca, was that when Jameson was hurting, he wanted to hurt *more*.

To prove that he could.

To prove that nothing mattered, when really it *all* mattered so much he could hardly breathe.

"I feel an aggressive hug coming on," Xander informed his brother. "Would you or would you not like the bear variety? I can also recommend our daily special, the Manly Snuggle Hug."

"Get out of my way, Xan."

"Not going to happen."

"I will go through you if I have to."

Xander lowered his hands to his side. No more mea culpa. No more ready stance. "You're spiraling."

"I mean it, Xander. Get out of my way."

"Manly Snuggle and/or bear hugs are still available, though supplies are limited, so you should get one while they—"

Jameson surged forward. Xander lunged sideways, blocking the way to Nash's bike.

"I don't want to hurt you," Jameson bit out.

"That's the thing," Xander said. He looked Jameson right in the eyes. "You won't."

If it came down to a fight, Xander would lose—*eventually.* They both knew it. Just like they both knew that none of Xander's brothers would ever hurt him as badly as Jameson would have to in order to win this fight.

"I hate you," Jameson grumbled.

"And I loathe your face!" Xander replied happily.

"You can't be everywhere, Xan." In other words: Jameson's inadvisable plan had been thwarted *for now.*

Xander was undaunted. "Or *can* I?" He wiggled his eyebrows dramatically and threw an arm around Jameson's shoulders. "Now, be honest: Where did that tackle rate in my top three?"

The Time with the Heartbroken Cowboy

There was an art to the rooftop tackle. Luckily, the sunrise painting the Texas sky over Hawthorne House in shades of orange and pink was downright inspiring. A muse, of sorts, as Xander moved silently toward his oldest brother, who was leaning up against the House's tallest stone chimney.

Easy does it...

"Don't even think about it, Xan." Nash didn't turn around. He just kept staring at the sunrise in the distance.

"I'm going to need you to move two inches to your left," Xander told him.

"Go back inside, Xander." Nash still didn't so much as turn his head.

"I have taken your suggestion under advisement, and after serious consideration, I—"

"Wasn't a *suggestion*, little brother."

Well, that was ominous! Xander, being Xander, was not deterred. "I have taken your order and implied promise of brotherly retribution under advisement," he amended amiably. "And yet..."

Nash finally turned around. In the early morning light,

Xander couldn't quite make out the set of his brother's features beneath the worn cowboy hat Nash wore tipped down over his brow.

All Hawthornes had their way of hiding.

"You try an' tackle me, and we're gonna be havin' words, Alexander." Nash's voice was slow and even, his Texas accent unhurried and pronounced.

Xander was well aware that no one with two brain cells to rub together would want to find themselves *having words* with Nash Hawthorne. And yet...

"I brought you something." Xander retrieved the object in question from one of his many pockets and tossed it at Nash's endearing, shadowed face.

Nash caught the paper booklet with one hand.

"It's a coupon book," Xander said helpfully.

Nash flipped through the book. "All of these just say *TACKLE*. All caps."

"You never know when you're going to need one," Xander told Nash. "I tackle with love, and those bad boys can be cashed in at your discretion. Now, if you could move one inch to your right and take two steps away from the edge of the roof..."

Nash was not persuaded. "Not happening."

"I really think you'll feel better if you let me do it," Xander argued.

"I'm fine." Nash's voice was low and smooth. "Promise."

Xander didn't trust that smoothness. He didn't believe it. "You and Alisa broke up. You're not fine. You're not even fine-adjacent."

"Heartbreak doesn't kill Hawthornes." Nash sounded certain of that. "And Lee-Lee and me—we're too different. Always were, I guess." Nash's voice wasn't smooth now. "What she wants, I can't give her. And Alisa Ortega..." Nash swallowed, his Adam's apple bobbling as he palmed his cowboy hat in a way that made Xander think Nash was desperately trying to hold on to *something*. "She deserves the world."

"I know." Xander understood. He *did*. They'd all seen this coming, but that didn't make it any easier. "*I know*, Nash, and I really think you'll feel better if you let me tackle you."

"Do not tackle me."

"You need a distraction."

"I need to get out of here. This place. This *house*."

Xander heard what Nash was really saying: He had to get away from their grandfather. Hawthorne House *was* Tobias Hawthorne, and Nash had never been able to take either for too long.

"So where are we going?" Xander asked cheerfully.

Nash pinned him with a look. "You're staying here." When Xander opened his mouth to object, Nash preempted that objection. "Someone has to look after Jamie and Gray. They're a mess."

As much as Xander wanted to argue with that, he knew that he couldn't. Xander Hawthorne was good at taking care of people. He nodded to the coupon book he'd given Nash. "Those are non-transferrable, by the way."

Despite himself, Nash *almost* grinned. "Try not to set anything on fire while I'm gone."

Nash had a bad habit of leaving—and a good habit of coming home. But something told Xander it might be a while before they saw each other again.

A muscle in Xander's chest tightened. "No promises—at least, none regarding fire." Xander met Nash's gaze. "I do promise to take care of Jamie and Gray."

He always had. He always would.

"Keep an eye on Lee-Lee, too." Nash looked down at the roof beneath their feet. "Don't let her work too hard."

"Gargantuan task," Xander said, "but it is possible that I also made a coupon book for Alisa."

Nash put his cowboy hat back on. "Now *that* I would like to see. I know the woman. She'll skin you alive at the first sign of tackling."

"Don't worry," Xander said confidently, "I am prepared to deploy Big Innocent Xander Eyes, among other contingencies."

Nash was still smiling, but his Adam's apple bobbed again.

Heartbreak doesn't kill Hawthornes, Xander thought.

Nash made the considerable error of starting back toward the trap door they'd both used to climb out onto the roof. *One step...two...*

Xander pounced. *Wa-bam!*

Nash went down. On top of him, Xander pumped a fist into the air. "That one was on the house."

And One Time He Didn't

Maxine Liu was absolutely, positively *not* going to show Xander Hawthorne her tattoo—the very nerdy, extremely secret tattoo she'd admitted to hours earlier in Hawthorne Chutes and Ladders.

Tell me more, Xander had said, *about this nerdy tattoo.*

But that was *not* going to happen! She and Xander were completely platonic! Which was why she was, at this very moment, stepping through the doorway into Xander's room. As a friend!

She was stepping through the door to his bedroom *as a friend.*

Avoiding looking at said friend, Max focused on the room instead. Complicated machines lined every inch of the walls like sculptures. Max watched as a dozen marbles ran down a long metal ramp and onto what looked like a tiny little Ferris wheel, which dumped them onto another ramp, which fed into a funnel...

"That one waters my cactus once a week," Xander said.

"Your cactus?" Max repeated.

Xander was absolutely unabashed. "His name is Mr. Pointy."

Of course it was. Max really, really needed not to look at Xander's face—the dancing eyes, the full, curving lips—so she glanced up at the ceiling instead.

Big mistake.

"*Fax me,*" she whispered, then told herself that absolutely was *not* an invitation, but . . . but. . . .

THE CEILING.

The ceiling was nothing but books. Thousands of them, spines down, defying gravity, seemingly nothing holding them in place.

"How are they . . ." Max couldn't help herself.

"Magnets," Xander said cheerfully. "Mostly."

This time, Max spared herself from looking at his jaw, cheekbones, and long, long Hawthorne lashes by looking down. The floor beneath her feet was made of whiteboard material, and there were handwritten notes scrawled all over it.

"You're working on something?" she guessed.

"I'm kind of working on everything," Xander admitted. "It's possible that I *also* have a lab-slash-workshop, but when you've got to science, you've got to science."

Max needed to *science.* She needed to *science* right faxing now. "Ahem." Max hadn't meant to say that out loud. *Change the subject!* she thought frantically. "So where do you sleep?" she asked.

Oh no.

Oh no.

That was not a good subject change. *Yes, Max. Ask your extremely platonic and well-muscled friend here about his BED.*

"Sleep." Xander nodded sagely. "Yes. I do the sleep."

"Where?" Max was digging herself a hole, and she just *couldn't stop*, because there wasn't a bed in this entire room, and now that she'd asked, she couldn't stop thinking about it. Besides, there was no reason in the world that the two of them couldn't just have a nice, reasonable, completely friendly and appropriate conversation about beds.

Xander gave a helpless little shrug. "What are your thoughts on blanket forts?"

Max's reply was immediate: "Right up there with book bouquets."

She knew she probably shouldn't have said that, but there was no unsaying it, so she just stood by and watched, with no small degree of fascination, as Xander approached a truly impressive collection of bobbleheads built into one of the machines on the walls. He tapped out a sequence, one head after another, like he was playing a very unconventional piano.

Suddenly, the floor beneath Max's feet began to part. She jumped to safety and stared as a hidden subsection of the room, recessed a good four feet into the floor, was revealed. It was rectangular in shape and twice the size of a king-sized bed.

It was also completely covered in blankets. Piles of them. Mounds of them.

Dozens of them. Max couldn't keep her eyes from darting to Xander's any more than she could keep herself from walking right to the edge. "May I?"

Xander inclined his head. "You may."

Max leapt. Xander followed on her heels and a moment later, they were both swimming in blankets. Literally.

"I don't like beds," Xander said.

Xander Hawthorne did not like beds. He *did* like blankets—and, she soon discovered, plushies. Nerdy ones. Adorable ones. A couple downright bizarre ones. *Is that a stuffed Tesla coil?*

Max had always pictured herself with someone dark and broody. A rogue assassin. A vampire of questionable morals. Someone with a checkered past and a heart in need of healing.

But there Xander was, with his blankets and his plushies and an entire ceiling covered in books.

Max sighed, and then she turned her head to look at him, which she *knew* was a mistake. "I believe I was a promised a *fort*."

One epic fort later, Xander threw out a challenge. A game.

Hawthornes and their games, Max thought.

"It's called Go, No Go," Xander intoned. "The rules are thus: I will present you with questions about your preferences, and you have to answer: *go* or *no go*." Xander disappeared under the sea of blankets for a moment, then popped back up holding a plush in each hand. "If your feelings on the topic are positive, you say *go* and hold up this narwhal. If you're not a fan, it's *no go* and this cupcake."

Max eyed the cupcake, the narwhal, and Xander in turn. "Why not just call it Yes or No?"

"Because at any moment," Xander replied, "I can flip things and yell *go* instead of posing the next question, and once I do, you have until I say *no go* to catch me."

Max gave him a look. "What happens if I catch you?"

Xander grinned. "You're not going to catch me."

"Spoken like a mother-faxing Hawthorne."

"I take it you're ready for your first question?" Xander rubbed his hands together dramatically. "*Star Wars?*"

"Go." Max held up the stuffed narwhal.

"Strawberries?"

"Go." *Narwhal.*

"Chocolate?"

"Go." *Narwhal.*

"Nutella?"

"Also go." Max made the narwhal dance a little this time.

Xander studied her with incredible focus and precision. "Scones?"

Max lowered the narwhal and raised the cupcake. "No go."

Xander clasped a hand to his chest like she'd shot him.

"Not sweet enough," Max opined. "Next question."

"You just need some additional scone-eating practice," Xander assured her. "A refined scone-tasting palette does not develop overnight."

Max narrowed her eyes. "Scones are like muffins that got confused."

Xander gasped. This time, it was Max's turn to grin.

"I'll let you redeem yourself," Xander told her gravely. "Robots?"

"Do the robots think they're human?" Max shot back.

"No?"

Max raised the cupcake high with no remorse.

"Yes?" Xander amended his prior response. Max rewarded him with a little narwhal dance.

"My turn." She tossed both cupcake and narwhal at Xander. He caught them. "Romance novels?" Max questioned.

"Which subgenre?"

Up until that moment, Max had been doing a really good job of holding it together. But this?

"What?" Xander said. "What did I say?"

"You." Max pointed at him. "Your opinion on romance novels depends on the subgenre!" Max stared at him and was reminded of why staring at Xander Hawthorne was not a good idea. "You, with the face! And the abs! And the blankets!"

"I also have a cactus," Xander reminded her.

"Mr. Pointy," Max said. And just like that, she knew: This was happening. "I should not do this. We should *definitely* not do this."

"Of course we shouldn't," Xander agreed. "And we shan't." He paused. "Or shall we?"

Max swallowed. *"This,"* she said. "Us. Go or no go?" Her heart was brutalizing the inside of her rib cage.

Go or no go, Xander Hawthorne?

Across from her, Xander raised the stuffed narwhal into the air.

"Go!" Max yelled, and just like that, the chase was on. Xander almost had her when she whirled around. "No go!" she said.

Xander froze.

Max arched a brow. And then, in blankets up to her knees, unable to resist for another *second*, she tackled him.

ONE
HAWTHORNE
NIGHT

A good suit was like armor. Grayson was the type to dress for battle—not a wrinkle in sight, layers between him and the world.

I, GRAYSON DAVENPORT HAWTHORNE, HAVE VIOLATED A
SACRED BOND OF BROTHERHOOD. WHEN A NINE-ONE-ONE IS
ISSUED, THE BROTHERS HAWTHORNE MUST RESPOND.

SO IT IS WRITTEN. SO IT MUST BE.

TO AVOID BEING NAMED DEFECTOR, I MUST ATONE. I DO
NOT KNOW WHEN MY ATONEMENT WILL HAPPEN. I DO NOT
KNOW WHAT IT WILL BE. BY SIGNING THIS DOCUMENT, I
HEREBY ATTEST: WHATEVER PENANCE IS DECREED, WITH THAT
PENANCE I WILL AGREE.

TIMES THREE.

SIGNED:

Grayson

WITNESSED THIS DAY BY:

Nash

Jameson

Xander

Grayson Davenport Hawthorne slept like the dead—when he slept at all. There were nights when he didn't, couldn't. But when things went quiet and still, when memories gave way to *nothing*...

He didn't even dream.

"Yup. He's out cold."

"Give me the puppy."

Something licked Grayson's hand. So much for blissful nothing—or an early night. *Another lick.* "That had better," he said sternly, his eyes still closed, "be the dog."

In response, his covers were torn back and said puppy was placed upon him.

"Get him, Tiramisu," Xander crooned from above. "Nuzzle those abs! Sniff those pecs!"

Grayson resigned himself to opening his eyes. He sat up, gathered the squirming puppy in his arms, and shot Xander the most austere of looks. "You are very lucky that I am holding an animal right now."

"An animal?" Jameson repeated, his lips twitching slightly.

Xander was outraged. "Is that any way to refer to Tiramisu Panini Hawthorne?"

Grayson had been heretofore unaware that the dog had a middle name.

"Tell her she's a good little pupper," Xander demanded.

Grayson rubbed the puppy's ears but did not allow his expression to betray even the slightest hint of amusement. "I will not."

"That right, little brother?"

Grayson looked to the doorway, where Nash was leaning against the wall—and that was Grayson's first true inkling about what was happening here, about why all three of his brothers were currently in his bedroom.

Whatever penance is decreed, with that penance I will agree...

Grayson eyed the squirming puppy in his hands. "You are a very adequate canine," he allowed, stroking her head.

Xander was clearly not satisfied. He gestured for Grayson to continue.

Grayson sighed. "Who's a good girl? You are. Yes, you. What a good little..." He glanced up at Xander, who nodded encouragingly. "Pupper."

"I would have also accepted *doggo*," Xander told him.

Grayson looked to the other two. "Happy?" he asked Jamie and Nash.

"Not as happy as we're going to be," Jameson replied. "The time for atonement has arrived."

Grayson bent to place Tiramisu gently on the ground. "Does this count as the first?" If memory served, he'd agreed to *three* acts of atonement.

"The puppy?" Nash drawled. "Hell no."

Grayson had expected as much. Hawthornes were not known for letting one another off easily. But a promise was a promise. Honor was honor. "I'll get dressed," Grayson said.

Jameson smirked. "That won't be necessary."

ATONEMENT NIGHT, 10:41 PM

A good suit was like armor. Grayson was the type to dress for battle—not a wrinkle in sight, layers between him and the world.

Boxer briefs decidedly did *not* count as layers.

Damn his brothers. It was December, and they hadn't even

allowed him *shoes*. He'd been dumped out of the Bugatti onto some country back road, dressed only in his underwear and with nothing but a suspiciously thick envelope, an index card, and very specific instructions: Give the envelope to the driver of the first car that stopped—and say nothing but the words written on the card.

This has Jamie's fingerprints all over it. In any other circumstance, Grayson would have been methodically plotting his vengeance, but tonight was different. *Family first* were words that landed differently now, but whatever misgivings Grayson had about their grandfather, he knew what he owed his brothers.

What they had always owed one another.

Xander had needed him, and Grayson hadn't come. He'd seen the 911 text, and he'd ignored it. If standing on the side of the road in an embarrassing state of undress was what it took to make amends, Grayson Davenport Hawthorne would damn well stand there and stare down anyone who *dared* raise a brow.

Headlights flashed. Grayson resisted the urge to cover his pelvic region. *When a Hawthorne walks into a room, he sets the tone.* The old man's lessons were forever etched in his mind. As irritating as Grayson found that, he nonetheless set his jaw. The trick to being nearly naked on the side of the road was the same as arriving to a party overdressed: Simply behave as though you and only you were appropriately clothed.

It was hardly Grayson's fault that the rest of the world had neglected to realize what a faux pas it truly was to wear more than just underwear on *this* road at *this* time of night.

A pickup truck came to a stop beside him. The passenger-side window rolled down. "Son," an old man barked out, "it looks like you've got yourself a situation."

Oh? Grayson would have liked to say in a steely deadpan. *I hadn't noticed.* Or perhaps, *I don't see how that's any business of yours.*

But rules were rules, and he could only say the words written on the card.

"Hello, kind stranger," he gritted out. "I seem to have misplaced my pantaloons."

The old man blinked. "You drunk, boy?"

Grayson gave a curt shake of his head. "I seem," he repeated, moving toward the truck and trying a different emphasis on the words, "to have misplaced my pantaloons."

Before the driver could roll up the window and force him to repeat this entire unfortunate situation with the next passing car, Grayson tossed the envelope through the open window and onto the passenger seat.

"Drunk as a skunk," the driver muttered. "I oughta call the sheriff."

"I seem to have misplaced my pantaloons," Grayson said in an icy tone that he hoped conveyed *I strongly advise against such action.*

Still muttering, the driver reached for the envelope. He opened it, and then his eyes went wide. He pulled out the bills and started counting them, then he came to a note—presumably, instructions from Grayson's cursed brothers.

"This for real?" the driver asked Grayson.

Rather than repeat that blasted line one more time, Grayson simply inclined his head.

The driver grinned. "In that case, son, hop on in."

ATONEMENT NIGHT, 11:14 PM

Grayson had entertained a myriad of possibilities about where his brothers might have instructed that he be taken next. An ice-cold body of water he would be required to jump into. A billboard in need of climbing. A country-club golf course whose sprinklers would turn on at the worst possible moment.

Grayson had not anticipated the possibility that he would be dropped off in a residential area, nor that someone would be waiting there for him, the look on her face oh-so-clearly communicating that Thea Calligaris was *never* going to let Grayson live this down.

The old man behind the wheel looked from Grayson to Thea but didn't say a word.

Wise choice. Grayson gave the man a parting nod, climbed out of the truck, and steeled himself for what was to come.

"Grayson Hawthorne." Thea greeted him sweetly, her full lips giving in to a smirk as she eyed his current state of undress. "I had you pegged for more of the thong type."

"You did not." Grayson kept his voice absolutely even. Another person had the advantage of you only if you let them.

"You have always," Thea replied solemnly, "been my least favorite Hawthorne."

"I am wounded," Grayson deadpanned.

Thea made a show of looking him up and down. "Not that I can see."

"Enough, Thea." Grayson arched a brow at her, well aware of how commanding his presence could be. "Why am I here?"

Thea met his eyebrow arch with one of her own. "Because I'm part two of your penance."

This had *Xander* written all over it. "Oh?"

Thea didn't buy his nonchalance for a moment. "Unless you don't want clothes?" she said innocently.

Grayson didn't rise to the bait. "I would hate to put you out."

"So courteous," Thea crooned. Then she turned and sauntered back toward her house, leaving Grayson no choice but to follow. "You can thank me when we're done," she added, with far too much satisfaction in her tone for Grayson's comfort.

He attempted to resist the urge to ask but failed. "Done with what, precisely?"

Thea looked back and aimed a most devious smile in his direction. "Your makeover."

ATONEMENT NIGHT, 11:18 PM

"I am not wearing leather pants." Of this, Grayson Hawthorne was certain.

"Yes," Thea replied with no small amount of smug triumph in her tone, "you are. Black leather pants, and fair warning: You may think they're a size too small, but that's only because they are very, very tight."

This was ridiculous. Almost as ridiculous as the fact that Grayson was standing there in his underwear, arguing with Thea Calligaris about pants.

Whatever penance is decreed, with that penance, I will agree.

"*Times three,*" Grayson muttered, reaching out to take those blasted black leather pants from Thea.

First, the underwear.

Then Thea.

Grayson shuddered to think what his brothers had in store for him next. Squeezing himself into the leather pants practically took an act of God. Fortunately, Grayson Hawthorne was not easily defeated.

"There," he snapped, once the task was complete. "Are we done here?"

"White T-shirt, ultrathin; black leather jacket, circa the eighties." Thea tossed the items at him as she spoke. Once he'd put them on, she rubbed her hands together. "Now, about that hair..."

"There is nothing wrong with my hair," Grayson stated tersely.

"But is anything about it really *right*?" Thea countered.

ATONEMENT NIGHT, 11:34 PM

Grayson Davenport Hawthorne drew the line at eyeliner. Or at least, that was where he drew the line until Thea brought in reinforcements.

"Avery." Her name escaped Grayson's lips the second she stepped into the room. Seeing her still did something to him. Perhaps it always would.

"Nice pants," Avery said, then snorted—literally snorted—and Grayson couldn't even hold it against her.

"I have no idea what you are talking about," he said calmly, but *damn it to perdition*, these leather pants were tight.

"Has Thea taken any photos yet?" Avery asked, unable to bite back a smile that nearly broke her face. A face he knew better than he should have.

Better than he had any right to.

Focus. Grayson replayed Avery's words in his head and scowled. "Photos?" he said darkly. "She'd better not have."

"More pout!" Thea demanded beside him, not even bothering to hide that she was now taking pictures by the dozens. "Give me more pout!"

Grayson turned, calmly considering murder. These things, when done, had to be done with a cool head. "Put the phone down," he told Thea.

"Narrow your eyes a little more. Growl, baby. Growl."

Grayson made a grab for the phone, but Thea was unexpectedly quick on her feet. "Avery," she called, clearly enjoying herself, "do his eyes!"

Avery's gaze landed on his. Grayson had spent a lifetime repressing emotions. Letting himself feel would take some getting used to.

Especially when what he was feeling was *this*.

"What exactly am I doing with his eyes?" Avery asked.

Thea supplied her with a stick of eyeliner. "Do your worst."

"She means best," Grayson corrected, because at least when he was correcting Thea, he wasn't too caught up in things that might—or might not—have been different, if *he* had been different.

"You'll let me do my best?" Avery queried skeptically, holding up the eyeliner with an arch of her brow. "With this?"

Letting her touch him really wasn't a good idea.

It wasn't a good idea at all.

"*Whatever penance is decreed,*" Grayson murmured, "*with that penance I will agree.*"

ATONEMENT NIGHT, 12:27 AM

Thea, Avery, and her security escort delivered him to an establishment called JOHNNY O'S, all capital letters. The flashing neon microphone on the building provided more than enough context for Grayson to determine what the night—and his brothers—held in store for him next.

"Karaoke," he muttered.

Beside him, Avery grinned. "Let the punishment fit the crime."

Karaoke had been Xander's request when he'd issued his 911. At the time, they had all been reeling, coping in their own ways with the discovery of the kind of man their grandfather had really been. Xander's method of dealing had involved his brothers—and karaoke.

Let the punishment fit the crime. "Which one of my brothers are you quoting?" Grayson asked Avery calmly.

Another smile. "All of them."

That did not bode well for what awaited him inside JOHNNY O'S. "Are you coming?" Grayson asked, and he let himself pretend that the question was directed equally at Avery and Thea.

Thea didn't even bother answering.

"We have been informed that this phase of Atonement Night is for the brothers Hawthorne and *only* the brothers Hawthorne," Avery replied. She lowered her voice. "They were afraid I would be too merciful."

Grayson allowed himself to look at her one more time. "You? Merciful?" She'd always been able to go toe-to-toe with him. "Somehow," he continued, as he made his way to the door, "I doubt that."

ATONEMENT NIGHT, 12:28 AM

Nash was waiting for him just inside the door. "That's quite a look you've got there."

Grayson made a valiant attempt at glaring his elder brother into submission, then looked past Nash to a bar and, beyond that, to a room where he could hear music playing. "Please tell me we have the place to ourselves tonight."

Jameson sauntered in. "We rented it out."

Grayson almost let out a sigh of relief, but he knew Jamie, and he very specifically knew *that* look.

"But then . . . ," Jamie continued, enjoying this far too much, "a bachelorette party showed up, and the bride was *so* disappointed that this fine establishment was closed for the evening."

Grayson glared bullets first at Jamie, then at Nash. "A bachelorette party?"

Xander bounded into the room, holding a hot-pink plastic champagne flute. "To Marina and Benny!" he declared, hoisting it jubilantly in the air. "Benny isn't here," he informed Grayson, "but Marina and her friends are going to *love* that outfit."

Of course they were. Just as they would likely enjoy whatever performances his brothers had in store for him.

"What am I singing?" Grayson asked, as if this entire turn of events were of utterly no significance.

"What *aren't* you singing?" Jamie retorted.

"We might have put together a set list," Xander explained. He handed a piece of paper to Grayson, who skimmed it with robotic precision, horror swelling in his chest.

"*Twenty-nine* songs?" he demanded.

Jameson smirked. "You object?"

It was on the tip of Grayson's lips to say that he damn well did. But rules were rules. A promise was a promise. Honor was honor. "No."

"Told you." Nash aimed a knowing look at Jameson. "Gray's a man of his word. And since I won our little wager, Jamie . . ." Nash angled his head back toward Grayson. "Looks like you only have to sing three songs."

"We each get to choose one," Xander said in a manner that made it clear the matter had already been discussed and decided.

Three brothers. Three songs. Grayson could do this—leather pants and bachelorette party notwithstanding.

"I, for one, will be making my song count." Jameson Winchester Hawthorne could not be trusted. "You'll be happy to hear, Gray, that I have spent weeks delving into decades of musical history, all in an attempt to find the *best* choice."

It was clear that when Jamie said *best*, he meant *most horror-inducing*.

"Honestly," Jameson continued, enjoying this far too much for Grayson's comfort, "I'm still deciding. Tell me: What are your thoughts on milkshakes and yards?"

Grayson felt his eyes narrow. "I neither recognize that reference nor want to."

"Like I said," Jameson replied with a wink, "I'm still deciding. Love the outfit, by the way."

A woman wearing a neon-green feather boa poked her head through the archway. "Woooo!" she yelled. "Let's get this party started!"

Grayson angled his eyes toward her. "Marina, I presume?" He didn't wait for an answer before turning back to his brothers. "What am I singing first?"

ATONEMENT NIGHT, 12:34 AM

Grayson was Armani suits and platinum cuff links; when it came to song choice, he favored Frank Sinatra, Bing Crosby, Dean Martin.

Nash was country; he'd chosen Taylor Swift. Not entirely surprising—but Grayson would have expected something a little more country than . . . *this*.

As "Shake It Off" began to play and the bachelorette party *lost its collective mind*, Grayson spared one last glare for his brothers.

ATONEMENT NIGHT, 12:43 AM

Grayson had all of one song to recover before he was informed that it was his turn again—Xander's pick this time.

"Well, Xan?" Grayson prompted.

Xander pressed the fingers on his right hand against the fingers on his left, adopting a meditative expression. "Picture this," he said dramatically. "The year is 2013. The movie..."—Xander paused dramatically—"is *Frozen*."

If looks could have killed, Xander would have been ashes. "You'd better not have," Grayson growled.

Xander threw an arm around him. "I'm an Anna. You're an Elsa. You know in your heart that this is true."

Nash and Jamie were *barely* holding it together.

"I hate you all," Grayson told his brothers.

As he climbed toward the stage for round two, Jameson called after him. "'Shake It Off.' 'Let It Go.' I think they're trying to tell you something, Gray."

ATONEMENT NIGHT, 12:59 AM

Jameson took his sweet time choosing the final song of Atonement Night. Grayson tried to imagine the worst song to sing—in front of a bachelorette party, while wearing tight black leather pants—but after the third or fourth horrifying option he'd considered, he forced himself to stop.

Marina and her friends were becoming increasingly rowdy.

"Please," Grayson told his brothers after one of the women approached him and lewdly complimented the fit of his pants. "End this."

"Jamie." Nash put a command into that one word.

"Fine," Jameson said. With a sleight of hand, he produced a small slip of paper and held it out to Grayson.

Steeling himself for what he was about to read, Grayson took it. "'The Wind,'" he read out loud, the words coming out perplexed. "Cat Stevens, 1971." It wasn't a song he was familiar with, but Grayson was fairly certain that it involved neither milkshakes nor yards.

"Here." Jameson handed Grayson his phone. "It's only fair that you listen to it once before you sing."

Grayson did, and something twisted inside him as he listened. It was beautiful in its own way and suited to his voice, a song about mistakes and what the heart wanted and not knowing how life was going to turn out.

First "Shake It Off." Then "Let It Go." And now—from Jameson of all people—this. It really was like his brothers were trying to tell him something.

ATONEMENT NIGHT, 1:43 AM

His atonement made, Grayson fell into bed, certain of two things: First, he would never again ignore a 911 summons from one of his brothers; and second, he would need to spend considerable time and resources scrubbing the internet of all evidence that this night had ever happened.

Leather Pants Grayson was *not* going to become a meme.

Lying back on his pillow, Grayson closed his eyes. He willed the nothingness to come. Then he felt a warm, wiggly body beside him. With no witnesses present, he didn't hesitate to cuddle the little beast next to him.

"Who's a good girl?"

$3CR3T $@NT@

"The best gifts," Nash said, glancing at Libby, a low, deep hum in his voice, "are the ones you don't even know you want."

Chapter 1

Less than a month after officially becoming the world's youngest billionaire, I woke up on December first to find my sister standing in the doorway to my bedroom, a black velvet Santa hat on her head and a cupcake in her hand.

"'Tis the season," Libby greeted. The cupcake was piled high with cream-colored icing and topped with a miniature gingerbread house.

I peeled back the corner of my covers.

Libby took the unspoken invitation, climbed into my bed, and lifted the cupcake toward my mouth. "Gingerbread," she told me. "With honey cream cheese frosting."

I took a bite and moaned, then went in for a second nibble, carefully eating around the tiny gingerbread house, which appeared to have...

"A teeny-tiny gumdrop graveyard," Libby confirmed, grinning. "Merry Christmas! And speaking of Christmas, someone— maybe multiple *someones*—decorated the House last night."

House, capital *H*. "Why does that sound like a warning?" I said.

"The use of mistletoe is...spirited." Libby was clearly aiming for diplomacy.

"Spirited?" I repeated.

"And creative. And... aggressive."

I read between the lines. "Jameson and Nash booby-trapped this entire forty-thousand-square-foot mansion with mistletoe, didn't they?"

"You say booby-trapped..." Right on cue, Jameson Hawthorne appeared in the doorway, his hair mussed. "I say Christmas at Hawthorne House is a contact sport." He gave me all of two seconds to process that, and then he tossed something at me.

I caught it—a small silver orb. The moment I closed my hand around it, the ball's metal shell began to shift and rotate, revealing a digital timer underneath.

That timer was counting down.

"Ummmm..." Libby looked up, somewhat alarmed. "What's it counting down to?"

Jameson leaned against the doorframe. "Secret Santa. We're drawing names today. Great Room. In..." He nodded toward the tiny clockwork marvel in my hand. "One hour, twelve minutes, and seventeen seconds."

Jameson's lips twisted into a familiar smile. That smile was trouble. The good kind.

"What's the catch, Hawthorne?" I slipped out of bed and began to make my way toward him.

"It is possible," Jameson allowed, "that Hawthorne Secret Santa has a few additional rules."

Chapter 2

*E*spionage. Risk.*" Xander's voice echoed dramatically through the Great Room. *"Defensive maneuvers. Competition."* Xander was enjoying this moment way too much. "This," he boomed, "is Secret Santa!"

"Well, that's not ominous at all," Libby said.

My gaze went to the elaborate cut-glass bowl sitting on top of the massive mantel—and then to the collection of objects *beneath* the mantel. "What's with the squirt guns?" I asked.

Nash sauntered toward the fireplace. The next thing I knew, he had a pistol-sized squirt gun in each hand.

Xander opened his mouth. "Hit me!"

Nash fired. *Bull's-eye.* "Festive water," Nash told Libby and me with a wink. "Courtesy of food dye."

Xander opened his mouth to show off a very green tongue.

Libby raised her hand, like a very earnest student in class. "Why does Secret Santa require squirt guns full of 'festive' water?" she asked.

The answer came from behind us. "Have you ever heard of the game Assassins?" Somehow, Grayson Hawthorne managed to make that sound like the world's most reasonable question.

Jameson, who prided himself on being a bit less reasonable,

elaborated. "In a typical game of Assassins, the players draw names. The name you draw becomes your target. The goal is to take out your target while avoiding being taken out yourself. Gameplay is spread out over days or even weeks. If you squirt someone and take them out, their target becomes yours. The game proceeds until there is only one assassin remaining."

"You see the obvious parallels," Xander told us.

"Between Assassins and...Secret Santa?" Libby was trying for diplomacy again. "I guess they both start out with drawing names?"

"Exactly!" Xander rubbed his hands together. "Now, for the distribution of supplies." He disappeared behind a wingback chair and reappeared with an enormous Santa bag from which he began distributing what at first appeared to be Christmas decorations. "You've got your reinforced garland," he said, piling a mound of it in my arms. "Your weaponized tinsel, your holiday drones, and, of course"—Xander lifted the single ugliest Christmas statue I'd ever seen out of the bag—"the Reindeer of Doom."

I had so many questions. "Start at the beginning," I told all four brothers.

Jameson smiled. "With pleasure."

It probably shouldn't have surprised me that Hawthorne Secret Santa was part Assassins, part Capture The Flag, and wholly competitive.

"So there is one way of permanently taking out another player and two ways of temporarily knocking them out of the game." Libby's expression was pure concentration.

"Correct!" Xander replied. "And what are those ways?" he quizzed.

"You can permanently take your target out of the game by getting them the perfect gift," Libby recited. "And you can temporarily take the person who has *your* name out of the game either by squirting them with any type of red or green liquid or using... one of these?" My sister glanced down at the highly festive arsenal she had been given.

"Ain't no weapon like a Christmas-themed weapon," Xander said. "If you can get the person who drew your name with your squirt gun or tinsel before they can sneak their gift into your base, then they're out of the game for three days, during which time, they can't go on the offensive against the person who drew *their* name." Xander grinned. "As an added bonus, once those three days have passed and the person targeting you is back in the game—if they've survived that long—they have to get you *two* perfect presents instead of just one."

It probably said something about me that this all made a twisted, Hawthorne kind of sense. *Get a perfect present for your target. Sneak it onto their secret base. Don't get caught. Protect your base from whoever drew your name—by any means necessary.*

"Okay." Libby nodded, putting on her game face.

I still had questions. "If you take your target permanently out of the game with a perfect present, you inherit their target, correct?" I verified.

"Correct." Jameson was enjoying this way too much.

"What qualifies as a perfect present?" I asked. Hawthornes were notoriously fond of technicalities and loopholes.

"The best gifts," Nash said, glancing at Libby, a low, deep hum in his voice, "are the ones you don't even know you want." The edges of his mouth crinkled with a subtle smile. "Maybe you don't even know it exists, but the moment you see it..."

"Perfection," Xander finished with a chef's kiss.

Libby slung her reinforced garland around her neck like a feather boa and shook her head. "Only you four could turn gift-giving into a competition."

"I told you two," Jameson said, looking directly at me, "Christmas at Hawthorne House is a contact sport."

"Now," Xander said dramatically, "before we draw names, a few parameters on the choosing of bases. Each player can have only one base. It must be in—or on—the House; it must be bigger than a motorcycle; and it must be marked to indicate that it is yours. If you choose to encode or otherwise mask said marking, so be it."

Libby was right: Only the Hawthorne brothers could have come up with something like this. I looked from Jameson to Nash to Xander—and then to the brother who had said the least since we filed into the Great Room.

"Hide your base well," Grayson advised. "Find ways of defending it without tipping off your opponent about its location."

"Tinsel bombs are strongly encouraged," Jameson added.

This was, quite possibly, the single most Hawthorne thing I'd ever heard of.

"Game ends Christmas morning," Nash told Libby and me, but he had eyes only for her. "Perfect presents take time."

Something occurred to me then: "What if there's more than one player left on Christmas morning?"

In one smooth motion, Grayson bent to pick up a squirt gun and tucked it into the inside pocket of his suit jacket. Then he answered my question. "There won't be."

Chapter 3

Xander was the first person to draw a name from the cut-glass bowl. When he read the slip of paper, he smiled, but it was the kind of smile that gave away *nothing*—Xander's version of a poker face.

Jameson drew next, then Nash, then Grayson, then me.

I looked down at the paper I'd just drawn. *Nash.* I didn't look toward him. I didn't look toward anyone. I just folded the paper in half and then in half again and then into a little triangle and tucked it into the front pocket of my jeans.

I'd have to make sure none of them tried to get ahold of it. In a game like this one, information was power.

Libby drew last. She read the name on her page, cocked her head to the side—and then a stream of red liquid hit her, right in the chest.

She'd been shot. With *festive*, red liquid.

"Hey!" Libby said.

"You drew my name." Grayson, squirt gun still in hand, arched a brow at her. "Did you not?"

Libby scowled at him. "There is no way you could possibly know that!"

"Am I wrong?" Grayson's tone made it clear: He knew he

wasn't. Without waiting for a reply, he tucked the gun back into the inside pocket of his suit.

Nash came up behind Libby. "Three days, Lib," he told her, wrapping his arms around her, cradling her body back against his. "And then you're back in the game."

Libby drew Grayson's name. I have Nash. My brain immediately started sorting through what that meant for everyone else. I looked around the room, studying the Hawthornes.

One of them had drawn my name.

"What happens if you shoot someone and it turns out that you're not their target?" I asked.

"Penalty." Grayson answered in one word.

Libby frowned. "What kind of penalty?"

"Trust me, darlin'..." Nash deployed a slow smile, the kind that might have looked lazy to someone who didn't know him. "You don't want to find out."

That was concerning coming from Nash, who was prone to understatements.

"Bases must be built and marked with your name by sundown." Jameson clearly wasn't avoiding looking at me. He was relishing it. "Libby, you'll need to construct your base, too. Given your sitting-duck status, you can't *actively* fight off a would-be present-giver, so your base's defenses are your best chance at staying in the game."

"I'll show you *sitting duck*," Libby retorted.

I started making my own mental to-do list. *Build a base. Hide it well. Spy on the others. Figure out who has who.*

And as if that wasn't a tall enough order, I also had to try to come up with a perfect present for Nash.

Chapter 4

I constructed my base in the passageway to the vault. Was that cheating, considering that none of the other players had access to that highly secure passageway? Of course not. They were Hawthornes. They'd figure something out.

The booby-trapping and marking of my base took a bit longer. I didn't have Xander's mechanical genius, but the tinsel bombs weren't that hard to figure out, and they were numerous. All it would take was *one*. As for marking the base with my name, I went with a classic: lemon juice. It was one of the simplest, cleanest forms of invisible ink. *And since heat is needed to reveal the message...* I smiled wickedly and planned for that contingency.

And then I covered my tracks.

The fact that the vault was hidden behind the elevator shaft made it easy enough for me to mask where I was coming from. Still, as I stepped out of the elevator on the top floor of Hawthorne House, well removed from my actual base, I couldn't help glancing back over my shoulder.

Espionage, Xander had said. *Risk. Defensive maneuvers. Competition.*

This was Secret Santa.

I spent the next six days trying to locate the other bases, running surveillance on my own base, and reading meaning into every detail of the way that Nash, Grayson, Jameson, and Xander interacted with one another. If I couldn't figure out who had drawn my name, the next best thing was figuring out *any* of the other players' targets. The fewer question marks there were in this equation, the fewer Hawthornes I would have to keep track of.

All of that was easier said than done. By December seventh, I had located only two bases: Libby's was in the walk-in freezer, and Xander's was *inside* one of the hidden staircases that descended into the tunnels. He'd somehow hollowed out the staircase, which would have made for a brilliant hiding spot were it not for the fact that Xander just couldn't help humming to himself when he was in engineering mode.

Based on the amount of humming I'd heard when I'd snuck out of bed at two in the morning to execute a grid search of the mansion, I could only conclude that Xander's base was *highly* booby-trapped.

Luckily, that wasn't my problem. Finding Nash's base was. Tailing him was next to impossible. Nash Hawthorne didn't miss a damn thing. The only distraction that he was even the least bit susceptible to was my sister, and Libby was currently spending all of her time hiding from Grayson, lest he take her out *again*. She'd already been shot *twice*—three days out of the game each time.

Grayson Hawthorne was not the type to leave anything to chance.

Since I couldn't count on Nash to lead me to his base, I had to resort to other tactics.

Namely: *Nan*. "I call," I said. I had a standing weekly poker game with the Hawthorne brothers' great-grandmother.

The old woman scowled at me. "Did I tell you that you could call?"

Somehow, I managed to keep a perfectly straight face. "No, ma'am."

Nan harrumphed. "Impertinent child." Her lips tilted very slightly upward on the ends. "*I* call."

I met Nan's eyes just long enough for her to realize I had a winning hand, and then I placed my cards on the poker table face down. "I fold."

Nan narrowed her eyes. "You want something."

I knew better than to beat around the bush. "I drew Nash in Secret Santa. I need to find his base. And I brought caramels." I reached out to lay four candies on the table between us.

Nan accepted my offering. She took her time eating the first caramel, then jabbed a finger in my direction. "You, girl." That was pretty much a term of endearment coming from Nan. "Hand me my cane."

I gave her a look. "Are you going to poke me with it?"

Nan offered no assurances. I handed her the cane, and she poked me with it. "Tell me, girl," she practically grunted. "Where does my grandson park that godforsaken death contraption of his?"

"His motorcycle?" I said dryly, and then I realized...I didn't know.

I spent three hours exploring the *outside* of Hawthorne House before I found a completely camouflaged garage—not the enormous, showroom-sized one that housed some of the most expensive automobiles in the world but a smaller, one-car garage that I hadn't even known existed. After spotting it on the mansion's exterior, I was able to find a hidden door to it off the massive laundry room.

I knew the second I stepped inside that this place was Nash's. I spotted multiple old guitars, a pair of beat-up motorcycle helmets, some truly muddy boots, and his bike, just as worn as the helmets. Beyond that, there was nothing to indicate that this might be his base—until I looked up.

And here I thought Xander was the mad scientist in the family. Nash had created what looked like a spiderweb of garland on the ceiling, holding a large platform aloft.

When Xander had said the garland was *reinforced* garland, he hadn't been kidding. That stuff was strong.

On the bottom of the platform, Nash had written his name. No code. No invisible ink.

I looked for a ladder and found none. Nash's base was out of reach—for now. Not daring to stay any longer, I turned to leave and came face-to-face with the business end of a squirt gun.

Nash.

He was the one who'd trained me to shoot, and I knew: *He doesn't miss.* But he hadn't taken the shot yet.

"Fancy meeting you here," Nash drawled.

I considered my options. "I seem to recall that there's a penalty for shooting someone if it turns out you aren't their target," I said.

"Sure is," Nash replied, staring me down.

As luck would have it, the Hawthorne pup chose that moment to pad into the garage. Fortunately for me, Tiramisu was almost as fond of me as she was of the boys. I wiggled my fingers by my side, and she bounded toward me. I picked her up, a little puppy shield.

"If you're entertaining ideas about Puppy Hot Potato," Nash warned, "I would recommend you reconsider."

"Wouldn't dream of it," I said from behind the puppy.

Nash was silent for a moment, and then he lowered his weapon by about an inch. "Whose name did you draw?" he asked.

I knew a test when I saw one. Whatever the penalty was for a wrong guess, Nash Hawthorne wanted to be sure, which meant that *I* needed a passable bluff. I couldn't say *Grayson* because everyone knew that Libby had Grayson. I had no idea who Nash had drawn or what he knew about the other players and their targets. But I couldn't afford to hesitate.

"Xander," I said.

Nash studied me. Tiramisu craned her neck backward and managed to lick my face. And then, out of nowhere, a song began to blare from the speakers.

I frowned. "'Grandma Got Run Over by a Reindeer'?"

Nash holstered his squirt gun in the band of his jeans. "That's the song that's played every time a player is taken out of the game for good."

Chapter 5

We soon discovered that the player in question was Libby. I found her sitting outside the walk-in freezer she'd used as her base, covered in tinsel.

"Caught in the explosion of one of your own tinsel bombs?" I asked.

Libby didn't reply. She was sitting cross-legged on the floor, cradling something in her lap. In one smooth movement, Nash hunkered down beside her, crossing his own legs and leaning back against the wall. My eyes were drawn to the object in Libby's hands. It appeared to be a picture frame.

"The perfect gift?" I asked.

Libby looked up at me with tears glistening in her eyes. "So damn perfect."

I sank down next to her, on the opposite side as Nash, to get a better look. The picture frame itself was simple, made of what appeared to be a high-quality silver. It was the picture inside the frame that had a breath catching in the back of my throat.

Libby couldn't have been older than eight or nine in the picture. She wore her brown hair long and loose, but a veritable rainbow of clip-in hair streaks—all of them neon—made her look more like the Libby I knew.

Beside her, there was a toddler. *Me.*

And beside me... "Mom," I said, my voice little more than a whisper. I had pictures of my mother, but not any from when I was this young.

"My ninth birthday," Libby told me. "Your mom had a friend take this picture." My sister—my *half* sister, though I never thought of her that way—brought a finger to the photo. Little Libby and Toddler Avery were both wearing reams of Mardi Gras beads. We were smiling.

I had no memories of this day, no memories of the days when Libby's mom had used mine as a babysitter at all, but Libby had told me before: Her ninth birthday, the only birthday she'd celebrated with my mom and me, had been the best day of her life.

And there it was, immortalized in a frame.

"Who?" I managed to ask. Who was Libby's Secret Santa? Which of the Hawthorne brothers had managed to get ahold of this picture after all these years?

Libby hugged the frame to her chest. "I have no idea."

My money was on either Jameson or Grayson. Nash had seemed as surprised by the gift as Libby and I had been, and the execution didn't feel like Xander to me. This had been the work of someone who noticed everything, someone who hadn't stuck around to see Libby open the present.

Someone who was playing this game to win.

If Jameson is the one who took out Libby, I thought, once I'd left Libby and Nash to their own devices, *then Jameson just inherited Libby's target: Grayson.* The wheels in my head turned a little further. *But if Grayson did it...*

I wondered what happened if a person ended up as their own target.

Regardless, it was clear to me that if Libby's present was the blueprint for what qualified as perfect, I had some work to do to take Nash out.

Big time.

I also needed a plan to get back to the garage without him catching me. One time, he might be able to chalk up to coincidence and me looking for Xander's base. But twice?

I'd be toast.

Hawthorne Secret Santa required *strategy*.

Over the next few days, as I strategized, it finally occurred to me to take advantage of the fact that, along with Tobias Hawthorne's fortune, I'd also inherited his security team.

"Hypothetically speaking," I said to Oren around December tenth, "if I asked you to start following me around the House again to guard against an impending threat, what would you say?"

"Threat of being temporarily taken out of the game?" My head of security *might* have been amused by the request, but he kept a mostly straight face. "I hear the boys have started using red and green eggnog instead of water in their guns, and I'm afraid eggnogging falls outside of my purview." He gave me a look. "I'm also not going to provide any reports on the specific Hawthorne or Hawthornes who may or may not have been tailing you."

In other words, someone *had* been tailing me. Maybe multiple someones.

I resisted the urge to look over my shoulder. "You're not going to help me," I summarized. "But I'm guessing you're not going to prevent me from accessing the security feeds, either."

Surrounded by monitors, I made myself right at home. I'd been scanning the feeds for all of five minutes when I felt someone else step into the room behind me.

"Why, Heiress, I'm shocked."

I kept my gaze on the monitors but couldn't help the way the edges of my lips crept upward, just hearing his voice. "No, you aren't."

Jameson made no attempt to mask the sound of his footsteps as he paced slowly toward me. "No," he admitted. "I'm not."

He lowered himself into the chair next to mine, angling his body so that his left knee brushed oh-so-lightly against my right one.

"Hardly sporting of you," he continued. "Almost as bad as hiding your base in the vault."

Busted. I kept my poker face firmly in place and turned to angle my eyes toward Jameson. I looked for the story told by the tiny details of his facial expression: Did he *know* where my base was, or was he guessing?

I considered my options, then played my next card. "Not *in* the vault," I said.

The slightest twitch of Jameson's lips told me: He hadn't been guessing. He knew where my base was—not in the vault, but in front of it. And that led me to one rock-solid conclusion.

"You didn't draw my name," I said. "I'm not your target." If I had been, he would already have made an attempt to take me out—and he probably would have succeeded.

I knew Jameson Hawthorne well enough to know that he wouldn't have any trouble at all finding a perfect present for me.

"You aren't my target," Jameson confirmed. "*Yet.*" That had the air of a promise. "I'm very good at Secret Santa," he told me. "If I take out enough targets . . ."

Sooner or later, he'd get my name.

I leaned forward in my chair and pushed Jameson back in his. "You didn't draw my name," I said, shifting my weight forward, "and neither did Nash." I paused, letting my eyes do my talking for me for just a moment. "Neither did Libby."

"If this is your attempt to distract me," Jameson said, "it is one hundred percent working and will continue to work more or less indefinitely."

I read between the lines of everything that had happened and everything he had and hadn't said.

"You drew Libby," I said. "You're the one who took her out." He was the miracle worker who'd found that photograph.

"I can neither confirm nor deny that statement." Jameson lifted a hand to brush my hair back from my face. "Your mom was beautiful," he said softly. "She had your smile."

In other words: He was definitely the person who'd found the photograph. A lump rose in my throat. "I think most people would probably say that I have hers," I told him.

"I have other pictures." Jameson brought his hand to my hair again, tucking another stray wisp behind my ear. "For you, Heiress— and not a part of the game."

Not a part of the game. When I'd first come to Hawthorne House, everything had been a game to him, and now...

"You're perfect," I said, my voice a little rough. "You know that?"

"I think you might be confusing me with someone else," Jameson quipped.

I gave him a look. "Never."

He gave me a look. "I keep thinking about last Christmas. You were still recovering from the coma."

Last Christmas, we hadn't played Secret Santa.

Last Christmas, we'd been together, but I hadn't been his and he hadn't been mine the way we were now.

"Just for the record...," Jameson told me, standing and reaching for my hand, pulling me inward, like we'd just been transported to a ballroom and this was our dance. "When I take out enough targets to inherit your name, my present will be *beyond* perfect." He smiled that dangerous, heady smile of his. "Also for the record: If you thought that this room escaped the mistletoe treatment..." He looked pointedly upward. "You were wrong."

Chapter 6

By December fourteenth, I was ready to make my move against Nash. Finding the perfect gift for our resident cowboy had proved to be the easier part of the equation. Getting close to the garage again without getting tinsel-bombed or eggnogged was harder. Luckily, I had an accomplice.

Nash had a history of finding Libby very *distracting*, and now that she was out of the game, my sister had a lot of time on her hands. I let her know when I was done and left one of my "holiday drones" in Nash's garage to observe his reaction when he found my present.

Conveniently, the rules in this game specified that each base had to be large enough to hold a *motorcycle*.

On the drone's video feed, Nash looked up at the broken-down, beat-up, literally-in-pieces motorcycle I'd bought him. "Needs some work," he murmured, but I knew: For Nash, the work was part of the appeal. "But," he continued, "she has promise."

He hadn't deemed it a perfect present yet, but he also hadn't found the helmet yet. The moment he did, I sent Libby a text: *NOW*.

She stepped into the room wearing a blue flannel shirt. "I believe," my sister told Nash, "that helmet's for me."

Nash executed an impressive vertical leap, grabbed the edge of the wooden platform, and managed to get the helmet in question down without disturbing the motorcycle he'd need to rebuild, practically from scratch.

I saw the exact moment he realized: "The motorcycle's not for me."

It was for Libby. "I thought you might like restoring it together," I said over the drone's audio feed.

Nash looked at Libby, looked back at his present overhead, and then raised the helmet toward the drone in salute. "Well played, kid."

I took that as an admission that my gift was *perfect*. As soon as I could manage it, "Grandma Got Run Over by a Reindeer" was blaring through the House.

In the aftermath, Nash informed me of my next target, the name that he had drawn. *Jameson*.

I had Jameson. Jameson had Grayson. Nash and Libby were out of the game. That meant that either Grayson had me and Xander had drawn his own name—in which case, I could only assume that we would have had to re-draw names, right at the start—or . . .

Xander had me, and Grayson had Xander.

Assuming that was true, I now had four tasks:

Finding the perfect present for Jameson.

Preventing him from discovering that I now had his name and taking me out.

Finding Jameson's base.

And taking out Xander before he could find mine.

On December sixteenth, scones proved to be the youngest Hawthorne brother's downfall. I shot him in the forehead mid-midnight snack. That bought me three days, after which, Xander was *nowhere* to be seen. Becoming increasingly paranoid—on all fronts—I decided to make use of the secret passageways and lay in wait for Xander near the vault, which was exactly what I was doing when I caught sight of Grayson moving silently and swiftly through the halls.

Toward his base? I wondered.

Grayson was Jameson's target, but if I succeeded at taking Jameson out, he'd be mine, and I'd need every advantage I could get. Flipping into stealth mode, I followed Grayson, all the way to the top floor—and upward still.

The roof? I hung back enough to make sure I was safe, then started the climb. The moment I did, Grayson stepped out of the shadows behind me.

"You doubled back," I said.

Grayson took another step toward me, then stopped, like there was an invisible wall between us. "You don't have me," he declared—not even a hint of a question mark in his tone. "Jameson does." He held open his suit jacket and glanced pointedly down at the pistol-sized squirt gun he'd holstered there. "No need for me to draw this, I suppose."

I pulled out my own gun and twirled it around my finger. No sense in letting Grayson Hawthorne get *too* comfortable in his own knowledge—or his presumed supremacy in this game.

"You seem pretty confident that I'm not distracting you *for* Jameson," I noted.

Grayson's silvery eyes locked on to mine. "I am not so easily distracted."

I glanced up at the ceiling and what I knew to be one of many trap doors to the roof. "I don't want to go up there, do I?"

If I'd learned one thing about Hawthorne Secret Santa so far, it was that Grayson Davenport Hawthorne was merciless. *Booby-trapped* was probably an understatement for what he'd done to his base.

"I assure you," Grayson replied austerely, "you do not."

I could hear the barest hint of humor hiding beneath that tone—and then I realized, belatedly, that there was something else in his tone, too.

Something…*suspect.* I thought about the way I'd spied Grayson, and then I realized…

"Are you distracting me for Xander?"

Grayson's expression gave away nothing until he spoke. "It is possible that the brother in question is unaware that he is my target."

It didn't take me long to connect the dots there. "You're distracting me to distract him," I accused.

"Would I do a thing like that?" Grayson rightened his suit jacket without so much as cracking a smile, but his eyes said it all.

Xander's sneaking a present onto my base.

I bolted, practically flying back toward the vault. When I got there, I found Xander tangled in garland and covered from head to toe in tinsel.

"I commend your use of tinsel bombs," he said solemnly.

"I have a friend who's taught me a lot about explosives." I smiled, and then, for good measure, I took advantage of the fact that my squirt gun was still in my hand and shot him with green eggnog.

"Betrayed by the Nog of Egg," Xander said mournfully. "So creamy. So violent."

I nodded to a present that seemed to have fallen at his feet. "Is that for me?" I asked. The wrapping paper was red and green and…*donut themed?*

"Indeed it is," Xander confirmed, smiling beneath all that tinsel. "But you can't have it yet. Rules are rules. I have to try again. On the bright side, if I survive the next three days as a sitting duck, I'll owe you *two* presents."

I thought about Grayson, who'd distracted me for the sole purpose of keeping Xander occupied. "I don't like your chances of survival, Xan."

Xander cocked his head to the side and then snapped his fingers. "Grayson?"

"Grayson," I confirmed.

"There is a reason," Xander sighed, "that he wins Secret Santa almost every year, and it's not just that he is very hard to shop for."

Without bothering to rid himself of the tinsel, Xander stood up. "I should probably go check out my base, but fair warning, Avery of My Platonic Heart, the moment a certain song signals what I am sure is my at-this-point-inevitable demise, Grayson's target will officially be...*you*."

Chapter 7

C hristmas was rapidly approaching, and Jameson, Grayson, and I were the only ones left in the game. I had Jameson. Jameson had Grayson. Grayson had me.

It had taken me some time to come up with the perfect present for Jameson, and it had taken me even longer to find his base, which I eventually located in the closed-off passageway behind my fireplace. Jameson's defenses were impressive, but Grayson was more than happy to help me take out his brother.

The moment that Jameson walked in to find *Grayson* caught in the booby traps he'd laid for me was sweet for so many reasons.

Rainbow tinsel was a good look for Grayson Hawthorne.

Surprise was a good look for Jameson.

Victory was an incredible look for me.

His gaze lingering on mine, Jameson ducked down to pick up the present I'd wedged through the motion-sensor-laden garland that surrounded his base. I'd chosen to leave Jameson's present right next to the object he'd used to mark his base: a travel-sized bottle of Jameson whiskey with the label peeled off.

Clever Hawthorne.

I watched as Jameson opened the envelope containing his gift from me. Inside, there was a flight plan and a travel itinerary.

The day after Christmas, he and I were headed to Tahiti.

Christmas Eve. I was Grayson's target. He was mine. Since all his brothers had a wish to see him dethroned from Secret Santa supremacy, I had no shortage of allies.

But he was Grayson Hawthorne.

Maybe that was how the two of us ended up in a standoff in the hallway in between our bases, weapons drawn, our gifts for each other in our free hands.

"Christmas is tomorrow," I said, ready to pull the trigger at a moment's notice. "If either one of us shoots, the other loses."

If both of us shot, and both of us hit our targets, we both would.

"I like my chances," Grayson told me.

I gave him a look that, by this point, he probably recognized all too well. "No. You don't."

Keeping his eyes on me the entire time, Grayson knelt. His present for me was large and unwieldly—at least four feet long, maybe eight inches wide, not that deep. But somehow, Grayson Hawthorne managed to place it on the ground without ever losing his balance.

Without ever taking his eyes off me.

My present for Grayson was smaller. I laid it on the ground beside his offering.

"I'll open yours," Grayson proposed. "You open mine." He was every inch the heir apparent, used to striking deals. "Loser drops their gun and submits."

I could only assume that by *loser*, he meant the person whose present was less perfect.

"Deal," I told Grayson.

I opened his present for me first. Beneath solid silver wrapping paper, garnished with a perfect navy bow, I found a wooden box made of cedar.

Four feet long, less than a foot wide, not that deep. I had no idea what was inside, but the second I opened the box, I was hit with the realization that I probably should have guessed what he'd gotten me.

"A longsword," I said, running my fingers along its blade.

"I'm told its first bearer was a woman," Grayson murmured. "Sixteenth century, give or take."

My fingers worked their way into round, hollow places in the sword's hilt, where I suspected there had once been jewels.

I liked it better without them.

"Now we have five," I said. In the center of the hedge maze outside, there was a hidden compartment that held four long-swords, originally purchased for the four Hawthorne brothers.

And now there were five.

My confidence in my own present wavered, just for a moment. But as Grayson began to unwrap it, I felt a surge of rightness.

Wrapping paper fell to the floor as Grayson turned the plain gray rock over in his hands. It was smooth—ocean smooth, the result of thousands of years of waves. The only parts of the rock that weren't smooth were the inscriptions, front and back.

On the front, I'd gone for a familiar Latin phrase. *EST UNUS EX NOBIS. NOS DEFENDAT EIUS.* It was something Grayson had said about me once. On the back, I'd opted for English, something that *I* had said to him.

IT GOES BOTH WAYS.

Grayson's fingers closed around the rock and he looked up, his eyes locking on to mine once more.

"Merry Christmas, Grayson," I said. I was on the verge of proposing a tie, but I didn't get the chance.

"Avery?" Grayson took a step toward me, and his lips curved into one of those very Grayson Hawthorne smiles, subtle but true. "You win."

WHAT HAPPENS IN THE TREE HOUSE

For a moment, the four of them stared out at the city. And then they jumped.

London, England
The day of Nash's bachelor party

Xander Hawthorne was a man of many talents.

"You have no vision."

"You have no decency."

Even from the hallway, Xander immediately recognized which one of those statements had been made by Jameson and which had been made by Grayson. Given that one of Xander's talents was Hawthorne mediation, he took the entire exchange as his cue to make an entrance.

"You have no baked goods!" he intoned, joining the melee and wheeling an enormous corkboard and assorted supplies into the room where his brothers were debating the evening's plans.

"I'm not hungry." Grayson frowned. "And where did you get that corkboard?"

Xander responded as one did in situations that called for subtlety and nuance: by tossing multiple objects directly at Grayson's head. "Have a scone! Hold my yarn!"

Grayson caught the scone with one hand and the skein of yarn with the other.

Xander blithely continued distributing supplies. "You, pushpins!" he told Jameson, tossing a small box of them his way. "Me, index cards!" Xander grinned. "Scones for all of us!"

Grayson eyed the board, the cards, and the yarn, ignoring the scones altogether. "We're planning Nash's bachelor party, not solving a murder, Xan."

Jameson gave the box of pushpins a twirl. "I like it."

"You would," Grayson muttered.

Gray might require some persuading, Xander thought. "Marker incoming!" He flung the marker at Grayson's forehead. Nothing said *persuasion* like a projectile thrown with love.

Grayson's hand caught the marker a second before impact.

Beside them, Jameson snapped his fingers. "I need my own marker and an index card," he told Xander, with an expression that could be described as either wicked…or *inspired*.

Grayson scowled. "Do *not* give him an index card."

"I will not," Xander replied solemnly. "I shall give him five index cards!" In the interest of fairness, Xander distributed the same number to Grayson and to himself. He tossed Jameson a marker, then uncapped his own and scrawled his first contribution onto one of his cards.

Grayson's eyes narrowed. "What in the name of all that is good and holy do you mean by *clubbing-slash-RBG*?"

Xander ignored the question. "I need a pushpin," he told Jameson, who responded by taking Xander's card and pinning it onto the board—alongside two of his own.

Grayson read Jameson's cards. He opened his mouth to object, but Xander intervened. Since he was out of projectiles, he opted for diplomacy. "We each get five cards and three vetoes," he suggested. "Once all proposals and vetoes have been finalized, the activities that remain on the board will be locked, and we'll use the yarn to plot out the night's progression from start to finish."

It was a good plan. A very Hawthorne plan.

"Deal," Jameson said immediately.

Grayson inclined his head—and then he stepped forward and mercilessly removed one of Jameson's cards from the board. "Veto."

This was going to be fun.

London, England
Some time later
Indoor ice-climbing facility

"So this is what five hundred tons of ice looks like," Jameson mused as all four of them walked toward the base of the towering frozen wall. Xander assessed the situation. The higher you went up the wall of ice, the more treacherous the climb became.

Excellent! Xander was pleased. "The ice is a metaphor," he said sagely.

Nash cocked a brow. "A metaphor for what?"

"Either your heart or your ass," Xander replied immediately. "It's hard to say which."

Nash snorted. "My heart ain't ice, Xan."

That was why they were here, why Nash had used his yearly 911, why the four of them were celebrating with one epic night. Nash Hawthorne had fallen in love. He'd let someone in. He'd *proposed*. To Xander, that seemed as breathtakingly magnificent as the massive wall of ice in front of them.

"You do realize," Grayson told Nash archly, "that you have just implied that your ass *is* ice?"

Nash tilted his head back, looked at the bell at the top of the climb, and gave the ice ax in his hand a little spin. "Let's make this interesting." Nash had taken off his trademark cowboy hat when they'd arrived at this establishment, but his tone was one hundred percent cowboy-proposing-a-shoot-off. "First one to the top…" Nash threw down the gauntlet.

Xander beat his brothers to filling in the blank. "Wins the right to choose our fake names for the evening! And last one to the top…"

"Has to wear the leather pants," Jameson cut in.

Grayson's right eyebrow twitched. "What leather pants?"

"*The* leather pants," Jameson replied. "I like to think of them as yours."

Xander adopted an angelic expression. "I might have brought them with me to London. A Hawthorne comes prepared!"

Refusing to rise to the bait, Grayson turned his attention to the ice wall, skimming his gaze over the most hazardous portions. "Since I do not intend on coming in last," he said finally, "I have no objection to the proposed wager. Nash?"

The man of the hour grinned. "Bring it on, little brothers."

Xander exchanged looks with Jameson and Grayson, and in the silent language of three brothers born in three years' time, they reached an unspoken agreement. *Nash is going down.*

He was the guest of honor at this little shindig. Those leather pants were rightfully his.

"You three done silently plotting against me yet?" Nash drawled.

"What's that saying of yours?" Jameson gave his own ice ax a twirl.

Xander and Grayson supplied the answer in a single voice: "There's no such thing as fighting dirty if you win."

London, England
Some time later
Skywalk Experience

Location: a billion-dollar stadium. Activity: not soccer—or football, as it was called on this side of the pond.

One by one, the Hawthorne brothers donned the appropriate harnesses.

Their guide cleared his throat. "Are you sure that you are

quite dressed for this activity, sir?" The man eyed Nash's cowboy hat—and his leather pants.

"You're right." Nash removed the hat with one hand and strode to the side of the staging area, where an eleven- or twelve-year-old girl sat by herself. She'd been sneaking awed looks at them since they arrived. Based on her puffy eyes, Xander was guessing the girl had gotten scared and bowed out of doing the Skywalk with her group.

He was also guessing she'd recognized the famous—and occasionally infamous—Hawthorne brothers.

Nash knelt in front of the girl. "Do me a favor, little darlin'?" He held the hat out to her, and the girl looked like she was going to faint—or possibly combust with joy. "Hold my hat."

With their harnesses clipped to the supports, Xander and his brothers began their ascent. Stage one of the climb took them around the outside of the stadium, slowly winding their way higher and higher.

The view was already astounding. Jameson was at the front of their group, Xander in the rear. But Grayson was the one who broke the awed silence of their climb.

"Would you rather," the most intense Hawthorne said, enunciating the words as the wind around them ticked up a notch, "die by falling to your death from a great height...or by tripping over your own two feet and hitting your head on a rock."

"Height." Jameson didn't even have to think about it.

Xander's imagination took hold. He visualized what that fall would be like, imagined seeing it coming, anticipating the *splat*. "Rock."

Nash weighed his options. "Rock," he said finally.

Grayson, as the person who'd issued the scenario, went last. "Height."

That surprised Xander a little, but before he could follow up, Jameson was tossing another scenario out like a grenade.

"Would you rather have your ex officiate your wedding...or have her marry one of your brothers?"

Xander, as always, appreciated Jameson's unique combination of creativity and deviousness. The question was clearly targeted at Nash, and the idea of Alisa officiating what would no doubt be a very goth wedding was *priceless*.

Nash groaned. "You're evil, Jamie." He paused. "And *wedding*. Definitely the wedding."

"I'm going to go with have her marry a brother," Xander declared, just to keep things interesting. If one wanted to get technical, he did not technically have an ex—though he *did* have a fake ex. "Keeping it in the family: the Hawthorne way."

"Very funny, Xander," Grayson said.

And so it went, scenario after scenario as they made their way to the top. *Would you rather discover that your inner monologue has somehow become a popular podcast or lose the ability to think in words at all?*

Would you rather sprout horns every time you experience sexual attraction or burst into noisy tears every time you try to tamp down an emotion?

Would you rather be incapable of lying or incapable of being lied to?

"Would you rather shave your head..." Xander posed as they approached the summit of the climb. "...or shave *Grayson's* head?"

"*What?*" Grayson was not amused.

Their guide chose that moment to delicately interrupt and direct them toward the next section of the Skywalk, which would take them out over a glass roof, the stadium visible more than a hundred fifty feet below. This time, Nash went first, and as he did, he posed a scenario of his own. "Would you rather get to see the old man again, just once, for an hour," Nash said, taking his time with the words, "or have him see you—everything your life is, everything you are—every day?"

It wasn't like Nash to bring up their grandfather. He and the old man hadn't been on the best terms for the years leading up to the billionaire's death. Of all of them, Nash was the one who'd most resisted becoming what Tobias Hawthorne wanted him to be.

Ambitious.

Fueled by purpose.

Extraordinary.

"I'd choose," Nash said quietly, "for him to see me."

"I wouldn't." That was Jameson, but Xander didn't hear the rest of his response, because for an instant, all Xander could think about was what he could do with an hour, what he would say to the man who'd raised him.

The man who'd kept his father from him for *years*.

"Xan?" Grayson's voice was quiet as they reached the end of the glass walkway, and Xander realized that he'd missed Grayson's answer. *I'm the only one who hasn't replied.* "I'd take the hour," he said, then he looked to Nash. "You'd really want him watching you *every day*?"

Nash didn't wait for their guide before he strolled up to the very edge of the stadium. All that was left now was the descent. The *jump*.

"Sure would," Nash drawled. "I'm livin' my life on my terms. Getting married to a girl of *my* choosing. Helping people, when and where I want to. Someday, Lib and me, we'll have a family, and our kids?" Nash's whiskey-smooth voice grew thick. "They will *always* be enough for me." Nash looked down at the drop and didn't so much as blink. "Let the great Tobias Hawthorne chew on that."

Xander joined Nash at the stadium's edge, followed by Jameson, then Grayson. For a moment, the four of them stared out at the city.

And then they jumped.

London, England
Some time later
A nightclub that shall remain nameless

Moped racing was the third activity of the night. By the time they'd sated the Hawthorne need for speed, it was getting late. *But not too late*, Xander thought wickedly, *for the next stage of the plan. Clubbing!*

"We're on the list." Grayson adopted an inscrutable expression as he met the bouncer's gaze.

"Last name is Thorne," Jameson added. He'd won at the ice climb, and that was the fake surname he'd chosen for them—an obvious abbreviation of their own.

"First names?" the bouncer grunted.

"Remington." Jameson gestured to himself, then nodded to Nash and Xander. "Dallas. Hawk. And…" Jameson grinned as he turned toward Grayson. "Sven."

The bouncer looked up from the list. "Sven?"

Xander admired the fact that Grayson's lips didn't so much as twitch.

"Is there a problem?" Gray asked, his tone exuding power and calm.

The bouncer looked back down at the list. "No problem."

Like clockwork, a hostess appeared to escort the four of them past the ropes. "Right this way, gentlemen."

Xander grinned. The VIP area awaited.

"What do you think, Sven?" Jameson said as the four of them slid into a booth behind yet more velvet ropes. "The dance floor calling your name?"

Grayson ignored the question, and Xander could not help but notice that the hostess seemed to be making a real effort *not* to stare at him—at all of them.

Fake names only go so far.

"What can I get you gentlemen to drink?"

Since this stop had been one of his contributions to the evening's plans, Xander took it upon himself to answer her. "What do you have that glows in the dark?"

A minute later, the hostess was out of earshot, and Nash shot the other three a look. "If we stay here, we're going to be recognized."

"All four of us?" Grayson said. "Together? Without question."

One Hawthorne could sometimes go incognito. But all four brothers? There was no way. Which was why, in Xander's opinion, there wasn't a moment to waste. "All the more reason to get down to it," he said.

Nash's eyes narrowed slightly. "Get down to what, exactly?"

"RBG," Xander replied, as if that was self-explanatory. But since his brothers were looking at him like his meaning somehow *wasn't* clear, he placed his phone in the center of the table, brought up the new app he'd been working on, and elaborated. "Random Boogie Generator. It's like a random number generator but with dance moves."

Silence descended over their table. Jameson recovered first. "Let's not forget," he told Nash, "this is *your* party."

Nash rolled with the punches. "What kind of dance moves?"
Xander smiled peacefully. "All kinds."

The waitress reappeared with a tray of glasses, the contents of which did indeed glow in the dark. After distributing them, she made her exit once more.

Nash surveyed the crowded dance floor. "This isn't exactly my kind of establishment, and that's not my kind of dancing."

Grayson was the one who replied. "We...dare...you." Each word was issued with the force of a gunshot. His eyes on Nash's, Grayson raised a glass. Xander and Jameson followed suit.

Accepting his fate, Nash did the same. He tossed back his drink and grinned. "Bring it."

London, England
The same nightclub
Twelve minutes later

The situation was thus: Nash on the dance floor. Cowboy hat? Check. Leather pants? Check. Ass? Shaking.

Letting his own body move to the beat of the music, Xander continued calling out dance moves as the RBG provided them, well aware that Nash was starting to draw an audience. "Hip thrust! Hip thrust!"

Nash complied. "We sure this is *random*?"

Jameson took the phone from Xander and hit the button. "Body roll!"

Xander grabbed it back. "Cha-cha!" He tossed the phone to Grayson next.

Gray caught it, hit the button, and met Nash's gaze. "Booty pop."

Nash popped that booty.

"Hip thrust!"

"Shimmy!"

Nash was *definitely* being recorded, and this was definitely ending up on the internet, but Hawthornes didn't do anything halfway.

"Pirouette!" Xander yelled over the now-roaring crowd. And then he hit the button one last time and grinned. "Shirt off!"

London, England
Outside the nightclub
A few minutes later

In the alleyway, Xander eyed the club's back exit, Jameson beside him, each of them holding a roll of duct tape. After a moment, the metal door opened, and Grayson slipped out.

"Did he see you leave?" Xander asked.

"He did," Grayson confirmed.

"Think he'll take the bait?" Jameson asked.

Grayson brushed an imaginary speck of lint off his suit. "What do you take me for, an amateur?"

Sure enough, Nash followed.

Did the four of them *have* to pounce the moment he came out the door? Strictly speaking, no. Did they *have* to overpower him, duct-tape him, blindfold him, and hoist him into the air? Also no.

But *did* they?

Certainly! Per the plan, they ditched the mopeds, stuffed Nash into the back of a chauffeured car, and instructed the driver to deliver them to the exact spot on the Thames where a speedboat was ready and waiting.

Did they *have* to tape Nash to the guardrails of the boat?

Yes. Yes, they did.

A high-speed boat ride, a few more alleyways, and a remarkable descent later, they arrived at the evening's last location: a medieval crypt beneath London, big enough to host a ball. The architecture was stunning. Tonight, the space was lit only by candlelight, a single table set up in the middle of the room, four chairs surrounding the table.

Jameson removed Nash's blindfold, and Xander *heard* the breath their brother took in as he absorbed their surroundings.

"Lib would approve," Nash said quietly, and Xander wondered if Nash was imagining getting married to Libby in a place just like this: eerie but beautiful—almost otherworldly.

"I can't believe you're getting married." The words were out of Xander's mouth before he'd even thought them.

"Wild horses couldn't stop me." Nash's gaze landed on the table, which held a single champagne bottle and four elaborate goblets.

"Black champagne," Grayson said, crossing the room to remove it from the ice, "in Libby's honor."

There was an emotion Xander couldn't quite pinpoint in Grayson's tone, in the lines of his face as he removed the cork from the bottle and poured the black champagne, which appeared closer to a very dark purple in color.

Swallowing, Grayson closed his fingers around the stem on one of the goblets. "To Nash," he said quietly.

Jameson brushed past Xander and claimed one of the goblets. He held it slightly aloft, his gaze landing on Nash's. Xander felt a shift in the air, like the winds of change.

In this moment, Nash and Libby—it was real. And tonight wasn't just adrenaline-fueled fun and leather pants and forcing

Nash to dance. It was a rite of passage. The end of an era and the start of another.

"Right after Emily died," Jameson said softly, his eyes still on Nash's, "you came home."

"And you," Nash countered, "stole my motorcycle."

Xander's eyes widened. *After I worked so hard to prevent it the first time?* "I can only assume," Xander said cheerfully, "that the ass-kicking that followed was epic?"

Jameson met Nash's gaze. "It was something." The memory thick in the air between them, Jameson raised his glass. "To Nash."

Feeling suddenly nostalgic, Xander claimed his own goblet of black champagne. He held it aloft and closed his eyes, and a moment later, he opened them. "Do you remember the time I climbed that tree?" he asked Nash.

"Which tree?" Nash replied calmly.

"Sequoia National Park." Xander could *feel* himself smiling. "I was five."

"The giant sequoia?" Nash groaned. "I *still* don't know how the hell you got all the way up there."

Now it was Xander's turn to meet Nash's eyes. "You got me down." A muscle in Xander's throat tightened as he raised his glass. "To Nash."

The four of them fell into silence for a small eternity, and then Grayson spoke. "The December that Xander was born," he said quietly. "The day he came home from the hospital."

Nash gave Grayson a look. "No way you remember that. You were two."

"I remember...you." Gray's voice was thick now. "Always you."

Xander felt that. They all felt it. This moment. This time in Nash's life. This change.

"Always," Nash said, his voice coming out rough and low. "Lib and me getting married won't change that. It won't change us. *This.*"

Silently, Grayson raised his glass all the way up. One by one, the others did the same.

"What happens in the tree house…," Grayson said, his voice thick with emotion.

"Stays in the tree house," Xander, Jameson, and Nash finished as one. All four of them took a drink of the black champagne. All four of them *felt* the moment—Xander knew they did.

This time, he was the one who broke the silence. "More champagne," he declared. "Then who wants to wrestle?"

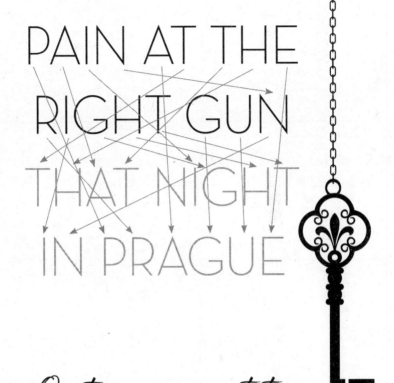

PAIN AT THE RIGHT GUN
THAT NIGHT IN PRAGUE

*Questions were meant to
be answered, mysteries solved.
And when your last name was
Hawthorne, there was always
one more mystery.*

Consciousness came slowly, like a wave over unstable sand. The first thing Jameson became aware of was the cloth bag over his head, its rough fabric scratchy against the skin of his face.

The second thing that penetrated the inky blackness of his mind was the feeling of his hands, bound at the wrists, his arms strung up over his head. He struggled against the binding and heard the clinking of metal.

A chain.

He was chained.

Fear came first, like ice in his veins, and then full awareness hit him all at once, as the crush of memory after memory began rushing in. *The Royal Suite. The wall behind the wall. Three lines. The pearls.* Jameson remembered the moment, the day before Avery had come to Prague, when he'd pieced it all together.

The map. He remembered finding the first passageway. And the second. Thinking—or trying to—made it easier not to feel. Fear was a beast that went for the jugular, if you let it.

Chains. I'm chained.

"You shouldn't be here." The voice was familiar, but Jameson's brain was hazy enough that he couldn't place it—other than that it belonged to a woman. *Or a girl.* He heard footsteps coming closer. He felt the tip of something sharp and metallic come to rest at the base of his neck, just over his collarbone.

A knife? No amount of fighting through his mental fog to *think* could prevent Jameson from tasting fear, like metal on his tongue. *A knife or—*

The blade—if it *was* a blade—dug into his flesh, bit by bit. With pain came clarity and the stubborn refusal to be afraid at all. In the blink of an eye, Jameson remembered what he'd been doing when the darkness had overtaken him.

Vinárna Čertovka. He'd been making his way through that most narrow of streets, Avery behind him, when he'd seen—*Not possible.*

He'd seen a ghost. A ghost who had, as he'd given chase, disappeared. A ghost who, almost certainly, had not expected him to follow beyond a hidden door.

"Alice." The second Jameson said his long-dead grandmother's first name, the person standing in front of him—the woman, the girl—began the task of meticulously cutting the buttons off his shirt, one by one.

Baring more skin.

More.

Jameson was hit by the sudden, sickening thought that she was broadening her canvas.

And then a new voice spoke, light and airy, calm and controlled. "That's enough." This woman, Jameson was sure, was older.

She sounded a bit like his aunt Zara.

"I think we can agree," the first voice said, bringing her weapon of choice to rest once more at the place where Jameson's collarbone dipped, the place she had already marked, "this situation merits more than *watching.*"

There was a moment of silence, and then the second voice, the older one—*Alice, the old man's Alice, the love of his damned life in that Hawthorne-men-love-only-once kind of way*—spoke again. "Tilt his head back."

Hands grabbed Jameson by the chin. This time, he didn't fight the fear. He *used* it, fighting with everything he had. And still, something was poured down his throat.

Thick, like syrup. Bitter, like fear.

Strong hands forced his jaw closed, blocked his ability to breathe through his nose. He fought swallowing the liquid.

Fought—and lost.

Within thirty second, darkness claimed him once more.

When Jameson came to, the air smelled of smoke. Not just *smelled*—he could feel the smoke on his skin, feel the *fire* closing in. The heat was already unbearable, the crackle of flames—*multiple flames*—jerking his body violently into survival mode. *Fight or flight.* There was no in between.

Jameson pulled against the chains that bound him, against the cuffs on his wrists. *No.* A Hawthorne didn't give up. Hawthornes *fought*.

The chains. The flames. Have to—

He kept fighting. He breathed—and tried not to.

Breathed—and tried not to.

In the distance, he heard voices. Three of them, calmly discussing the price of wheat.

Let me go. Saying the words would have meant taking another breath, and the smoke was so thick now that he couldn't afford to breathe.

He couldn't—

He breathed.

And not long after that, he stopped breathing.

The third time Jameson woke, there was no fire, no chains on his wrists, no bag on his face. He was outdoors on a rooftop terrace, sitting at a small, round table surrounded by the quaintest flower garden imaginable.

Sitting across from him was his dead grandmother. Jameson was struck by how very much she looked like Skye.

"You favor your grandfather," Alice Hawthorne said, her own thoughts running eerily parallel to his. "When he was young."

"You're—" Jameson's voice burned his throat.

"No one," Alice Hawthorne said, lifting a cup of tea to her mouth. So casual. So dainty. "I am no one, dear boy." He couldn't tell if that was affection in her tone or a warning—or both. "You have seen and heard nothing. Prague is a wonderful city, but it is not for you to explore." She set her teacup down, and it clinked lightly against the saucer. "I hear Belize is lovely this time of year."

Jameson's mind was the type that never stopped. Questions were meant to be answered, mysteries solved. And when your last name was Hawthorne, there was always one more mystery.

One more puzzle.

One more game.

But this—the cuts at the base of his throat, the smell of smoke still clinging to his body—did not feel like a game. He thought back, trying to remember anything before this moment, but suddenly, the last thing—the only thing—he could remember was coming out of Vinárna Čertovka.

Seeing Alice.

Giving chase.

And then—nothing.

Nothing, except for heat and pain and fear and, oddest of all, something about the price of wheat.

"Just to be clear here," Jameson said, searching his memory and finding almost nothing. "Am I dead?" He gave his grand-mother a look. "Because you are."

"As already established, dear boy, I am no one and nothing." Instead of reaching for her teacup this time, the impossibility that was an alive and well Alice Hawthorne reached for the napkin in her lap. When she brought her hand back up to the table, she was holding what appeared to be a shining gold compass.

She hit a hidden trigger, and its face flipped open. From inside the compass, Jameson's dead grandmother removed what appeared to be a small, iridescent bead that looked a bit like a pearl.

"There are ways, Jameson Hawthorne, to take care of problems."

His grandmother dropped the bead in *his* tea and then removed a second, identical one from the compass and set it down on his saucer. "That one you may keep, as a reminder."

Jameson stared at it. "Poison." He'd meant to make that a question, but it didn't come out that way.

"Quite untraceable, I assure you." Alice smiled a bit, and again, she reminded Jameson so much of Skye. "I understand that you are quite close to your brothers." The dead woman took another sip of her tea. "I also understand that there is a girl."

Avery, Jameson thought. The memory of the last few days with his heiress—of everything that had come before that and the lifetime of memories that they were supposed to have still to come—hit Jameson like a knife to the gut.

He jumped to his feet. "Stay away from Avery. And my

brothers." *An untraceable poison. An unmistakable threat.* Who the hell was Alice Hawthorne?

"I can sense that you might be on the verge of attempting a little threat of some kind, but I assure you, you needn't bother." Alice nodded again to the bead. *The poison.* "Go ahead. Take it. If there is one thing that loving a Hawthorne man taught me, it is that there are benefits to physical reminders of the past. To reminders of costs and risks, stories told and untold."

Jameson stared at her. "I don't understand."

"I know," Alice Hawthorne said. "If I thought you did, well, then we would have a problem." She let her gaze travel down to the cuts on his neck and then lower.

Jameson looked down at his own body. *Dried blood and ashes.*

There are ways, Jameson Hawthorne, to take care of problems.

"You really should be going," his grandmother said, finishing her tea. "It's nearly dawn now, and I believe your little heiress is getting quite antsy about your absence." Alice stood. "She'll have questions, I'm sure."

Jameson heard the threat inherent in that sentence. As much as he wanted to know what the hell this was—how the hell any of this was possible—Avery was the one thing that he would not, could not risk.

Fear wasn't just ice in your veins or a beast at your throat. Fear was loving someone so fiercely that there was no point in your heart beating if hers did not.

Jameson looked Alice Hawthorne directly in the eyes. "There's nothing to tell."

The old woman gave a soft *hmmm*, and as she began to walk away, leaving Jameson staring out at the city of Prague and the coming dawn, he couldn't bite back one more question—just one of all the thousands he had.

"The old man," Jameson called out. "Did he know?"

Silence was his grandmother's only reply, but Jameson's mind, wired as it was for puzzles and riddles and codes, came up with an answer of its own.

Who else would have drawn that map? The old man had known that his beloved was alive. That she was in Prague. The real question was what *else* Tobias Hawthorne had known.

What else there *was* to know.

Fire and pain and fear and the price of wheat. Memories hovered like ghosts over graves. Jameson didn't linger. He scaled down the building and snaked his way back through the streets of Prague.

And the entire time, he couldn't shake the feeling that he was being watched.

Acknowledgments

I am starting to feel like a broken record, because when I sit down to write acknowledgments for any Inheritance Games book, all I can think—and what I inevitably end up writing down—is that I am so beyond blessed to work with the incredible team at Little, Brown Books for Young Readers and with everyone at my literary agency, Curtis Brown, especially those who have been with me since my very first book. I don't think I will ever reach a point where I am not awed by how incredible all of you are at your jobs and how lucky I am to have your unparalleled expertise, instincts, and dedication behind me and these books.

For *Games Untold*, I am particularly grateful that when I said to my editor, Lisa Yoskowitz, "What if, instead of the book we had planned, I did an anthology of novellas and short stories, heavy on romance—and relationships of all kinds—that also advances the overall mystery in *The Grandest Game*?" she did not even bat an eye before going all in on the idea. Lisa, I cannot tell you how much joy it brought me to write these stories and share them with you first. That you loved them the way I do, right from the start, means the world.

I am also just *blown away* by the cover that the dynamite team of Karina Granda and Katt Phatt created for this book. I asked for romantic, and you gave me *beyond* romantic, the absolute perfect cover, which fits this book in every way. I'm also very indebted to the incredible sales and marketing teams that did double duty with two Inheritance Games releases this year! Thank you, Shawn Foster, Danielle Cantarella, Claire Gamble, Katie Tucker, Leah CollinsLipsett, and the rest of the HBG sales team for getting this book out there in so many ways, and to Savannah Kennelly, Bill Grace, Emilie Polster, Becky Munich, and Jess Mercado for your marketing and design brilliance! From the Hawthorne Vault to collectable cards, you make this process so much fun for me and for readers. And thank you also to my School & Library team of Victoria Stapleton, Christie Michel, and Margaret Hansen; I am so grateful to the librarians and educators who have supported this series and to all of you for getting it into their hands.

Thank you to Kelly Moran for your support across two releases this year, and to Marisa Finkelstein, Andy Ball, and Kimberly Stella for juggling overlapping deadlines on both books! And a special thank-you to the copy editor and proofreaders in this book, who went above and beyond to make sure that everything lined up with the rest of the series as it should: Erin Slonaker, Jody Corbett, and Su Wu. Thank you, Alexandra Houdeshell, for all that you do, and, as always, thank you, Megan Tingley and Jackie Engel, for creating and leading this unparalleled team.

I am also incredibly grateful to my publishers around the world and to the translators who have to work three times as hard with all my riddles and word puzzles! Thank you to Janelle DeLuise, Hannah Koerner, Karin Schulze, Jahlila Stamp, and all of the co-agents who have had a hand in bringing these books to readers all over the world, and to Anthea Townsend, Chloe

Parkinson, and Michelle Nathan for bringing me to the UK to celebrate the release of this book!

As I said at the beginning of these acknowledgments, I feel like I cannot help repeating myself book after book, but thank you to my agent of many years, Elizabeth Harding. I cannot tell you what it means to have you in my corner not just professionally but as someone who has known me since I was a teenager and seen me (and my career) through so many life changes. Thank you, Holly Frederick, for your work in film and TV rights on this project and so many others over the years, and to the teams that I cannot name working on those projects—you know who you are! And thank you to Eliza Leung and Manizeh Karim and everyone else at Curtis Brown—for everything.

Finally, I can't end these acknowledgments without thanking the family and friends who get me through deadlines and stress and wondering if I can do it with each and every book. Thank you to Rachel Vincent, for always being there, always being happy for me, always knowing the word I'm looking for, and always knowing the exact right question to ask to break me out of a writing slump. Thank you, Mom and Dad, for letting me use your house like a writing retreat, and for being there with food and company and hugs every time I come up for air. You're the best parents in the world, full stop, and the most incredible grandparents to my boys, and I truly could not have finished this book without you.

And on that note, thank you also to my boys, who *may* have inspired that scene where Xander is a sloth…and one or two others. Once you're old enough to read these books—*if* you read them—please do not adopt Hawthorne Secret Santa as your own. And thank you for not breaking any of your bones or any major parts of the house while I was writing this book.

Finally, thank you to my husband, who is undoubtedly the reason that no bones or major parts of the house were broken while I was writing this book. Thank you for your partnership, your love, your support, and your habit of asking exactly the right questions about any given book.

All questions have answers.

The mystery continues in
the Grandest Game series.

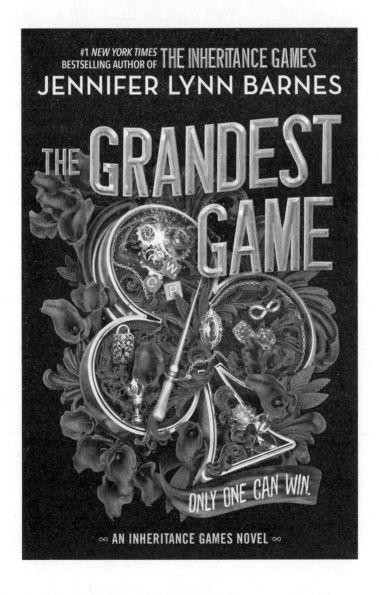

#1 *NEW YORK TIMES*
BESTSELLING AUTHOR OF THE INHERITANCE GAMES
JENNIFER LYNN BARNES

THE GRANDEST
GAME

ONLY ONE CAN WIN.

∞ AN INHERITANCE GAMES NOVEL ∞

JENNIFER LYNN BARNES

is the #1 *New York Times* bestselling author of more than twenty acclaimed young adult novels, including the Inheritance Games series, the Debutantes series, *The Lovely and the Lost*, and the Naturals series. Jen is also a Fulbright Scholar with advanced degrees in psychology, psychiatry, and cognitive science. She received her PhD from Yale University in 2012 and was a professor of psychology and professional writing for many years. She invites you to visit her online at jenniferlynnbarnes.com or on Instagram @authorjenlynnbarnes.